Maine Board of Agriculture

Eight Annual Report of the Secretary of the Maine Board of Agriculture 1863

SALZWASSER
VERLAG

Maine Board of Agriculture

Eight Annual Report of the Secretary of the Maine Board of Agriculture 1863

Reprint of the original, first published in 1863.

1st Edition 2022 | ISBN: 978-3-37500-653-2

Verlag (Publisher): Salzwasser Verlag GmbH, Zeilweg 44, 60439 Frankfurt, Deutschland
Vertretungsberechtigt (Authorized to represent): E. Roepke, Zeilweg 44, 60439 Frankfurt, Deutschland
Druck (Print): Books on Demand GmbH, In de Tarpen 42, 22848 Norderstedt, Deutschland

EIGHTH ANNUAL REPORT

OF THE

SECRETARY

OF THE

MAINE BOARD OF AGRICULTURE.

1863.

1863.

CLAPP'S FAVORITE PEAR.

[See page 266.]

BOARD OF AGRICULTURE...1863.

SAMUEL F. PERLEY, President.
SAMUEL WASSON, Vice President.
S. L. GOODALE, Secretary.

NAME.	COUNTY.	P. O. ADDRESS.
	Term expires January, 1864.	
S. F. Perley,	Cumberland,	Naples.
George A. Rogers,	Sagadahoc,	Topsham.
Ellis Fish,	Somerset,	Hartland.
Farnum Jewett,	Oxford,	North Waterford.
S. L. Goodale,	York,	Saco.
	Term expires January, 1865.	
J. C. Weston,	Penobscot,	Bangor.
Samuel Wasson,	Hancock,	Ellsworth.
Seward Dill,	Franklin,	Phillips.
J. W. Haines,	Aroostook,	Maple Grove.
Lyman Lee,	Piscataquis,	Foxcroft.
W. R. Waterman,	Washington,	Robbinston.
	Term expires January, 1866.	
Calvin Chamberlain,	Maine State Society,	Foxcroft.
Joseph Percival,	Kennebec,	Waterville.
Cyrus M. Pratt,	Androscoggin,	Greene Corner.
Sumner Leach,	Lincoln,	Warren.
——— ———,	Waldo,	———.

REPORT.

To the Senate and House of Representatives:

The Board of Agriculture convened at the State House in Augusta, January 21, 1863, in accordance with the provisions of law, and was called to order by the Secretary.

Messrs. Dill, Fish and Rogers were appointed a Committee on Credentials, who reported a quorum present. Permanent organization was then effected by the unanimous election of

SAMUEL F. PERLEY, *President.*
SAMUEL WASSON, *Vice President.*
S. L. GOODALE, *Secretary.*

Messrs. Weston, Chamberlain and Wasson were appointed a Business Committee to report subjects for the consideration of the Board.

Pending the Report of this Committee, several reports were presented upon subjects investigated during the interim since the last session of the Board.

Mr. Rogers offered the following Report upon

EXPERIMENTS IN POTATO CULTURE.

The Committee appointed to collect, compare and report upon the results of the experiments proposed by the Board at its last session, with reference to ascertaining the distance at which potatoes should be planted to secure the best results, have attended to that duty and report:

They have been able to collect the result of but eighteen experiments, conducted by eleven different individuals, in various sections of the State. These came in so varied forms, that, although each indicated the result of the experiment, it was found impossible to arrange them in a compact table. In almost every instance we have found that the closer planting produced the greater yield, though there were exceptions to this general result.

After having carefully examined and compared the returns of the several experiments, your Committee find that, although the close planting produced the greatest amount, yet the result indicated to us that the increased yield *did not* compensate for the extra seed and increased amount of labor required in cultivation.

The conclusion arrived at by your Committee is, that the returns indicate that two feet by three, produces a better result of crop, all things considered, than a greater or less distance; yet this should be varied somewhat, by the variety of potato intended to be grown.

A few of the experiments, although they may not coincide exactly with the conclusions arrived at by your Committee, were nevertheless so carefully conducted, and so faithfully and clearly reported, that we deem them worthy of being returned to this Board in connection with this report. We would call attention particularly to those conducted by Calvin Chamberlain of Foxcroft, and William D. Dana of North Perry.

Experiment by C. Chamberlain, Foxcroft.

The variety of potato planted, is known as the Orono or Reed. The planting was on May 9th. The land was in tough sod, and plowed in October, 1861. It had been mowed ten years, and in that time had received one slight top-dressing of phosphate of lime, and one of ashes. It had become much exhausted. The soil is a slate loam, dry and stony. The spring culture was simply harrowing. The rows were marked by drawing a chain. One peck of fish guano was scattered evenly in each row; the seed, one piece in each hill, was dropped on the surface and slightly covered. No rain fell after the planting, till June 18th. On account of the drought the hoeing and hilling was done soon after the most advanced tops appeared. The dressing was calculated at the rate of twenty-seven and a half bushels per acre, at a cost of $19.25. We state thus particularly for the purpose of showing the result of the application of a fertilizer not much known, except immediately on the coast. The potatoes produced in this experiment are of excellent quality—good and sound at this date (January.) Those marked *refuse* in the table, were the small ones, together with an occasional one of the largest size having discolored spots, showing disease. Less than eight per cent. of result is in this column.

The amount of seed per acre was found by the count of one bushel.

Number of hills.	Weight of good potatoes.	Refuse potatoes.	Total weight.	Bushels seed per acre.	Bushels yield per acre.	Missing hills.
245	258	25	283	22½	259½	19
171	219	18	287	15	217¼	5
182	227	14	241	11½	221	-
87	183	12	195	7½	178¾	1
248	213	9	222	-	208½	16
166	288	15	258	-	282	10
131	178	6	184	-	168¾	1
88	197	13	210	-	192½	-
243	182	27	209	-	191½	21
172	216	16	282	-	212¾	4
157	217	14	281	-	211¾	19
132	196	14	210	-	192½	-
248	198	16	214	-	196⅛	16
176	175	13	188	-	172½	-
124	174	13½	187½	-	172	8
87	136	12½	148½	-	136	1

Each of these lines of figures is the result of two rows forty-four yards long, each, or one-fifty-fifth of an acre.

In the third experiment an error in planting occurred, by which the one and a half foot distance was repeated, and the three feet distance left out.

Taking the averge of results, and we have—

Distance.	Bushels seed per acre.	Yield per acre.
1 foot	22½ bushels	213 bushels.
1½ "	15 "	209 "
2 "	11¼ "	188 "
3 "	7½ "	169 "

Deduction. The above table shows that seven and a half bushels planted at three feet distance produced one hundred and sixty-nine bushels, or over twenty-two and a half from one—that increasing the quantity of seed by three and three-fourths bushels, planting at two feet distance, gives an increase of nineteen bushels, or five and one-fifteenth bushels to each bushel of additional seed; that a further addition of three and three-fourths bushels seed—planting at one and a half feet gives a result of twenty-one bushels, or five and two-fifths for one. Lastly, increasing the seed by seven and a half bushels, giving a distance of one foot, and it results in an increase of only four bushels, or eight fifteenths of a bushel to one of seed. Comparing the one and a half feet with the three feet, and we have forty eight bushels more per acre with fifteen bushels of seed than with seven and a half bushels at three feet. The number of hills is given in the table, as found at harvest, because of there being many missing ones from drought and other causes. In the three experiments with the three feet distance, we have only two missing hills; in the four at two feet, nine missing; in the five at one a half feet, thirty-eight; and in the four at one foot, seventy-two.

Only one thing seems to be well settled by the above—that to plant this variety of potato with the above quantity of seed, at a less distance than one and a half feet is on the wrong side of correct practice.

Experiment made at North Perry, by William D. Dana, Esq., at the suggestion of the Board of Agriculture.

	Distance of hills in the row, feet.	Quantity of seed per acre in bus. of 60 lbs. each.	Yield per acre of large sound potatoes.	Yield per acre of refuse and few diseased ones.
1st. Experiment having reference only to distance, the quantity of seed being the same in each hill. Extra large or No. 1 potatoes (two to the pound) cut one eye in each piece, and one piece planted in hill,	1	25	450	50
	1½	17	250	15
	2	12½	188	37
	3	8	217	16
2d. No. 2 size seed, eight to the pound, planted as above, cut in four pieces, and one piece planted in each hill,	1	10	320	60
	2	5	230	30
3d. No. 2 potatoes cut in two pieces, one piece in a hill,	1	19	374	58
No. 2 potatoes cut in two pieces, two pieces in a hill,	2	19	319	45
No. 2 potatoes cut in two pieces, three pieces in a hill,	3	29	235	50
4th. No. 3 potatoes, seventeen to the pound, cut in two pieces, one piece in a hill,	1	11	277	39
No. 3 cut in two pieces, two pieces in a hill,	2	11	220	45
No. 3 cut in two pieces, three pieces in a hill,	3	11	189	33
5th. No. 2 planted whole, one in each hill,	1	37½	446	58
No. 2 planted whole, one in each hill,	1½	25	376	36
No. 2 planted whole, one in each hill,	2	19	308	30
No. 2 planted whole, one in each hill,	3	12½	237	27
6th. No. 3, seventeen to the pound, planted whole, one in each hill,	1	18	278	48
No. 3 planted whole, one in each hill,	1½	12	234	41
No. 3 planted whole, one in each hill,	2	9	227	25
No. 3 planted whole, one in each hill,	3	6	166	20

The variety of potato experimented with, is a rank and late grower, not given to rot—the tops being about four feet average length, and green and growing when dug, October 10, 1862. The manure was spread upon the ground and plowed and harrowed in. The rows at two and a half feet apart.

A remarkable degree of regularity will be noticed in these results, with the exception of the first lot, and they show, so far as they show anything—1st, that one foot by two and a half is better than any greater distance. 2d, that whole seed of medium size is better than cut. 3d, that the larger the seed, the larger the crop—all of which, with the exception of the last, agrees with my experience for thirty years past. In regard to the last point, in raising White Blue Nose potatoes, an early maturing and small foliaged variety, (the kind formerly cultivated almost exclusively here for market,) I never, in but one instance, could perceive that small seed was not equally as good as large. Perhaps the very different habits of the varieties may make the difference. The one growing with small amount of vines or tops, getting its full growth and ripening in September or August sometimes—the other growing a perfect swamp of tops, and never getting its growth or ripening—but withal a very good potato, and very free from rot. I have aimed at accuracy in this experiment—doing the work myself, and weighing the seed and crop, calling sixty pounds a bushel for convenience in reducing, one pound (1-60) bearing the same proportion to a bushel, that one hundred hills at three feet bear to an acre (1-60.)

North Perry, Oct. 11, 1862.

Some discussion having followed the reading of this report, on motion of Mr. Chamberlain, it was voted to continue the subject of potato culture as one of the topics for consideration during the interim. Messrs. Percival, Lee and Leach were appointed a Committee to report on this topic at the next session, and the following resolutions were introduced by Mr. Chamberlain:

Whereas, It is desirable that we should know more in regard to the best methods for the general culture of the potato, and whereas, the experience of past years has led to the cautious application of stable manure as a fertilizer for this important crop, thus inducing a practice of planting extensively for small returns, and whereas, it is important that we should learn at an early day the value of fish guano, and to what crops it may best be applied; therefore,

Resolved, That we pledge ourselves, so far as circumstances may permit, to conduct an experiment the present year, in the culture of the potato, using fish guano as a manure, in accordance with such suggestions as may be furnished by the Committee of the Board.

Resolved, That a general invitation is hereby extended to farmers to join us in the experiment, with the request that results be returned to the Secretary of this Board.

Mr. Chamberlain presented the following Report on

Flax Culture.

The Committee appointed at the last meeting of the Board, to investigate the subject of Flax Husbandry, have attended to the duty assigned, to the extent of their limited opportunities, and Report:

That it gives them great pleasure to find that this topic, of vital national importance, has received merited attention at the hands of the Government, and that a competent gentleman has been sent to Europe to investigate the cultivation and manufacture of flax; and that the facts thus elicited, together, with the present home status of this interest, are assigned a prominent place in the Agricultural Report of the Commissioner of Patents for 1861. It might seem that this investigation, conducted with all the means at the command of the Government, would have sufficiently ventilated the subject, without an additional effort on the part of humble individuals laboring for the greatest good of a single State.

It appears from the report above named, that but little remains to be done, when, by the aid of machinery, flax may be expeditiously treated in its several mechanical and chemical manipulations, and converted to ultimate uses.

In pursuance of our mission, one of your Committee, during the year took occasion to visit the State of Rhode Island, where we had in some way received the impression that the greatest success had been attained in the manufacture of flax fabrics. Our journey, (a very hurried one,) accomplished nothing further than to put us in communcation with a "Committee appointed by the Rhode Island Society for the encouragement of Domestic Industry," to investigate the subject of Flax culture and its preparation and use in connection with cotton and otherwise.

A member of that Committee, (Hon. James Y. Smith,) communicates to us the result of a meeting holden at Providence, October 2d, 1862, and we take the liberty to make the following extract from his letter: "We have memorialized Congress upon the subject, and asked Congress to aid us by making an appropriation to procure certain machinery to produce the desired result. The Committee of Congress on Agriculture has the subject under consideration, and may report at the next session.

A meeting was held to-day, to discuss the subject of Flax production and its manufacture. About thirty gentlemen were present, with our Senator and Representative. The discussion was animated and full, but no definite conclusions arrived at.

I will answer your several questions:

1st. 'The farmers of Maine would like to be informed in regard to the probable price that flax straw may bear in market at tide-water.'

This question could not be answered satisfactorily.

2d. 'Is such product lessened in market value by being ripened so as to mature the seed?'

I think the crop would be required to be cut before the seed was in full glaze. The largest oil manufacturers say the seed will produce more oil in this state than with seed fully ripened.

3d. 'Must the crop be pulled and bundled, or may it be cut with a scythe or cradle?'

The crop may be cut or pulled, but must be kept in straight layers.

4th. 'May it be threshed and then baled, as hay for transportation?'

It could not be used if the stubble is required to be cut in certain lengths before being separated from the woody portion of the stubble, and the fibre exploded by chemicals or otherwise.*

I don't think your farmers would be warranted in making a change until further progress is made. The West has millions of tons of stubble lying to waste, but of no use for this experimenting. The crop must be grown and handled with care to be used successfully for the new process of manufacture. I think it will come to be successfully used, but time must develop the subject."

From the tone of the above communication, gentlemen of this Board will conclude that we are not quite so near the *beginning of*

---

* We have been accustomed to use the word *stubble* as meaning that portion of the straw or stalk below where it is severed by the harvesting implement. Our friend applies it otherwise.

the end of this matter as they flattered themselves a year since. If, with the millions at the command of the manufacturers of Rhode Island they are at the present date besetting the halls of Congress for an appropriation "to procure certain machinery," we need no assurance that progress will not be rapid so far as it is open to the public.

However desirable it may be, as times have changed—to bring the flax culture back upon our farms, if its return is to be made dependent on the restoration of the domestic habits and primitive customs—the round of toil to which our mothers were subjected (God bless them,) then the people of Maine will never vote it back. But when manufacturers ask for flax, the farmers of this as well as the other free States, will listen to them.

It would take a great breadth from our bread-producing acres, to yield so much flax seed as to supply our wants for paint-oil and cake for feeding purposes. But the flax crop is so natural to our soil and climate, that a change would be extensively made if a demand should arise for flax straw. We might as well be dependent on other States for a little more flour and corn as to be constantly buying every gallon of drying oils that we use.

Your Committee as at present advised, see no reason that the Board should change its position on this topic, from that assumed at the last session; and that the words of a resolution passed by the Board, January 27th, 1862, still remain as the best expression that we have to offer to the farmers of Maine.

The resolution referred to is in these words:

Resolved, That we invoke the aid of manufacturers, with the capital and skill at their command, in placing our State in a condition less dependent on foreign aid in regard to clothing; and when they shall be prepared to pay remunerating prices for flax in the straw state, we pledge them that the soil of Maine and its cultivators will generously respond to the demand.

Mr. Haines offered the following paper on

The Value of Pedigree.

I assume that the Board clearly recognizes the value of purity of blood in all efforts to improve our live stock and that in requiring a report on the value of a recorded pedigree, the design is merely to show how this is reliable evidence of the desired purity of blood in the animal possessing it.

If it were necessary for me to urge upon the Board the value of pure blood in our breeding stock, I might cite many remarkable instances to demonstrate it, as I have had no little experience in the breeding of animals, particularly of neat stock, and I have had it forced upon my observation repeatedly, that the longer animals are bred in one line, and the purer their blood, the stronger and more surely do they mark their offspring; and I cannot refrain here citing as an example, the short-horn bull Leopard 2d, which originated in the celebrated Bates stock, because he was so widely known and had so much to do with establishing the character of neat stock in the Kennebec valley. He was a most notable instance of the value of fixed properties in a sire, the evidence of which I first obtained, when I bought him of E. P. Prentice, of Albany, N. Y., in a written pedigree tracing his descent entirely through pure-bred animals, and which was afterwards proved to the satisfaction of all who sought his service with their cows, by the unerring certainty with which he marked his get.

According to the dictionaries, a pedigree is *an account or register of a line of ancestors*; but to a breeder of live stock it has a wider significance. It here signifies that the animal possessing it has a record of a line of ancestors, who have been religiously kept in one race or breed, tracing their descent from unquestionable stock of the same character. By it, as Mr. Goodale says, in the introduction to his valuable book on the breeding of domestic animals, "satisfactory evidence is offered that the animal is of a pure and distinct breed, that it possesses certain well-known hereditary qualities." Finally it means to the live stock breeder a paper by the examination of which the absolute purity of breeding in the named animal may be made positively clear and undisputable.

It is the great safeguard which the purchaser may have against fraud. He has not to rely solely upon the word of the breeder; and if one should be so dishonorable as to attempt to deceive and cheat by palming off a fictitious pedigree with his animals, he must so "lie with circumstances of times, places and persons," that, by reference to the very authorities quoted, he may be readily detected.

To be complete, a pedigree must exhibit the breed and name of the animal, the date of its birth, the breeder's name and that of the present owner, the names of the sire and dam and their progenitor on both sides, back to herd-book numbers or to herds or flocks of acknowledged purity of blood, or well established studs, in every individual branch or root of the family tree; and this is what every reliable breeder in the country expects and is as much prepared to do as he is to furnish the animal which he has bred for sale.

If a man buys an animal as pure bred, and does not require therewith a written pedigree, full and complete, he must always be in doubt about its purity of blood and breeding, and in selling again, either the animal itself or its progeny, he must convey the same doubt and thus leave a door always open to dishonest practice, at the same time lending to it the advantage his name may give.

Herd books of the short horns and Devons have now been so long established that purchasers in either of these breeds may fairly *demand* that their selections shall trace directly on both sides to a record therein. And no breeder of live stock of *any* sort has a right to sell as "pure blood" any animal of which he cannot furnish a full and complete pedigree, tracing back in unbroken line to well established herds of unquestionable character. Purchasers should always demand this and failing to obtain it, ought, for their own sake, and that of honest and unreliable dealers, to forego the proposed purchase, however highly they may esteem the selected animal; for there are now throughout the country, honest and careful men who are struggling on in the straight and narrow way against a very unfair competition, and for their extreme care and exactness in the observance of rules and unwillingness to admit any but most thoroughly bred stock in their herds and flocks, are constantly subjected to the slanderous abuse and would-be witty flings of ignorant and unscrupulous dealers and breeders. I have heard breeders insinuatingly remark upon the herds of others that they did not care to own cattle of such aristocratic blood as required a pedigree; that they preferred good animals on their own hoofs, to having them good on paper; that they did not need a written history to inform them about the purity of an animal's blood, if they could but put their two eyes upon the animal, &c., &c.; and the reflection which I made was, that they were either very ignorant, or that they believed their audience to be so, and were themselves unscrupulous and unfair. Every purchase of an assumed "pure bred" animal which has not a written proof of its just claim to the title, is but an encouragement to the dishonest, and one more obstacle in the way of the honest breeder.

If an animal be bought for breeding purposes, a full and complete pedigree is as essential as a warranty of soundness, and should be no more neglected.

Mr. Perley presented the following paper on

WINTER CARE OF STOCK.

The leading object of this paper is to call the attention of farmers to and demonstrate the necessity of more abundant food and better care of their herds and flocks.

If a store animal receives food barely sufficient to maintain its weight, without gain or loss, it is manifest that the owner is losing daily just the worth of the food consumed and the labor of tending, deducting the value of its excrements. If the same animal diminishes in weight, the loss is the full sum of the worth of food consumed, the labor of tending and the pounds of diminution at its current value in the market, minus the value of its excrements. To make an actual profit the animal must increase in weight so that the pounds of gain, together with the excrements, shall be worth more than enough, at current values, to pay for all the food and the labor of tending; and the surplus so obtained is the actual profit. With milch cows, working horses and oxen, and breeding sheep, the case is different; they may yield their owner a profit in other ways, as in milk, labor or wool; but with all growing stock the facts are as above stated. The profit on the milch cow is the surplus value of her dairy products, increased by the value of her excrement, over and above the value of her food, and the labor of tending and manufacturing the milk into butter or cheese. The profit of the full grown ox or horse is the surplus value of his labor and excrements over and above the value of his food and labor of tending. And the profit of the sheep is the surplus value of its wool, excrements and lambs raised, over and above the worth of food and labor of tending.

Now if the above positions are correct, the farmer who allows his young stock to remain stationary at any season of the year, to "just hold their own," as he terms it, is actually losing the full value of the food consumed and the labor of tending, less the value of the manure. The milch cow which barely pays the expense of keeping and care, is a "dead head," yielding no profit. So of the ox, the horse or sheep. To make stock keeping in any of its departments profitable, each animal must return an income over and above its cost, else the farmer is simply changing the form of his product without increasing its value. There are some animals, ill bred brutes, which can never be made to yield a profit; such should be at once laid out for fox-bait, or, better still, incorporated in the compost pile, so that, being dead, they may be turned to some good account, for, while living, they make the farmer poorer every day. There are thousands of others which might, but do not yield a profit, and the fault that they do not, is entirely with their owners. A "plentiful lack" of good care and food is the reason. There are comparatively few animals which do actually yield a profit, either in growth, in labor, in dairy products or wool; and these are always found in the hands of careful, good feeders. But the profitless animals, it is believed, greatly outnumber those yielding a profit; outnumber them to a far greater extent than farmers are generally willing to admit; and this is the result of short pastures in summer, cold barns and a scanty supply of good, nutritious food in winter. In a climate like that of Maine, it becomes necessary for the herdsman and flockmaster, if they would keep their stock in a continually thriving condition, to provide food, other than pasturage, for more than half the year. From December 1st to April 30th, the animals upon the farm must, ordinarily, receive all their living from the winter's store; and the necessity is scarcely less imperious during November and May. The scanty feed in the pastures in the latter part of summer and early autumn, caused by the drouth usually occurring at that period, renders it highly important that at this season, too, feed of some kind should be supplied, else the stock will come to the barn in ill condition. The farmer who would see his stock continually gaining, or yielding a profit, must be prepared to feed, more or less, two-thirds of the whole year. This may seem a strong statement to some, but let him who doubts it, place his animals upon the scales once in every thirty days for a twelve month, and he will be convinced of its correctness. Farmers who rely upon a guess judgment, are very apt to misjudge the condition of their stock. Only a few days ago, the writer heard an experienced, good farmer, and a good judge, make the statement that his young stock actually gained more during the winter of 1861 and 1862, than during the summer following, and this without provender of any kind, the hay being of a poor quality, having been cut upon low, wet land. One of two things must be inferred from this statement, viz., that the summer's

FOUR COTSWOLD EWE LAMBS.

Bred and owned by CHARLES CORLISS of "Poplar Lawn," Haverhill, Mass. Exhibited at the "Essex Agricultural Society's Show," held in Georgetown, September 30 and October 1, 1862, and winners of the premium offered by the Society, for the best lot of Lambs.

gain was very small indeed, or that the farmer was mistaken in his judgment, most probably the latter. The writer has frequently called upon his herdsman to guess upon the gain or loss of individual animals since the former weighing, when again brought to the scales, and though the man—being a fair judge—had been with the animals every day, had constantly tended them and knew whether they had fed well or ill, yet he would as often guess very wild as near the mark. The girting chain is not a sure indicator of condition; often an animal, retaining well his girth, will show by the scales a gain or loss of twenty-five to fifty pounds in a period of a few days or weeks.

The degree of cold to which an animal is exposed has a very marked influence upon its condition, as may be shown by actual trial. For this purpose I desire to introduce some observations, (they hardly deserve to be called experiments,) made upon my own herd of neat stock during the past year. The herd consisted of twenty-three animals, viz: four oxen, working about half the time; eight cows, giving milk as indicated in the table; two heifers, two years old coming three; five yearlings, coming two; four calves, coming one.

I give below a page from my herd-book, containing a general summary, the result in gross of the food, total gain or loss per day, weight of milk per day, mean temperature and date of birth of calves. I embrace the whole neat stock upon the farm in these observations, for the reason that many farmers will say when questioned closely that they are aware that some of their animals are losing, but that others are doing well enough to make all up to a fair gain.

1861.	No. days between weighing.	Meal per day in quarts.	Roots per day in bushels and qts.	No. feeds per day Timothy or clover.	No. feeds per day meadow hay.	No. feeds per day corn stover.	Mean temperature.	Total gain, lbs.	Gain per day, lbs. and ozs.	Total loss.	Loss per day.	Weight of milk per day.	Birth of calves.
Nov. 30 to Dec. 14	14	14	6.0	1	2	2	31.3	474	36.8				
Dec. 14 to Dec. 30	16	20	6.4	1	2½	1½	24.1	191	12.0			40.7	
1862.													
Dec. 30 to Jan. 11	12	26	4.14	1½	1	2½	17.7	120	10.0			40.3	
Jan. 11 to Feb. 3	23	26	5.16	1½	2½	1	18.0	89	4.0			45.3	
Feb. 3 to Feb. 15	12	44	6.16	1½	2½	1	19.7	36	3.0			45.1	Feb. 8.
			Shorts										Change of herds-
Feb. 15 to Mar. 3	16	53	1.5	1½	2½	1	22.5			32	2.0	62.14	man one week.
Mar. 3 to Mar. 15	12	50	1.4	1	3	1	32.7	294	24.8			56.1	March 21.
Mar. 15 to Mar. 29	14	46	0.28	1	4		29.9	207	14.12			64.15	March 26.
Mar. 29 to Apr. 12	14	47	0.28	1	4		32.7			210	15.0	84.3	April 9.
Apr. 12 to Apr. 22	10	43	Pota's	2½	2½		46.5			383	38.5	84.3	April 17.
Apr. 22 to May 6	15	64	0.16	4			44.1	71	4.12			95.13	May 4.
May 6 to May 15	9	51	0.25	Grass.			54.2			93	10.5	104.11	
		Short pasturage with corn											Sept. 9—June 2.
May 15 to Nov. 26	195	fodder and pumpkins.						2011	10.5				Aug. 9--Nov. 26.

It will be perceived that from the first to the sixth weighing—i. e., from Nov. 30 to March 3, a period of ninety-two days, the forage feed continuing about the same, the grain feed being successively increased, while the mean temperature, (three observations each day,) fell from 31.3 to 17.07, and continued low for sixty days, there was a continual diminution in the gain of the stock, until, on the third of March, it became a positive loss. Then again the mean temperature rose to about 31 degrees, and for the next two weighings, a period of twenty-four days, carrying it to the 29th of March, there was a very fair gain.

After which time, the dropping and suckling of calves, the increased flow of milk and other irregularities, gave an irregular result, mostly a loss, although the temperature of April and May was favorable. Exact experiments can only be made under the personal care of an intelligent experimenter. Every circumstance and condition must be carefully noted and recorded. Too much reliance should not, therefore, be placed upon the foregoing observations, the feeding and care of the stock being all the while in the hands of another person. The results observed regarding temperature, however, accord so well with the generally received opinion that it cannot but strengthen that opinion, and lead farmers to provide warm shelter and an abundance of nutritious food for stock in severe weather. Animals, it is true, will eat enough food in very cold weather—they must do so or die, if this only is offered them ; but they will not, cannot gain, or yield a profit upon such food. In the above trial, the stock was full-fed most largely upon corn-stover and meadow hay. It consumed, in addition, 200 bushels meal, one ton cotton seed, one ton shorts, and 500 bushels roots. With this food, and it is believed to have been more liberal than is allowed upon most farms, the total gain from Nov. 30 to May 15, was only 764 lbs. To this should be added the worth of milk, labor of oxen and excrements ; yet with these additions, a balance sheet would show very much to the disadvantage of successful farming.

Next to exposure and positive suffering by cold and lack of food, irregular feeding, unkind treatment, and any other circumstances which create disquiet, are the causes of loss. No worrying of dogs, or ill-usage by thoughtless boys or ill-tempered men, should be allowed. Five minutes abuse while driving to or from the pasture,—while getting the animals to and confining them in their stalls during the operation of milking or currying, will probably cost the owner two-fold more than the labor of the man or boy, thus guilty, can be worth, and such herdsman or boy should be at once reformed or discharged from his place.

A constant supply of good water, easily accessible, and in a sheltered place for winter's use, is of the utmost importance to the health and consequent profit of farm stock. That from a spring or running brook is best; but this cannot always be obtained near at hand, and the practice of driving any considerable distance to water is always objectionable, particularly in severe weather. A well or cistern must often serve as a substitute for the running stream—from these the water should be freshly drawn and always free from offensive taste or smell. Many animals accustomed to pure water, will refuse that which is brackish or impure, until considerable suffering from thirst has been endured. This is a source of loss not generally appreciated by stock-owners.

These and several other points, scarcely less important, might be enlarged upon, but we will pursue it no further at present.

Now I hazard the assertion that not one herd in ten, take the State through—yes, I will say one herd in twenty—but leave the barn on the twentieth of May weighing less than when housed on the twentieth of November, and unless the excrements are reckoned higher than farmers generally value them, and unless the price of stock rules very much higher in spring than in the fall, all these nineteen out of twenty stock-owners have just thrown away their feed and labor, and with more courage than discretion are ready to engage in another hard summer's labor, that they may be able to do the same again. They find themselves in spring with the same number of animals, diminished in quality and gross weight, with a pile of manure, (that is, so much as has not been washed away to the neighboring stream,) in offset for the same animals in better condition the previous fall, and tons of hay or straw and bushels of meal and roots which those animals have consumed. There must be here a large balance upon the wrong side of the ledger, when the profit and loss is recorded.

Query. Would not the farmers of Maine act more wisely in keeping a less number of animals, feeding them more highly, and housing them more comfortably, thus securing a constant gain?

Mr. Waterman presented the following

On Rotation of Crops.

Among the many practical questions presenting themselves to the farmer for solution, there is probably not one ordinarily passed over more lightly, and, at the same time, of more importance, than the question of what crops he shall plant and sow from time to time. Very often it is settled by present convenience, chance, caprice, or perhaps more often by the way the farmer has become accustomed to do, without any fixed rule.

Experience has proved what might be very readily supposed, that the ordinary farm crops require to be changed round, or not cultivated for any great length of time, the same crop upon the same place.

To this there may be some few exceptions. Onions have been grown for a century upon the same spot, without diminution of the crop or deterioration of the soil. Carrots will admit of being grown quite a number of years successively upon the same spot. Buckwheat will sometimes produce better the second year than the first; oats and potatoes, in some cases, nearly as well. Grass may be raised for an indefinite length of time by top-dressing, and occasionally turning over the sod, manuring, harrowing, rolling and seeding down.

Now the demand which exists for a variety of products for home consumtion, and the uncertainty which attends all crops, seem to make it imperative to raise a variety of crops. Such being the case, we may, first, in deciding how the different crops shall be grown, inquire whether or not the same crop can profitably be raised upon the same ground for successive years—if so, it might be very much more convenient. The crops which involve in the process of cultivation and storing, a good deal of carting, might be grown convenient to the farm buildings. The corn, potatoes, or other hoed crops, could be raised on soil made easy by continued cultivation. The labor of turning over tough swards might all be saved. This might be, if the farmer could always return to his farm all that every crop takes out of it—which he cannot do, because, aside from the fact that were he obliged to do so, no farming (here in Maine,) could be made to pay, he cannot command all the elements of which his soil is deprived by the growing crops. Those elements, which are at his command, are not in the different forms which would be necessary in order for him to apply to each field the precise amount and kind of plant-food necessary for the particular crop allotted to that field and none other. Different plants require different sustenance. There is a recuperative power in nature which is continually at work to supply the waste of the soil; it may be slow, but none the less sure, and not the less to be regarded. While a certain crop is drawing upon the earth for what it needs to grow and thrive upon, this power is storing up resources for another and a different growth. An instance of this is seen in the fertility of land when first stripped of forest, and again in the rapidity with which forest growth succeeds to farm crops. This agency is of course in a great part lost if one undertakes to farm without change of products.

It being granted that a change is necessary, the question occurs, shall it be an indiscriminate change, or a systematic succession of crops recurring at regular intervals, or as it is called, a rotation of crops? Rotation cannot be used under all circumstances—indeed there are probably few farms in this State, certainly very few in the eastern part, where it can be strictly adhered to over the whole farm. It cannot be used upon new farms, nor upon rough, stony, or wet lands, until such are first cleared or drained. It may be the more an advantage in that it requires these improvements to be made, and where it may not be practicable, may be looked forward to as conducive to, and part of, a better system of cultivation. To be sure your amateur farmer, with his ample means and well read brain, can dig stumps, blast rocks, sink drains and build fences, so as immediately to establish such a rotation as suits his fancy; but the poor man who must make a living and reclaim his farm by the labor of his own hands will be a long time in arriving at the same results. He may often work over the same piece, when if he had more means, a new and tough one would be subdued. As for draining, without abundant capital, it must be a work of time.

The advantage of a rotation over a simple change of crops is not difficult to perceive.

The great staple here is the hay crop. We endeavor so to manure and cultivate our lands for one or more years under other crops, as to prepare them to bring grass for a number of successive seasons. Under the ordinary system these lands are mown so long as the crop will pay for cutting. It is considered economy to save all the grass, though the land be run down to utter unproductiveness. The lands which were the best when seeded down, remain down the longest, and so become equally exhausted. Now such a rotation as compels the breaking up of the sward at the expiration of a certain time, though there may still be some vitality in the grass roots, will be a safeguard against this depletion of the soil. Decomposed vegetable matter is the great fertilizer. A good sward is variously estimated to contain from twenty to thirty tons of vegetable matter—say it is but one-half, from ten to fifteen tons, and you have in an inverted sod a very valuable addition of the best of manure. Let your grass ground run out and the sod (on clay ground especially) becomes entirely gone; it has decayed too so gradually as to be of no perceptible benefit to the soil. So too if the land be kept up too long, the fibrous matter becomes entirely decayed, and, if the soil be sandy, it will lack adhesion and become too light. If it be a heavy soil, it will be too adhesive and become baked and lumpy; the rootlets bind the sand and divide the clay.

Any thing which helps to promote system in farming, is an advantage. Rotation will superinduce a more methodical management of other matters upon the farm. It is contrary to nature that a man should be strictly systematic in one particular and not at all so in others. The habit of regularity acquired in pursuing a rotation, will pervade and show itself in all the other operations of the farm. That man would be considered by all as a strange anomaly, who, while adhering to a wise rotation of crops, was still a thriftless and slovenly farmer.

A system of rotation leads to doing more upon the farm, as well as doing it better—to using more manure, as well as applying the same to better advantage. Under the indiscriminate change system, the farmer puts on what manure he can get and where it is most convenient—perhaps a small quantity—thinking it will do for this year, and next year he can go over it again. Under the rotation system he sees that he must have manure enough for a certain field—it must be a sufficient quantity, for it is to suffice for just so many crops, and the field can have no more until its turn comes round again.

It does away with the small patch practice, so destructive of time, with its short furrows, many turns and broken day's works, as well as the more pernicious practice of breaking up larger fields than can be manured, to be cropped and left in a condition more barren than before.

The particular succession which should constitute a rotation may be different in different localities, and depend somewhat upon the character of the farm to which it is to be applied. A simple rotation and one that has been tried successfully is, first, potatoes or other hoed crop, well manured, with clean cultivation; then a grain crop with grass seed, hay for three years, the hoed crop again, and so on. The land is gone over once in five years, and though one dressing may seem scanty for five crops, it is probably oftener than three-fourths of our fields are manured under the old system.

Perhaps on large farms it would be better to take off a crop of oats next after breaking up, then a hoed crop; corn where that succeeds well, then seeding down with barley, wheat, peas or buckwheat—the last, if sown sparsely with a light coat of manure is a capital crop to seed down with. The grass crop may look slim when the grain comes off, but the ground is left light, and if the buckwheat is taken off tolerably early, the grass will come on afterward and be sure to give a good account of itself when haying comes round; then, after three years of hay, introduce two years of pasture. If no pasture, then, especially upon clay loam, more than three crops of hay may profitably be taken off. By applying a dressing of bone dust, guano or fish pomace at seeding down, the field may hold out five seasons in grass. Pasturing is advisable even if it come after that. It is a notorious fact that the old pastures are fast becoming perfect barrens. They have been drawn upon largely and there is no ready way to restore the lost fertility. Now, if our fields can be pastured alternately, much of what is now used as pasture can be devoted to raising wood, as promising a rotation as any one can go in for. The forest growth of a country is universally allowed to affect the fall of rain—so much so that travellers believe that the only reason why Palestine has lost its ancient fertility is that fires have stripped the country of woods, and it is often swept by fires, which prevent the growth, so that there is no rain in summer, and vegetation dies for want of moisture. The summers of Maine certainly appear to be becoming dryer every year. If restoring a growth of wood to barren hillsides will bring refreshing showers to parched fields, it will be the best of rotations. The feed upon cultivated lands is of far superior quality, particularly for dairy stock. The trouble of scouring height and hollow, fell and forest to bring home the cows each night, is all saved. If sufficient pasture is not afforded for the whole farm stock, a selection can be made and such as are not needed often, or do not need the best feed, can be turned out upon the old pastures. Pasturing will eradicate many weeds that have escaped the plow and the scythe. The experience of some in this eastern part of the State shows this to be the case with white weed (ox-eye daisy) caraway and that pest of light lands, with half a dozen aliases, witch grass, couch grass, or whatever it may be called. For this purpose, as also enriching the soil by droppings, pasturing by sheep is best. We will here digress to say that where couch grass has fairly taken possession in pieces of any considerable extent, unless it is convenient to feed it to death with sheep (cattle will do) the better way is to let it have its way, turning it over once in a few years, or when it binds out, plowing shoal, putting on a dressing, harrowing down well and leaving it to come up again and flourish. It produces a good crop while the ground is rich, and cut early, makes fair hay.

Some cultivators disapprove of the latter grain crop, preferring to seed down immediately following the hoed crop, arguing that the land being saved the draft of the grain crop is in better order and will consequently bring more and better crops of grass. Though this course has some benefits, they do not appear sufficient to turn the scale. The first hay crop is apt to be less in quantity as well as not equal in quality, and more liable to be killed out the first winter. Then a crop of barley or other grain at the present high prices will more than make up any deficiency.

Sandy soils will require a rotation extending over less time than the one we have been considering. Such soils will not be likely to hold in grass more than two seasons, and will afford but indifferent pasture more than one year after. Upon extensive farms or those made up of widely differing soils, there can be no objection to using different rotations upon different parts. In this as in other things judgment must be used as well as system.

Where farming is carried on more extensively than in Maine, one year of fallow is made a part of the rotation. Upon an estate in New Jersey where wheat has been grown for a hundred and twenty years, and which the manager claims is steadily improving, the rotation is corn, clover, wheat, grass, fallow, oats. The corn is heavily manured and the wheat is well limed. The fallow is plowed many times during the season. Whether fallowing will pay here in Maine is a question which experiment can best decide. The old idea that land needs rest, is but little held to in these days; still the repeated stirring of the ground in warm weather, exposing the different particles to the action of the air, cleaning the soil of many annoying weeds and improving the mechanical character, while the restorative process of nature, before spoken of, is going on, must be beneficial and may be profitable.

It is not claimed that any one of the different successions mentioned is infallibly the best, or indeed that there may not be a better than either or all, or that any one way is best under all circumstances; but it is claimed, and fact and argument support the assumption, that upon every sufficiently cleared farm, some judicious system of a succession of crops, extending over not too long a series of years, ensuring a change before the soil shall have become exhausted under any one crop, must be adopted, to realize the greatest return for expense incurred, and at the same time most surely and steadily improve the soil.

What the rotation best adapted is will depend upon the nature of the farm, the locality, access to markets, the means of the farmer, and possibly, too, his tastes and disposition. The individual concerned must weigh these things and decide for himself as best he may. It is submitted whether it would not be better to spend money on well conducted experiments in this line, rather than to pay it out in premiums to sundry gentlemen for fast animals or big pumpkins, when oftentimes the simple reason why these gentlemen are more fortunate than their neighbors, is because they have more ample means to lavish upon a single animal or a single crop. It may do upon western prairies, where the decay of the gigantic growth of centuries has accumulated vast deposits of vegetable matter, to plant or sow the same crop year after year, and transport the increase to distant markets, bestowing upon bountiful nature no return; but upon our granite soil every care must be used lest the land deteriorate and fail to yield remunerative returns.

If the crop of last year has drawn so largely upon one particular element as to deprive the soil in a great measure of that element, a following crop of the same cannot succeed, and it is plain that one requiring different pabulum, in part, must be introduced, that the equilibrium may be restored.

The farmer must be on the alert to use every means to make his a paying business. Improvements are going on in all the arts of peace and war. The farmer must seize upon whatever benefits his calling or fall behind a progressing age.

Is it not time that the farmers of Maine adopted rotation of crops as one of the improvements of the age?

Mr. Rogers presented the following report on

THE AGRICULTURAL CAPABILITIES OF MAINE.

That the soil of Maine is as fertile and productive as that of the prairies or bottom lands of the West, no one asserts. But that it is capable when judiciously managed of richly remunerating the husbandman for all the labor, care and attention that he bestows upon it, the numerous well conducted farms, with their neat, tasty, and in many instances elegant, farm buildings that adorn our rural districts, abundantly testify.

The farmer of Maine has not so great a surplus for market, as his brother at the West, neither is it necessary; for his smaller surplus of barley, beans and potatoes, to say nothing of oats, apples, hay, &c., will yield a larger cash return than his western brother's big pile of wheat, corn and pork.

Although we import a large portion of our flour we are not without our exports. There was exported from the city of Bangor alone, the past year, upwards of 500,000 bushels of potatoes. The probable total export of the State for the same time, was at least 1,500,000 bushels, which at an average value of forty cents per bushel will amount to $600,000, besides leaving an abundant supply for our own population, more than sixty per cent. of whom are not producers. Maine is capable of producing with ease almost any quantity of these tubers for which she can find a market.

Barley, rye and oats in the larger portion of our State are certain crops, and may be cultivated to a much greater extent than has ever yet been done.

There are annually sent abroad thousands of tons of hay; and the trains upon our railroads weekly testify to the fact that Maine is largely a stock-growing State. The census returns show that she has made decided advances in this particular in the last decade, yet it is evident to any careful observer that very much more may yet be done in this direction. Indeed, precisely *here* is the place for improvement.

Stock husbandry, (including the dairy,) should be the prominent feature of farming in Maine. By making it such, farmers will be enabled the more readily to improve their farms, so that thus we can scarcely conceive of a limit to our capabilities in this respect.

Our State is well adapted to sheep husbandry; some portions of it peculiarly so. Probably no branch of farming yields a larger return for the capital invested and the attention bestowed than the keeping of sheep. It is somewhat surprising that our farmers have bestowed so little attention upon it. The experience of the older and more advanced agricultural nations goes to show that the keeping of sheep is indispensable to a good system of husbandry even among their densest population and on their highest priced land. And here allow me to extract from the preliminary report of the census of 1860, where in treating upon sheep, it is said, "they afford as much food for man in proportion to their consumption, as any other domestic animals. They are believed to return more fertilizing matter to the soil. In addition to these things, they, alone furnish wool. England proper has about five hundred and ninety to the square mile. The United States proper, (exclusive of territories,) have about forty-eight to the square mile."

In our own State there were returned by the assessors of three hundred and fourteen towns and plantations 334,820 sheep, which would give about ten to a square mile. But inasmuch as about two-fifths of the municipal officers in the State thought the matter of too little consequence for them to trouble themselves to make returns,—upon the supposition of our Secretary made in connection with the report of the returns, that they represented about three-fourths of our farmers, and productive acres, and allowing the proportion to hold good in those places from which no returns were received, we should then have 446,429, being about thirteen and one-half to a square mile, compared with the population less than 71 per cent.

In view of the foregoing facts, will any one presume to say that Maine has begun to develop her capabilities in this branch of husbandry? On the contrary have not our farmers paid too little attention to this matter for their own interest and the good of the State?

In order to develop our agricultural capabilities, we need good home markets and an easy transit from the interior and northern portion of our State.

To create the former, we should use our utmost endeavors to hold out to manufacturers and capitalists, the superior advantages we possess for manufacturing; to show them that we were evidently designed by nature to become a manufacturing State, and to induce them to occupy and turn to good account some of our numerous water-falls which are now unoccupied, or if occupied, are of comparatively little advantage to the occupants or the community.

The proposed Aroostook Railroad would open a communication into a fertile wheat growing country, and not only afford easy transportation for those already settled, but be a means of reducing the wilderness into fruitful fields, and do much towards enriching the State by developing its agricultural capabilities.

In connection with this topic, I would call the attention of farmers to the resources which our State possesses for furnishing plant food in the form of marine manures and more especially fish guano, which is now about being manufactured in large quantities, and at a moderate price, and which promises to be a valuable acquisition to our hitherto limited supply of fertilizers.

Mr. Wasson offered the following on

The Influence of the Agricultural Press.

Some fifty years ago, the first agricultural paper in this country was started at Baltimore. The idea of teaching farmers anything in that way, was hooted, as simply ridiculous. At the present time when sixty or seventy periodicals are devoted to farming, when hundreds of thousands of dollars have been spent on these publications, when the best talents practical and theoretical are employed to make them instructive and useful, with too many the idea is still simply ridiculous, and many more *expounders* in agriculture sympathize in harmony.

Agriculture is eminently an experimental science. The farmer needs the experience of others, together with his own, to establish new facts. The result of his own observations, coinciding with the observations of his neighbors, suggests new improvements. But the farmer from the isolated nature of his vocation—being a large portion of his time alone in the field—has but little time and less opportunity for social intercourse, and, by mere force of habit, becomes a kind of unsocial being. Having ears he hears not the experience and suggestions of others, and to the improvements around him he is a stranger. But through the medium of an agricultural publication, he sees at a glance what improvements his brother-farmers are making, and what has been the accumulated progress of the agricultural world.

The object of every farmer, is success with the least manual labor. He may be directed by his taste or capacities to some special department of agriculture, as the rearing of stock, or the cultivation of corn, or the culture of fruit, or a mixed husbandry, and in either case, the question is, how shall success be easiest and most successfully attained? A problem that may cost a lifetime to work out, when its solution, how some have succeeded, and why others have failed, may be found in any reliable agricultural journal. Therein the ways and means of others' prosperity become common property at a trifling expense.

Let every farmer ask himself, what would be the effect upon the public prosperity were the agricultural papers and periodicals and associations to become non-existent, the concentrated action, power and progress of the farmers dissevered, and each compelled to rely upon his own puny exertions,—such a "dissolution" would not only follow as the worst of traitors in their deepest rancor never thought of, but universal adversity would overflow the land.

The wealth of a country is based upon the surplus of its agricultural products, hence the debt of a government is paid in large measure from the cultivated lands of the country. And if *that* cultivation is to be carried on without associated effort, without concentrated action, without the agency of the agricultural press, the gloomy prospect becomes gloomier still.

In every other pursuit of life, success depends very much upon an exchange of ideas, which exchange is effected by the public press, becoming as it does a weekly summary of new ideas, discoveries, conditions and proximate methods; reflecting, not "as in a glass darkly, but face to face" the progress of the day. Saith the Latin proverb, *Nemo solus sapit*, no one is wise alone, a truth preëminently applicable to the farmer.

Of all the characters in the great drama of life, none are more unsuccessful or unwise than that man whose mind is already surfeited with his own individual egotisms.

The other great enterprises of life, the commercial, manufacturing, mechanical and maritime, have their monthly, weekly, semi-weekly, daily, morning and evening editions, an *epitome* to direct through the voyage of life. And can the ship of agriculture, upon that stormy sea, keep her reckoning, without quadrant, chart or compass?

The advice of the celebrated Bakewell to farmers was, "to spare no pains to know what others were doing;" and in this fast age, when everything is upon the high pressure principle,—when centuries are crowded into months, he who heeds not the advice, pays dear for the whistle. Solomon, the wisest of men, said, "get wisdom, and with all thy getting get understanding;" and another wise man has said, "reading makes the ready man, but practice the perfect man." So to the farmer; reading—book-farming, if you please—is an important auxiliary to success, the *sine qua non*, but *not* the *ultimatum*.

No farmer can hope for success at the present day in the vast field of agricultural competition, who does not know what improvements others are making; and *no man can know that does not patronize the agricultural press.* The reading and the non-reading farmer are as opposite as the very antipodes. The first farms by rule, reducing his labors to a system by well demonstrated agricultural theorems, avails himself of every improvement in husbandry, favors the introduction of labor-saving implements, believes that "blood *will* tell," and in the race of progress is ready to start with the age—the second, to use a cant phrase, "goes it blind," farms by accident; as his paternal ancestors did so does he, believes in making hard work harder, knows the natives are best, is sure that book-knowledge is a humbug, and agricultural societies a nuisance. With such qualifications he must inevitably be a mere visionary in theory and a loser in practice.

We are prompted to these expressions by no pecuniary interest or influence whatever, but solely a desire to better the condition of our fellow-husbandmen. To the farmer, *this* is the time to "try men's souls," and well may he take hold of the plow with serious thoughts. Superadded to the wants of Europe, which are emptying our immense granaries, is that of our vast army, with its increasing demands upon our flocks and fields, and when the proportion between consumers and producers is rapidly increasing against the producer, is an anxious present with a clouded future, unless every farmer will avail himself of every agricultural improvement. But a small portion of our knowledge can be derived from our own personal experience, hence the necessity of some cheap, practical aad direct method of adding to our fund of knowledge, which, fortuuately, is through the medium of the agricultural press.

Dr. Weston presented the following paper relating to the doings of

The Bangor Horticultural Society.

By Dr. J. C. Weston, Secretary.

The Bangor Horticultural Society is the oldest in the State. It was incorporated in 1849, and has therefore been in existence fourteen years. It has conferred a great benefit on all the surrounding country. By its exhibitions and awards of premiums, it has excited competition and stimulated the people to cultivate the very best varieties of pears, plums, apples, grapes, &c. It has developed a taste and rivalry in the cultivation of ornamental trees and shrubs and all the products of the best furnished gardens. Under its auspices every desirable new fruit, flower, and vegetable of native origin have early been introduced to the knowledge of the community.

It has had meetings for the discussion of such practical subjects as manures, draining, grafting, the best varieties of fruits and vegetables and the best method of cultivating them. It has also had valuable practical lectures.

A few years ago but one glass structure existed in the city for the cultivation of foreign grapes, built by Frederic Hobbs, Esq., the first President of the society. The beautiful clusters raised by his skillful cultivation and management appeared on the tables at our exhibitions to feast and delight the eyes of all beholders. The example was contagious. What had been done by one, others thought they might accomplish, and gradually twenty-seven other graperies sprung into existence, yielding thousands of pounds of delicious grapes, and adding thousands of dollars to the value of real-estate.

By the influence of this society, Bangor, like Damascus, has become a city of gardens, many of which are laid out in tasteful, picturesque forms, and make many a home beautiful and attractive, so that emigration has no charms for the occupants. They are firmly rooted to home soil and pay cheerfully the taxes to support a government which has given for a few years $150 annually to promote Horticulture, while they have invested thousands for the same purpose.

The most of our merchants and mechanics, when about to erect dwellings, purchase double lots, that each may possess his own garden, where he may sit under his own vine and fruit tree; and thus becoming interested in the culture of the soil, our men of wealth often enlarge the spheres of their operations, by purchasing farms in the adjoining country, and improving them according to the best system of modorn husbandry, and some instances might be mentioned where these farms pay a larger dividend than bank stock, or stock in trade, or manufactures.

The society has had an annual exhibition every year but one since its formation. In 1857, by invitation of the Trustees of the Maine State Agricultural Society, it united with that body in its exhibition at Bangor, and contributed its full share to make it interesting and attractive.

At its exhibitions, the best varieties of peaches, pears, plums, grapes, flowers and vegetables have been represented. Our plums, particularly, have been unsurpassed in color, size and quality. I have attended exhibitions in Boston, New York and Montreal, but have never seen elsewhere, such a variety of this fruit as in our own city, in years of plenty.

Last September, in spite of the severity of our winters, the specimens of pears and American grapes of open culture, exceeded in quantity those exhibited on any former occasion, evincing an increased interest in the cultivation of those fruits. The Delaware, Hartford Prolific and Rebecca were nearly ripe on the 17th day of September, but the Concord, Diana, and Isabella had not colored, except on girdled branches.

Apples appeared in greater abundance than ever before. Two members, each, exhibited ninety varieties. Raising so many kinds is not so profitable to the orchardist as a select few of the best quality; but we have every year offered premiums for the largest and best variety of this and other fruits, with a view of ascertaining what kinds are best adapted to our climate and soil. The principal producers of fruit were requested to furnish the Secretary lists of apples, pears, plums and grapes which each had found by experience to be the very best for general cultivation in Bangor and vicinity, taking into consideration hardiness and productiveness of trees and vines, and quality of fruits. By inspection of these lists, it appears that a majority agreed in recommending the following apples: For summer—Bell's Early, Red Astrachan, William's Favorite, except for light soils, Benoni and High Top Sweeting. For autumn—Duchess of Oldenburg, Porter, Gravenstein, Winthrop Greening or Lincoln Pippin, Hubbardston Nonsuch, and Fameuse or Snow apple. For winter—Blue Pearmain, Yellow Bellflower, Rhode Island Greening, Ribston Pippin, Tolman's Sweeting, Baldwin grafted into large trees, and Northern Spy. Some two or more of the minority have concurred in recommending Early Harvest, Sweet Bough and Sweet Quincing for summer. Fall Jenneting, Sweet or Golden Russet, Killam Hill and Maiden's Blush, for autumn, and Jewett's Red, Mother, Danvers Winter Sweet, (in strong rich loams,) Esopus Spitzenburg, Roxbury Russet, and Red Everlasting, for winter and spring. One each also recommends Summer Rose, Fall Pippin, Hawley, Northern Sweet, Shop, Minister, Wine Apple, Nonsuch, Vandevere and Ladies' Sweet.

Of these varieties, it is apparent that the first eighteen are the most popular, and they are recommended for general cultivation in our locality; while the others promise well and deserve a further trial to secure the favorable consideration of orchardists.

The Duchess of Oldenburg is one of the most hardy of all trees, and doubtless would flourish in the most Northern part of Maine, if engrafted on native stocks. It is a constant bearer—the fruit, though surpassed in flavor by other varieties, is of good quality and suitable for cooking at an early age. The Blue Pearmain is also very hardy, but rather a slow grower. The Baldwin is tender when grafted into small trees, but succeeds well when inserted in full grown native stocks. The first trees of this kind introduced from Massachusetts, some thirty years ago, required some time to become acclimated. When they first bore, the fruit was entirely green, not possessing a particle of the red color peculiar to this apple, but in a few years it acquired it. This is not the case with grafts inserted on native stocks, but they produce from the first, well colored fruit, not quite equal in flavor and size to those of its native state, but will keep until a later period in the spring.

The tree of the Rhode Island Greening is apt to decay early at the heart in some localities, from some cause or disease not ascertained, and this peculiarity in the estimation of some has diminished its value. The Esopus Spitzenburg succeeds well in warm virgin soils containing a sufficient supply of potash and lime, particularly when engrafted in the top of a well-grown native tree, but the growth is slow and the fruit inferior on old impoverished lands.

The Red Everlasting is said to be one of the most sprightly and fresh of all late dessert apples.

The Northern Spy has rapidly acquired the favor of our orchardists. Its flesh is mild, juicy and fresh after long keeping and commands the highest price in the market. The tree is of rapid, upright growth and needs judicious pruning when young, that it may form open heads, and its fruit may be fully exposed to the sun, as it is insipid in the shade.

Our fruit-growers, when selecting trees in a nursery, give a preference to those which throw out their limbs horizontally—for experience has taught that those branches which grow from the trunks at an obtuse angle, are stronger at the point of juncture, and less inclined to split off than those which form an acute angle. Crotched trees are rejected, on account of this liability to split apart.

One of our nurserymen, Mr. A. Noyes, has been very successful in growing the apple on the paradise stock, by which it is very much dwarfed, so that the trees can be raised six or eight feet apart. They are well adapted for gardens and bear abundantly, but are more suitable for the amateur than the orchardist.

The apple tree cannot be made to grow well in light sandy soils, where the white pine has flourished for a long series of years, and where there is a deficiency of potash, unless the land is first enriched with a compost of ashes, lime, muck and stable manure, and after the trees are set out, it is necessary to mulch the ground under them to prevent evaporation until they make sufficient progress to shade it completely, and it is important to encourage the limbs to grow as low down as possible. In this way only can complete success be attained in such localities. The compost just mentioned is a good manure for the apple tree in any locality. A preference is given to oyster shell lime, when it can easily be procured.

Our best and most popular pears are Doyenne d'Ete, Dearborn's Seedling, Tyson, Bartlett, Fulton, Flemish Beauty, Beurre d'Amalis, Louise Bonne de Jersey, Urbaniste, Seckel, if grafted in the top of a thrifty growing tree, St. Ghislain, Winter Nelis, Easter Beurre, and Vicar of Winkfield for cooking. The Doyenne d'Ete is tender on the quince stock, but is hardy on the mountain ash.

In severe winters, some of the branches of the Bartlett are killed when unprotected; but it is hardy when grafted on the wild pear stock. The fruit, however, is sometimes insipid. The Louise Bonne de Jersey and Vicar of Winkfield, in some localities, are also tender. The rest are comparatively hardy.

In the city gardens, pears have been grown, principally, on the quince stock. The trees are headed back and the branches encouraged to grow near the ground. Early in September the ends of the branches are cut off to check their further growth and cause the wood to ripen, but with all our care, the more tender varieties are sometimes killed down to the snow. But it has been discovered that pears are hardy when grafted on the wild pear stock or "shad-bush." One of the members of this society, Mr. Jefferson Stubbs of Hampden, has used this stock for the last ten years. He already has a pear orchard of two hundred and fifty trees, and intends to add two hundred more next spring. He transplants the trees from the woods, cutting off all the branches when they are tall, so as to force the latent buds to start, and after they have grown a year or two, he inserts the grafts, and they take effect as readily as on other stocks. He claims that they bear early and constantly, that they are perfectly hardy, that he has not lost a single tree from the effects of winter. He has already had experience with the Madeleine, Tyson, Buffum, Pratt, Bartlett, Flemish Beauty, Onondaga, Louise Bonne de Jersey, Seckel, Beurre Diel, Urbaniste, and Winter Nelis. Pears generally prove more hardy, also, on the mountain ash and pear stocks, than on the quince, but the quality of some is inferior.

Plums. Our most experienced cultivators recommend the Green Gage, Washington, Jefferson, McLaughlin, Imperial Gage, Smith's Orleans, Lawrence's Favorite, Washington Seeoling, Purple Favorite, Bleeker's Gage and Lombard, and the Damson and Yellow Egg, for preserving. The first-named are decidedly the best. The Columbia is a large and handsome plum; but its meat is rather coarse and sometimes lacks flavor, and the tree is an awkward and scraggy grower.

Grapes for open culture. The Delaware for our climate is the best and most desirable of all grapes. It is hardy as an oak, is sure to ripen its fruit, however unfavorable the season, and its flavor surpasses all others. Every farmer ought to possess it. The Hartford Prolific is also very hardy, early and productive—

will thrive in the open field, even with careless culture, wherever corn will grow. The Rebecca is of excellent flavor and generally ripens its fruit; but is less hardy, and requires a dry, protected location. The ends of the branches do not always mature. The Diana and White Sweet Water, Logan and Concord, if trained against a wall and protected from the early frosts of autumn, will also mature in most years; but the Isabella, even under the most favorable circumstances generally fails. When girdled it will color before the last of September, but seldom becomes sweet and good. By removing part of the branches, and judiciously thinning the berries from the remainder, the ripening of grapes may be hastened at least a week. If a third are removed, the fruit will be larger and better.

Cherries. No cherry is perfectly hardy in Bangor, except the Kentish or early Richmond. These become quite sweet, if allowed to hang on the tree some time after they become red. In favorable seasons, the May Duke, Elton, Black Eagle, Downton, Honey Heart, and Downer's Late have been raised.

Grafting. The modes of grafting practiced by our horticulturists, differ somewhat from those employed elsewhere. By one method the stock or limb is scarped off at an angle of about forty-five degrees. The scion is split up two or three inches with one side thicker; the inside of the thicker part is made smooth with a sharp knife, and the end sharpened on the outside, and the bark of the stock opposite the scarf with a thin sliver of wood is cut down and it is thrust under it. The thin part is brought down over the scarf and inserted beneath the bark as on the opposite side. The bark is then bound over the forks of the scions by strips of grafting cloth, which is also passed neatly over the cut surface. The scion unites readily with the stock on both sides; the juncture is perfect and the wound speedily heals.

Another mode introduced to the knowledge of the community by George P. Sewall of Oldtown, is the following: Cut a T in the bark on the upper side of the limb, in the spring, after the leaves have pushed and when the bark peels easily; scarp off the scion on one side and sharpen its point by cutting off a little each side of the round part, that it may slide down well, and then press down the scion; put a little grafting wax over the corners, and bind around strips of list. As the scion grows, the ends of the stock or branch are gradually shortened and the binding loosened.

When the scion becomes long and heavy a piece of list is passed around it and the branch to confine it and prevent the wind from blowing it out before the union is strong and perfect. Finally in a year or two the branch is entirely removed and the scarp made in the act being underneath, heals more readily. The advantages of this method are: that the growth of the tree is not checked; the process is quickly performed, and it is very successful, particularly on thrifty trees.

Grafting by approach has been used for the grape vine, when two branches of different vines are near each other, or a vine in a pot can be obtained. The bark and a sliver are removed from the sides, so that when brought in contact, they will closely fit and they are bound together until a union is effected, and then the branch which is to be discarded is removed and the connection with the vine which has been used for the scion is severed.

Of currants, a new variety, the Versaillaise, surpasses all the others, It is very large and the bush is a great bearer. Red and White Dutch have long been cultivated, and the Red and White Grape have been introduced.

Some twenty kinds of gooseberries have been cultivated, but none have escaped the mildew except the Houghton's Seedling, and this variety cannot be too highly commended.

Raspberries. Red and White Antwerp, Knevett's Giant, Fill Basket, Franconia, Brinkle's Orange and Catawissa have proved the best. The Catawissa is an everbearing variety and differs essentially from the others. Instead of producing its fruit chiefly on the old wood, it bears mostly on wood of the current year's growth and continues until prevented by frost. Its size is large and color deep crimson.

Strawberries. The Wilson's Albany, Cutter's Seedling, Austin Shaker, Hooker's, Boston Pine and Downer's, have all succeeded well in our vicinity, and have been prolific. For productiveness and profit the Wilson's Albany stands first and the Cutter's second. For flavor, the Hooker's and Downer's are the best. The Cutter's and Downer's have strong stalks, which are not apt to bend to the ground under the weight of their fruit.

One cultivator, Mr. J. P. Sinclair, brought into market the last season (1862) six hundred and forty boxes, the produce of five kinds, and Mr. A. Noyes raised about six hundred quarts of the best varieties.

It is estimated that twenty-five hundred bushels of the smaller fruits have been raised the last year in Penobscot county.

What the Bangor Horticultural Society has accomplished for all the surrounding country, similar associations can effect in their several localities, until, from these common centres, a benign influence shall go forth which shall encircle the whole State. By ascertaining the varieties best adapted for every soil and place, by collecting the lessons of experience, by diffusing knowledge in respect to the cultivation of fruits, and *especially the apple*, an increased interest may be excited, so that Maine, at no distant day, may not only raise enough for home consumption, but also a surplus for a foreign market, and thus may add hundreds of thousands of dollars to the valuation of property. A consummation so desirable is worthy our warmest zeal—our most persevering efforts.

On motion of Dr. Weston, the following resolve was unanimously adopted:

Whereas, It is the province of the Board to prescribe and determine the duties of the Secretary, and whereas the more extensive culture of fruit in the State is extremely desirable, therefore

Resolved, That the Board of Agriculture recommends to the Secretary, in addition to his other duties prescribed by statute and by former votes of the Board, an investigation of the subject of Fruit and Fruit Culture in Maine, during the current year, and the preparation of a leading paper on the subject, to be included in his next annual report.

The following communications were presented and read:

From Joseph M. Smith, Anson.

My flock of sheep in the spring of 1862, was composed of sixty-seven ewes, four wethers, and forty lambs (or one year olds.)

From my ewes I raised sixty lambs; I sheared seven hundred and thirteen pounds from the whole flock, which I sold at fifty cents per pound, amounting to the sum of . . $356 50

Sold ten old sheep for	30 00
One ewe, ...	6 00
Ten lambs, $6, ...	60 00
One for	9 00
One for	8 00
One (ewe) for	9 00

One (ewe) for	$5 00
Four for	32 00
Was offered $6 per head for thirty-eight, amounting to	228 00
Total income, ...	$743 50

Equal to $6.70 per head.

The above sheep were Spanish Merinos, and samples of the wool were presented with the statement.

An experiment in the use of Superphosphate of Lime.

S. F. PERLEY—*Dear Sir:*—At your request, I send you the following statement of my experiment with *Superphosphate of Lime and pumpkins among corn.* About the middle of May last, I plowed a field that had been in grass five years, and the yield had become so reduced that it was unprofitable for hay. After plowing, I spread on stable manure at the rate of seven or eight cords per acre, and harrowed it in. I also procured of Kendall & Whitney, a barrel of Coe's Superphosphate, and mixed it with about half its bulk of plaster, and directed a quantity, perhaps two or three spoonfuls, to be put in each hill of corn and slightly covered before dropping the seed. When the man at work dropping the fertilizer had gone over nearly half the field, he came and told me that the Super-phosphate would not hold out to go over the whole at the rate directed. I told him to diminish the quantity so as to make it go over the whole, except six rows through the middle of the field to be left without any. But on these six rows I directed him to put about the same quantity of plaster to a hill that in the mixture would go upon the rest of the field, so that I might fairly test the effect of the Superphosphate. I gave the boy who dropped the corn some pumpkin seeds to plant with it, and being a liberal handed boy, he bestowed all his pumpkin seeds on the first sixteen rows. At the first hoeing I had a gill or more of ashes put on each hill through the field.

The result. After the corn was up nearly large enough for the second hoeing, one of my neighbors remarked that a strip of my corn through the middle of the field *looked as though it had fainted away.* There was a marked difference in the growth through the whole season. At harvesting, the yield was as follows:

Six rows without Superphosphate, eight bushels of ears good corn, three small or unripe.

Six adjoining rows with Superphosphate, eleven bushels of good ears, two small or unripe.

Sixteen rows with pumpkins, twenty bushels of ears good corn, six small or unripe.

With Superphosphate, one and five-sixths bushels of ears good corn, per row.

Without Superphosphate, one and a third bushels of ears good corn, per row.

With pumpkins, one and a quarter bushels of ears good corn per row.

Giving half a bushel to a row more with Superphosphate than without; and the pumpkins more than neutralized all the good effects of that fertilizer, although they were planted on that part of the field which had the most liberal supply of it. The crop of pumpkins was not worth half as much as the corn was damaged by them. The six rows with Superphosphate which were measured, grew in that part of the field which had the reduced quantity.

I suppose there is nothing gained by putting plaster with Superphosphate of lime, as in the manufacture of that article from bones and sulphuric acid, sulphate of lime or gypsum is formed, and becomes a portion of the article as sold.

Yours truly,

M. Gould.

North Bridgton, Jan. 22, 1863.

Mr. Rogers gave the result of an experiment he had made with concentrated manure upon potatoes. The soil a clayey loam; the land prepared and seeded in every way precisely alike, the only difference in treatment being in the different kinds of manure applied.

A given number of rows produced with no manure, seven-eighths bushel.

American guano, one and a half bushels. Increase seventy-one per cent.

Coe's Superphosphate, two bushels. Increase one hundred and twenty-nine per cent.

The concentrated manure was applied at the rate of about five hundred pounds per acre, and a larger proportion of merchantable potatoes were found in the rows manured with the American guano.

Profits of three Cows.

Dr. WESTON—*Dear Sir*:—As you have a sample of our cheese, it occurred to me that a statement of the products of my three cows might not be amiss.

Accordingly, I have gone over my cash book and gathered the amount of sales of dairy produce for 1862. I kept the past year, three cows, one of which calved in September, 1861, and has been farrow since.

514 gallons milk sold, averaging 14 cents, . .	$71 96
263 pounds butter sold, averaging 19½ cents, . .	51 28
345 pounds cheese sold, averaging 9 1-6 cents, .	31 62
365 gallons milk used in family at 10 cents, . .	36 50
98 pounds butter used in family at 19½ cents, .	19 11
42 pounds cheese used in family at 10 cents, . .	4 20
2 veal calves sold, ...	8 00
90 pounds cheese on hand (now worth) 12 cents, .	10 80
	$233 47
The estimated cost of keeping the cows for 1862, at $40 each, ...	120 00
Balance in favor of cows, labor, &c., . . .	$113 47

In the above statement, I have not taken into account the value of the sour milk and whey fed to the cows. I do not consider my cows extra ones. Neither do I think the above statement shows better profits than most farmers *might* realize with proper care and attention. But I do not believe that one farmer in twenty can make so good a statement. My crops are principally hay and grain. I commenced in 1861, keeping sheep; think they pay the best of any stock. And this reminds me that we "sheep keepers" demand of the Board of Agriculture all the influence you can exert with the Legislature to give us additional protection from *dogs and cattle at large.*

Respectfully,

W. W. JOHNSON.

Brewer, Jan. 20, 1863.

The Business Committee having reported, and Committees having been appointed to investigate the several topics presented, Dr. Weston, for Committee upon First Topic, submitted the following Report and Resolutions relative to

Agricultural Education.

What further means should now *be adopted to promote Agricultural Education in Maine?*

No one, like the fabled Minerva, makes his entrance on the stage of life fully developed and prepared to engage successfully in any avocation. All need that mental discipline which shall give them quickness of perception, a retentive memory, a habit of thinking and reasoning, and language to express their ideas. All require that physical training which shall produce a healthy development of their whole physical organization, so that a sound mind may dwell in a sound body; and all need that moral instruction which shall prompt a ready obedience to laws, both human and divine.

Such a comprehensive preliminary training is important for all ranks and conditions of men, for the most limited capacity, as well as the mightiest intellect; for the most humble laborer, as well as the most exalted ruler. By means of it, all are better prepared for the actual duties of any profession, art or business.

Knowledge, when practically applied, becomes a power—a lever which shall move the world, and send it onward in a career of progress and advancement. No matter how low the occupation, how menial the employment, intelligence elevates and ennobles. It secures, in the best manner, the most beneficial practical results, with the least fatigue, the least possible expenditure of strength. The greater the intelligence, the greater the success in any pursuit.

Besides the general discipline required by the great mass of mankind, a *special* education is necessary not only to fit students for the professions, but also adapted to the wants of that largest and most important class of the community, comprising the agriculturist, the mechanic and the merchant.

Youth, it is generally conceded, is the most favorable period to acquire this knowledge. It is the age of leisure, of exemption from the cares and perplexities of business. Ideas then received are stamped with an indelible impress on the fresh tablets of the memory. Correct moral principles then instilled, grow with the growth, and strengthen with the strength, until they become incorporated with the very being. Youth is emphatically the spring-time of life. The seeds of knowledge then sown will the more surely germinate, and at maturity yield an abundant harvest of usefulness.

The State has provided for the education of all the children and youth, by establishing common schools, where the rudiments of knowledge may be learned by both poor and rich. It has instituted academies, where higher attainments may be made. It has founded colleges, where a small fraction of the young men who have the time and means, can avail themselves of the thorough course of preparatory discipline afforded by classical studies and mathematics. It has added special schools of Divinity, Law and Medicine, to qualify them for the practice of either of the learned professions.

These have all been connected together like separate links in the same chain. The goal continually in view, in the great race of life, by those who aspire to a liberal education, has hitherto been to reach at least one of the professions, or take their chance in the mazes of politics. Hence the whole course of instruction is subservient to this great end. The academy takes its pupils from the common schools, and drills them principally in the pure mathematics and the dead languages. They then enter college, and devote a large proportion of the time to the same classical studies. At length they graduate after some seven years constant discipline; but having expended so much time and capital in this preliminary training, they think they cannot afford to engage in any common industrial pursuit, and have no inclination for it. Custom, supposed interest and pride, all prompt them to enter such special schools as shall best qualify them for the practice of the profession selected. Thus it often happens that the supply exceeds the demand, and the professions are crowded. Some monopolize the business, while others obtain little patronage; yet the latter, from want of the requisite practical training, are unfitted for, and disinclined to, any other occupation, and in some instances become the drones of the community.

It is not intended to disparage, in the least degree, the system of education adopted in our academies and colleges. It is doubtless the best which the experience and wisdom of ages could establish, for those who design to devote their lives to some regular profession, or the pursuit of literature; but it does not supply the wants of a large majority of young men who need an education for agriculture or the mechanic arts.

It is not creditable to our country, that while we have surpassed most European nations in the number of our common schools and colleges, we are greatly behind them in institutions designed to teach the innumerable applications of science to agriculture, and throw a charm around this noble employment. Only New York, Pennsylvania, Maryland, Michigan and Iowa have each established one, and even all these are not in successful operation. New England is entirely destitute. And yet three-fourths of the people of the United States are agriculturists;* and it has been estimated that nine- tenths of the fixed capital of all nations is invested in the same pursuit. Statistics collected in the State of New York, show, notwithstanding the enormous wealth of the metropolis, the agricultural interest pays four-fifths of all the taxes.† Although England is called a manufacturing country, yet the returns of her income tax show that two thirds of all the net income from the industry of the nation is derived from agriculture.

Daniel Webster, after observing with his keen intellect the prosperity of agriculture in England, thus speaks of its great relative importance: "No man in England is so high as to be independent of this great interest—no man so low as not to be affected by its prosperity or decline. The same is true, eminently, emphatically true with us. Agriculture feeds us; to a great extent it clothes us; without it, we could not have manufactures, and we should not have commerce. These all stand together like pillars in a cluster—the largest in the centre, and that largest is AGRICULTURE."

An interest of such vital, intrinsic importance, underlying and contributing to the prosperity of all others, especially deserves the fostering care of government. It ought to make as ample provision for the education of the masses for practical life, and particularly for agricultural pursuits, as it has hitherto made for those intended for professional and literary life. Recognizing, then, and appreciating the fact that a large proportion of its citizens must devote themselves to the cultivation of the soil, it should prepare them to engage in it, intelligently and successfully, by such instruction as shall make them thoroughly understand their business.

---

* See Patent Office Report on Agriculture for 1861, page 5.

† See Report on Agricultural Education, by Hon. Henry F. French, page 277 of the Transactions of the Mass. Society for Promoting Agriculture, 185J.

The State has already partially attended to this duty. It has established a Board of Agriculture, whose especial office is to investigate and discuss all such subjects relating to agriculture and horticulture, and the arts connected therewith, as they may deem expedient, to disseminate among the people useful facts, discoveries, improvements and theories, by reports and essays, and to make such suggestions and recommendations to the Legislature, from time to time, as the interests of agriculture may seem to require.

The State has also incorporated agricultural and horticultural societies, and has annually appropriated money to be offered in premiums for the best animals, crops, dairy products, improvement of soils and manures, &c.; and has required in return, from each society, a full and accurate statement of the process or method of rearing, managing, producing and accomplishing the same, together with its cost and value, with a view of showing the profits or benefits derived or expected therefrom; also the leading features of the annual exhibition, the character of the efforts of the society for the advancement of agriculture, the prominent crops grown in the county or district, the success attending their culture as compared with former years, and the obstacles met with; and generally upon the condition, prospects and wants of agriculture, so far as they may be able to ascertain them, together with any reports of committees, essays, addresses, or other papers presented to the society, containing matters of general interest.

The State, by means of the scientific survey, is giving us some adequate conception of our own resources for agriculture, manufactures and commerce; of our physical geography, agricultural capacity and geology; of our zoology, botany and entomology; of our soils, mines and quarries.

By these several methods, useful knowledge has been obtained and diffused, which, like leaven, is permeating the community and silently working out beneficial results. Agricultural journals and farmers' clubs have coöperated, and we already see the good effects, on comparison of census returns of the State for 1850 and 1860, in the increase and value of farming implements, live stock, and farm products.

The State has thus provided for the instruction chiefly of its *adult* population. But the time has come when it ought to take another step in advance, if it would keep pace with the progress of other nations. It ought now to give all its children and youth an opportunity to acquire a knowledge of the principles of practical agriculture. In all our district schools, besides the common branches now required to be taught by statute, such as reading, writing, spelling, arithmetic, grammar and geography, easy primary lessons in chemistry should be given on the properties of elementary substances, their mutual combinations, the modes of separating them, with the application of such knowledge to the explanation of natural phenomena and to useful purposes in the arts of life. Also a knowledge should be imparted of the first principles of natural philosophy or of the laws of motion and mechanical forces; of botany, or the structure and growth of plants; of physiology, or the requirements of plants and animals; of geology, or the origin and nature of soils.

If suitable elementary treatises on these subjects cannot be obtained, the teacher might talk familiarly about them fifteen or twenty minutes daily, and illustrate the first principles by a few simple experiments, and thus afford agreeable relaxation, awaken an interest and develop a taste for these studies.

In all our High schools, these sciences should be more thoroughly taught, more amply illustrated; their relations to the useful arts more fully explained, and more time devoted to their investigation.

But most of all, there is an imperative necessity that the Legislature should now found an Agricultural College, with an experimental farm and accomplished instructors to teach all its pupils in the lecture room, in the laboratory, and in the field, all the innumerable applications of science to Agriculture and the Arts; to accustom them to the best methods of cultivation, and the skilful use of the best farm implements; to acquaint them with the best farm buildings and the different breeds of animals; to enjoin upon them system, and habits of careful observation and reflection; in fine, to make them compehend all the principles, the whole science of husbandry with all its practical details, and the reasons for them, and at the same time to give them a fondness for this noble occupation.

Thus the brain and the hand, the heart and the muscle would all unite in its prosecution and would conduct its operations with success and profit. Intelligence would then be wedded to labor; the first minds of the age would engage in agriculture, instead of rushing into the professions, when it was apparent that capital and labor might be invested in it with as much certainty of paying a remunerating dividend as when ventured in any other business.

Demonstrate to the community that farming would be profitable, and capital would flow abundantly into this channel, and so capital, intelligence and labor, would all coöperate to bring agriculture to a high degree of perfection; then, and only then, will it thrive—when this confidence is secured, and the necessary means freely applied.

A class of men like the stewards of England would be educated, who might be employed by the wealthy to superintend the farms they purchase, when, advanced in years, they engage in a new branch of business for which they have had no previous experience and training, and so by aid of such an overseer incur no risk of disastrous failure.

Already there is a demand for such men which cannot now be supplied. The College contemplated alone can furnish the agents who shall be entrusted with the funds awaiting investment, and who can obtain for their services a larger compensation than the average income of professional men.

Teachers and lecturers would be properly qualified for our schools of various grades who may radiate the light of science and intelligence to our remotest borders. Thus "many shall run to and fro and knowledge shall be increased."

For want of this scientific knowledge our whole country has seriously suffered. Our most fertile fields have been impoverished by an unwise system of husbandry. During a long series of years, cattle and grain have been conveyed away to a distant market; the products of their final decomposition have flowed down our sewers into rivers, and been lost in the ocean, and no equivalent has been returned to the soil to repair the waste. Our soils once abundantly possessed all those mineral constituents essential to the growth of plants.

True wisdom, which scientific knowledge imparts, would have taught the farmer to ascertain the chemical ingredients of the products transported, and would have prompted him to return a sufficient amount in the form of manures. Then their primeval fertility would not have been impaired; then we should not have to regret the disastrous effect of the "spoliation system," as it has been significantly called.

In many of the oldest States the average product of wheat has decreased one-half in less than fifty years, while in Great Britain during the same period, it has increased one hundred per cent. in consequence of a more intelligent cultivation.

From these facts, the inference is unavoidable that the older farms have degenerated; that some of the elements in the soil, essential to the constitution, health and growth of the great staples of the country, have been diminished by continued cropping and need to be restored.

An Agricultural College would teach our farmers how to ascertain what is requisite to render an impoverished soil again rich and productive, and how to increase their crops without impairing the fertility of their fields.

Such institutions are especially needed in all the States to give a new impetus and prosperity to all the productive interests of the country in this great emergency. We are in the midst of a great revolution, not only social and political, but industrial and economical. There has been no rebellion in the history of the world equal in magnitude to the present. Nearly two millions of men are arrayed against each other in deadly strife for conquest and power. Every single individual has daily wants to be supplied. Each soldier must be fed and clothed. His wages too, must be regularly paid. If sick, he must be nursed and healed. If disabled, he must be pensioned. The expenses of this war affect both the present and extend far into the future.

Money goes, and must continue to go in a perfect flood. We are piling up a debt of scores of millions every month, and it will continually increase until the wicked rebellion is crushed. This national debt, like a great incubus, will rest heavily upon the productive resources of the country. We must sustain it, and be taxed to provide means for its payment. Hence these interests should be appreciated and fostered, that they may be able to bear the burden and finally extinguish the debt.

Impressed by these considerations, the present Congress, (the 37th,) notwithstanding the heavy responsibilities and arduous duties occasioned by the war, has recognized the importance of agriculture and kindred pursuits, and with far reaching sagacity has established a National Department of Agriculture at Washington. It has also found time to mature and pass "An act donating lands to the several States and Territories which may provide Colleges for the benefit of Agriculture and the Mechanic Arts," and which express their acceptance thereof, with the annexed conditions, prior to July 2, 1864.

By the provisions of this act an amount of public lands is offered to Maine equal to 30,000 acres for each of its members of Congress, according to the last apportionment. As we have five Representatives and two Senators, this would give 210,000 acres as our portion.

It is also provided that ten per cent. accruing from the sale of these public lands, may be expended for lands, or building sites, or experimental farms, whenever authorized by the Legislature, and that the remainder "shall be invested in stocks of the United States, or of the States, or some other safe stocks, yielding not less than five per centum upon the par value of said stocks; and that the moneys so invested shall constitute a perpetual fund, the capital of which shall remain forever undiminished, and the interest of which shall be inviolably appropriated, by each State which may take and claim the benefit of this act, to the endowment, support and maintenance of at least one college, where the *leading* object shall be, without excluding other scientific and classical studies, and including military tactics, to teach such branches of learning as are related to agriculture and the mechanic arts, in such manner as the Legislatures of the States may respectively prescribe, in order to promote the liberal and practical education of the industrial classes in the several pursuits and professions of life."

The course of study is exceedingly liberal. While those branches of learning intimately connected with agriculture and industrial arts; with military tactics are expressly enjoined, other scientific and classical studies are not excluded. Thus it may be an institution where an education, both special and comprehensive, can be obtained. It combines the theoretical and practical, the intellectual and physical. "It furnishes the means of a positive increase of human knowledge in the departments bearing on agriculture and manufactures, and the medium of teaching, not only farmers, but those who shall become teachers and improvers of the art of farming." Here all the sons of Maine may seek that preparatory discipline required to fit them for all the diversified occupations of life. Here, by the military drill, and by labor on the farm, they may attain that physical strength and development so essential to vigorous health, energy and success in any pursuit.

This provision for physical education is one of the most important features of the bill. In our haste to develope the mind we have forgotten the body. The one has been constantly forced by a kind of hot-bed process, while the other has been neglected or cramped in all its powers, and so we are dying for want of physical culture. It is the great American want. The National Government now offers the military drill and prescribes instruction in military tactics.

If such discipline and knowledge had generally been imparted, the present war would not have found us all unprepared. It might have been prosecuted more successfully, terminated more speedily, and saved millions of money and thousands of lives.

The errors of the past are irremediable. The present and future can only be molded by our influence. The time has not yet come to deprecate the military spirit. The lion has not yet shown any disposition to lie down peaceably with the lamb, hence we cannot safely turn the swords into plowshares or the spears into pruning hooks, however desirable such a consummation may be to agriculture, but we must, at least for the present, be a nation of soldiers or give up our liberties. Hence, in the proposed institution, ample instruction in military science must be imparted, and all the students required to practice all the exercises the manual of arms directs. This exercise by the military drill, and daily labor upon the farm or in the work-shop, would secure ample physical development and preserve the health, while the mind is intently applied to the acquisition of knowledge, and thus not only would sedentary habits be prevented and the constitution be unimpaired, but the muscles of the body and the faculties of the mind would be strengthened and developed at even pace, the one reacting upon and promoting the vigor of the other, and the whole man would be prepared in the best manner for the arduous duties of subsequent life.

As the National Government has offered to the State such a munificent gift, it devolves on the Legislature to determine whether it will accept it with the annexed terms and conditions. "It is rare that a question of more immediate or more far reaching consequences is submitted to its action."

If it would obtain this bounty, it must provide the college and furnish the necessary buildings. Vast benefits to the age and to the race hang on the decision. The time has already arrived to locate the lands. The acceptance must be signified within two years, and the college must go into operation within five years from July 2d, 1862. A measure of such intrinsic importance, both present and prospective, must receive the favorable consideration of the Legislature. It cannot afford to refuse a donation so beneficent.

Assuming, then, that an agricultural college is to be founded, in accordance with the provisions of the act, the questions of location, buildings, departments, &c., must be considered. And while it would be premature at this time to decide upon any fixed definite plan, it may be well to mention some details by way of suggestion, that may properly be considered when arrangements are made to put the college into operation, with the hope that they may serve as a ground work upon which others may rear a more finished structure.

Instead of connecting it with some classical institution already established for another purpose, and making the agricultural subordinate to the literary department, it ought to be located entirely independent of any other school, in some place which is central in respect to geographical position, population and social advantages, where enough land comprising the greatest possible variety of soil susceptible of improvement by cultivation, can be obtained to constitute a suitable farm.

The *farm* is indispensable. It is the most appropriate arena to impart and illustrate important lessons, to interrogate nature, witness all her processes and operations and gain valuable instruction. By means of it the principles of science can be directly applied to agricultural operations, so that by the union of science and experiment, the results produced will indicate the precise practical value of these principles, and aid the student to obtain a correct knowledge of the best and most profitable methods of cultivating and managing a farm. He will institute experiments to test disputed modes of culture, to ascertain the adaptation of our climate and certain soils to particular crops of desirable plants, the fertilizing properties of various manures, and will determine other questions of vast importance, requiring accurate and methodical investigation. And an annual report is required to be made of the progress of each college, recording any improvements and experiments made on the farm, with their costs and results, and such other matters as may be supposed to be useful, and a copy sent to all the other colleges, so that each may be the recipient of the knowledge attained by all the others.

A suitable building should be provided containing lecture and recitation rooms, library, laboratory, room for the various departments of Natural History, with accommodations, at first, for some one hundred students, so planned that it can easily be enlarged or extended, when necessary, by the addition of wings.

The library, chemical and philosophical apparatus, the instruments for surveying and leveling, mensuration and drawing, the different kinds of woods, and models of fruit might be gradually collected as they are needed. Our Scientific Survey might furnish specimens of the botany, mineralogy and geology of the State, to which additions may afterwards be made.

A model barn is needed, with apartments for all the various uses of the farm. The live stock should be such as the different branches of husbandry require, and ought to include thorough bred animals, or specimens of all improved breeds that their merits and characteristics may be observed and ascertained.

In the proposed institution the various departments of instruction will include:

1st, Practical Husbandry.

2d, General and Agricultural Chemistry.

3d, Botany, Vegetable Physiology and Horticulture.

4th, Zoology, Animal Physiology and Entomology.

5th, Geology, Mineralogy and Meteorology.

6th, Mathematics, Surveying, Engineering and Mechanics.

The Superintendent ought to be a thorough practical agriculturist, one who will not simply travel in the monotonous routine of the dead past, but believes in science and progress, and is prompt to avail himself of any improvements, and has that peculiar tact and judgment and intelligence that shall qualify him to oversee and direct the labors of others.

He will require all the students to work on the farm or in the gardens some three hours daily, to become acquainted with all the details of practical husbandry, to use the various tools with their own hands, and perform all kinds of work required in the management of the farm and stock. He will teach them *how* to dig, to plow, to plant, to hoe, to drain, &c., in the best manner, while the Professors of the college will enable them to understand exactly *why* each is to be done, or the reasons for the operations, so that labor may be applied to the best possible advantage.

Some five Professors will be required of the highest natural and acquired talents, each devoting himself specially to one of the departments of science and thoroughly exhibiting all its relations to Agriculture and the Mechanic Arts.

The annual revenue derived from the national bounty will pay the salaries of all the professors needed to instruct the several classes. It will also secure occasional or regular courses of lectures from the most eminent scientific men of the country, not connected with the college. Indeed, if economically expended, it will defray all the expenses except those incurred for the erection of the buildings. For these the State must provide, assisted, perhaps, by private benefactions. It is asked to expend a few thousand dollars with the certainty of realizing millions in the increased intelligence and consequent advancement of agricultural and all kindred industrial pursuits.

It will then provide a school whose doors will ever stand open to all who have obtained the necessary preliminary knowledge. No time need be expended in the attainment of any branch of learning, not having a close relation to practical pursuits.

The college will drill them some four years, and will then bestow its honors by conferring a degree of Bachelor of Science, as honorable, as useful, as any title ever bestowed by man; or it will allow those whose time and means do not permit such protracted study, to select those branches more closely related to their future business.

The Department of Chemistry will comprise instruction in respect to chemical forces, laws of combinations, properties of bodies, the facts and phenomena belonging to Inorganic and Organic Chemistry, all being amply illustrated by experiments. In Analytical Chemistry instruction will be imparted in respect to the analysis of soils, minerals and preparation of artificial manures.

In the prosecution of this analysis, the student must have daily practice in the laboratory, applying with his own hands the tests required to ascertain the composition and properties of bodies, thus securing a practical knowledge of the methods employed in these investigations.

Agricultural Chemistry will be principally taught by lectures, illustrated on the farm as well as in the laboratory, whenever the subject will permit, on the formation and composition of soils, composition of plants as determining the chemical condition of the soil, composition of the air, and its relations to vegetable growth, connection of heat, light and electricity with the growth of plants, nature and sources of the food of plants, chemical changes attending vegetable growth, chemistry of the various processes of the farm, as plowing, draining, &c., exhaustion of soils, and methods of chemically improving them, by mineral, vegetable and animal manures, and by indirect methods, rotation of crops, chemical composition of various crops and their uses as food, feeding, housing and care of stock, the chemistry of the dairy, nutritive and fattening qualities of the different articles of food and its preparation for animals and man.

In Botany, the student must first become intimately acquainted with structural and physiological botany with the aid of living and dried specimens, diagrams, and microscopes for the examination of minute structure. He then may proceed to the investigation of systematic botany, by dissecting and inspecting a sufficient number of our native plants to become acquainted with the more important natural families.

A Botanical Garden, containing specimens of every tree, shrub and plant, which will endure the climate, and an ample Herbarium would greatly assist in obtaining a knowledge of this science. The relations of botany to Horticultural operations, and the principles concerned in those operations can be intelligently explained and comprehended in the gardens and grounds.

There the student can have abundant practice in propagating plants from seeds, in budding, layering and grafting. He may also by cross breeding obtain new varieties of fruits, by removing the anthers from the blossom of one tree, and dusting upon its pistil pollen from the stamens of the flower from another tree, and subsequently planting the seeds obtained from the resulting fruits. In this way many new and desirable fruits, ornamental shrubs and flowers have been obtained. This is only one of the many applications of science.

Zoology and Animal Physiology. Instruction in this department would consist of recitations and lectures, illustrated as far as practicable by specimens of native and foreign animals, diagrams, by dissections of animals, and inspection of minute structure by the microscope, to make the student familiar with the appearance and relations of the various organs of the system in health, and the changes produced by disease. He may be led to the investigation of the Anatomy and Physiology of the organs of locomotion, digestion, circulation, respiration and reproduction; the systematic arrangement of animals in classes, families, &c., their habits, the Natural History of domestic animals, including the characteristics and peculiarities of different breeds and their value for particular purposes; the history and habits of the Insects injurious to vegetation, and the means of obviating and lessening their ravages, with the birds, reptiles and parasites which destroy them. He will study the economy of domestic animals, including the principles of breeding, rearing, and management; the diseases of animals, their nature and treatment, and the mode of administering medicines.

Geology, Mineralogy, and Meteorology. By recitations properly illustrated, and by familiar lectures on the relation of these sciences to agriculture, the student learns how all soils were originally rock, and have been gradually produced by its abrasion, disintegration and decomposition to form the great seed-beds of the world; how some seven or eight of the four hundred and thirty-four kinds of minerals constitute nineteen-twentieths of the whole crust of the earth, of which quartz, which gives strength to the stems of all grains and grasses, constitutes alone, nearly one-half. By studying the geological strata, those broad leaves of the book of nature, he learns where to find valuable quarries, minerals and manures; and discerns at a glance the agricultural capacities of any particular section for valuable plants and trees.

As all plants derive a great part of their sustenance from the atmosphere, a knowledge of those forces of nature which affect their growth comprehended under the term of Meteorology is of great utility. By it the student ascertains that the agricultural capacities of a country depend upon its climate and moisture as well as upon its soils; that soils differ greatly in their power to absorb and radiate heat from the sun, as also in their ability to absorb and retain rain and dew, according to their geological structure and state of cultivation, and thus affect the climate; also that distance from the equator, elevation and distance from the ocean, the currents of the Gulf stream, the prevailing direction of the winds greatly influence the temperature and the amount of moisture. Having learned these lessons and the mean temperature of any region by long observations, the farmer is taught to adapt his crops to it. Even if the season is too short to bring any plant to perfection, he may overcome the difficulty by preparing the soil by drainage for the earlier reception of the seed, and forcing its growth by stimulating manures; or if a summer drowth is apprehended, its deleterious effects may be avoided by the earliest possible planting and by deep tillage, so that the crops may be well rooted and grown before the soil becomes dry.

Mathematics, Surveying, Engineering and Mechanics. This department would involve instruction in algebra, geometry, trigonometry and conic sections applied to surveying, leveling, topographical surveying and plotting, with the use of compass, level and other instruments in the field; in mechanics and engineering especially as applied to agricultural machinery and processes, to rural architecture, arches, framing, road making, bridge building, etc., with drawing and design.

In the course of instruction, declamation, composition and debating would be included; and it is extremely desirable to add all those branches that are most closely allied to manufactures and commerce, and thus afford an education to the sons of our mechanics and merchants as well as the farmer.

Although we deem it inexpedient now to determine upon any fixed definite plan, for which ample time is allowed, yet we entertain no doubt that the very terms of the act donating the lands indicate an institution entirely distinct and radically different from any other heretofore founded in the State; for had it contemplated or desired its connection with any other schools, the grant would have doubtless been expressly made for the purpose of increasing the facilities of those already in operation.

It is also equally clear that a scientific education will as effectually prepare our young men for practical life, as a classical training would qualify them for literary pursuits or professional life. Hence there is no necessary connection between the two systems, and it is sufficiently obvious that an independent college was designed. We therefore append to this report a series of resolutions which comprehend the leading features indicated by the act or which are palpably necessary in themselves.

As we look through the long perspective aisles of the future, we catch a glimpse of a coming golden age; when every branch of natural science, every art, every weapon of obsolete warfare, shall contribute to bring the art of agriculture to perfection; when our vast area shall become one great, fertile garden, teeming with busy manufacturing villages and cities, and our keels shall plough every sea, transporting our surplus materials, enhanced in value by the cunning fingers of our artisans and exchanging them for the products of more favored climes. It is now in our power to hasten a consummation so devoutly to be wished, by promoting scientific education and diffusing intelligence, so that Maine, in accordance with her proud motto, shall take the lead in the onward career of progress and improvement.

Resolved, That the Board of Agriculture respectfully and earnestly recommend to the Legislature the early acceptance of the grant of public lands tendered by act of Congress, in aid of agricultural and mechanical education.

Resolved, That the fund arising from this grant will not be, in the opinion of this Board, more than sufficient for the suitable endowment of *one* efficient school of the kind contemplated.

Resolved, That the college indicated by the act of Congress above mentioned, is essentially unlike either of the existing colleges in the State, they being properly *literary* institutions, while this should be primarily designed and purposely adapted for the education and training of pupils for *industrial pursuits* in after life.

Resolved, That such a school should not be incorporated with any of the existing literary institutions of the State ; because they are designed for, and are adapted to, a different style of education and training, and also because a liability would thereby be incurred of an overshadowing influence from, or of ultimate absorption into, the institution to which it is attached.

Resolved, That an industrial college should possess as a part of its apparatus, a farm and a work-shop which are as indispensable for practical instruction as philosophical or chemical apparatus is for scientific instruction. And the farm should embrace such a variety of soils and of surface as should constitute it, as near as may be, a fair epitome of the State.

Resolved, That the school should occupy a location easily accessible, and as nearly central to the State as may be, considering both geographical position, population and social and other advantages.

The above resolves were the occasion of protracted and animated debate and were unanimously adopted.

Mr. Chamberlain, for the Committee to whom was referred the Second Topic, viz: "What action shall be taken under the provisions of law authorizing the Board of Agriculture to prescribe for what objects or purposes a portion of the State bounty shall be offered in premiums," presented the following Report:

This question is predicated on section fourteen of the act approved March 19, 1862, in the following words: "Every society which receives bounty from the State, shall award in each year, by way of premiums or gratuities, or shall expend for the purchase of seeds, implements, or breeding animals, a sum not less than the bounty so received, for the encouragement and improvement of agriculture, horticulture or the mechanic arts, and it shall be competent for the Board of Agriculture to direct for what objects and purposes premiums shall be offered to an extent not exceeding one-half the bounty of the State."

To determine whether any action is now called for in the premises, let us look a little into the operations of our agricultural societies to see if any suggestions or directions from the Board would be well timed under the act that thus links the duties of the Board to the active operations of these societies.

In 1859 the twenty-four county societies received from the State $4,590.56, and paid in premiums $6,783.87. Of this sum $3,403, or one-half of the whole, was awarded on live stock. The total amount awarded for grain and root crops was $549.45, or less than one-sixth the sum distributed for the encouragement of improvement in our domestic animals.

In 1861 the total amount of premiums offered by the twenty-seven societies was $10.032. Of this amount, $1,114, or a fraction over one-tenth was for grain and root crops.

In 1862 the amount of premiums offered on grain and root crops fell to $814, of which only $316 was awarded. About one-fifteenth of the money paid by the State to these societies, goes to encourage the production of those crops which make up a large portion of our own sustenance and that of our domestic animals. The general feature of the prize lists, giving prominent encouragement to improvement in our domestic animals, has not changed in the history of the societies; except latterly, much money has been paid for the exhibition of fast horses. We have shown above, that in one year, one-half of all the awards was for live stock—the other half being distributed for the encouragement of general farm improvement, experiments in draining, subsoil plowing, plowing at exhibitions, for reclaiming waste and wet lands, for manures and experiments with them, for orchards and nurseries, and for other special improvements on the farm, for fruit, dairy and other products, for agricultural implements and the encouragement of the mechanic arts.

The time *was* when improvement in the animals on the farm was the great desideratum. A realization of the comparative low condition of Maine in this regard, the magnitude of the undertaking to secure a sure and speedy improvement, and through this means to raise the general character of our husbandry, led to associated efforts, and finally to the construction of our agricultural societies. What was a leading object at the outset would naturally remain such till Anglo Saxon perseverance compassed the end.

Of the paltry sum of $316 paid in the whole State in 1862 for the encouragement of grain and root culture, how large a portion was probably bestowed for preconcerted and carefully conducted experiments aiming at discoveries in general laws, and the establishment of facts for our future guidance?

The peculiar and unfortunate condition of affairs in our country, prompts us to put forth new efforts; and wherever mental or physical force has hitherto laid dormant, every patriotic impulse dictates that it shall now be made available for the common weal.

In whatever channel our agricultural societies may have directed their efforts, with good results, it is foreign to our intention to divert those efforts to the detriment of any special interest. It might seem an unfavorable time to urge any material change from the "mixed husbandry" hitherto prevailing, to that course of practice indicated by the Secretary in his recent reports, whenever new products are proposed and a wider range in practice naturally suggested.

The State policy in the aid extended to agricultural societies, is a compensating policy. The property of the State—the cash in its treasury—is exchanged through the agency of these societies, for products coming through *human brains*, in the shape of valuable knowledge, to be applied to the production of material wealth, and ultimately the restoration of the cash to the treasury with large increase. Whether the return be immediate or through a longer cycle, is not material. We do not question the soundness of the State policy in this regard. Men do possess brains enough, and may grasp knowledge enough to make farming and mechanical pursuits both intellectual and interesting. The expansion of the soul, the interior growth is not necessarily cramped and fettered by being wedded to the soil. We may be educated to a love of nature, so as to appreciate her daily surroundings, and to delight in searching to know her laws. Every crop raised on our farms may be made an exceedingly interesting experiment.

Intellect is dulled by excessive physical labor, and now when men are scarce, farm arrangements should be perfected so as to economize strength. Mind should quicken—thus extending the long arm of the lever at which we stand to do our work.

Applying these thoughts to the matter in hand, we are forced to the conclusion that at present an undue proportion of the money bestowed in premiums, is awarded on live stock. The statements accompanying the presentation of stock at our exhibitions, are, in the aggregate, of little value. The intrinsic worth of the animal itself is a sufficient incentive to the careful farmer to select from the best breeds within his reach; and the proof is entirely wanting, that the continuous payment of premiums has not latterly effected anything for the introduction of new and better breeds, anything for instituting comparisons between different breeds, by sufficient data, to settle questions of preference for specific purposes, or even to determine the general question of profit or loss.

In another direction there are unexplored fields that we approach with much curiosity, where the border of the veil of obscuration is but just raised by science, where we are invited to step in and pursue our investigations and gratify curiosity by experiment alone—the fields of vegetable life—the crops of the farm. Here, even, where we all are anxious to know more, where we all confess ourselves but children, we are gaining, year by year, but little knowledge.

The prize lists of the societies name a mere pittance for premiums, for the reason that so few of them are applied for. They are not competed for because they are so small. They hold out no inducement in compensation for the time required in conducting anything like a careful experiment.

An acre of wheat is grown on one of Maine's verdant hill tops. Its yield is thirty-fold. Mother nature was propitious. The early and latter rain descended gently. Insect life in its neighborhood did not appropriate it. The straw grew tall and strong and bright.

Besides the elements of its structure supplied from the atmosphere, carbon, hydrogen, oxygen and nitrogen, it *chanced* to find in the soil, and which it appropriated, about one hundred and eight pounds of soluble silica, thirteen pounds phosphoric acid, nineteen pounds potash, eight pounds lime, and a less quantity of sulphuric acid and magnesia.

The grain was full and fine, for besides its atmospheric elements, it chanced to find within the range of the roots, silica, phosphoric acid, sulphuric acid, lime, magnesia, peroxide of iron, potash and soda.

We find in our book of record, that this crop was a premium crop; and we are informed that the ground was plowed and harrowed previous to being sown. How much more than this simple announcement, do the great bulk of the returned "statements" required by law, contain?

A crop of potatoes is a very exhausting one, when the tops and tubers are entirely removed from the soil. A large crop takes more than four hundred pounds of incombustible matter from an acre, more than half of which is potash. Turnips, mangolds and carrots abstract from four hundred to six hundred and fifty pounds of inorganic matter, about one-half of which is potash and soda. But what is worthy of consideration, is the fact, that these crops may be extended very much beyond our present practice, and all be consumed at home with great advantage, thus returning to the soil the precious mineral elements taken from it and with them a great deal more of fertilizing substances obtained by these crops from other sources.

The most successful husbandry in the world, as proved in grain products and an increased fertility of soil, deals in vast quantities of roots, and this mainly with a view to increase the stock of manure on the farm.

The opinion of your Committee remains the same as when expressed on former occasions—that if stock husbandry is to receive special attention—if the number and value of our domestic animals shall be increased, if we are to produce more meat, milk, wool and bread, it must come mainly through the increased production of roots in a well considered rotation. This matter is vastly suggestive of thought, but we abstain from extended remarks, feeling our incompetency even to attempt the giving directions or even advice to such a people as our constituents, where matters of such magnitude are pending. We will simply name the objects for which it seems to us desirable that increased encouragement should be given at the present time: 1st, cheese-making. 2d, orchards and nurseries. 3d, wheat and corn culture. 4th, root crops. And we respectfully submit the following preambles and resolutions:

Whereas, it is the opinion of the Board that Dairy Husbandry has not received that attention in this State that it claims in consideration of our inherent advantages and capabilities for the manufacture of cheese and butter; and whereas, from the information communicated in the last Report of our Secretary in respect to the most approved modes of practice in the principal dairy regions of the country, it is believed that cheese of uniformly good quality may be manufactured in Maine; therefore

Resolved, That we recommend to the several Agricultural Societies to devote such portion of the bounty of the State, as their several circumstances may seem to require, to premiums for the best conducted and fully reported experiments in making cheese and butter.

Whereas, it is the opinion of the Board that the climatic and other influences in the last few years, causing a decline in the number and condition of our fruit trees, may not again operate for a long series of years, and should not discourage us, nor weaken our efforts to become large exporters of fruit; and whereas, it is desirable that the trees required for the extension of our orchards should be produced at home; therefore

Resolved, That we recommend to the societies to offer premiums, to be awarded at the end of two, three or more years, for best and most fully reported experiments in renovating and improving orchards now existing, and for the setting and culture of new ones, and also for the rearing of nurseries embracing such varieties of apples, pears, plums and small fruits as are approved for the several localities.

Whereas, the most of our lands that have long been cleared of wood, fail to produce a remunerating crop of wheat or corn, except they be carefully worked and liberally fed; and whereas, maximum crops cannot be expected till we have learned much more than we now know concerning the demands our crops make on us in the preparation of their seed-beds, and more in respect to the best ways and means to supply those demands; and whereas, more light and knowledge in this interesting field of inquiry can only be expected through further experiments; therefore

Resolved, That we recommend the offering of liberal premiums for the best conducted experiments in the culture of wheat and corn.

Whereas, it is the opinion of the Board, that the root crops have not received that attention, in the "mixed husbandry" prevalent in the State, that their value and importance demand; and whereas, it has been demonstrated that the art of agriculture in its highest condition deals very largely in these crops; and whereas, it is desirable that when change shall be effected in our practice, it shall be such that an increase in the fertility of our soils shall legitimately follow; therefore

Resolved, That we recommend to the societies to offer increased premiums for the best conducted experiments in the culture of potatoes, carrots, mangolds, parsnips and turnips.

Resolved, That the several Agricultural Societies *be directed* to offer not less than one-fourth of the State bounty annually received by each, in premiums upon *crops,* either of grains or of roots, and that premiums be offered for the *largest crops grown at least cost.*

Mr. Percival, from the Committee upon the Third Topic, reported as follows:

The Committee to whom was assigned the following subject—"What unusual demands on the farmers of Maine grow out of the present condition and prospects of our country?"—met in council, considered and discussed in a careful manner the subject, but before committing our conclusions to paper in the form of a report, we glanced over the last Annual Report of our Secretary, just laid on our table, and there (on page 44) we found a report on the same subject, in which this matter is fully and ably treated. Many important and valuable considerations and suggestions are given, and it seemed to us that nearly everything was there said that the subject demanded, leaving little for us to do but to call attention to that report.

On page 211 of our Secretary's Report, he has summed up the whole matter, finished up what he did not say in his former one. He there forcibly and properly reminds us that the last call for men for our army took a large proportion of the men from the producing classes. That help which the farmer must have, will, in the nature of things, be scarce and dear; therefore, the necessity of early and well matured plans, unusual care in the economy of our time, and of bringing to our aid all the appliances within reach, in the way of improved labor-saving implements and machinery.

He has also reminded us that while there are many less hands to perform the labor of the farm, there are few less mouths to feed, or bodies to clothe, therefore, we need to manufacture and economise in every possible manner, every fertilizing material, and apply it in such a way, and to such crops as are most needed, and will give the largest and most profitable return, and also that we shall encourage and sustain all those organizations and institutions that tend to elevate and improve the calling we represent. Your Committee cordially and heartily endorse all our Secretary there says as to our "duties and prospects."

In the report before mentioned, it was urged that more attention be given to sheep husbandry. The result has already proved the sagacity of that recommendation. The price of sheep and wool have seldom, if ever, been higher than now, and must continue to be high for some time to come; and we recommend to the farmers to continue to improve and increase his flocks, and at the same time to look about him and learn if possible if there are not some crops that may be more cheaply and easily cultivated, that will supply the deficiency of short pastures. We recommend for this purpose the English turnip for early fall feeding; and for winter the Swede or Rutabaga, the Lupine, the California Pea, and the Vetch or Tare.

One of the characteristics of the Yankee farmer is to run into extremes; and while we recommend him to increase his flocks in all prudent ways, we would caution him against doing it to the neglect of other important interests.

Heretofore a large proportion of the exports from our State have consisted of beef, neat cattle, and horses, which your Committee believe have never paid so large remunerative prices as wool at its lowest point. Yet it is not prudent for us to abandon the raising of neat stock and horses, and give our attention exclusively to sheep. The raising of good horses has always paid the farmer. Our Secretary has, in the report just issued, demonstrated satisfactorily to our minds that we may profitably become larger manufacturers of dairy products; and we must have good cows, and oxen to do our work and make our beef. It is only the thousands of miserable and worthless animals that have never half paid for

COTSWOLD BUCK "DR. KANE."

Bred by G. C. HITCHCOCK, New Preston, Conn. Sired by "Cedric." Now owned by CHARLES CORLISS of "Poplar Lawn," Haverhill, Mass.

the care and cost of raising, that we would have to give place to sheep, or some animal that will pay.

No pains or reasonable expense should be spared to improve our neat stock. Much, very much has already been done, and yet there is abundant room for more, and without any great outlay of money, but simply by a careful selection of our best cows, and breeding to such improved and thorough-bred bulls as we may have in our State.

The past has been a fruitful season. Nearly all our crops have yielded abundantly, especially so is it with the grain crops, which are now bringing unusually high prices, particularly barley and oats. And here again is a demand on the farmers, not to get excited by these high prices, and rush into the growing an unusually large breadth of these grains to the neglect of other crops, without first considering whether the circumstances which induced this state of things may continue any great length of time.

The high price of many farm products, and indeed of almost everything in the country, has created a sort of speculative mania in the land; and there is danger that the farmer, in his eagerness to become suddenly rich or to accumulate money more rapidly, may invest his hard earnings in some outside enterprise of doubtful utility, or in stock that may or may not pay, instead of the legitimate one of improving his flocks, herds and farms, or supplying himself with better farm implements, which never fail to pay a large per cent. on the investment. On the whole, your Committee do not see that there are any *new demands* made on us as *farmers* by the unfortunate condition of our country, but that those already existing are intensified. But we are to remember while straining every nerve to add to our own and the wealth of the country, the other and higher demands upon us as citizens.

Mr. Wasson, for Committee on Fourth Topic, reported as follows:

Protection of Sheep Husbandry.

The Committee having this Topic under consideration, submit the following:

For a succession of years the farmers of Maine, through the medium of the Board of Agriculture, have come to the capitol, as regularly as the Mussulmen assembled at Mecca, to invoke legislative aid and protection in behalf of the interests of sheep husbandry. The natural advantages of the State—and none other is better adapted to sheep husbandry of a high character than Maine—have been earnestly and faithfully portrayed and presented. The causes which make sheep raising both unremunerative and hazardous, have been as fully and as truthfully explained. Those *canine* causes still continue like "war risks" to *eat* up the profits. The essence of legislative interference has been too much like British neutrality.

Every man has the right to claim from the government under which he lives, protection in the enjoyment of his property. That right has been exercised, and that protection has been claimed, at the hands of those who have been called to preside over the political and economical interests of the State. The assumption has been unimpeachably established and shown beyond denial, by the farmers of the State, that the losses from wild animals, disease and accident, are not equivalent to the losses from the depredations of dogs. Facts and figures multiplied to an almost unlimited extent testify to the truth of the assertion. Supplications, remonstrances and petitions, have failed to induce the Legislature to abate the grievance or remove the aggressors.

Cotton, the great source of supply for the textile fabrics of the world, being cut off by the rebellion, woolen fabrics for a long time must take the place of many for which cotton has hitherto been considered essential. We have never grown wool enough to meet the home demand, even when cotton was accessible; and the entire policy of our State has been of a character to diminish rather than increase the growth of this product. In proof of this, is cited the "act" of last winter, taxing dogs, provided *the several towns shall agree thereto*, a proviso without precedent or parallel in the whole history of taxation.

No elaborate report is required to vindicate the importance of our cause, or the justness of our claims. The extraordinary circumstances by which we are surrounded, afford no new argument in favor of the protection of sheep husbandry. And again we ask of the Legislature such protection for this important branch of our industry as the case demands. We herewith submit the following resolution:

Resolved, That the interests of the State, demand at the hands of the Legislature, protection to sheep husbandry.

The Resolve was unanimously adopted.

Mr. Percival, for the Committee to whom was referred the Fifth Topic, Viz: "How has the introduction of thorough-bred animals affected the milking properties of our cows," submitted the following Report:

No data can be obtained by which definite conclusions can be arrived at on this question, and we can only give our opinion in the matter and a few reasons for "the faith that is in us." In our judgment this introduction has produced a very beneficial effect on our dairy stock. We do not deny that there have been and now are many good and some extraordinarily good dairy cows amongst what are termed natives. But that as a class, on the whole, they are as good as the thoroughbreds or grades, we deny. The Herefords have not seemed to improve the dairy qualities of the animals with which they have been crossed, and we are not aware that any great merit is claimed for them in this respect, and yet we believe their introduction beneficial. The Durhams have been longer in our State, and consequently have been the greater means of improvement than any other breeds introduced. We believe their grades have almost uniformly surpassed the original native stock and often the thoroughbreds in this respect.

On searching for reports of celebrated cows, we have found them as five to one in favor of the grades of this breed over the native; and so of the Ayrshire. The Devons, although not having been bred with us with much reference to their dairy properties, have improved upon the natives, if not in quantity, certainly in the quality of their milk. The Jerseys are a new breed with us, but from what we know of them, we have no doubt their introduction has done us good.

In consultation with Amasa Stetson, Esq., who was for many years largely and successfully engaged in manufacturing butter for the Bangor market, in the town of Stetson, keeping from forty to sixty cows, he informed me that he found grade Durhams the most profitable cows he could keep. This is in accordance with my own experience, having owned a grade cow, of medium size, that yielded, in twenty-eight days, 57½ lbs. butter—16½ lbs. being her largest yield in one week—on good grass feed alone, which was quite equal to the celebrated Oak's cow, whose largest yield was 19½ lbs. in one week, when she was largely fed on meal. One of this cow's progeny, sired by an Ayrshire bull, has proved quite equal to her dam. Any quantity of instances can be given of grade Durhams and Ayrshires of superior milking qualities.

Before the introduction of foreign animals, but little attention was paid to the improvement of neat stock. When Thorougbred Bulls were brought among us and larger prices demanded for their use, the attention of the farmer was called to the subject—comparisons were made between these animals and only the best selected for crossing. It not only led to more careful selections in breeding but to more generous care and treatment in the way of warm barns and better feed.

Much has already been accomplished, and yet there is abundant room for further improvement in this direction. We cannot have grade animals without thoroughbreds. We believe that as much depends upon having bulls from good dairy ancestry as cows, and as it is a fact that there is a great difference in families of the different breeds as to their dairy qualities; if butter and cheese is the desired object, we advise the purchase and use of only such animals as have been bred to this point.

Mr. Chamberlain, for the Committee on the subject of Manures, reported as follows:

New and Increased Fertilizers.

We take the liberty to join to our topic as expressed in its widest application, the same thing, only clipped a little, which was assigned us for consideration in the last interim.

We couple them for the reason that we have now only time to treat the subject with extreme brevity. Our topic, then, contemplates the inquiry whether we have availed ourselves of all those substances within our reach recognized as fertilizers, and to the extent that it may be applied with good results.

Chemistry teaches that sixty-four primary elements, (so far as at present known,) enter into the composition of soils and go to build up the structure of vegetable and animal organisms.

A chemical analysis detects certain elements in plants; the plants get them from the soil. If the soil is deficient in them they must be supplied; and for this supply we procure such elements as were previously derived from the soil, or we get them otherwise from nature's great storehouses.

The principle involved in this simple cycle is the basis of the art and science of manuring crops. When these principles were first perceived, scientific men predicted a sure and swift development of the art of agriculture. But science is a materialist. It stops short where the natural elements are merged into life.

Science, whis is a name for exact knowledge of facts and principles, of effects and their causes, and is obtained by the observation and experience of many observers, has rendered us essential service through chemical research, but it leaves us to explore the most interesting field, the world of life, without aid from chemistry proper.

Fertilizers are divided into two great classes, viz: Inorganic, or Mineral, and Organic, or Vegetable and Animal products.

The inorganic fertilizers most known in this State, are lime, plaster, wood ashes, phosphate of lime, and salt. All these with the single exception of wood ashes are enhanced in price in most localities by a cost of transportation. The value and importance of each is now generally appreciated. Salt, in all places removed from the ocean, is a valuable fertilizer when applied in small quantities to grass as well as to all cultivated crops and garden vegetables, particularly to mangolds, asparagus and cabbage, it is thought to be highly beneficial. It is an essential aid in the compost heap.

All salt found damaged in our marts of trade and in the fisheries, should be saved for the soil. Wood ashes can now be had in very small quantity compared with the demand.

Our granitic and sienitic rocks contain about the same percentage of potash as wood ashes. They also contain lime as well as other elements found in all fertile soils, but they are locked up from our use. Regardless of any peculiar theories which may have been broached regarding it, we would like to see an extended experiment with granite heated and reduced to powder.

From some experiments made under our own observation, we have a strong faith in it as a valuable amendment to any soil. In all places where these rocks and wood abound, they can be reduced at a moderate cost. It may prove to bear the cost of preparation and transport as well as plaster.

In the class of *organic manures*, vegetable and animal, and their mixtures, we include the waste portions of all our cultivated crops, the natural vegetation of the country, such as the grasses and weeds, the leaves of trees, marine vegetation, animal excrement, fishes, the flesh of animals, hoofs, hair, skins and blood. We have all had a degree of practical education in saving and applying this class of fertilizers.

We need not look beyond our own immediate neigbborhoods to see the most reckless waste of many of these precious substances.

The life-giving elements are being drained from our farms and are borne on the current of every rivulet and creek that flows near our factories, tanneries, and slaughter-houses,—to say nothing of the rivers of drainage from our cities—all bearing to old ocean, the very foundation of our material prosperity, while scarcely an effort is put forth to dam up and divert any of these streams.

As an illustration of waste,—on one occasion one of your Committee bought a quantity of manure under the name of *superphosphate of lime*, at a cost of over fifty dollars per ton—which proved a good investment—and the article was made up with a large percentage of tanner's waste.

At the same time two tanneries were in operation within a mile of our land, so constructed and worked, that all the waste was "sluiced" into the river. In a single instance, with much difficulty, we obtained a few bushels of "fleshings," from a lot of "slaughter hides," for a compost heap. And these mills still work on, like nearly all the larger tanneries in the State, year after year, with thousands and millions of our industrial capital running to waste through their hungry maws.

The value of marine manures, to which the attention of those farmers not directly upon the coast has recently been directed, proves to be considerable; and it becomes an important question, to be solved as soon as possible, what can we afford to pay for *fish guano* at our gates.

Of the many waste substances of the farm that are valuable fertilizers, and which are more frequently suffered to be wasted, we can now only mention,—*First,* Soap Suds. This is a most grateful application, to be made at any season of the year to the surface of any lands about the house that are required to contribute to our pleasure or our sustenance through the vegetation they sustain, whether it be the lawn, the flower border, the vegetable garden, vines, shrubbery or fruit trees. *Second,* Bones. These are now receiving increased attention, since farmers have discovered that their cows are suffering from the lack of soluble phosphate of lime in the soil of the pasture and the hay field, and consequently a deficiency of that sustenance in the grasses. It has been carried off in the formation of milk and bones, and very little of it has been returned.

To supply the cow in her extreme necessity, her owner gives her bone-meal. The better way is to feed the soil. We who have had a care in this direction, do not see a diligent cow losing an hour of precious time on a summer morning, chewing a bone for the morsel of phosphate she may detach from its surface.

Many now save all the bones and throw them into a tub with moist ashes, where they become decomposed and made ready for use as a fertilizer. But the larger portion of the soluble phosphates from our farms goes beyond our reach, in our stock, milk, and crops sold. The bones that accumulate with our consuming population are mostly sold to go abroad—lost to the State.

Finally, as we are forced to stop at a point not very far from whence we started, we only add that we need several bone mills, to encourage a general gathering of old bones, and to entirely arrest all export of that substance.

We want to see *marine manures*, in long trains, moving inland over all the lines of conveyance, till it reaches every farm.

We want to see every man and woman more awake to the importance of improved habits in saving and applying plant food. To awaken interest in this direction is to do good.

Mr. Pratt, for Committee, presented the following Report on

Fruit Culture.

There may be other questions of more importance to the farmers of Maine than the cultivation of fruit, but certainly it is one of the most important and is deserving of much more attention than has been paid to it by the farmers of Maine generally. The consideration of fruit opens so wide a field for investigation, embracing as it does the apple, pear, plum, cherry, and all the smaller fruits, (the cultivation of which is almost entirely neglected by the farmers of Maine,) that your Committee have been compelled to narrow down their investigation to that of the apple. The apple without doubt stands at the head of the list of fruits both in point of usefulness and profit; yet many orchards are going to decay which might with trifling expense be made a source of profit. Few efforts comparatively are being made to rear new orchards or to resuscitate old ones, a fact which every one who has the welfare of our State at heart must deeply deplore. If we attempt to discover the causes which have led to this state of things we shall find them to be various, and differing in different localities.

One of the principal causes of discouragement in putting out new orchards has been brought about by the purchase of miserable, worthless trees from parties out of the State, instead of buying of nurserymen here, of whom we have a plenty of honest and reliable men. Another cause of discouragement is improper location and treatment. Some have planted on flat and heavy soils, without a suitable preparation by underdraining, and the trees have soon become stunted and worthless. Others have planted on rich sandy soils, which has induced a rapid growth of wood, and consequently an early decay. Such orchards while they live will occasionally produce a large crop, but are not to be depended upon. Still another cause of discouragement is to be found in the ravages of the borer.

The first of the above mentioned causes can be overcome by simply purchasing of honest and reliable nurserymen of our own State; or, if one prefers to raise his own trees, by selecting seeds from rugged and vigorous growing varieties, and planting in moderately rich soil, letting them remain until they have attained sufficient size to transplant into the nursery or orchard.

The second may be overcome by planting on high, rocky and moist soils, of which this State furnishes an abundance.

The third and last difficulty is one which is not so well understood generally as either of the others.

There are some localities where this pest of the orchard does little harm, but there are many more where he does work, and cultivators are not aware of it. The jack knife and wire are the best remedies known.

The decay of our old orchards is to be attributed mainly to injudicious pruning, want of nourishment, and perhaps in some measure to a few unfavorable seasons which we have recently had.

The question then arises can they be restored? We answer yes, in a large number of instances; and we cannot better explain how, than by citing an instance which has come under the observation of one member of the Committee. Mr. J. M. Richardson of Androscoggin county, restored such an orchard by simply mulching with brakes to the depth of ten inches, and in some instances the application of a small amount of barn yard manure. Mr. Richardson is more successful than almost any other man in his town in the cultivation of the apple. He mulches his young trees not only to make them vigorous and healthy, but to protect them from mice.*

* If Mr. Richardson finds deep mulching *to prevent* the ravages of mice or vermin, his experience differs very materially from that of some other cultivators.—[ED.

The importance of giving more attention to the cultivation of the apple, may be shown by the extent to which it enters into our daily food in the shape of sauces, pies, tarts, &c., scarcely a meal being eaten without it in some one of those forms; but it may be still more forcibly impressed by showing how handsomely it fills the pocket of the producer. The County of Franklin in the year 1859, with a population of 20,000, exported $92,000 worth of apples, showing in some measure what may be done in favorable situations. In deciding to what extent we should enter into the cultivation of the apple, we should consider our proximity to market, and the adaptation of our soil to that purpose. In the selection of varieties, those living near large markets may cultivate with profit the summer and fall varieties, while those at a greater distance from market will find it more for their interest to cultivate the winter and spring varieties. We have thus hastily glanced at the subject of fruit culture in Maine, and if any of the ideas here advanced shall be of any practical use to the cultivators of fruit, the object for which this report has been written will have been accomplished.

AGRICULTURAL STATISTICS.

It will be recollected that the Legislature passed an act two years ago requiring assessors to make return to the office of the Secretary of State, of Agricultural Statistics according to the facts as they existed on the first of April in each year. Returns were received the following year from three hundred and fourteen (314) towns and plantations. From one hundred and ninety-one (191) none were received. The requirement being a novel one and its purpose being at first but imperfectly understood, it was hoped that the returns would become more perfect and complete in the future. The hope has not been realized thus far, for during the past season returns were received from only two hundred and thirty-seven (237) towns and plantations, while from two hundred and sixty-eight (268) or more than one-half, none were received. In this state of the case much doubt was felt as to the expediency of bestowing the very considerable time and labor necessary to prepare an abstract for public use. No provision was made by the act itself for any method by which they could be made available to the agricultural community, and if done at all it must be by volunteer and gratuitous labor. The value of statistics depends in the first place upon accuracy and completeness. These are certainly lacking in regard to the last; but their value also depends not less upon uninterrupted continuance during a considerable term of years.

It is this latter consideration, mainly, which induces me here to present the following abstract of the returns—incomplete as they are—for if the plan of collecting them be continued, and its execution be properly improved, even these may furnish a very acceptable contribution to the data from which, hereafter, most valuable practical deductions are to be drawn. For the present we merely remark that an examination and comparison of these with those of last year will exhibit numerous points of interest and furnish many instructive suggestions.

ANDROSCOGGIN COUNTY.

Towns.	Number of bulls.	Heifers under four years old.	Cows four years old and upwards.	Steers under four years old.	Oxen four years old and upwards.	Number of common mixed or native sheep.	South Downs and grade South Downs.	Improved long-wooled sheep.	Merinos and grade merinos.	Pounds of wool produced.	Number of wool skins.	Pounds of dressed flax produced.	Swine, without distinction of age, sex or breed.	Colts under four years old.	Horses four years old and upwards.	Number of bushels of Indian corn produced.	Bushels of wheat.	Bushels of rye.	Bushels of barley.	Bushels of oats.	Bushels of buck-wheat.
Durham, ...	10	218	557	250	274	1275	-	-	-	3745	212	15	201	48	249	6537	223	144	652	13465	23
Greene, ...	12	204	295	146	148	1216	-	232	-	4750	138	8	273	41	148	4564	1135	165	2144	5091	97
Lisbon, ...	7	157	329	174	186	675	19	98	113	3620	625	35	183	47	180	2836	423	226	1846	7111	11
Leeds, ...	20	226	555	408	333	620	230	333	750	5617	68	31	233	60	194	7631	1396	317	3348	8400	136
Poland, ...	24	348	672	178	256	1359	93	44	83	5917	11	16	231	82	228	10571	1837	1289	2199	11457	68
Webster, ...	3	201	315	234	181	357	220	245	375	3200	40	-	111	23	145	3493	396	81	3690	3051	-
	76	1154	2723	1390	2078	5482	552	952	1321	26849	1094	105	1232	281	1144	35632	5410	2222	13879	48575	325

ANDROSCOGGIN COUNTY, (Continued.)

Towns.	Bushels of potatoes.	Bushels of turnips.	Bushels of carrots.	Bushels of beets.	Bushels of apples.	Tons of upland hay.	Tons of interval hay.	Tons of bog and salt hay.	Pounds of butter.	Pounds of cheese.	Pounds of honey.	Pounds of maple sugar.	Gallons of maple syrup and molasses.	Value of poultry and eggs produced.	Bushels of beans.	Bushels of peas.	No. of sheep killed by wild animals.	No. of sheep killed by dogs.	No. of sheep injured by dogs.	Amount of damage to sheep by dogs.
Durham, ...	26574	214	410	164	1535	2935	1561	-	53715	6822	600	-	-	269	712	244	-	10	15	45
Greene, ...	17412	2049	574	309	16425	1812	392	-	24542	31472	423	300	29	1210	474	134	-	10	20	50
Lisbon, ...	14767	2034	395	1072	6408	1893	198	20	35985	1535	390	-	-	2227	593	246	-	7	12	35
Leeds, ...	21988	884	195	317	13967	2025	1000	120	27950	19120	330	40	93	2931	542	206	-	-	6	22
Poland, ...	60732	2235	904	241	10665	2863	209	306	74490	9450	1020	166	98	3686	1084	187	2	6	-	40
Webster, ...	17193	1691	535	308	7321	1543	421	70	28035	1210	62	-	-	1920	509	189	-	1	2	6
	158666	9107	3013	2411	56321	13071	3781	516	244717	69609	2825	506	220	12243	3914	1196	2	34	55	198

AROOSTOOK COUNTY.

Towns.	Number of bulls.	Heifers under four years old.	Cows four years old and upwards.	Steers under four years old.	Oxen four years old and upwards.	Number of common mixed or native sheep.	South Downs and grade South Downs.	Improved long-wooled sheep.	Merinos and grade merinos.	Pounds of wool produced.	Number of wool skins.	Pounds of dressed flax produced.	Swine, without distinction of age, sex or breed.	Colts under four years old.	Horses four years old and upwards.	Number of bushels of Indian corn produced.	Bushels of wheat.	Bushels of rye.	Bushels of barley.	Bushels of oats.	Bushels of buck-wheat.
Ashland,	6	90	111	75	24	556	–	–	–	2152	109	4	107	34	75	17	1604	446	820	6884	2491
Linneus,	9	221	225	136	97	1246	–	–	–	4469	287	48	169	56	128	578	1777	305	423	11954	8337
Maysville,	14	138	178	82	70	778	–	–	–	2334	72	–	163	60	109	53	2900	660	942	7925	3359
Weston,	7	73	130	37	71	471	–	–	–	1200	100	–	100	31	71	21	950	55	142	4289	2068
Crystal plantation,	2	37	61	45	44	350	–	12	–	1053	20	–	103	10	24	129	930	349	667	2950	1811
Fremont plantation,	2	68	93	64	86	191	10	25	–	679	38	–	65	8	47	40	2224	244	654	12285	1039
Island Falls plantation,	5	27	46	29	18	140	5	2	–	441	13	–	44	7	29	147	1150	142	521	1834	253
Macwahoc plantation,	2	8	35	10	16	100	–	–	–	375	20	–	30	12	25	175	380	100	190	2000	90
Mapleton plantation,	9	36	98	14	38	110	–	–	–	91	–	–	80	13	37	40	2387	313	588	2880	1330
Reed plantation,	1	4	10	6	2	30	–	–	–	105	8	20	9	2	8	–	60	–	–	300	100
Washburn plantation,	–	105	98	50	37	275	–	–	–	736	35	–	89	23	58	2	784	318	312	2645	1801
	57	807	1085	548	503	4247	15	39	–	13635	702	72	959	256	611	1202	15146	2892	5159	56046	22679

AROOSTOOK COUNTY, (Continued.)

Towns.	Bushels of potatoes.	Bushels of turnips.	Bushels of carrots.	Bushels of beets.	Bushels of apples.	Tons of upland hay.	Tons of interval hay.	Tons of bog and salt hay.	Pounds of butter.	Pounds of cheese.	Pounds of honey.	Pounds of maple sugar.	Gallons of maple syrup and molasses.	Value of poultry and eggs produced.	Bushels of beans.	Bushels of peas.	No. of sheep killed by wild animals.	No. of sheep killed by dogs.	No. of sheep injured by dogs.	Amount of damage to sheep by dogs.
Ashland,	6803	1073	63	61	13	615	59	10	8495	1788	50	480	47	299	41	619	1	3	–	6
Linneus,	11045	1760	98	59	524	2053	–	–	20442	2295	200	296	93	1161	215	233	–	–	–	–
Maysville,	9233	1110	42	59	7	927	287	–	15735	695	50	860	40	288	86	328	–	2	–	7
Weston,	3000	300	–	–	200	594	–	–	9700	200	200	–	–	164	40	60	–	–	–	–
Crystal plantation,	4375	876	24	21	171	382	120	–	5820	1534	30	84	143	223	87	119	–	–	–	–
Freemont plantation,	7015	4700	10	12	–	290	–	–	5525	–	45	155	124	816	–	–	–	–	–	–
Island Falls plantation,	2912	850	46	42	7	213	17	–	3376	915	20	265	152	360	183	27	–	–	–	–
Macwahoc plantation,	4310	175	200	50	100	142	75	–	3850	200	375	–	–	300	30	50	–	–	–	–
Mapleton plantation,	3096	5117	14	4	–	181	–	–	935	80	–	30	15	152	24	48	1	–	–	–
Reed plantation,	900	175	5	6	60	40	15	–	800	–	–	–	–	50	9	3	4	–	–	–
Washburn plantation,	3072	1795	15	2	–	316	37	–	6397	790	–	50	–	156	10	12	–	–	–	–
	55761	17931	520	316	1082	5753	610	10	81475	8497	970	2225	614	4909	725	1499	6	5	–	13

CUMBERLAND COUNTY.

Towns.	Number of bulls.	Heifers under four years old.	Cows four years old and upwards.	Steers under four years old.	Oxen four years old and upwards.	Number of common mixed or native sheep.	South Downs and grade South Downs.	Improved long-wooled sheep.	Merinos and grade merinos.	Pounds of wool produced.	Number of wool skins.	Pounds of dressed flax produced.	Swine, without distinction of age, sex or breed.	Colts under four years old.	Horses four years old and upwards.	Number of bushels of Indian corn produced.	Bushels of wheat.	Bushels of rye.	Bushels of barley.	Bushels of oats.	Bushels of buck-wheat.
Casco, ...	17	210	285	146	176	483	–	–	–	1627	–	–	257	27	145	5890	1355	145	88	2624	30
Falmouth, ...	10	73	440	56	209	425	–	–	–	1534	–	–	236	24	144	4800	250	20	2814	1035	–
Gorham, ...	17	173	651	122	272	1153	–	–	–	2943	–	–	353	32	374	8483	523	121	5804	6323	54
Gray, ...	11	154	443	90	159	498	–	–	5	51	1	–	205	42	192	4793	438	343	2265	3367	31
Harrison, ...	12	240	452	260	206	851	–	–	–	2500	30	25	226	50	220	19500	2400	575	300	5000	40
New Gloucester, . .	20	340	795	142	268	1170	–	–	–	3940	260	25	242	52	235	6320	280	173	1720	4532	37
North Yarmouth, . .	17	96	395	28	116	400	40	100	30	1450	315	20	300	40	200	5000	310	253	2567	8023	37
Otisfield, ...	11	185	407	197	232	1042	–	–	–	3043	36	54	217	44	162	7854	2672	448	307	4152	128
Raymond, ...	15	203	283	129	144	661	–	–	–	1880	27	2	135	28	99	4740	1335	161	36	2081	51
Sebago, ...	6	126	260	141	136	554	–	–	–	1337	22	–	113	29	98	4143	1160	94	–	1048	8
Standish, ...	8	263	476	131	267	707	–	21	–	2672	187	–	200	43	240	6159	681	405	1215	4194	13
Windham, ...	17	237	559	64	229	418	49	160	–	3260	3	22	290	34	393	6934	402	72	3835	5987	49
	161	2305	5446	1506	2414	8362	89	281	35	26237	881	146	2774	445	2502	84616	11806	2810	20951	44366	478

CUMBERLAND COUNTY, (Continued.)

Towns.	Bushels of potatoes.	Bushels of turnips.	Bushels of carrots.	Bushels of beets.	Bushels of apples.	Tons of upland hay.	Tons of interval hay.	Tons of bog and salt hay.	Pounds of butter.	Pounds of cheese.	Pounds of honey.	Pounds of maple sugar.	Gallons of maple syrup and molasses.	Value of poultry and eggs produced.	Bushels of beans.	Bushels of peas.	No. of sheep killed by wild animals.	No. of sheep killed by dogs.	No. of sheep injured by dogs.	Amount of damage to sheep by dogs.
Casco,	14125	645	850	127	6450	960	–	330	28500	3550	560	575	60	1260	747	162	–	–	–	100
Falmouth,	15100	2005	2215	210	3685	3377	75	140	20730	2080	225	–	–	2522	436	78	–	–	–	–
Gorham,	36690	1236	1213	417	21514	4400	216	194	72305	3325	850	27	–	3939	1284	262	–	–	–	–
Gray,	19530	1508	419	352	6985	1555	570	–	31787	2240	310	100	–	940	814	159	–	–	–	–
Harrison,	32526	2000	300	150	10425	2000	175	–	34835	6000	400	30	75	2000	842	200	–	–	–	–
New Gloucester,	24725	1500	600	209	1025	2199	1002	–	26040	7428	109	237	120	1540	430	241	–	–	–	–
North Yarmouth,	6728	1673	573	391	3041	2560	40	152	23673	15675	43	35	–	2685	507	109	–	–	–	–
Otisfield,	24845	1407	306	28	11197	1501	20	317	29693	8090	–	330	128	1532	881	142	6	12	4	50
Raymond,	12297	1241	933	98	7358	904	–	320	30060	854	40	171	–	1281	582	122	–	–	–	–
Sebago,	11089	124	86	–	4319	723	–	262	8122	635	75	204	–	463	492	57	–	–	–	–
Standish,	23441	568	1076	115	61159	1521	465	–	35942	500	65	278	27	5901	846	236	–	1	–	–
Windham,	31112	1196	626	698	10334	2804	163	–	38210	1465	938	25	–	2771	917	209	–	36	–	101
	252308	15103	9197	2795	147482	24504	2726	1715	379897	51838	3615	2012	410	26834	8777	1977	6	49	4	251

FRANKLIN COUNTY.

Towns.	Number of bulls.	Heifers under four years old.	Cows four years old and upwards.	Steers under four years old.	Oxen four years old and upwards.	Number of common mixed or native sheep.	South Downs and grade South Downs.	Improved long-wooled sheep.	Merinos and grade merinos.	Pounds of wool produced.	Number of wool skins.	Pounds of dressed flax produced.	Swine, without distinction of age, sex or breed.	Colts under four years old.	Horses four years old and upwards.	Number of bushels of Indian corn produced.	Bushels of wheat.	Bushels of rye.	Bushels of barley.	Bushels of oats.	Bushels of buck-wheat.
Chesterville, . .	9	214	311	279	171	1706	134	349	257	5158	180	96	131	28	139	3913	1438	197	1794	3622	45
Farmington, . .	18	688	577	655	447	4000	205	1000	5000	35147	285	175	243	115	480	9095	2604	160	3573	13511	185
Freeman, . . .	11	155	270	161	188	1639	11	23	3041	13692	150	169	86	50	97	1391	2032	123	1756	4422	158
Jay, . . .	20	353	705	700	438	2592	–	–	300	10122	–	1000	250	51	247	6600	1000	300	1500	13200	100
New Sharon, . .	10	267	466	327	261	1530	199	90	4713	16344	195	220	206	77	252	6089	2250	190	4382	7435	52
New Vineyard, . .	2	294	200	291	211	6068	–	–	–	15000	75	–	112	43	129	1850	1502	37	1797	4566	–
Rangely, . .	12	94	105	127	96	1213	10	80	20	4801	81	–	66	38	45	–	5757	85	906	4044	40
Eustis plantation, . .	5	86	89	100	58	316	–	176	984	4949	87	45	60	15	58	18	747	143	1670	2358	973
Perkins plantation, .	3	31	42	29	34	422	–	–	–	1089	9	–	13	7	15	188	551	–	810	867	–
Washington plantation, .	2	11	20	13	16	74	–	–	–	250	–	–	7	3	5	160	294	7	298	165	–
	92	2193	2785	2682	1920	19560	559	1718	14315	106552	2762	1705	1174	427	1367	29004	18176	1242	18486	54190	1553

FRANKLIN COUNTY, (Continued.)

Towns.	Bushels of potatoes.	Bushels of turnips.	Bushels of carrots.	Bushels of beets.	Bushels of apples.	Tons of upland hay.	Tons of interval hay.	Tons of bog and salt hay.	Pounds of butter.	Pounds of cheese.	Pounds of honey.	Pounds of maple sugar.	Gallons of maple syrup and molasses.	Value of poultry and eggs produced.	Bushels of beans.	Bushels of peas.	No. of sheep killed by wild animals.	No. of sheep killed by dogs.	No. of sheep injured by dogs.	Amount of damage to sheep by dogs.
Chesterville,	15253	1018	481	171	10707	1882	116	438	15631	3152	215	118	458	1907	403	69	-	7	-	21
Farmington,	31730	1855	378	174	40034	4833	1465	741	49652	12502	1054	1520	1736	2974	1205	460	-	2	12	30
Freeman,	11165	973	225	47	6243	1857	8	173	11078	1180	510	-	108	599	319	279	12	14	2	30
Jay,	26500	1000	100	350	2600	5000	280	-	3500	7000	2000	200	500	1000	1300	500	-	-	-	-
New Sharon,	22952	2358	298	127	14757	3174	411	482	30075	10135	1399	872	590	2213	1108	247	-	14	18	53
New Vineyard,	7000	565	58	50	8000	2100	-	-	15665	1300	150	-	300	640	240	63	-	-	-	-
Rangely,	2257	141	14	44	-	903	-	-	8090	1600	684	10	-	607	5	32	-	6	10	10
Eustis plantation,	6315	448	25	28	100	569	251	-	7897	875	-	-	10	531	-	-	-	-	-	-
Perkins plantation,	1680	190	93	18	42	320	12	-	3475	175	-	-	18	120	38	21	-	-	-	-
Washington plantation,	795	-	25	-	320	134	-	-	532	-	-	-	-	2150	18	7	-	-	-	-
	125647	8548	1697	1009	82803	20768	2543	1834	145595	37919	6012	2790	3720	12771	4636	1678	12	37	40	144

HANCOCK COUNTY.

Towns.	Number of bulls.	Heifers under four years old.	Cows four years old and upwards.	Steers under four years old.	Oxen four years old and upwards.	Number of common mixed or native sheep.	South Downs and grade South Downs.	Improved long-wooled sheep.	Merinos and grade merinos.	Pounds of wool produced.	Number of wool skins.	Pounds of dressed flax produced.	Swine, without distinction of age, sex or breed.	Colts under four years old.	Horses four years old and upwards.	Number of bushels of Indian corn produced.	Bushels of wheat.	Bushels of rye.	Bushels of barley.	Bushels of oats.	Bushels of buck-wheat.
Brooksville, . .	15	91	295	138	140	1450	300	-	-	6135	1500	-	63	26	56	200	200	-	3000	500	200
Cranberry Isles, . .	1	14	43	6	11	233	-	-	-	698	12	-	13	-	3	-	-	-	79	33	-
Eastbrook, . .	2	45	57	20	45	132	-	-	-	420	158	-	30	9	21	110	154	-	190	617	-
Eden, . . .	7	61	258	45	93	869	-	-	-	3093	328	-	39	23	65	126	240	29	531	259	-
Gouldsborough, . .	10	35	351	52	139	1113	-	-	-	4212	220	-	67	6	56	40	50	-	150	100	-
Hancock, . . .	8	119	187	60	70	980	7	12	-	2940	339	-	102	21	54	301	337	2	1101	917	17
Mariaville, . .	3	70	123	36	96	307	-	-	-	966	116	-	20	9	44	169	272	119	65	1152	36
Mount Desert, . .	2	100	188	28	88	1194	-	-	-	4776	450	-	49	6	35	25	125	-	200	200	2
Orland, . . .	3	200	290	133	139	852	-	-	-	8119	217	-	85	109	87	758	199	23	3280	2850	-
Otis, . . .	6	36	46	15	11	152	-	-	-	430	50	-	23	6	25	115	120	80	90	1021	20
Penobscot, . .	27	190	372	135	120	1465	-	-	-	4395	632	-	113	40	70	396	215	-	2885	3046	70
Surry, . . .	7	166	230	44	100	1036	-	12	17	3322	436	4	66	18	56	340	236	72	1670	1866	40
Tremont, . . .	10	92	279	100	112	985	-	-	-	2500	184	-	84	10	49	41	237	-	359	-	-
Verona, . . .	6	47	63	30	20	173	-	-	-	559	32	-	44	7	9	19	21	20	222	352	5
No. 33, Middle Division, .	1	18	20	12	16	-	-	30	6	129	10	-	21	2	8	-	69	-	218	280	-
	108	1284	2612	854	1180	10941	307	54	23	35694	4084	4	769	492	638	2640	2475	295	14950	13193	390

HANCOCK COUNTY, (Continued.)

Towns.	Bushels of potatoes.	Bushels of turnips.	Bushels of carrots.	Bushels of beets.	Bushels of apples.	Tons of upland hay.	Tons of interval hay.	Tons of bog and salt hay.	Pounds of butter.	Pounds of cheese.	Pounds of honey.	Pounds of maple sugar.	Gallons of maple syrup and molasses.	Value of poultry and eggs produced.	Bushels of beans.	Bushels of peas.	No. of sheep killed by wild animals.	No. of sheep killed by dogs.	No. of sheep injured by dogs.	Amount of damage to sheep by dogs.
Brooksville, . .	9800	1500	600	300	500	750	240	40	3600	500	400	-	-	1000	250	300	-	-	-	-
Cranberry Isles, . .	1767	100	-	-	-	76	-	-	3075	-	-	-	-	402	-	30	-	-	-	-
Eastbrook, . .	2000	150	75	60	150	78	20	-	3600	500	150	200	50	75	-	-	-	-	-	-
Eden, . . .	6823	845	399	157	280	414	240	5	18058	-	-	-	-	1265	187	121	52	2	-	-
Gouldsborough, . .	2500	700	100	90	40	400	200	25	600	-	-	-	-	100	80	100	50	20	-	75
Hancock, . . .	8656	1480	222	96	1136	615	92	9	23210	50	250	20	-	2176	157	231	19	17	-	-
Mariaville, . .	4844	250	60	78	1419	438	21	-	8091	260	369	-	-	481	155	124	18	8	4	11
Mount Desert, . .	2500	600	150	75	50	650	-	-	1880	-	-	-	-	500	50	100	-	1	-	-
Orland, . . .	13562	1895	1290	265	1310	1466	53	-	27600	700	974	-	-	1876	384	362	-	-	-	100
Otis, . . .	2810	228	103	40	150	219	11	-	6635	-	450	84	-	392	63	96	2	3	-	-
Penobscot, . .	10995	678	100	450	2068	931	100	15	19472	1650	-	-	-	877	698	491	108	-	-	234
Surry, . . .	12756	3868	568	276	504	834	-	2	4624	194	150	14	-	1870	336	376	-	106	20	324
Tremont, . . .	4744	2254	1050	153	-	285	23	-	7963	-	-	-	-	3285	73	74	-	48	-	200
Verona, . . .	2742	191	52	78	21	266	-	-	4414	-	8	-	-	394	38	63	-	6	30	18
No. 33, Middle Division, .	1345	28	27	16	286	116	50	-	2150	-	-	-	-	117	39	33	-	-	-	-
	87854	14767	4796	1737	7914	7538	950	96	134970	3854	2751	318	50	13810	2510	2201	249	211	54	962

KENNEBEC COUNTY.

Towns.	Number of bulls.	Heifers under four years old.	Cows four years old and upwards.	Steers under four years old.	Oxen four years old and upwards.	Number of common mixed or native sheep.	South Downs and grade South Downs.	Improved long-wooled sheep.	Merinos and grade merinos.	Pounds of wool produced.	Number of wool skins.	Pounds of dressed flax produced.	Swine, without distinction of age, sex or breed.	Colts under four years old.	Horses four years old and upwards.	Number of bushels of Indian corn produced.	Bushels of wheat.	Bushels of rye.	Bushels of barley.	Bushels of oats.	Bushels of buck-wheat.
Albion,	12	233	462	366	240	3256	-	-	-	9768	150	-	206	63	222	5997	2934	478	5418	7201	227
Augusta,	31	369	951	161	258	1791	255	69	101	5782	2560	5	623	151	583	5927	524	440	9620	14570	405
Belgrade,	6	175	483	210	252	3732	-	-	-	13058	-	-	219	63	208	6833	2104	247	5178	7526	74
Benton,	8	200	291	194	122	1944	-	-	-	5056	62	-	133	52	140	3950	670	490	4856	15845	129
Chelsea,	5	50	267	200	120	168	-	-	-	572	-	-	200	25	150	1200	25	150	3000	2300	50
China,	16	380	755	520	303	2260	304	520	1480	10200	250	-	399	93	349	7850	1818	218	10408	5556	275
Fayette,	12	205	318	221	210	1104	235	62	96	4011	102	-	122	42	138	4024	1471	61	2360	2907	32
Hallowell,	6	46	198	40	74	288	-	-	130	1772	50	-	220	18	160	1170	176	90	2752	795	-
Litchfield,	15	90	661	120	224	800	300	-	-	4000	100	100	300	45	300	2700	450	225	937	3437	25
Manchester,	7	116	277	118	146	1550	-	-	54	3638	86	20	125	59	159	3046	153	157	3725	3753	35
Monmouth,	13	277	602	243	283	1164	75	200	75	4510	248	50	271	40	230	7000	1600	325	5000	3651	143
Pittston,	13	227	564	194	206	607	102	196	144	3046	32	-	163	75	495	4024	330	281	4545	3918	21
Sidney,	16	294	573	271	238	4390	15	-	9	12773	216	-	298	69	288	8731	820	156	9271	12573	162
Vassalborough,	20	306	897	300	281	2855	160	254	112	7728	278	-	310	104	287	10059	910	313	13141	7108	46
Vienna,	6	155	280	308	170	1396	225	110	250	5621	151	21	128	31	119	3085	1884	133	1649	2653	71
Wayne,	8	121	374	254	126	100	200	181	400	3111	500	8	117	35	138	4584	1153	116	1759	2892	-
West Gardiner,	16	126	444	137	144	1088	-	-	-	3422	29	-	210	28	193	3487	134	109	3415	7244	65
Windsor,	12	160	540	420	242	1836	-	-	-	6426	1000	-	232	76	153	3863	602	150	4541	6807	52
Winthrop,	20	500	603	445	450	2531	140	71	190	6915	409	103	314	78	307	4101	1870	562	6117	7470	43
Unity plantation,	1	13	17	18	16	89	-	-	-	197	2	20	12	4	8	300	68	-	146	410	-
	243	4043	9557	4740	4125	32949	2011	1663	2941	111706	6225	327	4602	1151	4627	91931	19696	4701	97838	118617	1855

KENNEBEC COUNTY, (Continued.)

Towns.	Bushels of potatoes.	Bushels of turnips.	Bushels of carrots.	Bushels of beets.	Bushels of apples.	Tons of upland hay.	Tons of interval hay.	Tons of bog and salt hay.	Pounds of butter.	Pounds of cheese.	Pounds of honey.	Pounds of maple sugar.	Gallons of maple syrup and molasses.	Value of poultry and eggs produced.	Bushels of beans.	Bushels of peas.	No. of sheep killed by wild animals.	No. of sheep killed by dogs.	No. of sheep injured by dogs.	Amount of damage to sheep by dogs.
Albion,	26320	2066	704	754	17403	2842	250	61	26932	3345	916	281	129	2944	987	244	-	8	-	40
Augusta,	61891	4321	613	1904	11033	5366	577	17	50552	4093	2172	12	7	4063	979	314	-	8	7	28
Belgrade,	40412	951	255	155	20604	2975	318	-	32178	7955	947	295	20	2767	1450	204	-	-	-	10
Benton,	20490	477	205	119	3286	2282	-	120	30150	4505	1070	65	-	2041	-	-	-	-	-	-
Chelsea,	11000	200	75	75	1000	1500	400	-	12000	-	500	-	-	500	200	100	-	10	-	40
China,	31798	1505	540	650	18231	3880	332	-	44838	9060	767	76	61	5342	1333	411	2	20	19	70
Fayette,	13932	709	707	173	12228	2001	-	246	18571	10614	275	184	201	2164	450	135	-	5	-	20
Hallowell,	5410	400	200	400	6500	1120	-	-	21275	275	250	-	-	850	190	80	-	-	-	-
Litchfield,	16000	750	475	450	24000	630	300	50	18435	3241	100	200	50	2339	400	150	-	-	-	-
Manchester,	13305	923	288	115	12890	1885	-	-	21145	3750	500	36	95	1825	460	99	-	12	-	60
Monmouth,	30000	1119	300	345	17795	2564	473	225	42000	18666	475	455	200	2811	1300	300	-	4	24	25
Pittston,	24144	1165	538	361	7444	3250	479	-	38835	1425	1620	384	-	2409	505	407	-	14	-	72
Sidney,	33011	2558	759	626	23812	4502	519	-	43143	18077	1253	39	80	4156	1397	327	-	3	6	21
Vassalborough,	36394	1682	466	628	23153	5120	-	-	6225	9659	940	-	-	4690	1113	222	-	11	-	38
Vienna,	12545	1425	352	69	10864	1582	470	-	17889	2850	165	60	644	2183	561	139	-	2	2	12
Wayne,	10635	616	63	172	10363	1198	410	-	22625	10523	346	60	232	1933	326	52	-	17	4	84
West Gardiner,	24866	1348	690	287	13720	2288	371	-	39269	7020	1427	-	-	3252	700	384	-	1	-	3
Windsor,	103673	1112	308	324	10689	2936	275	-	37331	4220	455	-	-	3948	896	450	-	-	-	-
Winthrop,	36120	3009	1581	516	5013	4110	219	-	51187	13818	694	911	105	3582	480	340	-	27	-	65
Unity plantation,	1344	12	5	-	412	88	-	22	933	100	-	-	-	124	74	28	-	-	-	-
	553290	26348	9098	8123	249440	52119	5343	741	575513	133186	14872	3058	1824	53423	13801	4387	2	142	62	588

KNOX COUNTY.

Towns.	Number of bulls.	Heifers under four years old.	Cows four years old and upwards.	Steers under four years old.	Oxen four years old and upwards.	Number of common mixed or native sheep.	South Downs and grade South Downs.	Improved long-wooled sheep.	Merinos and grade merinos.	Pounds of wool produced.	Number of wool skins.	Pounds of dressed flax produced.	Swine, without distinction of age, sex or breed.	Colts under four years old.	Horses four years old and upwards.	Number of bushels of Indian corn produced.	Bushels of wheat.	Bushels of rye.	Bushels of barley.	Bushels of oats.	Bushels of buck-wheat.
Appleton,	14	348	454	206	234	1628	-	-	-	5205	196	-	208	44	157	3498	409	747	2850	4484	29
Camden,	34	344	730	121	267	1278	-	-	-	4977	423	-	502	40	333	1306	488	535	3715	2426	-
Cushing,	7	87	172	52	67	537	-	-	-	1698	175	-	69	10	36	321	71	128	1000	208	-
Friendship,	3	68	150	36	52	369	-	-	-	861	127	-	28	8	41	169	23	89	699	151	-
Hope,	6	156	335	82	136	851	-	-	-	2290	91	-	150	20	115	1882	454	317	2800	749	40
Rockland,	3	80	381	24	76	108	-	-	-	-	-	-	157	14	393	396	196	2	1316	286	-
South Thomaston,	10	130	256	36	46	407	-	-	-	1793	35	-	236	15	81	235	653	188	1387	616	-
St. George,	13	172	311	28	100	808	-	-	-	2474	320	-	47	6	99	113	62	6	534	211	-
Thomaston,	2	100	280	30	35	120	-	-	-	300	-	-	117	15	160	277	87	26	796	53	-
Vinalhaven,	6	25	175	10	78	2000	-	-	-	7050	350	-	100	15	12	62	120	-	475	68	-
Warren,	28	434	489	231	206	1277	40	2	31	4072	309	-	257	52	219	3363	404	784	3864	3067	83
Washington,	11	240	377	243	242	1009	-	14	-	2651	92	-	153	43	158	2514	611	606	1890	6761	36
	137	2184	4110	1099	1539	10392	40	16	31	33521	2118	-	2024	382	1806	14136	3528	3428	21326	16880	188

KNOX COUNTY, (Continued.)

Towns.	Bushels of potatoes.	Bushels of turnips.	Bushels of carrots.	Bushels of beets.	Bushels of apples.	Tons of upland hay.	Tons of interval hay.	Tons of bog and salt hay.	Pounds of butter.	Pounds of cheese.	Pounds of honey.	Pounds of maple sugar.	Gallons of maple syrup and molasses.	Value of poultry and eggs produced.	Bushels of beans.	Bushels of peas.	No. of sheep killed by wild animals.	No. of sheep killed by dogs.	No. of sheep injured by dogs.	Amount of damage to sheep by dogs.
Appleton,	28593	1347	243	548	9116	2498	-	499	53265	3149	487	192	2	2707	810	318	1	2	2	4
Camden,	18836	3589	1410	1321	7929	3315	356	54	73000	-	-	-	-	6957	-	-	-	-	-	-
Cushing,	6283	1177	134	130	155	610	-	145	17475	-	-	-	-	1698	99	102	-	-	-	-
Friendship,	6349	940	69	114	114	357	154	15	9873	60	25	-	-	800	19	61	2	-	-	-
Hope,	16745	974	239	273	6716	2048	285	-	33393	4695	561	48	16	1794	499	260	-	-	-	-
Rockland,	9803	1725	531	1582	1067	897	-	-	22560	400	90	-	-	1052	294	108	-	2	-	6
South Thomaston,	9581	2761	88	780	209	915	105	54	27130	1820	-	-	-	1665	195	176	11	3	-	32
St. George,	9902	3124	154	178	-	857	131	7	27648	-	-	-	-	1570	13	21	-	9	1	28
Thomaston,	3571	1298	35	240	190	710	-	30	-	-	-	200	-	-	25	-	-	-	-	-
Vinalhaven,	2000	932	45	50	-	250	50	-	2000	600	-	-	-	1475	-	-	-	-	-	-
Warren,	23074	2458	425	730	6700	2516	227	723	50294	6010	68	-	-	3545	627	382	-	17	18	83
Washington,	20121	1203	198	71	6110	832	274	-	17637	1443	350	84	11	997	478	193	-	-	-	-
	154858	21528	3571	5317	38306	15805	1582	1527	332275	18177	1581	524	29	24050	3059	1621	14	33	21	153

LINCOLN COUNTY.

Towns.	Number of bulls.	Heifers under four years old.	Cows four years old and upwards.	Steers under four years old.	Oxen four years old and upwards.	Number of common mixed or native sheep.	South Downs and grade South Downs.	Improved long-wooled sheep.	Merinos and grade merinos.	Pounds of wool produced.	Number of wool skins.	Pounds of dressed flax produced.	Swine, without distinction of age, sex or breed.	Colts under four years old.	Horses four years old and upwards.	Number of bushels of Indian corn produced.	Bushels of wheat.	Bushels of rye.	Bushels of barley.	Bushels of oats.	Bushels of buck-wheat.
Alna, . . .	3	172	281	210	155	622	-	-	-	1201	89	-	87	40	121	1317	54	213	2657	879	-
Bremen, . . .	2	102	183	56	114	581	-	-	-	1549	128	-	57	9	44	682	31	35	1259	749	-
Dresden, . . .	13	209	418	151	230	700	-	-	-	2285	132	-	173	35	110	2803	132	243	3497	2053	95
Edgecomb, . . .	6	120	286	99	176	626	-	16	-	2481	242	6	113	17	74	1473	8	166	2713	610	-
Jefferson, . . .	23	450	500	401	375	1500	100	300	25	4992	343	8	200	50	200	4402	543	363	3948	5100	4
Newcastle, . . .	14	218	386	236	142	900	25	-	-	3600	522	-	200	65	161	2106	120	300	5000	500	20
Nobleborough, . .	12	183	321	271	160	531	-	-	40	1900	251	30	162	15	125	5000	160	325	4121	1030	-
Waldoborough, . .	19	545	800	310	473	1472	18	16	-	4726	444	88	334	32	283	2171	272	809	6321	2157	49
Whitefield, . .	8	403	645	310	324	1627	37	20	-	4742	149	-	265	59	257	4116	407	261	5544	7438	46
Wiscasset, . . .	10	150	300	129	188	623	4	-	15	1922	230	125	174	20	100	1700	118	56	2500	296	-
	110	2552	4120	2173	2337	9182	184	352	80	29398	2630	257	1765	342	1475	25771	1845	2771	37060	20912	214

LINCOLN COUNTY, (Continued.)

Towns.	Bushels of potatoes.	Bushels of turnips.	Bushels of carrots.	Bushels of beets.	Bushels of apples.	Tons of upland hay.	Tons of interval hay.	Tons of bog and salt hay.	Pounds of butter.	Pounds of cheese.	Pounds of honey.	Pounds of maple sugar.	Gallons of maple syrup and molasses.	Value of poultry and eggs produced.	Bushels of beans.	Bushels of peas.	No. of sheep killed by wild animals.	No. of sheep killed by dogs.	No. of sheep injured by dogs.	Amount of damage to sheep by dogs.
Alna,	9185	690	116	156	2390	1420	256	-	14371	200	100	75	-	364	260	167	-	4	-	16
Bremen,	6533	547	221	370	787	804	136	48	14958	175	-	-	-	1467	93	58	-	-	-	-
Dresden,	18848	1318	166	285	5929	2522	705	-	36140	-	206	-	-	2277	295	235	-	5	10	25
Edgecomb,	8367	735	216	314	8753	1311	962	52	20680	110	90	-	-	1660	251	95	-	2	-	9
Jefferson,	22290	156	141	8565	1956	494	805	805	27572	1021	290	4	5	3021	664	199	2	6	9	14
Newcastle,	11520	1065	200	800	4000	3000	100	500	38600	4000	500	-	-	4000	400	120	-	40	-	80
Nobleborough,	11782	1600	600	785	9121	2431	507	100	3000	450	250	355	60	45	760	310	-	6	3	20
Waldoborough,	27859	3716	218	1027	5624	3516	162	504	68108	1300	310	278	14	4763	466	463	-	62	65	316
Whitefield,	33554	1447	193	241	8530	2841	200	604	41532	610	302	364	87	3111	760	387	-	33	12	120
Wiscasset,	9014	621	381	487	2500	2058	99	181	30633	-	333	-	-	4200	275	365	-	-	-	-
	158952	11900	2452	13030	49590	20397	3932	2794	295594	7866	2381	1076	166	24908	4224	2399	2	158	89	610

OXFORD COUNTY.

Towns.	Number of bulls.	Heifers under four years old.	Cows four years old and upwards.	Steers under four years old.	Oxen four years old and upwards.	Number of common mixed or native sheep.	South Downs and grade South Downs.	Improved long-wooled sheep.	Merinos and grade merinos.	Pounds of wool produced.	Number of wool skins.	Pounds of dressed flax produced.	Swine, without distinction of age, sex or breed.	Colts under four years old.	Horses four years old and upwards.	Number of bushels of Indian corn produced.	Bushels of wheat.	Bushels of rye.	Bushels of barley.*	Bushels of oats.	Bushels of buck-wheat.
Albany,	22	236	219	222	150	1914	–	–	–	5571	103	5	104	25	88	3173	1172	422	8	4484	82
Andover,	12	230	272	203	197	1878	108	–	2	4756	144	–	159	67	193	1702	1392	3559	1259	6784	2781
Bethel,	32	648	610	620	347	3888	–	–	–	11037	66	–	265	722	264	8012	2333	1101	1069	10646	717
Byron,	4	90	94	110	64	504	40	100	–	1601	21	–	41	13	41	366	588	80	173	1026	800
Canton,	21	316	341	348	129	770	60	984	12	5647	600	80	150	80	136	6055	1213	544	1015	7593	111
Dixfield,	22	222	301	301	221	1822	34	–	–	5314	32	29	138	53	102	3546	1342	409	706	5980	171
Fryeburg,	27	493	514	552	398	1499	19	–	–	3038	11	50	251	70	265	8991	384	504	115	10605	511
Gilead,	9	131	143	118	78	706	–	–	–	1802	51	–	77	17	63	2047	356	237	228	2753	263
Grafton,	4	35	33	14	28	163	–	–	–	320	–	–	27	4	20	–	110	180	–	500	–
Greenwood,	18	200	253	196	207	1585	–	–	–	4755	50	53	129	46	104	3019	1230	370	682	3893	103
Hanover,	4	57	79	50	56	900	–	–	–	1996	28	64	58	23	35	1034	125	255	453	927	430
Hartford,	21	351	441	402	299	2408	145	8	94	9256	140	25	239	65	180	7602	2892	295	1479	4606	72
Hebron,	9	192	280	137	212	1186	–	–	–	3344	67	–	103	30	89	3021	373	158	1692	2696	50
Hiram,	16	306	391	252	270	794	–	192	–	3044	18	100	220	40	148	9828	2227	483	122	3793	34
Lovell,	16	192	331	249	212	959	–	–	–	2306	13	151	168	46	127	1542	1411	753	176	2944	129
Mason,	4	48	45	69	26	243	–	18	–	646	14	33	33	8	17	611	227	168	6	577	142
Mexico,	15	189	194	219	117	1178	32	32	10	3116	39	102	94	20	44	2520	778	491	371	2885	450
Newry,	8	192	149	155	90	839	–	–	–	2517	30	28	82	24	86	820	508	490	130	1405	110
Norway,	33	456	546	372	294	1612	6	79	2	5312	108	71	329	55	195	8857	2112	260	1813	10572	39
Paris,	41	517	670	580	413	2644	56	–	–	9254	327	–	300	75	293	14000	2317	413	3780	8806	59
Peru,	17	357	376	500	248	2016	100	203	175	5868	110	–	176	66	133	6768	1963	775	394	4555	235
Porter,	5	291	369	280	260	671	–	–	–	1363	–	–	223	45	140	10207	1712	396	6	2372	15
Roxbury,	1	63	70	45	54	401	–	–	–	1126	13	32	40	11	39	405	268	169	554	1468	191
Sumner,	13	439	536	548	340	2708	240	–	–	8443	300	–	183	58	215	7422	2315	606	1014	7016	47
Sweden,	12	162	262	158	116	–	–	–	640	1841	20	–	132	32	108	4809	1223	484	28	2812	23
Upton,	7	42	58	56	61	358	–	–	–	1032	–	–	53	8	23	5	449	112	354	1090	1018
Woodstock,	15	200	315	250	246	3746	–	–	–	9400	450	–	130	74	93	2611	2550	426	350	3980	100

Franklin plantation,	5	60	74	83	54	300	50	75	124	1850	25	50	38	15	31	1689	815	115	94	351	10
	413	6625	7503	7089	5487	37692	890	1691	1069	115555	2780	973	3912	1792	3272	120659	34385	14245	18071	117209	8283

OXFORD COUNTY, (Continued.)

Towns.	Bushels of potatoes.	Bushels of turnips.	Bushels of carrots.	Bushels of beets.	Bushels of apples.	Tons of upland hay.	Tons of interval hay.	Tons of bog and salt hay.	Pounds of butter.	Pounds of cheese.	Pounds of honey.	Pounds of maple sugar.	Gallons of maple syrup and molasses.	Value of poultry and eggs produced.	Bushels of beans.	Bushels of peas.	No. of sheep killed by wild animals.	No. of sheep killed by dogs.	No. of sheep injured by dogs.	Amount of damage to sheep by dogs.
Albany,	5580	947	561	43	3165	1100	125	400	17155	4456	250	150	14	756	150	125	25	5	–	20
Andover,	[illegible]0915	1836	316	131	3007	1477	502	–	14978	3092	155	235	73	948	204	128	4	–	–	–
Bethel,	46505	749	564	50	8439	2910	1237	–	32425	4430	1120	6360	162	1762	196	184	–	–	–	–
Byron,	5326	200	140	60	1240	360	378	–	3940	1585	–	–	–	149	95	35	–	–	–	–
Canton,	20691	1802	240	156	11143	1334	583	334	25026	20549	700	50	156	1962	491	171	5	12	1	24
Dixfield,	10544	463	–	81	10041	1838	324	–	11490	16980	60	557	148	374	466	140	33	–	–	–
Fryeburg,	24860	737	737	147	3487	486	1325	1690	32910	9617	–	15140	2550	1951	539	62	–	15	3	65
Gilead,	8180	587	69	25	3805	148	670	272	89[illegible]	3265	30	1300	75	466	63	–	6	12	–	24
Grafton,	2500	300	50	–	–	125	110	–	1500	–	–	–	–	–	–	–	7	–	–	–
Greenwood,	16875	543	152	90	5014	1293	122	–	16225	2365	585	862	6	2469	289	100	–	–	–	–
Hanover,	5900	239	47	17	1880	169	185	155	3500	1840	70	1412	88	317	157	67	9	18	9	27
Hartford,	23924	1668	479	228	21528	2260	541	–	29490	16217	358	264	285	2272	649	213	–	–	–	–
Hebron,	15084	875	217	100	11113	775	985	–	15025	7070	58	1685	318	1254	209	50	–	–	–	–
Hiram,	18148	371	119	55	9920	1846	164	94	30454	3415	–	–	64	1362	791	39	–	21	10	97
Lovell,	13758	925	287	121	4586	1153	20	301	18040	2305	405	100	77	720	394	104	–	2	–	8
Mason,	3012	469	59	28	158	322	28	–	3800	420	90	437	17	292	51	73	10		–	–
Mexico,	7893	615	126	78	5980	1133	176	–	10220	5277	331	–	84	997	341	94	29	–	–	6
Newry,	8912	90	20	7	306	508	217	189	4017	365	–	1427	25	150	50	20	56	4	7	40
Norway,	32497	1212	1032	194	24175	2843	518	–	41710	11795	415	329	174	25[illegible]1	710	298	–	24	–	75
Paris,	28600	1300	700	150	23800	2978	500	–	38100	3746	510	270	300	2046	673	170	–	–	–	–
Peru,	17568	1768	705	93	3318	1475	1000	98	25889	17371	508	501	235	1711	308	110	–	–	–	–
Porter,	16285	920	120	41	13699	1246	394	–	13450	3900	–	1020	48	1609	759	50	–	–	–	–
Roxbury,	3740	351	113	11	2200	227	339	13	3477	550	–	21	15	234	92	36	27	–	–	–
Sumner,	22500	995	761	250	19900	2272	1289	–	27900	16900	900	775	125	850	573	158	–	–	–	–

OXFORD COUNTY, (Continued.)

Towns.	Bushels of potatoes.	Bushels of turnips.	Bushels of carrots.	Bushels of beets.	Bushels of apples.	Tons of upland hay.	Tons of interval hay.	Tons of bog and salt hay.	Pounds of butter.	Pounds of cheese.	Pounds of honey.	Pounds of maple sugar.	Gallons of maple syrup and molasses.	Value of poultry and eggs produced.	Bushels of beans.	Bushels of peas.	No. of sheep killed by wild animals.	No. of sheep killed by dogs.	No. of sheep injured by dogs.	Amount of damage to sheep by dogs.
Sweden, . . .	13340	438	170	53	3918	889	9	69	15965	3535	-	-	87	739	270	43	-	-	-	-
Upton, . . .	3680	222	107	4	-	179	25	-	1985	1600	-	400	32	-	-	10	12	6	-	30
Woodstock, . .	21310	1000	1100	400	3900	1848	100	-	14885	4961	500	225	75	-	550	960	-	-	-	-
Franklin plantation, .	4374	193	66	11	761	600	20	17	6715	1045	25	40	30	329	-	-	-	-	-	-
	432456	21815	8457	2624	200483	33794	11882	3632	479386	168661	7070	33560	5263	28710	9070	3440	222	121	30	416

PENOBSCOT COUNTY.

Towns.	Number of bulls.	Heifers under four years old.	Cows four years old and upwards.	Steers under four years old.	Oxen four years old and upwards.	Number of common mixed or native sheep.	South Downs and grade South Downs.	Improved long-wooled sheep.	Merinos and grade merinos.	Pounds of wool produced.	Number of wool skins.	Pounds of dressed flax produced.	Swine, without distinction of age, sex or breed.	Colts under four years old.	Horses four years old and upwards.	Number of bushels of Indian corn produced.	Bushels of wheat.	Bushels of rye.	Bushels of barley.	Bushels of oats.	Bushels of buck-wheat.
Bangor,	16	315	756	56	96	483	19	48	1	691	4033	1	489	66	669	516	415	182	7852	4546	144
Bradford,	36	309	382	250	154	1780	–	–	–	5139	197	–	206	53	249	2456	1011	167	2961	6705	1100
Bradley,	2	67	111	40	53	192	–	–	–	449	16	–	56	13	57	226	167	9	570	586	32
Brewer,	2	114	280	73	26	254	–	–	–	830	11	–	120	26	190	213	40	83	2177	3939	84
Carroll,	8	128	173	93	88	646	–	150	–	2126	91	130	93	28	86	825	1708	98	1896	8006	501
Charleston,	8	277	440	–	166	2280	140	–	–	9680	200	1	218	43	252	4500	1600	50	5514	7001	375
Chester,	7	103	88	70	52	390	–	–	–	1101	35	–	54	13	30	498	650	20	292	3001	549
Corinna,	9	297	485	270	222	3339	–	–	–	9295	214	95	237	59	249	4225	3080	170	2736	10161	124
Corinth,	27	399	524	247	230	3085	73	–	–	9619	711	–	301	83	296	4170	865	238	8042	12489	445
Dixmont,	33	332	419	285	199	3845	–	–	–	11024	187	–	222	73	201	2826	2015	169	5277	14083	41
Edinburg,	1	5	18	10	10	56	–	–	–	198	10	–	8	1	2	20	93	–	16	157	35
Enfield,	8	108	173	66	52	329	–	125	–	1358	82	–	58	19	67	352	564	36	387	4474	587
Exeter,	6	126	–	66	255	3557	9	–	74	11083	1801	–	268	75	306	4848	2063	63	5087	17112	94
Garland,	19	374	469	266	238	2340	–	–	46	6333	102	8	202	71	211	2943	2935	139	4004	8562	232
Glenburn,	14	247	287	108	94	672	111	142	10	2249	79	–	94	55	134	433	303	127	2971	3924	255
Hermon,	21	321	461	171	59	1330	12	–	35	3565	146	–	174	60	232	937	457	159	4332	7685	260
Holden,	4	135	227	154	127	1024	8	11	–	3810	191	–	86	37	109	935	521	104	2160	2881	35
Hudson,	6	107	128	82	77	868	29	–	–	1648	56	–	102	19	82	642	185	75	613	2116	144
Mattawamkeag,	4	47	55	12	29	153	–	–	–	341	42	–	34	5	25	101	230	27	420	1306	220
Maxfield,	2	43	66	29	20	243	–	–	–	450	5	–	17	9	25	150	355	–	45	968	450
Newburg,	5	338	440	286	134	2865	–	–	–	7763	421	–	178	53	249	1662	851	320	4879	13092	49
Newport,	10	152	410	270	180	2000	100	600	400	12400	560	–	250	56	210	3050	2560	175	3150	7200	–
Oldtown,	10	129	317	25	40	350	42	43	3	1047	591	–	251	34	232	554	30	151	2251	4349	108
Orrington,	14	263	431	55	74	793	38	30	–	2551	325	–	149	–	170	309	305	166	5473	4003	88
Patten,	8	148	167	180	68	922	–	–	–	2291	46	30	123	37	102	212	1972	196	2251	9370	1686
Stetson,	–	–	357	447	168	2074	–	–	–	4109	151	–	144	26	158	2232	1178	233	2002	10041	164
Veazie,	2	31	85	20	12	4	6	–	–	35	–	–	63	8	55	75	–	55	1062	1907	–

PENOBSCOT COUNTY, (Continued.)

Towns.	Number of bulls.	Heifers under four years old.	Cows four years old and upwards.	Steers under four years old.	Oxen four years old and upwards.	Number of common mixed or native sheep.	South Downs and grade South Downs.	Improved long-wooled sheep.	Merinos and grade merinos.	Pounds of wool produced.	Number of wool skins.	Pounds of dressed flax produced.	Swine, without distinction of age, sex or breed.	Colts under four years old.	Horses four years old and upwards.	Number of bushels of Indian corn produced.	Bushels of wheat.	Bushels of rye.	Bushels of barley.	Bushels of oats.	Bushels of buck-wheat.
Webster,	-	11	13	13	12	24	-	-	-	179	12	-	4	4	5	106	238	-	179	1104	75
No. 2, Grand Falls,	1	7	17	6	16	-	-	-	24	75	-	-	2	1	4	77	172	26	20	543	-
	294	5290	8164	3660	2951	35218	579	1047	573	113539	10295	264	4203	1027	4657	41003	26563	3238	78619	171061	7477

PENOBSCOT COUNTY, (Continued.)

Towns.	Bushels of potatoes.	Bushels of turnips.	Bushels of carrots.	Bushels of beets.	Bushels of apples.	Tons of upland hay.	Tons of interval hay.	Tons of bog and salt hay.	Pounds of butter.	Pounds of cheese.	Pounds of honey.	Pounds of maple sugar.	Gallons of maple syrup and molasses.	Value of poultry and eggs produced.	Bushels of beans.	Bushels of peas.	No. of sheep killed by wild animals.	No. of sheep killed by dogs.	No. of sheep injured by dogs.	Amount of damage to sheep by dogs.
Bangor,	32125	5327	1936	793	1079	2908	216	300	28705	905	1213	-	-	3031	420	417	-	9	18	81
Bradford,	39600	1516	666	175	2620	2177	-	-	32987	978	2903	293	45	2832	716	770	-	-	-	-
Bradley,	6077	340	161	277	276	353	-	198	7710	425	13	-	-	806	89	107	3	5	-	16
Brewer,	9991	692	1184	173	175	1207	64	-	10145	667	827	-	-	860	135	127	-	5	-	30
Carroll,	12286	1248	551	35	473	710	20	-	14000	6631	81	179	146	406	217	149	5	1	1	4
Charleston,	55129	1147	505	200	2804	2501	125	-	40100	3050	1500	1000	-	2500	-	-	-	-	-	-
Chester,	5315	207	107	38	734	426	136	-	5925	965	690	-	15	280	98	406	2	1	-	10
Corinna,	46657	934	483	324	9419	2432	77	-	31808	12557	3194	567	102	2156	1109	1452	9	2	4	700
Corinth,	85907	1475	386	282	10790	3547	278	21	54289	13035	5034	85	114	2188	1154	1875	-	12	4	75
Dixmont,	46570	754	298	405	14405	2511	423	14	40960	6234	2348	130	50	2927	814	231	-	4	2	20
Edinburg,	830	35	32	12	60	125	50	-	925	-	-	-	-	40	13	16	7	-	-	-

Enfield,	7361	297	233	85	1709	397	65	–	12450	–	405	165	20	655	163	621	–	–	–	–
Exeter,	66203	1045	514	294	3827	3258	75	–	45539	6319	3042	521	163	2854	1403	1455	–	–	–	–
Garland,	47866	1371	507	229	8171	2888	53	–	40709	6296	2293	399	228	1943	1049	271	1	4	1	12
Glenburn,	20945	2094	333	105	1247	1107	211	180	20786	865	1226	–	–	946	209	399	4	7	–	33
Hermon,	33313	1152	410	209	2130	2019	383	–	46656	1700	1997	28	–	1422	449	543	–	7	–	45
Holden,	19696	276	246	135	3796	1356	167	–	24818	3365	995	–	11	693	263	182	–	–	–	–
Hudson,	14393	1097	340	60	1489	680	281	–	11210	573	2105	–	16	1110	256	161	1	–	–	3
Mattawamkeag,	3277	267	180	35	34	273	42	–	5600	–	125	–	–	200	83	42	8	–	–	–
Maxfield,	3525	85	5	28	1364	262	10	–	3210	317	215	145	4	108	50	8	3	–	–	–
Newburg,	53615	1089	261	321	12551	2583	489	93	32225	2010	1495	1629	137	3423	713	263	3	30	7	140
Newport,	30460	550	710	–	4570	2140	160	–	30185	9210	1865	–	–	1760	455	200	–	10	50	100
Oldtown,	23769	3079	1436	1552	1000	1185	–	237	24718	–	216	200	–	1864	–	–	–	–	–	–
Orrington,	27839	940	630	256	4248	2051	75	–	29478	803	587	–	–	1533	468	303	–	2	1	–
Patten,	10172	1397	55	44	364	932	–	–	10215	1905	75	30	10	492	142	535	31	2	–	10
Stetson,	27650	440	196	–	2337	1614	75	–	35890	4675	1734	500	50	350	608	100	–	3	1	15
Veazie,	8791	185	245	54	60	392	–	–	8500	225	150	450	–	297	79	173	–	–	–	–
Webster,	1156	357	20	20	27	61	40	–	900	–	–	110	4	67	35	7	–	–	–	–
No. 2, Grand Falls,	471	–	–	–	30	60	2	–	400	–	–	–	–	200	–	–	–	–	–	–
	929499	29396	12125	5041	91789	41848	3517	1043	652043	84040	36328	5431	1015	34816	10090	10808	77	107	87	601

PISCATAQUIS COUNTY.

Towns.	Number of bulls.	Heifers under four years old.	Cows four years old and upwards.	Steers under four years old.	Oxen four years old and upwards.	Number of common mixed or native sheep.	South Downs and grade South Downs.	Improved long-wooled sheep.	Merinos and grade merinos.	Pounds of wool produced.	Number of wool skins.	Pounds of dressed flax produced.	Swine, without distinction of age, sex or breed.	Colts under four years old.	Horses four years old and upwards.	Number of bushels of Indian corn produced.	Bushels of wheat.	Bushels of rye.	Bushels of barley.	Bushels of oats.	Bushels of buck-wheat.
Barnard,	6	28	38	16	29	127	-	-	-	310	13	-	22	8	12	166	250	3	112	500	40
Bowerbank,	1	20	33	36	20	176	-	-	-	528	20	-	15	5	9	390	235	62	125	770	-
Blanchard,	7	50	64	42	18	442	-	-	-	988	34	25	26	10	29	188	157	35	1106	1312	179
Brownville,	10	122	207	74	74	858	-	12	1	2293	134	-	124	51	110	1013	1161	-	1987	8254	978
Guilford,	21	146	243	104	120	1326	-	-	7	4800	70	12	177	52	133	1267	1492	24	2288	6039	9
Greenville,	8	70	88	39	50	325	-	-	-	882	21	-	42	10	59	-	383	25	727	2969	69
Medford,	14	65	87	62	44	280	-	17	-	975	16	-	53	9	42	237	589	30	257	2582	287
Milo,	15	210	300	175	132	1425	-	-	-	3758	108	51	206	62	140	1676	1798	45	1800	6787	890
Sangerville,	15	197	290	242	161	3544	-	-	-	13126	97	1	184	56	171	1790	2564	74	5365	11147	60
Sebec,	6	240	304	208	162	1665	-	-	140	2823	16	-	151	42	157	1761	5701	42	2642	11183	119
Shi.ley,	1	45	72	5	53	586	-	-	1	1822	37	-	27	16	33	6	485	13	1022	3328	291
Williamsburg,	3	39	42	19	180	138	-	-	-	423	12	-	14	6	24	181	388	-	251	810	421
	107	1232	1768	1022	1044	10892	-	29	149	32728	481	89	941	327	919	9175	15206	353	17682	55681	3333

PISCATAQUIS COUNTY, (Continued.)

Towns.	Bushels of potatoes.	Bushels of turnips.	Bushels of carrots.	Bushels of beets.	Bushels of apples.	Tons of upland hay.	Tons of interval hay.	Tons of bog and salt hay.	Pounds of butter.	Pounds of cheese.	Pounds of honey.	Pounds of maple sugar.	Gallons of maple syrup and molasses.	Value of poultry and eggs produced.	Bushels of beans.	Bushels of peas.	No. of sheep killed by wild animals.	No. of sheep killed by dogs.	No. of sheep injured by dogs.	Amount of damage to sheep by dogs.
Barnard,	3700	93	83	8	600	182	7	-	2275	100	500	-	3	65	52	47	2	1	-	-
Bowerbank,	1585	215	30	30	390	260	-	-	3300	825	300	350	30	152	30	60	-	-	-	-
Blanchard,	3240	616	45	26	582	333	65	-	6320	2120	70	100	10	219	55	43	8	-	-	-
Brownville,	14891	2034	257	103	2237	851	7	14	18490	3025	630	253	36	782	250	294	6	2	-	6
Guilford,	17273	616	137	62	5011	1368	27	-	16063	5520	265	181	81	591	266	81	-	-	-	-
Greenville,	4833	60	-	16	28	399	20	-	5118	615	-	-	-	116	10	5	-	-	-	-
Medford,	6445	102	48	6	346	431	48	51	5755	340	268	12	-	248	93	150	26	-	1	-
Milo,	20550	830	157	53	1530	1496	-	-	18662	2985	1430	-	-	1681	449	711	24	1	1	3
Sangerville,	39165	219	193	38	7810	2119	-	-	19598	6035	2050	-	-	1256	465	1056	-	-	-	-
Sebec,	24530	492	58	-	6675	1676	8	-	23165	3550	780	225	93	1804	557	322	-	-	-	-
Shirley,	5120	305	4	5	62	327	-	-	4400	520	-	305	30	200	1	21	1	3	6	18
Williamsburg,	2832	127	35	38	624	381	2	-	3560	575	290	-	12	210	74	51	-	-	-	-
	144164	5769	1047	385	25895	9823	184	65	106706	26220	6584	1426	295	7324	2299	2841	67	7	8	27

SAGADAHOC COUNTY.

Towns.	Number of bulls.	Heifers under four years old.	Cows four years old and upwards.	Steers under four years old.	Oxen four years old and upwards.	Number of common mixed or native sheep.	South Downs and grade South Downs.	Improved long-wooled sheep.	Merinos and grade merinos.	Pounds of wool produced.	Number of wool skins.	Pounds of dressed flax produced.	Swine, without distinction of age, sex or breed.	Colts under four years old.	Horses four years old and upwards.	Number of bushels of Indian corn produced.	Bushels of wheat.	Bushels of rye.	Bushels of barley.	Bushels of oats.	Bushels of buck-wheat.
Arrowsic, . . .	4	40	80	50	60	300	-	-	-	900	20	-	60	8	20	240	-	-	400	50	-
Bowdoinham, . .	8	209	286	159	120	1205	-	3	2	4142	500	45	225	29	173	3265	518	205	6202	3432	6
Georgetown, . .	10	34	175	36	82	320	-	-	-	960	75	-	-	3	24	120	50	10	150	60	-
Perkins, . . .	3	19	35	6	22	115	-	-	-	343	13	-	14	4	8	389	60	34	236	516	-
Richmond, . . .	5	218	426	244	134	796	-	198	-	2262	212	20	114	25	146	1788	300	138	2888	3464	-
Topsham, . . .	19	132	305	150	224	1087	61	214	-	3939	380	57	178	25	120	3125	365	242	3113	2515	113
West Bath, . . .	3	73	131	30	30	146	-	-	-	474	86	-	67	6	58	392	42	-	1338	32	17
Woolwich, . . .	10	334	496	290	252	1296	-	-	-	5184	50	-	164	33	120	2558	68	159	4576	397	-
	62	1059	1934	965	924	5265	61	415	2	18204	1336	112	822	133	669	11875	1403	788	18903	10466	136

SAGADAHOC COUNTY, (Continued.)

Towns.	Bushels of potatoes.	Bushels of turnips.	Bushels of carrots.	Bushels of beets.	Bushels of apples.	Tons of upland hay.	Tons of interval hay.	Tons of bog and salt hay.	Pounds of butter.	Pounds of cheese.	Pounds of honey.	Pounds of maple sugar.	Gallons of maple syrup and molasses.	Value of poultry and eggs produced.	Bushels of beans.	Bushels of peas.	No. of sheep killed by wild animals.	No. of sheep killed by dogs.	No. of sheep injured by dogs.	Amount of damage to sheep by dogs.
Arrowsic, . . .	1000	100	-	50	500	240	50	150	2500	-	-	-	-	200	50	20	-	-	-	-
Bowdoinham, . .	10264	7264	1117	684	9224	2854	475	-	21375	990	1025	-	-	50	651	312	-	16	42	71
Georgetown, . .	1000	40	-	-	100	500	-	-	8750	-	-	-	-	200	20	10	-	-	-	-
Perkins, . . .	1202	27	19	141	142	293	12	17	2300	-	-	-	-	168	57	-	-	-	-	-
Richmond, . . .	16761	432	117	130	2223	2852	236	-	28969	645	395	-	-	1162	393	239	-	3	-	9
Topsham, . . .	18220	1396	265	1028	9122	1852	216	716	30061	561	295	21	26	527	570	235	-	6	7	23
West Bath, . . .	5130	674	66	577	682	625	15	15	11102	232	-	-	-	1106	118	86	-	-	-	-
Woolwich, . . .	21000	528	210	357	3450	3166	675	100	32160	-	-	-	-	1250	375	150	-	-	-	-
	73577	10561	1794	2967	25443	12382	1679	998	137217	2428	1715	21	26	4673	2234	1052	-	25	49	103

SOMERSET COUNTY.

Towns.	Number of bulls.	Heifers under four years old.	Cows four years old and upwards.	Steers under four years old.	Oxen four years old and upwards.	Number of common mixed of native sheep.	South Downs and grade South Downs.	Improved long-wooled sheep.	Merinos and grade merinos.	Pounds of wool produced.	Number of wool skins.	Pounds of dressed flax produced.	Swine, without distinction of age, sex or breed.	Colts under four years old.	Horses four years and upwards.	Number of bushels of Indian corn produced.	Bushels of wheat.	Bushels of rye.	Bushels of barley.	Bushels of oats.	Bushels of buck-wheat.
Anson,	15	392	407	478	264	–	–	–	11944	35705	82	48	250	100	252	5228	2006	202	4791	15273	256
Athens,	5	–	489	839	308	4261	–	–	–	4000	100	150	236	82	207	2500	1000	50	6000	9000	275
Bingham,	16	163	244	155	141	1350	–	–	702	5652	60	104	143	34	136	1715	1218	197	3814	8600	212
Brighton,	7	143	183	203	138	1515	–	–	–	3732	57	110	113	30	76	875	1270	111	1113	2550	259
Cambridge,	4	153	158	120	90	1962	–	–	–	4720	61	–	108	22	67	1373	1972	16	989	5205	18
Concord,	4	26	143	46	88	811	–	–	1520	5609	46	–	115	29	61	469	883	709	842	669	255
Cornville,	10	362	356	460	218	5662	–	–	200	11389	148	75	170	93	263	3063	1101	67	1660	9469	60
Detroit,	7	106	157	81	60	820	4	12	11	2242	55	–	61	26	79	1352	491	72	1357	1921	15
Embden,	10	250	320	339	142	3202	–	–	–	10586	88	157	1193	44	129	3243	2502	399	3528	8003	662
Fairfield,	10	270	603	182	312	6595	–	–	–	16061	98	30	304	87	363	4783	922	182	9447	9498	82
Harmony,	17	247	324	264	212	3241	–	–	–	8392	132	14	159	48	145	3488	2126	52	3145	7009	147
Hartland,	5	147	214	188	138	1574	10	12	110	4631	75	10	142	36	24	2997	1149	218	2780	3352	77
Madison,	14	278	453	364	267	1823	–	–	5271	23250	142	102	302	84	229	4811	2104	501	10107	15430	395
Mercer,	10	164	316	236	188	2984	15	–	330	11251	82	50	146	25	158	4020	820	85	3600	6782	24
Moscow,	5	182	213	173	123	2636	–	–	850	6533	132	62	137	33	88	997	2052	557	3207	6449	2391
New Portland,	18	326	348	172	291	–	–	–	9830	30216	123	153	164	65	174	4788	2783	159	3287	9309	77
Norridgewock,	9	225	470	284	222	756	95	–	6974	23063	123	42	239	101	287	4290	1336	437	6885	12103	171
Palmyra,	15	378	503	310	262	1951	342	298	1277	10223	237	147	328	112	220	5185	2406	263	6033	7990	375
Pittsfield,	8	223	305	177	177	3196	–	–	–	5320	27	–	136	42	127	3763	1049	289	4021	6072	25
St. Albans,	14	345	414	356	210	3396	–	–	–	10022	136	148	268	73	212	5663	3646	659	3931	6739	250
Skowhegan,	13	430	698	378	302	775	370	1296	3750	18347	528	–	386	112	452	4926	1291	555	9583	8082	–
Smithfield,	8	109	223	220	184	1503	–	–	143	4563	229	–	188	23	69	3397	874	149	3312	3779	29
Moose River plantation,	3	31	29	13	14	161	–	–	–	445	14	–	22	4	12	–	223	–	331	2858	30
No. 2, R. 2,	2	30	42	30	30	572	8	–	–	1896	19	–	12	11	18	300	295	29	150	500	43
	229	4980	7792	6178	4301	47745	844	1618	42912	261268	3064	1402	8132	1196	3788	73227	36519	5838	106903	167542	6128

SOMERSET COUNTY, (Continued.)

Towns.	Bushels of potatoes.	Bushels of turnips.	Bushels of carrots.	Bushels of beets.	Bushels of apples.	Tons of upland hay.	Tons of interval hay.	Tons of bog and salt hay.	Pounds of butter.	Pounds of cheese.	Pounds of honey.	Pounds of maple sugar.	Gallons of maple syrup and molasses.	Value of poultry and eggs produced.	Bushels of beans.	Bushels of peas.	No. of sheep killed by wild animals.	No. of sheep killed by dogs.	No. of sheep injured by dogs.	Amount of damage to sheep by dogs.
Anson,	39339	837	62	100	13812	4070	183	70	30323	7660	1666	-	355	2564	962	412	30	37	-	130
Athens,	22550	500	300	-	-	3000	50	-	-	-	-	-	-	-	1000	2500	-	-	-	-
Bingham,	13140	1550	25	60	6100	1419	325	92	12640	2150	855	2525	75	1458	440	510	16	4	-	75
Brighton,	10352	784	112	54	4777	1263	15	-	13755	1400	150	150	26	1079	263	160	3	-	-	-
Cambridge,	11430	96	48	15	2231	876	8	-	12195	2863	150	38	22	558	295	-	-	-	-	-
Concord,	8816	556	109	28	1239	1297	181	-	7405	1900	346	430	211	439	240	177	17	29	-	88
Cornville,	27661	818	168	78	10181	3360	100	19	26707	10196	2660	440	249	2456	716	465	-	-	-	-
Detroit,	12944	412	220	270	611	873	179	104	15106	2305	1436	-	4	848	350	365	1	5	-	20
Embden,	22051	1276	212	123	14786	2017	174	275	19232	4171	630	308	474	1950	650	505	-	-	-	-
Fairfield,	40225	1711	-	230	16246	3056	-	-	42530	31660	1255	500	407	2905	796	198	-	18	-	45
Harmony,	21942	995	174	91	12000	2203	-	-	20395	3082	1459	254	218	1163	733	532	5	4	-	24
Hartland,	19312	1028	153	220	6054	1700	100	-	30053	3051	1700	238	44	1919	533	257	10	3	-	-
Madison,	57360	1349	236	89	7051	9567	1574	73	33895	8710	1950	-	189	3189	1194	341	-	1	-	-
Mercer,	32872	501	48	100	10610	2234	101	256	22030	4750	720	24	222	1578	736	200	-	2	2	7
Moscow,	10997	2354	121	91	5282	1554	176	-	17400	3795	225	4336	137	2162	330	212	7	12	-	48
New Portland,	22832	1224	230	133	13509	3299	399	159	28185	5209	943	210	154	1915	776	304	10	20	-	47
Norridgewock,	47663	1309	264	278	12689	3332	-	372	23360	10175	1542	101	274	2012	912	427	-	-	-	-
Palmyra,	42084	890	635	304	7844	3111	289	-	35054	10837	3130	128	91	4066	1078	722	-	8	2	36
Pittsfield,	20585	786	449	309	2579	1853	134	-	12785	3340	2125	-	-	923	587	242	-	-	-	5
St. Albans,	41035	787	349	139	9156	3100	70	-	35414	10180	991	84	156	2355	922	293	1	-	-	-
Skowhegan,	48908	1416	792	170	29450	4325	-	-	29405	17545	712	-	648	2415	979	230	-	-	-	-
Smithfield,	19467	260	58	17	6192	1072	-	147	12460	3078	1305	-	33	454	652	575	4	41	41	169
Moose River plantation,	2200	250	14	13	-	144	53	-	825	50	-	250	14	51	-	23	-	-	-	-
No. 2, R. 2,	1400	129	8	6	270	300	15	-	1950	340	-	100	-	150	75	69	16	20	11	60
	603165	21798	4777	2914	193812	59885	4026	1567	485604	149337	25950	9306	4021	38899	15169	9717	128	204	56	787

WALDO COUNTY.

Towns.	Number of bulls.	Heifers under four years old.	Cows four years old and upwards.	Steers under four years old.	Oxen four years old and upwards.	Number of common mixed or native sheep.	South Downs and grade South Downs.	Improved long-wooled sheep.	Merinos and grade merinos.	Pounds of wool produced.	Number of wool skins.	Pounds of dressed flax produced.	Swine, without distinction of age, sex or breed.	Colts under four years old.	Horses four years old and upwards.	Number of bushels of Indian corn produced.	Bushels of wheat.	Bushels of rye.	Bushels of barley.	Bushels of oats.	Bushels of buck-wheat.
Belmont,	3	92	195	164	54	640	-	-	-	1200	225	-	36	26	75	800	140	40	1500	1500	-
Frankfort,	6	142	250	107	101	901	61	-	-	2333	139	-	83	33	127	377	341	73	2166	3581	25
Freedom,	8	123	186	132	122	1277	-	-	240	3172	28	-	101	36	92	1199	1175	46	2286	2118	37
Islesborough,	8	262	200	70	74	711	33	-	19	2074	153	-	45	11	45	502	326	86	966	507	-
Knox,	12	208	298	234	172	2498	-	5	30	6082	165	12	198	66	157	1988	1844	257	4168	4620	38
Lincolnville,	20	395	529	297	206	1962	-	-	-	5357	337	-	194	43	206	2281	959	103	3333	2718	-
Montville,	7	434	532	400	256	3047	-	-	-	8479	329	-	210	43	235	3169	2215	286	6069	6422	-
Morrill,	17	144	167	125	98	963	4	9	19	3103	232	19	127	25	104	1394	75	140	2240	2922	26
Northport,	8	81	165	95	36	968	-	-	-	1875	273	-	72	20	86	576	231	21	994	1406	231
Palermo,	7	233	278	164	168	1838	3	100	-	4658	96	-	198	48	150	3160	1292	103	2900	3414	72
Prospect,	14	125	185	104	78	-	-	-	-	2274	167	-	124	22	58	610	66	-	1849	1700	49
Searsport,	18	103	433	62	146	650	200	163	240	4064	1008	12	196	54	154	517	520	71	2312	3893	97
Swanville,	11	190	283	139	102	960	-	-	-	3360	800	-	126	61	80	600	1000	-	2100	2500	-
Troy,	24	270	369	284	197	3253	-	-	-	9570	116	-	185	38	188	3808	3043	380	3588	10792	22
Waldo,	5	170	207	152	114	1097	-	52	-	2455	50	-	120	30	98	765	140	10	1808	3515	6
Winterport,	17	242	292	201	108	1525	200	800	-	8294	336	-	208	66	246	808	390	100	6922	12897	-
	185	2804	4469	2730	2012	21292	501	1029	548	69410	4554	43	2123	622	2901	22556	13757	1716	45101	64305	603

WALDO COUNTY, (Continued.)

Towns.	Bushels of potatoes.	Bushels of turnips.	Bushels of carrots.	Bushels of beets.	Bushels of apples.	Tons of upland hay.	Tons of interval hay.	Tons of bog and salt hay.	Pounds of butter.	Pounds of cheese.	Pounds of honey.	Pounds of maple sugar.	Gallons of maple syrup and molasses.	Value of poultry and eggs produced.	Bushels of beans.	Bushels of peas.	No. of sheep killed by wild animals.	No. of sheep killed by dogs.	No. of sheep injured by dogs.	Amount of damage to sheep by dogs.
Belmont,	10000	200	150	200	1200	1000	400	–	19500	500	500	50	–	1200	100	100	–	50	50	150
Frankfort,	14933	675	288	269	3686	1469	38	3	16904	500	165	–	–	779	221	208	–	13	5	74
Freedom,	12415	513	174	62	4759	1092	109	4	4765	689	458	10	80	512	280	86	1	5	15	17
Islesborough,	7479	1989	230	116	1161	840	32	7	10780	5590	10	–	–	757	223	128	–	5	1	–
Knox,	37752	900	212	114	8607	2722	144	77	25413	4125	1817	1604	18	2116	667	322	10	35	10	103
Lincolnville,	21122	1213	450	278	9704	3515	548	192	44833	4250	392	–	–	3128	848	220	–	–	–	–
Montville,	34373	2221	478	313	19833	3554	416	–	52758	4520	800	1000	300	3493	700	400	–	–	–	–
Morrill,	23508	643	310	181	4269	1084	284	60	19000	840	288	625	33	1450	330	139	–	15	8	56
Northport,	9300	269	170	119	3835	1258	239	–	7360	480	218	–	–	1140	198	106	25	–	–	–
Palermo,	24795	636	588	232	9991	2007	316	228	29610	1569	25	440	123	2113	566	245	–	10	–	40
Prospect,	10464	618	587	297	3514	1056	–	52	18755	–	265	20	–	1538	320	221	–	–	–	–
Searsport,	21390	3435	1631	1351	5130	2139	–	45	36830	75	699	60	–	1496	309	329	10	30	25	150
Swanville,	9000	2000	1200	200	2500	2100	200	–	22640	500	1100	–	–	1000	300	295	–	7	2	23
Troy,	39691	492	316	203	9856	2373	174	3	35880	5580	1462	74	133	3128	858	413	–	–	–	–
Waldo,	16510	733	410	115	2538	1294	330	–	13400	3500	870	110	–	1000	255	210	–	12	–	30
Winterport,	67265	955	800	400	10801	2970	–	–	45335	–	1450	–	–	2036	387	138	–	–	–	–
	359697	17492	7994	4450	101384	30573	3230	671	372763	32718	10519	3973	687	26886	6503	3560	45	182	116	643

WASHINGTON COUNTY.

Towns.	Number of bulls.	Heifers under four years old.	Cows four years old and upwards.	Steers under four years old.	Oxen four years old and upwards.	Number of common mixed or native sheep.	South Downs and grade South Downs.	Improved long-wooled sheep.	Merinos and grade merinos.	Pounds of wool produced.	Number of wool skins.	Pounds of dressed flax produced.	Swine, without distinction of age, sex or breed.	Colts under four years old.	Horses four years old and upwards.	Number of bushels of Indian corn produced.	Bushels of wheat.	Bushels of rye.	Bushels of barley.	Bushels of oats.	Bushels of buck-wheat.
Alexander,	15	174	164	68	41	423	-	-	-	1368	95	-	61	89	42	51	104	39	940	1730	773
Centerville,	7	29	62	8	26	186	-	-	-	329	14	-	23	6	12	12	17	-	157	105	2
Cherryfield,	10	81	170	30	55	480	-	-	-	700	429	-	60	16	95	10	50	-	967	80	15
Cooper,	8	106	173	120	48	377	-	-	-	1154	77	-	58	18	61	98	172	14	308	1108	604
Danforth,	5	76	86	36	50	313	-	-	-	1000	18	-	31	20	36	74	597	41	44	3249	1539
Jonesborough,	16	80	147	43	54	326	-	-	-	978	102	-	47	10	33	-	80	-	726	-	5
Lubec,	5	209	444	145	78	1323	-	-	-	2476	221	-	40	12	61	-	72	-	913	632	7
Marion,	2	21	33	18	20	83	-	-	-	166	20	-	15	5	9	-	8	-	95	88	27
Pembroke,	9	163	336	114	58	829	13	55	20	2968	247	10	188	38	159	50	25	-	3185	2612	348
Robbinston,	24	167	235	87	50	583	9	6	-	1880	184	-	69	28	73	67	230	59	1872	1486	1101
Wesley,	6	99	119	50	42	168	-	-	-	516	39	-	100	2	38	120	95	28	200	761	332
Whiting,	4	50	100	20	50	281	-	-	-	843	10	-	40	10	25	-	-	-	700	50	75
Codyville plantation,	2	32	30	36	34	177	-	-	-	531	32	-	18	10	15	28	30	15	100	482	120
Big Lake plantation,	1	10	7	10	18	70	5	-	-	125	30	-	9	-	-	50	100	-	-	300	180
	114	1297	2106	116	583	5619	27	11	20	15034	1518	10	719	264	659	552	1580	196	10307	12683	5118

WASHINGTON COUNTY, (Continued.)

Towns.	Bushels of potatoes.	Bushels of turnips.	Bushels of carrots.	Bushels of beets.	Bushels of apples.	Tons of upland hay.	Tons of interval hay.	Tons of bog and salt hay.	Pounds of butter.	Pounds of cheese.	Pounds of honey.	Pounds of maple sugar.	Gallons of maple syrup and molasses.	Value of poultry and eggs produced.	Bushels of beans.	Bushels of peas.	No. of sheep killed by wild animals.	No. of sheep killed by dogs.	No. of sheep injured by dogs.	Amount of damage to sheep by dogs.
Alexander,	11210	699	112	54	1623	707	–	232	14643	–	285	–	–	593	137	80	2	2	–	–
Centerville,	940	47	72	14	23	78	27	–	1135	–	–	–	–	46	29	27	11	–	–	–
Cherryfield,	6788	654	702	275	460	549	2000	18	14756	100	–	–	–	225	120	180	10	7	10	27
Cooper,	8652	575	297	68	272	448	93	–	13330	75	72	105	9	395	130	76	4	–	–	–
Danforth,	4262	385	34	25	60	447	10	4	8400	530	–	56	20	477	56	62	4	–	–	10
Jonesborough,	5931	642	68	63	219	479	110	112	14700	–	–	–	–	361	24	49	17	–	–	–
Lubec,	9321	2211	702	225	101	921	–	41	16650	–	–	17	5	972	31	52	–	33	–	74
Marion,	2250	198	105	12	138	130	15	–	3400	–	–	–	–	99	54	25	25	12	14	25
Pembroke,	14561	1963	484	140	309	917	15	10	24414	80	120	–	–	245	108	148	38	20	2	–
Robbinston,	16216	3484	171	86	547	911	34	25	20371	105	142	–	57	1290	196	159	2	1	3	5
Wesley,	4200	278	56	31	75	262	366	–	10835	100	50	–	–	187	50	24	9	–	–	–
Whiting,	2500	250	100	100	–	500	150	–	15000	–	200	–	–	500	20	40	30	20	–	50
Codyville plantation,	1050	1075	95	–	68	98	180	–	1700	–	–	–	–	60	13	10	–	5	–	13
Big Lake plantation,	1000	80	70	–	80	70	–	100	500	–	20	–	–	30	20	–	–	–	–	–
	97381	12541	2868	1093	3975	6517	3000	542	165634	1790	889	178	91	4374	988	932	152	100	29	189

YORK COUNTY.

Towns.	Number of bulls.	Heifers under four years old.	Cows four years old and upwards.	Steers under four years old.	Oxen four years old and upwards.	Number of common mixed or native sheep.	South Downs and grade South Downs.	Improved long-wooled sheep.	Merinos and grade merinos.	Pounds of wool produced.	Number of wool skins.	Pounds of dressed flax produced.	Swine, without distinction of age, sex or breed.	Colts under four years old.	Horses four years old and upwards.	Number of bushels of Indian corn produced.	Bushels of wheat.	Bushels of rye.	Bushels of barley.	Bushels of oats.	Bushels of buck-wheat.
Acton, . . .	11	221	475	437	260	783	-	-	-	2369	100	-	176	36	164	7293	1340	295	1398	1482	-
Biddeford, . . .	14	177	521	79	144	393	3	-	7	1455	76	-	303	34	401	6060	363	41	3142	2046	12
Kittery, . . .	11	132	338	170	238	330	-	-	-	1000	150	-	240	50	120	4121	20	30	400	40	-
Limington, . . .	21	281	590	315	300	750	154	-	-	2200	-	-	274	47	251	5000	1500	500	250	4000	-
Newfield, . . .	19	216	327	275	224	435	-	-	-	1415	81	-	202	38	126	7893	1153	118	87	1894	-
Parsonsfield, . .	16	246	684	1101	462	819	18	6	57	1503	147	-	304	69	246	9714	3396	285	1125	3468	33
Saco, . . .	22	206	818	119	276	801	8	-	-	2690	68	-	523	39	423	8507	304	36	3948	1271	-
Shapleigh, . . .	12	250	500	205	325	485	-	-	-	1460	65	-	142	49	131	5245	275	105	250	1565	-
Wells, . . .	11	240	581	206	460	1336	29	4	-	4680	208	-	280	53	159	10030	253	174	4925	1006	10
	137	1969	834	2907	2689	6132	212	10	64	18772	895	-	2444	415	2021	54863	8604	1584	15525	16772	55

YORK COUNTY, (Continued.)

Towns.	Bushels of potatoes.	Bushels of turnips.	Bushels of carrots.	Bushels of beets.	Bushels of apples.	Tons of upland hay.	Tons of intervale hay.	Tons of bog and salt hay.	Pounds of butter.	Pounds of cheese.	Pounds of honey.	Pounds of maple sugar.	Gallons of maple syrup and molasses.	Value of poultry and eggs produced.	Bushels of beans.	Bushels of peas.	No. of sheep killed by wild animals.	No. of sheep killed by dogs.	No. of sheep injured by dogs.	Amount of damage to sheep by dogs.
Acton,	16488	578	646	168	17198	1526	766	–	27104	9731	–	1751	198	2052	578	58	–	–	–	–
Biddeford,	24162	1395	2266	653	6101	1940	200	185	25222	610	164	112	12	2562	1037	98	–	3	5	10
Kittery,	15800	660	1200	320	2904	1560	300	150	26000	430	200	20	3	2410	205	50	–	–	–	–
Limington,	15000	1000	500	300	10000	2000	1000	–	20000	5000	–	1000	300	2000	1000	300	–	–	–	–
Newfield,	17418	534	870	210	11211	1210	929	–	28028	3483	20	800	456	1782	–	–	–	–	–	–
Parsonsfield,	27024	1404	879	417	12677	1455	1542	–	17378	5137	150	2880	180	1618	1149	207	9	–	–	14
Saco,	28877	1818	1369	1538	12100	3077	489	666	62170	175	50	827	28	3993	1070	160	3	29	6	118
Shapleigh,	13850	445	300	55	2410	1670	485	–	40842	1175	84	1345	300	1242	450	75	–	15	12	55
Wells,	29674	249	9557	154	11067	2026	647	389	22645	100	–	–	–	1922	849	18	–	9	10	12
	188293	8083	17587	3815	85668	16464	6358	1390	269389	25811	668	8739	1477	19581	6328	966	12	56	33	209

AGGREGATE RETURN OF AGRICULTURAL STATISTICS IN THE SEVERAL COUNTIES, 1863.

Counties.	Number of bulls.	Heifers under four years old.	Cows four years old and upwards.	Steers under four years old.	Oxen four years old and upwards.	Number of common mixed or native sheep.	South Downs and grade South Downs.	Improved long-wooled sheep.	Merinos and grade merinos.	Pounds of wool produced.	Number of wool skins.	Pounds of dressed flax produced.	Swine, without distinction of age, sex or breed.	Colts under four years old.	Horses four years old and upwards.	Number of bushels of Indian corn produced.	Bushels of wheat.	Bushels of rye.
Androscoggin,	76	1154	2723	1390	2078	5482	552	952	1321	26849	1094	105	1232	281	1144	35632	5410	2222
Aroostook,	57	807	1085	548	503	4247	15	39	–	13635	702	72	959	256	611	1202	15146	2892
Cumberland,	161	2305	5446	1506	2414	8362	89	281	35	26237	881	146	2774	445	2502	84616	11806	2810
Franklin,	92	2193	2785	2682	1920	19560	559	1718	14315	106552	2762	1705	1174	427	1367	29004	18176	1242
Hancock,	108	1284	2612	854	1180	10941	307	54	23	35694	4084	4	769	492	638	2640	2475	295
Kennebec,	243	4043	9557	4740	4125	39949	2011	1663	2941	111706	6225	327	4602	1151	4627	91931	19696	4701
Knox,	137	2184	4110	1099	1539	10392	40	16	31	33521	2118	–	2024	282	1805	14136	3528	3428
Lincoln,	110	2552	4120	2173	2337	9182	184	352	80	29398	2630	257	1765	342	1475	25771	1845	2771
Oxford,	413	6625	7503	7089	5487	37692	890	1691	1059	115555	2780	973	3912	1792	3272	120659	34385	14245
Penobscot,	294	5290	8164	3660	2951	35218	579	1047	573	113539	10295	264	4203	1027	4657	41003	26563	3238
Piscataquis,	107	1232	1768	1022	1044	10892	–	29	149	32728	481	89	941	327	919	9175	15206	353
Sagadahoc,	62	1059	1934	965	924	5265	61	415	2	18204	1336	112	822	133	669	11875	1403	788
Somerset,	229	4980	7792	6178	4301	47745	844	1618	42912	261268	3064	1402	8132	1396	3788	73227	36519	5838
Waldo,	185	2804	4469	2730	2012	21292	501	1029	548	69410	4554	43	2123	622	2901	22556	13757	1716
Washington,	114	1297	2106	116	583	5619	27	11	20	15034	1518	10	719	264	659	552	1580	196
York,	137	1969	834	2907	2689	6132	212	10	64	18772	895	–	2444	415	2021	54863	8604	1584
	2552	41778	67008	39659	36085	277970	6881	10925	64073	1028102	44429	5509	38595	9652	33055	618842	215899	49319

AGGREGATE RETURN OF AGRICULTURAL STATISTICS, ETC., (Continued.)

Counties.	Bushels of barley.	Bushels of oats.	Bushels of buck-wheat.	Bushels of potatoes.	Bushels of turnips.	Bushels of carrots.	Bushels of beets.	Bushels of apples.	Tons of upland hay.	Tons of interval hay.	Tons of bog and salt hay.	Pounds of butter.	Pounds of cheese.	Pounds of honey.	Pounds of maple sugar.	Gallons of maple syrup and molasses.
Androscoggin, . .	13894	48575	325	158666	9107	3013	2411	56321	13071	3781	516	244717	69609	2825	506	280
Aroostock, . .	5159	56046	22679	55761	17931	520	316	1082	5753	610	10	81475	8497	970	2225	614
Cumberland, . .	20951	44366	478	252208	15103	9197	2705	147482	24504	2726	1715	379897	51838	3615	2012	410
Franklin, . .	18486	54190	1533	125647	8548	1697	1009	82803	20768	2543	1834	145595	37919	6012	2790	3720
Hancock, . .	14950	13193	390	87854	14767	4796	1737	7914	7538	950	96	134970	3854	2751	318	50
Kennebec, . .	97838	118617	1855	553290	26348	9098	8123	249440	52119	5343	741	575513	133186	14872	3058	1824
Knox, . .	21326	18880	188	154858	21528	3571	5317	38306	15805	1582	1527	332275	18177	1581	524	29
Lincoln, . .	37060	20912	214	158952	11900	2452	13030	49590	20397	3932	2794	295594	7866	2381	1076	166
Oxford, . .	18071	117209	8283	432456	21815	8457	2624	200483	33794	11882	3632	479386	108651	7070	33560	5263
Penobscot, . .	78619	171061	7477	929499	29396	12125	5041	91789	41848	3517	1043	252943	84040	36328	5431	1015
Piscataquis, . .	17682	55681	3333	44164	5769	1047	385	25895	9823	184	65	106706	26220	6584	1426	295
Sagadahoc, . .	18903	10466	136	73577	10561	1794	2967	25443	12382	1679	998	137217	2428	1715	21	26
Somerset, . .	106903	167542	6128	603165	21798	4777	2914	193812	59885	4026	1567	485604	149337	25950	9306	4021
Waldo, . .	45101	64305	603	359697	17492	7994	4450	101384	30573	3230	671	372763	32718	10519	3973	687
Washington, . .	10307	12683	5118	97381	12541	2868	1093	3975	6517	3000	542	165634	1790	889	178	91
York, . .	15525	16772	55	188293	8083	17587	3815	85668	16464	6358	1390	269389	25841	668	8739	1477
	540775	990448	58795	4255478	252087	90993	58027	1361387	370238	61343	19141	4458778	821970	124830	74843	19968

AGGREGATE RETURN OF AGRICULTURAL STATISTICS, ETC., (Continued.)

Counties.	Value of poultry and eggs produced.	Bushels of beans.	Bushels of peas.	No. of sheep killed by wild animals.	No. of sheep killed by dogs.	No. of sheep injured by dogs.	Amount of damage to sheep by dogs.	Remarks.
Androscoggin, .	$12243 00	3914	1196	2	34	55	$198 00	Returns received from 6 towns—8 wanting.
Aroostook, .	4909 00	725	1499	6	5	-	13 00	" " " 11 towns and plantations—52 wanting.
Cumberland, .	26834 00	8777	1977	6	49	4	251 00	" " " 12 towns—13 wanting.
Franklin, .	12771 00	4636	1678	12	37	40	144 00	" " " 10 towns—16 wanting.
Hancock, .	13810 00	2510	2201	249	211	54	962 00	" " " 15 towns—25 wanting.
Kennebec, .	53423 00	13801	4387	2	142	62	588 00	" " " 20 towns— 9 wanting.
Knox, .	24050 00	3059	1621	14	33	21	153 00	" " " 12 towns— 5 wanting.
Lincoln, .	24908 00	4224	2399	2	158	89	610 00	" " " 11 towns— 5 wanting.
Oxford, .	28710 00	9070	3440	222	121	30	416 00	" " " 27 towns and plantations—15 wanting.
Penobscot, .	34816 00	10090	10808	77	107	87	601 00	" " " 29 towns—34 wanting.
Piscataquis, .	7324 00	2299	2841	67	7	8	27 00	" " " 12 towns—14 wanting.
Sagadahoc, .	4673 00	2234	1052	-	25	49	103 00	" " " 8 towns— 3 wanting.
Somerset, .	38899 00	15169	9717	128	204	56	787 00	" " " 24 towns and plantations—13 wanting.
Waldo, .	26886 00	6503	3560	45	182	116	643 00	" " " 16 towns—10 wanting.
Washington, .	4374 00	988	932	152	100	29	189 00	" " " 14 towns and plantations—36 wanting.
York, . .	19581 00	6328	966	12	56	33	209 00	" " " 9 towns—17 wanting.
	338211 00	94327	50274	996	1371	733	5904 00	Returns received, in all, from 237 towns and plantations, and from 268 they are wanting.

ON THE MANUFACTURE OF CHEESE

AS AN ARTICLE OF EXPORT, BY MEANS OF ASSOCIATED DAIRIES.

A large portion of my report last year was occupied with a consideration of the dairy, and more particularly with the manufacture of cheese. The extensive introduction into this State of a branch of industry so profitable as this is at the present time, and promises to be in the future, appears to me a matter of so great importance, that it is deemed a duty to submit some farther remarks on the subject at the present time. In order to correct any erroneous impressions previously received, to obtain additional facts, and to ascertain with certainty the developments of another year, I again went over the principal cheese dairying districts of the United States during the past summer. Although comparatively little was learned to add to the report of last year, in regard to the best process of manufacture, a good deal was ascertained regarding the importance of dairying as a branch of rural industry, and the progress of associated action in carrying it on.

In the first place, there can be no doubt that it is, at the present time, profitable beyond any other branch of stock husbandry.* The belief is entertained by many of our most intelligent farmers, that the amount of vegetable food which will produce one gallon of milk when fed to a good milk cow, as now used by farmers generally in the rearing of young stock to sell, does not actually secure to them a return of more than four cents; many set it as as low as three cents and a few as high as five cents. Now a gallon of good milk will make a pound of cheese, and good cheese has been bringing, for a twelve-month past, from twelve to sixteen

* The opinion was confidently expressed by many farmers on the Western Reserve, (Ohio) where cheese-dairying and sheep-husbandry have long been the leading pursuits, that at the present prices of both, cheese-making was decidedly the more profitable of the two.

cents; * and some has been sold even higher still. The necessary cost of manufacture is less than two cents per pound, and, with the best of facilities, but little exceeds one cent; thus leaving the dairyman from ten to fourteen cents for the same food which has brought to our stock farmers only four or five cents; and even allowing that the price of cheese should fall to former rates, the gain would still be very considerable.

An inquiry naturally arises here, if the farmers of Maine become dairymen who will buy all the cheese? To which it may be replied that they will not all do so; for the profitable production of milk demands good pastures abounding in springs of pure water, and yielding a pretty steady supply of grass, together with facilities for making good the very possible deficiences caused by droughts, by means of a supply of other succulent food. It is not all the land upon which sheep and cattle can be reared, nor where corn and wheat are plentifully produced which can be judiciously devoted to the dairy. There is a good deal of land in Maine which will do better for sheep and for other uses than for the production of milk, and there are immense districts throughout the United States, particularly in the South and West, where dairying will never prevail to any extent, for the simple reason that farmers there can buy butter and cheese to better advantage than to make it. At the same time we have hundreds of thousands of acres of land in Maine where good milk can be produced as cheaply, considering the price of land and labor, as it can in Vermont, New York, or anywhere else.

Next, what and where is the market for cheese? First, some can be disposed of at home, in place of the two millions of pounds or thereabouts which has been annually brought into the State for years past, and thus a leak of two hundred thousand dollars, more or less, be stopped. This is an item worth considering, but it is not all. Cheese is exported to the West Indies, to South America, to California, and to other places. Formerly a large quantity went to the Southern States. Let us hope that before long we may send thither a great deal more than ever before. When in the Western Reserve last August, I was informed by a large dealer that the call for cheese from Cincinnati, Louisville, and

* At this present writing, (first week in November,) I notice quotations of factory cheese, in New York, 14½ to 16 cents.

other places, to be sent South was urgent and so large as to affect prices considerably even there. But the principal market abroad is in England. In Great Britain there are thirty millions of inhabitants, more or less, and they eat a great deal more cheese than the same number of Americans, whom we can supply with manifest advantage to them and to us. The manufacture of cheese has long been pursued there extensively. The county of Chester has been famous for centuries, insomuch that it is usually called Cheshire, which is merely a slight contraction for Cheese-shire. The northern counties of England and the neighboring counties in Scotland have also been largely engaged in it. But the price of land is so dear that no farmer in England can produce a gallon of milk at a less cost than six pence sterling, — equal to twelve cents of our currency when exchange is at par, and considerably more now that gold is at a premium. Of course no dairyman there can sell cheese for less than the cost of the milk and the pay for making it up. It is also a fact that meat sells in Great Britain at much higher prices than it does here, and the British farmers have their hands full, and more too, to make meat enough for home consumption, and large quantities of cured meats, beef, pork, bacon, &c., are annually imported. What reason, then, can be imagined why we may not furnish them all the cheese required, with mutual advantage? Our facilities are such that we can surely make it cheaper than they. There is no difficulty in sending it thither in prime condition, and at a cost of only about one cent per pound; including freight, insurance, commissions, and all charges attending transportation.

It required a long time to create the demand which now exists in England for American cheese, and to Herkimer county, New York, belongs the credit of accomplishing it. It was mainly effected by bringing a high degree of skill to bear upon the manufacture generally, thus producing not only a good article, but one uniformly good, or as near uniform as is possible, when made in many families. Cheese had been sent abroad in small amounts for many years, but when once, by good quality and uniformity, it had secured a firm foothold, the amount exported increased with astonishing rapidity. By gradually increasing steps it had come to be nine millions of pounds in 1859. In 1860 it amounted to twenty-three millions; in 1861 to forty millions, and the amount has increased steadily since then.

That this export demand governs the price of cheese in this country is demonstrated by the fact that in June, 1862, prime cheese was bringing, in Herkimer county, eight cents per pound, but as soon as specie payments were suspended and gold bore a premium, the price of cheese advanced with even step; when gold fell, the price of cheese receded, when it rose again, cheese advanced, and all the while just in proportion to the current rate of exchange; and this shows, satisfactorily enough, that to cancel indebtedness or to pay for goods purchased in England, the cheese was as good as the gold, and answered the same purpose exactly. With a market of so great capacity open to us, it is as certain as anything in this uncertain world, that the manufacture of cheese in this country will increase immensely, and I see no good reason why the farmers of Maine may not come in for a share of the profits as well as to go without it.

On the other hand it must be admitted that we are not in possession of the requisite skill, and it cannot be diffused through a large number of families at short notice. Should the manufacture be extensively introduced into the families of Maine farmers, several years of study and of practice must elapse before the product, as a whole, would compete successfully in the foreign market; and at the same time it would greatly increase household labors, and add heavily to burdens already heavy enough.

These have the look of serious obstacles, and if they be insurmountable ones, cheese-making must necessarily make very slow progress. But it is believed that the plan alluded to in my report of last year (pages 81–82) is capable of effectually obviating them both. The advantages of association in the conduct of various branches of art and manufactures, are sufficiently understood and appreciated; but the farmer has hitherto considered himself excluded from a participation in them by reason of the nature of his occupation. To a considerable extent this is undoubtedly true, but it admits of some exceptions, and here is a notable one, not merely in theory but abundantly proved so by facts. In the manufacture of cheese, considerable time must necessarily elapse after the milk comes in before the curd goes to press. The process cannot be hastened without serious injury; during much of this time, where only the milk of ten to fifty cows is employed, there is little or nothing to do but to note the progress making, and with the proper facilities it is scarcely more work to make up the milk of fifty cows than the milk of ten; and so it is comparatively little more to make up that of five hundred than of fifty. About ten years ago, Jesse Williams, living near Rome, Oneida county, New York, conceived the idea of turning this to practical advantage by making up the milk of his neighbors into cheese, together with his own. The plan worked well, and before long he increased his facilities so as to make up the milk of four hundred cows or more. Farmers are usually cautious, and slow in changing long established customs and practices, but the advantages of this new notion were so evident and indisputable that gradually similar establishments were set up, until when I was there last year it was said there were ten of these "cheese factories" within a circle of about ten miles.

At the time of my visit the present year, the number was found to be largely increased, and so recently had many of them been established that it was not easy to ascertain with certainty how many were actually in operation. From various sources, however, a list was obtained of the following:

Rome, (Jesse Williams,)	600 cows.
do (Spencer Allen,)	500 "
do (Greenfield,)	400 "
do (Cady & Chandler,)	300 "
do (Crosby & Huntington,)	400 "
Delta, (F. Smith,)	600 "
Lee, (W. D. Sexton,)	500 "
do (Geo. Wood,)	300 "
Lee Centre, (P. Charton,)	400 "
Florence, (Saveny & Coventry,)	500 "
West Branch, (Williams,)	300 "
Westernville, (Hill,)	300 "
Verona, (Hill,)	300 "
do (Buck,)	500 "
do (Weeks,)	400 "
do (Durham,)	300 "
Verona Centre, (Lampher,)	200 "
New Hartford, (Sherman,)	300 "
Trenton, (H. J. Fowler,)	800 "
do (H. Miller,)	600 "
do (W. W. Wheeler,)	300 "

Deerfield, (Lewis & Horn, superintendents,)	700	cows.
Marcy, (Wilcox,)	600	"
do (Tanner, Wood & Ashly,)	1000	"
Kirkland, (Blackstone,)	500	"
Hampton, (Williams, Adams & Derry,)	300	"
Lowell, (H. S. Rose,)	500	"
Remsen, (W. Mitchell,)	400	"
do (D. Thomas,)	400	"
Holland Patent, (T. Pierce,)	600	"
Steuben, (W. Brooks,)	400	"
Floyd, (J. Davis,)	350	"
Vernon, (Clark,)	350	"
Boonville, (Jackson,)	600	"
Stittville, (J. W. Rathbone,)	700	"
South Trenton, (Whitaker & Curry,)	600	"
Whitestown, (Williams & Smith,)	650	"

Besides the above, all of which are in Oneida county, five are in operation in the adjoining county (Herkimer)—all established the present year. Mr. Frazee, who last year carried on the one mentioned in the above list as Crosby & Huntington's, last spring started one in Cortland county intended for fifteen hundred cows, and establishments upon the same plan are known to have been started in other States during the present year.

Thus it will be seen that a radical change in the system of cheese manufacture has been extensively introduced, and is making rapid progress. The advantages of the new system and an account of its details are very ably and fairly stated by X. A. Willard, Esq., of Little Falls, New York, in a paper on "The Associated Dairies and Cheese Manufactories of New York," written for the Transactions of the New York State Agricultural Society, proof sheets of which he has sent me. Mr. Willard, who is well known as one of the most intelligent and successful dairymen of Herkimer county, was so kind as to accompany me in visiting several of these establishments, and I am happy to acknowledge my indebtedness to him for valuable assistance in studying their details and operation, and for numerous other courteous attentions, as well as for the extensive quotations from his paper, which we give below. Mr. Willard says:

"The advantages claimed for the factory system are superior

quality, uniformity, higher prices, saving by buying at wholesale such materials as salt, bandage, annatto, boxes, etc., and finally, relieving the farmer and his family from the drudgery of the manufacture and care of cheese.

It is not pretended that a better quality of cheese can be made at the factory than in families, but that it is quite as fine as the best, and therefore above the average of that manufactured in small parcels. Some of the causes which conspire to depreciate the quality of cheese when made in single dairies are not present in the factory system.

The agent, or superintendent, makes it his business to see that all parts of the work are properly performed. He employs skillful workmen; his interest and reputation are at stake, prompting him at all times to do his best. He knows that neglect or mistakes will not be tolerated, and the desire to satisfy persons interested, in order to secure their patronage, stimulates him to make every exertion to build up and sustain a reputation for "fine goods." He has every convenience at hand for manufacturing to advantage, and makes the business a specialty and a sole employment. He is not liable to be disturbed with other matters which might serve to call his attention away from time to time, to the prejudice of the immediate work at hand.

The same rule must hold good with him as among those engaged in other professions and arts, for he who gives his whole attention and energies in a certain direction is likely to become more skilled, and arrive nearer to perfection in his calling, than he who is striving to do many and diverse things well at the same time; more especially in cheese manufacture under this system, as a high degree of skill is expected, and jealous and interested eyes are daily watching and noting every mistake and shortcoming. Uniformity and fine quality are therefore more likely to obtain under this system, and whatever progress can be made toward improvement, will naturally develop itself more rapidly here than among persons scattered over a broad extent of country, and who are so occupied with a variety of work as to have little time to spend in the improvement of any one particular branch.

The factories, so far as we are acquainted, have acquired a high reputation for fine quality and uniformity. At some of these establishments we have seen a large number of cheeses, making in the aggregate more than one hundred thousand pounds, so uniform in appearance as they lie on the tables, that the most practiced eye could scarcely detect any difference in their manufacture. Such a quantity of cheese, uniform in size and quality, will usually command a higher price in market over that of single dairies, from the fact that in the latter an allowance is always made by the purchasers for unequal or imperfect cheese. Factory cheese generally sells at a price above that of single dairies equal to the whole cost of manufacturing. In November, 1862, long dairies, made in families, of good quality, were selling at from ten cents to twelve and a half cents per pound, while factory cheese, of Oneida, sold at fourteen cents per pound, and the large size, those weighing from 700 to 1,000 pounds each, brought in some instances as high as seventeen cents per pound.

We have alluded to some of the causes that operate to increase the price of well made factory cheese over that of private dairies. Another may be added, in the less time, trouble and expense of purchashing. The whole quantity made from six hundred or a thousand cows can be bargained for and bought at no more time and expense than a "twenty cow" dairy. This item amounts to a considerable sum in the aggregate, as experts are employed by the principal commission houses in cities, by shippers and dealers, to select and purchase cheese, under salaries ranging from $500 to $1,000 per year. Others, again, get a certain percentage on what they buy. These sums, of course, come out of the producer, and hence by so much must depreciate the price of cheese. Another saving is also made in buying the materials used, such as bandage, salt, annatto, boxes, etc., at wholesale instead of retail.

We come now to consider the most important advantage to farmers in this union arrangement. It is the relief from the drudgery of cheese making, and the constant care and attention necessary in properly curing and fitting the cheese for market. It would be difficult to estimate this in dollars and cents, since health enters into the account more largely than is generally suspected.

It is believed, and we speak advisedly, that the old method of cheese making has done more to injure the health of women in cheese dairying districts than any other cause. Much of the work about the dairy ought to be performed by men, but too often the manufacturing and most of the care of cheese are left wholly to females, overtasking their strength by hard and exhaustive labor, thereby laying the foundation of weakness and disease.

As the same process is to be gone through with in manufacturing cheese, whether the quantity of milk be large or small, and as nearly the same time also is occupied, it will be seen that what requires the labor of a great many persons to do when cheese making is divided up in families, can be accomplished with but a few persons on the factory system, some five or six being sufficient to do the work about an establishment manufacturing the milk of a thousand or more cows.

The principal objections urged against cheese factories are: difficulty of detecting adulterated milk, the carrying of milk to the factory and liability of sour milk, difference in quality of milk arising from the manner in which cows are fed and managed, and the loss of the whey. As the milk is weighed or measured at the factory, and each credited with the amount daily furnished, it is evident that when there is a considerable quantity a dishonest person could add water, and thus increase the amount to be credited. Such cases have occurred, and the individuals cheating have been summarily expelled from the association.

Some object to the labor and trouble of carrying milk to the factory, and the necessity of keeping to regular hours for its delivery under all circumstances of weather, inconvenience, and disability from other causes, since no delay at the factory can be made for the milk of a single dairy without hazarding the acidity of a large quantity, at least that contained in one vat, besides deranging, in some degree, the regular factory work.

Without extra care and cleanliness as to the pails and milk cans, there is liability of sour milk from time to time, which of course would not be received at the factory. The cans for carrying the milk, it may be observed, are somewhat difficult to cleanse and to keep sweet, and the confinement of the milk, and its agitation while being carried, in hot weather, renders it susceptible to change, especially if there be the least taint of acidity about the cans.

Then there is the loss of whey, which is regarded by some to be an important item in the way of pork making, or as a feed for cows, for the whey is usually the property of the person who runs the factory; but were it given to the farmer, as it sometimes is, there is the trouble and expense of carting it home."

Regarding the organization, selection of a site, &c., Mr. Willard says:

"Cheese factory associations are organized in neighborhoods of ten or a dozen or more farmers.

When it is proposed to start a factory, several persons who are neighbors to each other get together and talk over the matter among themselves. If enough are found willing to turn in their dairies together, so as to make a fair start, (say three hundred cows,) a committee is appointed to look further into the matter, to visit factories, and get all the information on the subject that can be had. A favorable report from the committee being had, they then organize, choose directors, and adopt some general rules or plan for the guidance of the association. The next step will be the selection of some experienced cheese maker as superintendent, and the place for the erection of the factory building.

Generally some person proposes to put up the buildings on his own account, and to manufacture and take care of the cheese at a fixed price per pound, demanding a contract on the part of the farmers to furnish the milk of the requisite number of cows for a certain number of years.

The milk of about four hundred cows, it is believed, is the smallest quantity that can be employed by the manufacturer, (when cheese making is his sole business,) in order to obtain a fair living compensation for services, while the milk of a thousand cows can be manufactured at but little extra expense comparatively.

In choosing a place for the erection of the factory buildings, two requisites are sought—good water and convenience as to access and distance for the dairies furnishing the milk. The site, above all, should command an abundance of pure cool spring water, and the supply should be unfailing as well as abundant. This is regarded by those who have had longest experience at the business as imperative. Its temperature should not be above 50° Fahr. unless the supply is very plentiful, in which case a temperature of 52° or 53° might serve.*

Even in family cheese making a considerable quantity of water is needed in various ways about the dairy, for cooling milk, cooking the curd and keeping the utensils and buildings clean and

* At one factory which I visited in Ohio, the spring had failed; consequently, not having cold water to reduce the temperature of the milk it was made up both night and morning, thus involving double labor, and even more, for it required longer cooking, and (not being acquainted with the use of sour whey with milk too sweet) an inferior product also.—[S. L. G.]

sweet; but for the factory the quantity of water should be abundant and unfailing. It is usual to have a considerable stream of water passing under the manufacturing room, so as to carry off the drippings of whey and refuse slop, so that there be no accumulation of filth or taint of acidity hanging about the premises. Where whey and slop are allowed to collect from day to day about the milk room, the stench at times becomes intolerable, and must do great damage to the milk, which absorbs taints of every character with great readiness. Hence means must be taken to have all the refuse matter swept beyond the reach of the premises.

Some factories are being built where dependence for water is placed upon wells of large capacity, but these are as yet experiments to be tried. At all events, it will be seen that much more labor will be required, with greater liability to taints, than where spring water, passing in a considerable stream under the building, can be had.

Where it is admissible, the manufacturing room should be located with a bank on one side, several feet in height, and forming a road on which the teams drive and deliver the milk through the receiving windows, thus giving the proper descent to the weighing or measuring apparatus, and from thence to the vats. Where the bank is wanting, a platform must be raised for the purpose indicated.

If it is proposed to employ some one person to collect and deliver all the milk, then the factory should be located at a point where the work can be effected at the least trouble and expense.

The buildings to be erected will consist of a manufactory or place for making the curd, a press room, dry house or curing rooms and an ice house.

The dry house should be a separate building, so as not to be affected by dampness, and in case of fire, that the cheese may be more readily removed. At one of the establishments near Rome, Oneida county, recently erected, and where the milk of six hundred cows is used, the size of the buildings is as follows: Manufactory, 26 by 26 feet; story and a half; press room, 39 by 13 feet; dry house, 26 by 100 feet; two stories high. Cost of the buildings, with fixtures, about $2,500.

These buildings consisted in nothing but frames shingled and covered with rough siding, and even not lathed and plastered.

The curing house, where it is not proposed to lath and plaster should be sided with matched floor plank, and provided with ventilators at the sides and top.*

One of the best arranged plans for building and fixtures that I have seen is that of the new factory of Frazee's, at Truxton, Cortland county, which goes into operation the present year. Mr. Frazee formerly conducted a factory near Rome, and had there made a considerable improvement over the original or early built factories. The new buildings are a great improvement over the Rome establishment.

This factory has a capacity for manufacturing the milk of fifteen hundred cows, and was expected to start with that of twelve hundred.

Mr. Smith, who has charge of the manufacturing department of the Truxton factory, in a note, says: "The manufacturing room is 32 by 40 feet, and contains seven vats, 15 feet long by 3½ feet wide, of six hundred gallons capacity each. There will be two places by which the milk can be emptied, so as to keep the wagons waiting the least possible time. The milk will be *weighed* instead of being measured. Adjoining the work room is the press room, 50 by 16 feet; there are ten presses on each side. The sink containing the curd stands on rails, so as to be run into the press room opposite the presses. There is a space of four feet behind the sink, so the hands can work the curd and not interfere with those who are dipping it out.

"The engine, of eight horse power, stands in a separate building. There is a (horizontal) main steam pipe, six feet from the floor, to which are attached six steam pipes connecting with the vats; the hands can in this manner go around either end of the vats.

"The buildings are on a level, so the cheese can be run from the press room on trucks into the curing house, between the counters; no carrying of the cheese, as at the original Frazee factory.

"The back side of work room is built of masonry, and the water, fifty feet fall, brought into a large reservoir directly under the platform upon which stand the receiving cans. Under the work room is laid flagging, over which flows a stream of water to keep it free from any matter that might collect there if the soil under the building was soft.

* For plan of these, see report of 1862, page 110.

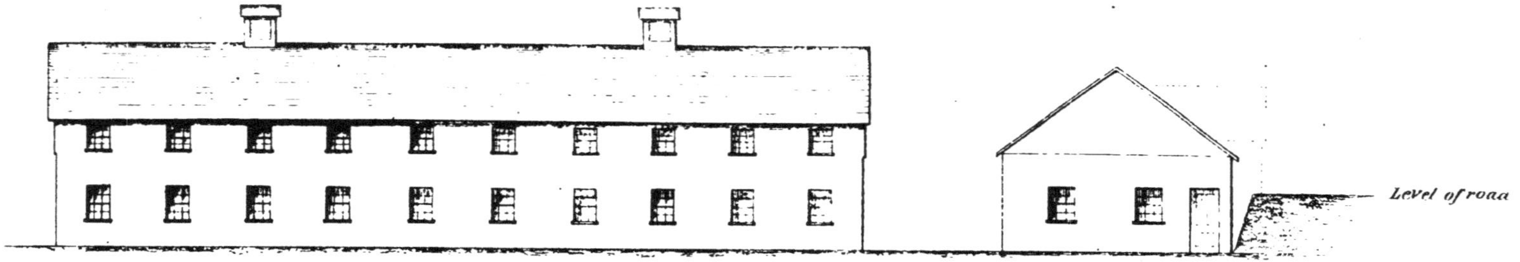

EXTERIOR OF CURING HOUSE

INTERIOR OF CURING HOUSE

Scale, 24 Ft. to the Inch.

Scale. 6 Feet to the Inch.
Cheese lying on the ranges.
Cheese partly turned.

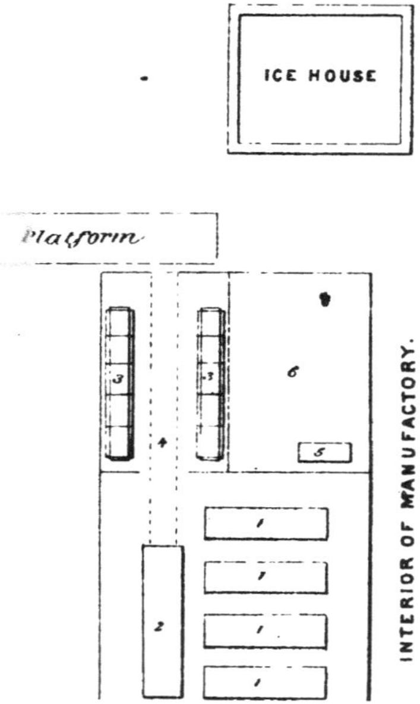

INTERIOR OF MANUFACTORY.

1 Vats.
2 Sink.
3 Presses.
4 Track.
5 Boiler.
6 Woodshed.

"The whey vats will be a long distance from the buildings, for we believe the milk will absorb any impurities of the atmosphere. Hog pens will be dispensed with entirely, for past experience proves to us that if cheese is properly made there is not enough nourishment left in the whey to make it profitable for pork raising."

The accompanying cut shows the ground plan and buildings of the factory near Herkimer, Herkimer county, under the supervision of Mr. H. Farington, who for many years has been widely known throughout the dairy region as an extensive cheese dealer. The cut shows the bank alluded to, where the teams deliver the milk. The floor of the manufacturing room should incline a little towards the centre, so that, in cleansing, the slops may be discharged into the creek.

The Herkimer factory has facilities for manufacturing annually 300,000 pounds of cheese. The manufacturing room is 28 by 48 feet, and the curing house 28 by 100 feet, and two stories high. There are four tin cheese vats, placed inside an equal number of wooden vats, the milk in which is heated by steam; each vat holds four hundred gallons.

The ice house has capacity for holding one hundred tons of ice. The cheese at this factory is pressed in a twenty-three inch hoop, and will weigh one hundred and fifty pounds each. This factory is built on the improved plan, and all the internal arrangement quite convenient.

In most cheese factories steam is used for warming the milk and cooking the curd. In some there is merely a steam boiler set in brick work and provided with pipes, while in others there is an engine also, usually of from four to eight horse power. The milk as received is conducted into vats of from four hundred to six hundred gallons capacity, each. These vats are made double, the inner one being of tin and the outer one of wood, with a space between of about two inches. This space is for the reception of water, and is provided with pipes conducting from the boiler, and so arranged that when steam is let on it may be distributed through the water as evenly as possible.

It is generally supposed to be cheaper thus to use steam, than to employ an apparatus similar to that described in the report for 1862, as the most desirable for family use; and very probably it may be cheaper at the outset, but if Ralph's Oneida Vat and Heater are employed, (which, in some important respects, appears to me to be the preferable one,) the daily expense of fuel would be much less, all risk of explosions or other accident from steam wholly avoided, as well as the loud and very disagreeable noise caused by the steam as it is driven into the water of the outer vats.

The factory of Mr. Spencer Allen, near Rome, is supplied with Ralph's Patent Vats. There were three of them which I saw in operation when there the past summer. Their capacities were severally six hundred gallons, five hundred and forty gallons, and four hundred gallons, which served to make up the milk of four hundred and ninety-six cows. Only one of these had the hot water tank attachment, which was found to suffice for all three. My observation of the working of these vats led me to coincide fully with the opinion expressed by Mr. Allen of their superiority over the vats heated by steam.

For a detailed description of these Vats, see report for 1862, pages 99–100.

The presses at these establishments are of the simplest character, and consist in nothing but a stout iron screw, with the proper wood work attached for holding it in position, and a platform on which the hoop holding the curd rests when put in press.

Several of these presses are frequently connected together by framing the uprights of each press to stout beams, or square pieces of timber running nearly the whole length of the press room. The screws when turned up pass through the upper beam and are turned down on the cheese with an iron lever, from time to time, until the desired pressure is acquired, and the work of pressing accomplished.

When the cheese is turned in press it is bandaged with a kind of thin dressed cotton cloth, similar to bleached goods, but manufactured specially for the purpose. This style of bandage, when carefully pressed on, gives to the cheese a remarkably smooth and neat appearance. Thick, heavy bandage, it may be proper to observe, should not be used on ordinary sized cheese, as it is more liable to produce mould. The bandage having been properly put in place and the hoop slipped on, circular caps of cotton cloth, the size of the cheese, are added at top and bottom, so as to give a perfectly smooth surface to the new cheese when it comes from the press, and care is taken that it be pressed true, and that the rind be closed in all its parts, for a badly pressed cheese can never afterwards be made to assume a handsome appearance.

It is claimed that the screw can be managed more readily in pressing the cheese to a perfect shape, that it is less expensive, and occupies less room than other devices for the purpose, and hence is best adapted to factory use.

When some person is at hand to watch and attend to the pressing, the inconvenience in using this character of press is perhaps not so much felt, but in family cheese making, where help is limited, they would be considered a nuisance, for the farmer requires a press that will follow up its work, and do the pressing faithfully without watching.

At some of the factories the screw is beginning to be regarded as objectionable on this account, since they can receive no attention during the night. Hence strong presses, like 'Oyston's Herkimer County,' * are being in some places substituted. The main advantages of the screw are its trifling cost, its strength, and the small space it occupies; in other respects it is believed to be inferior to other devices for compressing the curd.

The hoop in which the cheese is pressed is of pine staves, bound with heavy band iron, and very carefully made, the inside being turned or worked down true and smooth.

A good proportioned cheese is in height about half the size of its diameter, and the hoop therefore should be high enough to conveniently hold the curd and accomplish this end. When a hoop of

---

* Described and figured in last year's report, page 107.

twenty-three inches in diameter is used for cheese weighing one hundred and fifty pounds, it should be at least fourteen or fifteen inches high, and be provided with iron handles on the sides for convenience in moving and slipping it from the cheese.

Messrs. Ralph & Co., of Utica, New York, have devised and are manufacturing metal hoops, which are very convenient, and admit of a closer fitting follower than wood, which shrinks and swells. Some of them are of tin, heavily but neatly banded, while the latest pattern are of galvanized iron.

A suggestion in regard to properly constructed milk caps for delivering milk, may perhaps be deserving of a passing notice.

Cans holding from forty to sixty gallons will be of convenient size, and should be well and nicely made from the best of tin. The cover should be with a rim, and tapering so that it may be pressed into the can, and down to the milk, making a close fit. In the centre of the cover is a three-quarter inch hole for the air to escape while pressing the cover to its place; it is then to be closed with a cork. A faucet is provided near the bottom for conducting out the milk into the receiving cans at the factory, where it is weighed by the superintendent. Formerly the milk was measured, but latterly weighing seems to be in favor.

The platform where the receiving cans are placed stands higher than the vats, and as fast as each dairyman delivers milk it is weighed and conducted into the vats by merely opening the faucets. This platform commands a view of all parts of the manufacturing room, is provided with desks, and it is here the books are kept for noting the quantity of milk delivered, and the calculations made for the quantity of rennet, annatto and salt to be used for each vat of milk.

Tables and racks of convenient height for handling the cheese are arranged in the curing house, on which the cheese is placed as it comes from the press, and where it remains during the process of curing. Each cheese when it is placed on the table receives a record of its weight and date neatly marked on its bandage.

The wood best adapted for the table bed is hemlock. It should be smooth and level, and made of well seasoned stuff. Pine is sometimes used, but being more or less resinous is apt to impart something of its flavor to the cheese; the cheese also adheres to it more closely than hemlock. Wood like basswood is objectionable, doing damage to the cheese, and should not be used, for it adheres so closely to the cheese as not to be readily loosened, marring the rind and oftentimes taking out considerable portions of the cheese. It may be proper to say that the table bed, where the cheese rests, should never be painted.

The recent invention of the cheese rack is a great improvement over the table. The cheese rack consists of scantling, four inches by five inches, with the corners beveled or cut so as to be 5-sided; these are framed the proper distance apart at the ends, and set on legs of the desired height, forming a skeleton table. Round covers, of inch hemlock or pine, bound with stout elm rims, three or four inches wide, set upon the racks and hold the cheese. When the cheese is to be turned, a spare cover is placed on top, and the cheese and covers turned over; the cover now on top is removed, rubbed with a cloth, and is ready to be applied to the next cheese. The rims of the covers protect the edges of the cheese in the process of turning; and a part of the cheese, swinging down in the open space between the timbers and the rims, resting on the beveled sides, renders the operation not only easy, but it insures safety to the cheese. A large cheese can be turned with as much ease on a properly constructed rack as the loosening of a smaller cheese on the table preparatory to being turned. Large cheese are difficult to handle on a table, and are liable to have their edges broken, or in other ways marred in turning.

The sink, where the curd is drained and salted, should be convenient to the vats, movable, being provided with rollers and placed on a track leading to the press room, so that the curd may be dipped directly into the hoops where it is to be pressed.

This will not only be a saving in time and labor, but will avoid occasional losses in dropping particles of curd or spilling it by accident, which is liable to occur when it is carried by hand from one room to another. It will be scarcely necessary to observe that the whey vats should be a considerable distance from the manufacturing room; for as milk is very susceptible to taints, and is affected by the state of the atmosphere, every means must be taken to promote the most favorable condition in the milk for the production of fine cheese.

In starting a manufactory some little anxiety may be had in regard to the most suitable size of the cheese to be made. This, doubtless, may be controlled somewhat, from time to time, by the market for which the cheese is manufactured. The home trade, during hot weather, prefers medium sized cheese; but for shipping to Europe, there seems to be a growing demand for cheese of larger size.

During the season of 1862, cheese weighing from one hundred and twenty to one hundred and fifty pounds were in favor for the foreign trade; and this size is, perhaps, all things considered, most convenient for factory make. They are easily handled, and in case of accident either at the factory or in carrying to market, the loss is not so great as on the larger cheese.

The factory charge for manufacturing cheese is one cent per pound; rennet, salt, bandage, annatto and boxes, as well as the carting of cheese to market, being charged to the association and paid by each dairyman in proportion to the quantity of milk furnished during the season. All other expenses, including the care of the cheese while curing, &c., is paid by the manufacturer.

To run a factory using the milk of six hundred cows will give constant employment to at least four persons, half or more of whom may be females.

At one of the factories near Rome, New York, in 1862, the price paid for the services of a man and woman, who were the foremen of the establishment, was one dollar each per day and board; others received from two dollars to four dollars per week; and I was informed that the actual cost of manufacturing the milk of six hundred cows for the season, was seven hundred dollars. It is presumed this sum did not cover interest on capital invested for buildings and fixtures, but was the amount paid out for labor, board, fuel, &c.

From these data it will be easily estimated what amount of money can be realized from the business of manufacturing. Allowing that the 600 cows produced on an average 400 pounds of cheese each, there will be in the aggregate 240,000 pounds. The cost of a well constructed factory will not be far from $3,000.

We have, then, 240,000 pounds at one cent,		$2,400
Cost of running factory,	$700	
Interest on buildings, &c.,	180	
Annual wear and tear, or depreciation of property,	200	
		1,080
Profits,		$1,320

Now, for 300 cows, nearly the same expenses would be incurred, and the factory account would stand thus:

120,000 pounds cheese at one cent, . . .		$1,200 00
Expense of running factory, . . .	$700 00	
Interest on capital invested, . . .	180 00	
Annual depreciation of buildings, fixtures, &c.,	200 00	
		1,080 00
Profits, ...		$120 00

We do not pretend to give the exact figures in the above estimates, but it will be seen that a factory manufacturing the milk of a less number than 300 cows will not be a very paying business, unless the manufacturer can have most of the work performed by members of his own family.

When a factory is located in a neighborhood where all or nearly all the dairymen are on one road, some one of the number may be employed to gather up the milk of the several dairies, and deliver it at the factory. Neighbors living near each other may take turns, each delivering one day out of the week. When men are hired to gather up and deliver the milk for a neighborhood during the season, the price usually paid for such delivery is one dollar per cow.*

In cheese manufacture an important point to be considered is the proper management of the evening's milk; and in order to do this to the best advantage, the state of the atmosphere must be observed at the time the milk is placed in the vats. The milk room should be cool, airy, and free from impurities. In hot and sultry weather much care and attention must be given to the evening's milk, to have it well exposed to the atmosphere and thoroughly cooled down before it is left at rest for the night. When there are large quantities of milk to be attended to in hot weather, it will be better to spread it thinly over a considerable surface, rather than deeply, as in filling the vats. The temperature of the evening's milk should be so reduced that it will stand in the morn-

* Although in most cases the milk delivered at any one factory is made within one or two miles, yet it is often carried three miles, and in a few cases I found it carried five miles; the dairyman saying this was less trouble than to make it into cheese at home, and as the factory cheese brought two and a quarter cents more per pound than that made at home, while the charge for making it was only one cent, he saved a double gain by doing so.—[S. L. G.]

ing at about 62° or 63°, and it should be reduced to at least 62° before leaving it for the night. At the factories, where the carrying of the milk and the mingling it together from several dairies has doubtless a tendency to hasten its acidity, there is more necessity for care and attention than in families; or rather there is more danger of too much acidity.

It may be proper to observe, that the requisite degree of acidity in milk at the time of setting it with rennet, for cheese, is imperfectly understood by the generality of cheese makers, and must be learned by well and carefully conducted experiments. It is not possible to make so good a quality of cheese from milk recently drawn from the cow, or from any milk that has been kept too sweet, as from milk that has acquired proximate acidity. Neither will it be possible to obtain the greatest quantity of curd from the milk so manufactured. Such milk will require the addition of a small quantity of sour whey.

At the factories, it is believed, there is more danger from too much acidity than otherwise, since there are many causes to hasten that condition of the milk which are not present in family dairies. In the factories it is usual to cool the evening's milk to about 60°, by letting in water between the vats, by the use of ice, and by lifting and stirring the milk. This, under all circumstances, is or should be attended to. The lifting and stirring of the milk and exposing it to the atmosphere not only serves to cool it down to the desired temperature, but in another way operates favorably on the condition of the milk for the production of fine cheese, since the stirring and lifting process allows the animal odor to pass off more readily. If a considerable quantity of milk directly from the cow be placed in the vat and cooled down without proper exposure to the atmosphere, it retains more or less of this taint, and more especially if the cream soon rises to the surface, forming a barrier of escape, and holding it in the milk.

Some idea may be had of the effect of this animal odor by placing milk recently drawn in a vessel where it is closely confined and excluded from the air. In a few hours it becomes fetid and putrid. In family dairies too little attention is given to this point in the treatment of milk."

The process of manufacture at these establishments is substantially the same as that set forth in the report for 1862, pages 90–110. Some trifling deviations are made in consequence of difference in the condition of the milk and the larger quantity operated upon. Thus, as for obvious causes, before alluded to, the milk, when received at the factory, is nearer the point of sensible acidity than when put into the family vat at home; and also because five or six hundred gallons of milk in one vat will not lose its heat so rapidly as a small quantity, it is set, i. e., the rennet is added, at a lower temperature, say 82° or 83° instead of 88° or 90°, as in family manufacture.

At the factories the making of cheese is proceeded with more leisurely* than is usual in families. It is their work for all day, and no inducement exists to hurry through the process. The heat used in cooking the curd is raised *very* gradually, and is never allowed to exceed 98°. The curd is also handled with great care throughout the cooking process, which saves any loss of butter in it, while its long steeping in the whey is supposed to contribute to that peculiar, nutty, sweet flavor which is considered indispensable in a strictly first-rate cheese. This lack of hurry and its attendant evils might properly enough be classed with the advantages of factories over private dairies, since in the latter there is ever a very natural and almost irrepressible desire not to expend more time on the process than can be afforded, or conveniently spared from other pressing calls.

Whether or not it is best for the farmers of Maine to engage largely in dairying is for them to decide. I have endeavored, in the last report and in this, to lay before them, fairly and fully, such facts and suggestions as seem worthy of being weighed in arriving at a decision. If this be in the affirmative, the next question is whether it shall be mostly butter or cheese which shall be made. At present, prices are altogether in favor of cheese. If cheese is to be made a leading aim, the question next arises, whether it shall be by private or by associated dairies; and here the advantages of the latter are so great in the case of those commencing the business and unacquainted with its manufacture, as to admit of no hesitation; since by employing a few persons who are skilled in the art, and at a trifling expense, they may at once reach all the benefits and advantages enjoyed by old dairying districts, and which

*If there appears to be danger of the milk souring before the cooking can be *properly* finished, the process is hastened somewhat, but only as a choice of evils, because a too rapidly cooked curd is less objectionable than a sour one.

otherwise could not be easily, cheaply, or speedily attained. My own conviction is, that in many neighborhoods a change might be made, with comparative ease, from the stock at present kept upon farms, to dairy cows, sufficient to furnish an ample supply of milk within moderate distances, and that the introduction of associated dairies, in good grazing districts, would be attended with much larger returns for the vegetable food consumed by the stock than is now obtained.

FRUIT CULTURE.

"*Forward in the name of God, graffe, set, plante and nourish up trees in every corner of your groundes; the labor is small, the cost is nothing, the commoditie is great; yourselves shall have plenty, the poore shall have somewhat in time of want, to relieve their necessitie, and God shall reward your good mindes and dilligence.*"

Thus wrote honest old Gerarde, more than two hundred and fifty years ago; and no better advice can be given to the farmers of Maine at the present time. There are few situations in the State,—probably not a single farm,—where fruit enough to add a healthful luxury to the farmer's store may not be readily grown, with a little painstaking; and there are very considerable districts so admirably adapted by nature to its production, that no other crop so well repays the labor and cost of culture. Apples, especially, may be grown with profit, to supply more largely the home market (it has never yet been properly supplied), *and for exportation also*, for our Northern grown fruits are among the best keeping and finest flavored in the world, and will command the highest price whereever apples can be carried; and with cargoes of ice they have been safely carried to the farthest points of the globe. The greater firmness of flesh which Maine grown apples possess, gives them a great superiority for shipment, over those grown in the Middle States. Apples sent from Portland to Cuba in slow sailing vessels, have arrived in much better condition than those sent from New York by steamers; and they can be sent after more southern grown fruit has gone out of market. It is true that our orchards have suffered serious injury within the past six or eight years, most unusual damage, so that some of them, in fact many of the older and more neglected ones, are unproductive and profitless; still facts abundantly sustain the assertion that, take twenty or forty years together, in suitable locations in Maine, no other branch of farm business has given, or promises to give in years to come, more ample returns than the judicious and skillful culture of fruit. If we may judge of the future by the past, there is little probability of as serious harm occurring again for one generation at least, as only one other instance of extensive damage is known to have occurred since the settlement of the State.

At the last session of the Board of Agriculture, I was instructed to make this a leading topic of the present report. Perhaps it may be thought by some that the publication of so many books on the same subject as have been issued during the past fifteen years, and which are accessible to such as seek information regarding it, should supersede the necessity of such a labor. If it were only general information which is wanted, this might be so, but such is not the case. We need the knowledge adapted to our own situation, and which they do not furnish. It is information regarding the *local* character of any fruit, which the orchardist especially requires, before he can decide whether to enter upon its extensive cultivation or not. By far the greater number of fruits are specially adapted to some locality, soil or climate, or to some combination of these. Nearly all develope their true worth only within a limited area, and sometimes within narrow limits; away from the soil or climate or other conditions which meet the peculiar wants of any one fruit, that fruit becomes inferior in quality, more or less unproductive, or otherwise profitless. Gerarde said truly in 1597: "Every clymat hath his own fruite, far different from that of other countries." Downing in 1845 wrote as follows:

"Those fruits which succeed perfectly in one section of the country, are sometimes ill adapted to another."

Jaques, in Worcester county, Mass., a little later, puts it strongly as follows: "If there are pears which ripen finely at Salem, but will not succeed in Boston; if the climates of Western New York and the shores of the Hudson differ so widely as to affect the quality of several varieties of different species of fruits, one might easily infer—what it has cost the writer something to learn—that whoever would succeed with fruit trees, in the hill country of the eastern States, may rely with tolerable safety upon the uncertain testimony of his own neighborhood, while the profoundest wisdom that has ever recorded the experience of other countries, would only mislead and bewilder."

Now it happens that the works on fruit culture by Downing, Thomas, Barry, Elliot, Manning, Cole and others, were all written for districts west and south of Maine, and most of them further from our southern limit than "Salem is from Boston," or "the shores of the Hudson from Western New York," and so may we not conclude, that to gather together, to collate, and to disseminate the results of experience *at home*, may be a needful and useful work?

Simply to prepare reliable lists of the best fruits adapted to the various sections of one State situated as ours is, so large as to embrace more than four degrees of latitude,* on the very border of orchard culture, too, and as many of longitude—great diversities of soil, surface and climate—might well occupy a life-time; and besides this, not only in the selection of varieties, but in *practice also, both in the nursery and orchard, different methods*, in some respects, *must be adopted*, if we would be successful, from those which prevail in other States.

It is therefore with much diffidence that the attempt is made; and were it not that twenty-five years experience in the culture and management of nursery and orchard trees, together with large opportunities for observation in this and in other States, may lessen the incompetency brought to the task, it would scarcely be undertaken at all.

Why Orchard Trees do not generally succeed so well as formerly.

It is a common and very just remark that orchards do not thrive now as they did when the country was newer. For this there must be adequate reasons, and it behooves us to ascertain, if we can, what they are, with a view of obviating them. In the first place, then, I would remark that the early plantations were set in a virgin soil, full of vegetable mould from the decay of forest trees and leaves for centuries, containing in abundance all the elements necessary to a thrifty growth. Thousands of trees have since then been set upon lands greatly exhausted by repeated croppings, with insuffi-

*The southern limit of Maine—say at Kittery and Elliot—is in latitude about 43° 5′; Saco and Alfred, about 43½°; Bridgton, New Gloucester, Wiscasset and Thomaston, about 44°; Dixfield, Waterville, Searsport and Ellsworth, about 44½°; Bingham, Exeter, Oldtown and Perry, above 45°; Patten, 46°; Houlton, a trifle further north; Presque Isle and Ashland, about 46° 40′; and the northern limit of the State about 47° 20′. Latitude alone, it is to be remarked, however, is not an exact guide to climate, as many other circumstances modify it not less—such as elevation, proximity to water, prevailing winds, &c., &c.

cient returns, and they have literally starved, not being able to obtain from it the food which they required, and consequently they languished and at length perished. This, it is evident, may be obviated by proper manuring, and for this purpose nothing is better than a compost of leaf mould with wood ashes and lime. If leaf mould cannot be had, muck from a hard wood growth, well decomposed by exposure to a winter's frost, and mixed with quicklime slaked with water in which common salt has been dissolved until it is saturated, is a good substitute. Muck from a wet swamp, composed largely of decayed mosses and leaves of evergreens, possesses considerably less value, but still is worth using, if no better can be had. It needs, however, a longer exposure, and larger additions of mineral matter. Stable manure may be mixed with the above compost to advantage, but, as a general rule, farm-yard manure is more needed for other crops than for fruit trees, and if used freely, it is liable to induce a late and unripened growth of wood. This is to be carefully avoided, for unless the shoots become fully mature, the tree cannot be relied upon, either for hardihood sufficient for our severe winters, nor for productiveness. These remarks concerning stable manure, it should be added, apply chiefly to nursery trees and to young orchards. When trees are in full bearing, and especially if the orchard is in grass, farm-yard manure may be applied to advantage.

Again, the earlier planted trees were generally *well sheltered* by the native forest growth. The value of shelter, in such a climate as ours, has never been sufficiently appreciated. In many localities this single circumstance alone may cause the difference between a stunted growth when exposed to all the blasts of winter and the blighting winds and gales of summer, and a vigorous healthful growth when properly secured against them. The success which has attended the planting of rows of evergreens, is really surprising to those who have not observed the results, or have not sufficiently reflected upon the subject; and warrants the belief that no more judicious investment can be made for young orchards in exposed situations, than the planting of evergreen screens, simultaneously with, or better still, previous to, the planting out of fruit trees. In some countries this subject is so well understood, that no success would be looked for with many varieties without such protection; and with it, there is no doubt that some kinds might be successfully grown with us, which now prove tender and unreliable without it.

Another reason may be found in the fact that new soils of naturally a rather tenacious character, but occupied to a considerable extent with roots, more or less decayed, do not suffer from the presence of stagnant water beneath the surface, to the same extent that the same lands will suffer from this cause after the roots of the former growth have completely decayed, and the soil has fallen into a more compact and less pervious condition than before. Here, too, the remedy is obviously indicated by the nature of the trouble, viz: THOROUGH DRAINAGE. Under-draining is absolutely necessary to success in fruit culture in all soils which retain water in a stagnant condition within two or three feet of the surface. Fruit trees cannot thrive with wet feet all the year round. To attempt their culture upon retentive soils without draining, is to throw away time and money. Every observing person knows that our best orchards are upon strong rocky or stony soils, *with a dry or porous subsoil*, which allows all surplus water to pass readily away. Rarely do orchards thrive even tolerably upon clayey or other naturally retentive soils, unless underlaid by a porous subsoil, or upon hillsides free from springs where the descent answers in part the purpose of drains.

Another reason of much force in this connection is, that the trees first planted *were seedlings*, which had grown four, five, or six years upon the farmer's own land, or in the immediate neighborhood, on similar soil, and there being plenty of them, only the best and most vigorous were planted out permanently. The simple fact that they had thus grown upon the spot is conclusive evidence that they were hardy, thrifty, and adapted to the soil and climate; and this not because, as many suppose and some have asserted, that a tree or plant by reason of having grown from a seed in any given locality, thereby acquires a character or constitution especially adapted to that locality, for this is false, the fact being that all the characteristics of a plant to be grown from a seed—as, for instance, whether its fruit shall be large or small, green or red, sweet or sour, as also whether the plant itself shall be vigorous or feeble, hardy or tender—*are all determined during the formation of the seed*, before it germinates at all, or anywhere, just as much as it is determined in the seed whether the plant to be grown from it shall produce an apple or a pear, a cucumber or a cabbage; but because, having grown vigorously for a series of years in a severe climate, the possession of hardihood and vigor are demonstrated by actual proof of the fact. Meantime all the tender ones which might have started in the same seed bed have perished, all the feeble ones have been rejected, and neither of them will give any future trouble. It is undoubtedly true that the efforts of nature *through the seed grown in a given locality* are towards such a variation as shall be best adapted to that locality, just as it is the case of Indian corn; only more plainly in the latter case because more rapidly; we can get several generations of corn from seed before an apple seed will produce its first fruit.*

Now what are the facts regarding the fruit trees planted in later years? While some have been grown as formerly, and grafted after being planted out, and some have been purchased of respectable nurserymen at home, thousands upon thousands have been planted which were grown hundreds of miles away, in a milder climate, often grafted with sorts, which, however well adapted to other localities, are tender or otherwise worthless in our soil and climate; and what is worse yet, frequently grafted upon bits of root, and so possessing little vitality compared with seedlings, but being stall fed by high manuring or a naturally rich soil, run up quickly into pretty trees to look at, and saleable only to those who know no better than to believe the plausible stories of irresponsible pedlars who hawk them over the country. Is it any wonder that a large proportion of such trees prove mere cumberers of the ground? The remedy in this case is too obvious to be dwelt upon.

To account for the fact that some varieties of fruit have apparently degenerated, certainly do not succeed so well now as formerly, Mr. Knight, a distinguished horticulturist of England, advanced a theory which was for a time quite popular, and is yet believed by some to be correct. His theory was that every seedling tree has a natural limit to its life, that within such limit there will be a period of vigor succeeded by inevitable decline, corresponding to the increasing feebleness of old age in an animal; also that every tree that has been propagated from it, whether by layering or by buds or grafts, is in fact merely an extension of the original seedling, and carries with it all its peculiarities and liabilities. The

---

* *Therefore* plant seeds of your best fruits, and if you cannot or do not wish to have all the seedling trees remain until fruiting in the natural way, take a scion from such as promise best, and graft it towards the end of a limb of an old tree. It will soon bear, and your fruit is thus tested at an early day.

period of vigor and of decline may be extended by influences favorable to the health of any particular tree, as it may also be shortened by unfavorable influences; but he holds that sooner or later, it must develope the decline and decay incident to old age, and finally become extinct.

Other eminent horticulturists, among whom are Lindley and Downing, dissent from the views of Mr. Knight, and believe that no such resemblance exists between the life of a tree and of an animal. They hold that a bud, equally with a seed, contains the germ of a new life; and that when a bud, or a cutting or layer having upon it several buds, strikes root into the earth, it becomes a new plant, as really as if grown from a seed. They believe that if a bud or a scion is engrafted upon a seedling stock and unites with it, striking its roots first into the stock instead of directly into the earth like a cutting, that such tree starts anew with all the vital energy of the parent plant. One of them* says: "With the exception of their integuments, a bud and a seed are the same thing. A seed is but a bud prepared for one set of circumstances, and a bud is a seed prepared for another set of circumstances—it is the same embryo in different garments. The seed has been called therefore a 'primary bud,' the difference being one of *condition* and not of *nature*. It is manifest then that the plant which springs from a bud is as really a new plant as that which springs from a seed; and it is equally true that a seed may convey the weakness and diseases of its parent with as much facility as a bud or a graft does. If the feebleness of a tree is general, its functions languid, its secretions thin, then a bud or graft will be feeble—and so would be its seed; or if a tree be tainted with disease, the buds would not escape, nor the trees springing from them. * * The conditions in which a bud grows render it liable to extrinsic ills not incidental to a plant springing from seed. A seed emitting its roots directly into the earth is liable only to its own ills; a bud or a graft emitting roots through the alburnum of the stock on which it is established, into the earth, is subject to the infirmities of the stock as well as its own. Thus, a healthy seed produces a healthy plant. A healthy bud may produce a feeble plant because inoculated upon a diseased branch or stem."

Accordingly, the advocates of the latter theory account for the

* Rev. H. W. Beecher, in Horticulturist, Oct., 1846.

deterioration of certain varieties by supposing them to be more or less *diseased*;—that they are troubled with something analogous to what physicians call "tubercular diathesis," or a scrofulous condition in man. Such a habit is hereditary in man, and we find the progeny of some degenerate kinds of fruit, whether they come of seed or by grafting, to inherit the diseased habit of the parent. Such a condition might arise originally from various unfavorable influences, or, more likely, from a combination of them;—as, for instance, from insufficient food, or from too stimulating food, inducing a succulent and unripened growth of wood; from too severe a climate, or from continued propagation upon unhealthy or unsuitable stocks. They belive, moreover, that as the scrofulous habit, unless very virulent, may be overcome by a judicious course of treatment, so this deterioration of certain varieties of fruit is not incurable, like old age, but that restoration to full health and vigor is possible.

The practical deductions from these differing theories are not nearly so much unlike, as the theories themselves. Both alike teach the importance of endeavoring to sustain and extend healthy existence—to plant in fitting soils and situations, to supply appropriate food in sufficient quantity, shelter to the trunk from the scorching rays of the sun,* and to the leaves from blighting winds—protection, so far as practicable, from the attacks of enemies like insects, vermin and parasites; to eschew all needless mutilations under color of pruning; in a word, to bestow such judicious care and treatment as shall result, so far as the result is under our control, in continued vigor and productiveness.

Is Fruit Culture Profitable?

The remark was made just now, that notwithstanding the very unusual and severe drawbacks to the growth of fruit, which were experienced a few years past, and which probably may not be repeated in the lifetime of the present generation, it has been and promises to be in the future, as profitable a branch of farming as any which can be pursued among us. The neglected appearance of the older orchards, generally, throughout the State, would suggest that such is not the common faith, but rather that the growth of fruit is best attended to by *letting it grow*, and doing nothing

* Best done by low branches.

either to help or hinder it; or that little or no thought is given to the subject.

I have my own opinion on the subject and have stated it above. It seems proper to add the testimony of others, from various parts of the State. To obtain this, a circular was sent out last summer to several hundreds of orchardists, in which, among other inquiries, was the following: "What would you estimate to be the comparative returns from an acre of apple trees, say one hundred, *well cared for*, during a period of twenty or thirty years, and from an acre of similar soil devoted to other crops, and receiving the same amount of care, labor, and manure, during the same period?"

I have reason to believe that most of the replies came from men whose experience and observation are such as to enable them to speak advisedly on the subject. It is evident that the question was variously understood, and this fact may account, in part, for the diversity of the replies.

Below are some of them, from different sections, the least favorable and the more favorable,—as nearly as possible a fair sample of the whole,—and first I will quote from a communication from a gentleman living in latitude between 45° and 46°, not far from forty miles from Bangor, and where I have seen evidences of as severe injury from the hard winter of 1856-7, as I have in any part of the State. "Before 1847 my chief study of apples was how best and most expeditiously to gather and dispose of a thousand bushels, more or less, each fall, and how fastest to work a big cider mill. Since then I have set, with my own hands, more than a hundred thousand scions, in various orchards in this county. I ought to have learned more in regard to apples in northern Maine than I really know. I have passed through several towns of this county during the past season, and I have not seen an orchard of any age that is cultivated and cared for as indicated in the tenth question of your circular of July last. Consequently that question cannot be answered where no data exist for its solution. The little orchard where I now reside, was first set ten years since. Many of the trees failed by the effects of the hard winters. All vacancies were filled as they occurred, and all the trees had a circle of four feet well hoed around them and an occasional application of some fertilizer. The last two seasons the whole ground has been plowed and planted, and the improved condition of the trees shows that the former treatment was very far below what is meant in the expression, 'well cared for.' * * * *

"The raising of apples may be made a source of large profit on the majority of farms in this county, both for home consumption and for market, and many farmers are now realizing extensively from this source. I am satisfied that no crop of the farm is more deserving of, or will better pay for good care."

Another in the same county says, "I cannot state definitely, but the orchard would be more than double the profit of any other crop."

I know of no better section of the State for orchards than Oxford county, but one reply received from that county gives by far the lowest estimate received from any source, viz: "With fair success, an orchard may be as profitable in thirty years from planting as the same amount of culture of other crops. I should be unwilling to set it higher, though no doubt there are many instances of much greater profit from an orchard." This reply probably refers to the income yielded by orchards on an average, and as they are, rather than to what would be were they "*well cared for.*"

Another in the same county says, "I have fifty trees in a pasture which have yielded me a hundred dollars a year on an average of the last ten years." I do not know how much room these trees occupy, or how much expense is bestowed upon them—but if not more than an acre, and the amount is the net profit, that acre is as good, while it holds out, as sixteen hundred dollars at interest; and it is probably taxed for a good deal less than that sum.

From a very intelligent orchardist in Lincoln county we have as follows: "One acre of orcharding on suitable soil, with proper care and attention, will produce three times the amount in value of any other crop we usually cultivate on our farms with the same amount of labor and manure."

From Waldo county we have the opinion "that an acre of apple trees, in good bearing condition, on the right kind of soil and location, will yield an average annual net profit of fifty dollars during a term of twenty years; and that the net profit per acre of corn or potatoes will not exceed twenty-five dollars per year for the same period."

From Penobscot county comes the reply: "Decidedly in favor of fruit."

An enthusiastic cultivator in Kennebec sends the following:

"An estimate of the comparative returns from an acre of apples and an acre of other crops must be mere guess work, for I have no accurate data upon which to speak with certainty. If high, rocky side hills, such as are usually devoted to pasture, and often furnish the best location for an enduring and productive orchard, are selected, the returns from an acre in good bearing condition would equal that from thirty acres in pasture. If good tillage land is taken and kept in tillage, with a trifling addition of manure for the trees, there would be but little diminution of the tilled crops during ten years. It could not be expected that during the first seven years on the tilled land and ten years on the pasture, the returns would more than pay the cost of trees, planting and subsequent care. For the following twenty or thirty years, I estimate the net returns from an acre of orchard equal to that from ten in tillage or thirty in pasture."

Another, not many miles distant from the last, says: "Devote an acre of land to apple trees, say one hundred, and for ten or fifteen years other crops could be cultivated on the same ground without much hindrance from the trees, and for a period of twenty or thirty years my opinion, is that 'other crops' taken from the land, if as 'well cared for' as an orchard should be, will more than pay for all extra manuring and trouble, so that, according to this reasoning, I believe it safe to reckon the additional value of an acre of apple trees to be the value of the fruit, deducting the cost of gathering and marketing. I should estimate the income for that period of time to be from three to five times more than from other ordinary farm crops."

One in Cumberland county, living near their best market (Portland), says: "To compare the product of an acre of apple trees with the same amount of land in other crops, and receiving the same labor, manure and care, will depend more upon the character of the soil than locality in the State. Land that is well adapted to corn will usually grow good apple orchards; but it is a waste of labor and money to try to grow trees on land not suitably drained, or on land naturally unfitted for trees. Five or six hundred dollars is not more than a fair value for a well grown young orchard covering an acre of land. No other crop generally grown could remunerate the owner of land purchased at one-half, or perhaps one-quarter of those prices. Market gardening, in advantageous positions, would perhaps prove profitable at so large an outlay for land, but this is because the labor of cartage of vegetables and manure to and from the city is made less by more than the interest on the price of the land."

Another in the same county, but living some forty miles from the city, says: "Your tenth question can only be answered *correctly* by reference to a diary of facts kept through a series of years. I answer, *generally*, I believe in this locality, the same amount of care, labor and manure applied to an orchard will produce double the profit they would if applied to any other crop usually cultivated. Orchards here are sadly neglected, my own among the number. Better care would pay well."

A cultivator in Sagadahoc county says: "I am unable to state the difference in dollars and cents, but I am sure the comparison would show a large percentage in favor of fruit." And another in the same county says: "I cannot answer the question with precision, but I am fully persuaded that my orchard for the last twenty years has yielded me much larger profits than the same ground would if devoted to any other crop with the same outlay for the same period."

The only reply from Androscoggin county is, "That the comparison would be four fold in favor of apples."

A farmer in York county, of considerable experience with fruit, and living twenty miles or so from a seaboard market, makes the following estimates: "In answering your tenth inquiry, much depends on the situation and nearness of market, and the natural fertility of the land for orcharding. The best orchard lands lie back from the sea, lakes or rivers; consequently away from markets, and the best grass land is not the best orchard land, and good orchard land is good for corn or other grain; and hay or grain is worth nearly as much twenty miles back from the seashore as it brings in the seaport markets; but apples at that distance bring much less than in good markets. Then there are other considerations. The apple crop of a good orchardist does not sap his farm if taken off and sold, like hay or grain. Now, to be fair about the matter, I will calculate for the orchard land in this town. One acre properly prepared for trees is worth one hundred dollars. One hundred trees, five years from planting, the land to be cropped to pay the expenses during that time, including manures and interest, one hundred dollars. The yearly expenses subsequently as follows:

Three cords of compost, at $5, . .	$15 00
Cultivating it in with horse, . . .	2 00
Care and attention, ...	25 00
Decay—to set new or keep good, . .	25 00
Taxes and interest, ...	18 00
	$85 00

This estimate is for *good* culture.*

Five bushels per tree is a fair average crop, taking twenty or thirty years together, and twenty-five cents per bushel a fair average price for them in the orchard—

Making the annual income, . . .	$125 00
Deduct annual expense, . . .	85 00
Leaves a net profit for each year of . .	$40 00

Good apples often bring much more than I have set these at, and what is gained by marketing I am willing to call profit in trade and lay it out for manure, or grain to make manure, to go on grass lands.

An acre of grass land in good culture I also call worth one hundred dollars—the annual expenses I reckon as follows: Three cords of manure once in three years is equal to—

One cord, (for one year), . . .	$5 00
Harvesting the hay, ...	5 00
Taxes, $1; interest, $6, . . .	7 00
Annual expense, ...	$17 00
Crop, two tons of hay at $10 per ton in the barn, ...	$20 00
After-math, ...	3 00
Making, ...	$23 00
Deduct expenses as above, . . .	17 00
Net profit, ...	$6 00

If these figures are correct, there would be thirty-four dollars yearly in favor of the acre of orchard over the acre of grass, or six hundred and eighty dollars in twenty years."

* How many orchards in this State receive fifty dollars' worth of care and attention *annually* including what replanting is needed, or half of it?

I have often seen statements of great productiveness and profit attending fruit culture—of fifty, sixty or more bushels of apples on a tree in one season—of as many dollars received from the crop of a pear tree—of a thousand dollars from an acre of pears in a year; and there is good reason to believe many of these statements to be strictly true; but I would never quote them as having any bearing on the profits of simply good orchard culture—such culture as I would recommend to the farmers of Maine, and such as they can bestow, if they will, to a very considerable extent; and for the simple reason that such cases are exceptional ones, being sometimes the result of a fortunate combination of accidents, and, at other times, of a high degree of skill and a lavish expenditure of labor and manure in preparation, connected with the most favorable natural conditions.

But such statements as are quoted above, based, as they are, on the observation and experience of plain, sensible farmers among us, not given to exaggeration, and who, by their own testimony, have rarely bestowed, or seen bestowed by others, as good culture and attention as yields the most profit, may be relied on as fully sustaining the proposition which I maintain, viz: That no other crop, nor any other branch of rural industry, promises more satisfactory returns in Maine than fruit culture, if judiciously pursued. It is believed to be safely inside the fact to say that good orchards, at, or nearly approaching maturity, on suitable soils, treated as well as other crops are treated, will pay an average annual net profit of fifty dollars per acre; say the interest of eight hundred dollars. Why then cultivate whole farms with hard labor for a net proceed of how much? I do not know how much your farm pays of *net profit* per acre. Is it five dollars? ten dollars? twenty dollars? Reckon and decide as you find sufficient cause. Neglected orchards don't pay much. Why should they? Would corn or potatoes pay better with such neglect?

Before entering on the more practical portion of our subject it may be well to devote some thought to the physiolgical principles involved in it, in order the better to understand the why and the wherefore of suitable practice.

General Principles of Horticulture as connected with Fruit Trees and their Culture.

A tree is a living, organized body made up of various parts or organs. The root, the stem, and the leaf, comprising those which it needs for growth, are called the organs of Vegetation. The flowers, together with the seed which comes from them, are called the organs of Reproduction. These take no part in the nourishment or growth of the tree, but on the contrary are exhausting in their effects upon it. Their special office in the operations of nature is to reproduce and perpetuate the species. Incidentally, in the case of the trees we are about to consider, to yield, for the use of man, a supply of fruit, wholesome, nourishing and delicious.

The *root* grows downward into the ground, usually branching again and again, until terminating in fibres or rootlets, the extremities of which are known as spongioles, from their delicate, spongy texture. The office of the root is to absorb nourishment for the support of the tree. This it does by means of the spongioles, the sponge-like extremities. What is known as the *collar*, is the point of junction between the root and the stem. The *stem* is that part which starts from the collar and grows upwards.* There is usually a correspondence between the growth of the roots and the stem—for instance, if the main roots grow directly downward, the stem will tend directly upward. If they are mainly on one side, the tree will grow more to that side. The original or main root of a seedling pear or apple usually penetrates the earth in a vertical direction. If this root be cut or otherwise disturbed, it will at once send out lateral branches, and the tendency upon the tree will be to form a more spreading top. If a tree is designed to furnish an upright trunk for timber, it would be bad policy in any way to disturb the tap root. If, on the contrary, the tree be designed for the production of fruit, it is well to encourage the formation of lateral or horizontal roots, as this tends to the production of a well developed and spreading top. Besides this correspondence in the style of growth, there is much of intimate relation and mutual dependence between the stem and the root. As the roots collect and furnish food to the stem and leaves, so these, in their time, transmit nourishment to the roots, by virtue of which they

---

* The branches are, as it were, repetitions of the stem, and for present purposes may be considered part of it.

extend and strengthen, each depending upon the other for sustenance, and even for existence. There is reason to believe that every root so formed has its corresponding part above, and that every extension of the stem has its corresponding roots, and that whatever affects one of these affects the other. Were this truth realized by orchardists, we should see less misuse of the knife and saw in mangling trees under color of pruning; and we should see a wholly different plan followed in the grafting of grown trees from that so often adopted, of at once removing the whole top. We shall have occasion to refer again to this in treating of pruning and grafting.

A stem possesses the property of forming along its surface, divers minute vital points, of the same nature as the one in which the stem itself originated. These become *leaf-buds*, each one capable of becoming a stem or a branch like the one upon which it was formed, and capable also of becoming, under favorable circumstances, an independent plant or tree. Each of these buds is usually nourished by a leaf which springs from the bark just below the bud, the latter growing in the axil thus formed.

It is by means of these leaf-buds that propagation by budding, by grafting, by cuttings or by layers, is effected. When a bud, or a scion with several buds on it, is inserted into another plant, under favorable conditions, they produce wood which unites with that to which it is joined. A cutting or a layer placed in the soil, emits roots into the soil. In either case we have a new plant, possessing leaves precisely similar to those of the parent stock. Sometimes, and oftener with some species than with others, these vital points or buds are formed and developed along the root and shoot upward from it. These are known in the nursery as root suckers, and are sometimes resorted to for propagation of fruit trees, especially the plum and pear, but they make trees much inferior to seedlings, and should never be used where seedlings can be obtained.

The leaf buds of fruit trees rarely push into growth during the season in which they are formed. The succeeding year a part of them grow into branches, but not all. As the original embryo remains for a time latent in the seed, so leaf-buds may remain dormant for an indefinite length of time without losing their vitality. The terminal bud and those near the end of the shoot, if the wood be fully ripe, and has not been injured by the winter, are most readily excited into growth, and those nearest its base are the most sluggish. Leaf-buds sometimes remain dormant for years; they may even be covered up by succeeding growths of wood, and yet by severe pruning may be forced into growth and develope into branches.

The *leaves* constitute the foliage of the tree. A leaf is an appendage to the stem, and has a leaf-bud in its axil. It consists of an expansion of the cellular rind of the bark, through which are distributed veins, or tough woody fibres, like ribs, and over all is an epidermis or skin. Through this skin respiration, perspiration and absorption take place. The office of the leaf is analogous to that of the stomach and lungs in animal life. The tree does not get its food wholly from the root. A portion of it is obtained by the leaves from the air. This, with what comes from the root, through the stem, dissolved in sap, is here exposed over a large surface to the action of sunlight, air and other external agencies, by which, in connection with vital action, the crude materials are elaborated and digested, and returned to the general circulation to be assimilated, and go to form root, wood, leaf, seed and fruit.

If it were proper to say that one organ is more necessary than another, when all are indispensable, we might give this distihction to the leaf, but this we may certainly affirm, that the *functions of the leaf are essential to the healthy existence of the plant*, and that whatever disturbs their free and normal action diminishes its health. Some persons, ignorant of this, have been so foolish as to strip a grape vine of its leaves, with an expectation of hastening the maturity of the fruit by the admission of more light and air. The fact is, that sunlight and air influence the ripening of the fruit indirectly, and by their action upon the plant through its leaves. By ill management the leaves on a vine may and often do become so numerous and crowded as to prevent a proper discharge of their functions. In such case the early removal of a part, by allowing the more perfect development of a suitable amount of foliage, will be found beneficial.

In spring the opening of the leaf-buds is accompanied by the extension and increased action of the spongioles of the root, and the action of the leaves upon the roots and of the roots upon the leaves, throughout the whole season, is constant and mutual. Cut off all the spongioles from a tree in full growth, and the foliage at once withers and dies. Let the leaves be destroyed by a blight or removed by design, and growth is at once suspended, the action of the root is suspended, and the maturing of its fruit is suspended. Without the full and healthy action of the leaves, a tree cannot possibly mature either its wood or its fruit. The peculiar characteristics of any fruit, as it's size, flavor, texture, keeping qualities, &c., are doubtless due to some peculiarities of the leaf which determine the nature of the nutriment supplied to the fruit, and which is elaborated or manufactured, as it were, in the leaf. These peculiarities of the leaves in different varieties of the same species are so obscure that no one from an examination of a leaf could determine the properties of the fruit to be produced by it; but the fact appears to be certain, for if we would reproduce any given varieties, we can do so only by means of leaf-buds. By inserting into another tree, a single bud, or a scion bearing several buds, we can determine the future foliage, and so be sure of perpetuating the desired variety of fruit.

For aught which appears thus far in considering the *Organs of Vegetation*, it would seem that a tree might go on to grow and extend itself upwards and outwards and downwards indefinitely, and stop growing only when a supply of nourishment should fail. But such is not the case. After a period of growth, varying with different species and varieties, and somewhat also with the conditions under which they are grown, they arrive at puberty, and now a new series of organs appear and come into action, viz: the *Organs of Reproduction*, or those by which it multiplies or increases in number. In the case of the trees we are considering these consist of the flower and the fruit containing seeds.

Flowers come from buds just as branches do, but in this case, instead of elongating into branches, the leaf-buds first undergo a transformation into flower-buds. In the peach and the quince this change takes place towards the end of the first season, and the fruit is borne on wood of the preceding year's growth. In the apple, pear and plum it takes place commonly the second or third year, and it is usually the smaller and less fully developed buds near the base of the previous year's shoot which are thus changed in their form and nature, while the more vigorous ones push into branches. What causes this transformation of leaf-buds into flower-buds is not known; but we may learn something of the circumstances usually attending it, and of the results flowing from it; as, for instance, that seedling trees usually are slower in coming to productiveness than grafted ones; such as are situated in moist, rich soils, thus favoring rapid growth, are more tardy in bearing than the same kinds would be if growing in a soil less favorable to rapid growth. If one species be grafted upon another which furnishes a more abundant supply of sap, as when the plum is worked on the peach stock, growth is more rapid, and bearing is retarded. The reverse of this is also true; when one species is worked on another of slower growth, as the pear upon the quince, productiveness is hastened. The wood-producing and the fruit-producing forces are, as it were, antagonistic to each other, and, as a general rule, whatever favors the one tends to lessen the other. Whatever produces excessive vigor is favorable to the formation of leaf-buds; while, on the other hand, whatever tends to diminish luxuriance, without injuring the health of the plant, favors the production of flower-buds instead of leaf-buds. An apparent exception to this rule is found in the fact that a scion from a young seedling tree may be made, by grafting it upon a mature healthy stock, to produce fruit at an earlier age than it would otherwise have done, but this is doubtless owing to the presence in the mature stock of a sufficient quantity of secreted matter fit for the development and maintenance of the flowers when produced. The bending downward of limbs, or training by any mode which checks the free circulation of the sap, induces fruitfulness. So does transplanting or root pruning, because, the roots being injured, sap is less abundantly supplied in the following season to the leaves, and thus being less able to grow, they do not consume the nutritious matter lying in the branches and which they would have expended had they grown with their previous vigor; consequently the nutritious matter accumulates and fruit buds are formed.

If the blossom buds of one year are all removed or destroyed, the crop the next year is more abundant; and a very abundant crop of one year is usually followed by barrenness the succeeding year. Many kinds of apples have a tendency to bear only in alternate years. This is owing to the exhaustion which follows the production of more fruit than the tree is able to produce continuously, so requiring a season of rest in which to recruit its energies. This may be easily remedied, or the bearing year changed, while the trees are young, by removing the bloom buds or the young fruit as soon as formed. In repeated instances the bearing year has been changed by this method from the "even" to the "odd" year, with great increase of profit to the orchardist.

Blossom buds draw heavily upon the tree for nourishment, and they return nothing to it; therefore flowering as well as fruiting is an exhaustive operation. I have noticed with some pears, as the Duchess d'Angoulene for example, that an abundant bloom in spring ushered in a barren season; while a very moderate bloom has frequently been followed by a plentiful crop.

There is often, and especially with those just commencing the culture of fruit, a strong desire for early and plentiful bearing, but such persons should remember that unless their trees first attain a suitable degree of strength and maturity, and have, as it were, laid up sufficient capital to honor the drafts made by flowering and fruiting, feebleness, premature old age and decrepitude will be the sure result. The removal or thinning out of fruit on young trees is often one of the most judicious and best paying operations of the fruit garden or orchard. It would not be practicable to do this to advantage on a large scale, with trees arrived at maturity, but while the orchard is young a regular habit of bearing in some, and a change in others to the years of usual scanty bearing is easily accomplished.

Flowers consist of floral envelopes, the *calyx* and *corolla*; and of sexual organs, the *stamens* and *pistils*. The *calyx* is the outer covering or lower envelope, usually green, and resembling ordinary leaves. The *corolla* is the inner envelope, of brighter colors and more delicate texture, and form the most showy part of the blossom. The several parts of the *corolla* are called petals.

The sexual organs are of two kinds; the outer ones called *stamens*, being the male organs; and the inner ones called *pistils*, which are the female organs. A stamen consists of a slender column or stalk, called a *filament*, which bears on its top a rounded body or case termed the *anther*, filled with a powdery substance which it discharges and drops upon the pistil. The pistil consists of the *ovary*, the hollow portion at the base, which contains the ovules or bodies destined to become seeds; the *style*, or erect portion, and the *stigma*, a small glandulous body on its summit, and which receives the pollen or fertilizing powder from the anthers.

Plants are called *hermaphrodite* when both stamens and pistils exist in the same flower. This is the case with most of our cultivated fruits. They are called *Monœcious* when the male and female flower are separately borne on the same tree, which is the case with the filbert. They are called *Diœcious* when the male flowers are found on one plant and the female on another, which is the case with some varieties of the strawberry, but not with all.

Impregnation is effected by the action of the pollen or fertilizing granules, which, when the flowers first open, is covered by a delicate membrane about the anther. This membrane soon bursts open and scatters the pollen, a portion of which falls on the stigma of the pistil and penetrates through the style to the ovary. Here impregnation is effected and a new embryo plant soon commences formation. Sometimes, where the ovary is composed of several cells, as in the apple and pear, impregnation is only partially effected, and hence the development of the fruit is only partial and one-sided.

Hybridization is performed by fertilizing the pistil of one species or variety with pollen from the stamens of another. Many precautions are necessary to insure success, the principal of which are first to remove the stamens from the plant intended for the mother before they shed any pollen upon the pistil; and next, after the proper application of pollen from the destined male parent and at just the right time, to guard the flower from accidental impregnation from other varieties.

As soon as the ovary is impregnated and begins to swell, the petals, stamens and other parts of the flower, no longer required, fall off, and the fruit *sets*, as we say. It now continues to receive food, and gradually arrives at maturity.

Propagation and Nursery Treatment.

First by seeds. Fruit trees are grown from seeds mainly for the purpose of obtaining stocks upon which to bud or engraft the choice varieties; sometimes for the purpose of obtaining new varieties. The seeds of the apple, the pear, &c., will always produce their own *species*, but not the same *varieties*; that is to say, apple seeds will always grow into apple trees, and never into pears, and pear seeds will produce pear trees and not apples; but the seeds of a Rhode Island Greening or of a Roxbury Russet may not be relied upon to produce a greening or a russet. It is by means of variations, primarily induced by the conditions attending culture, that we now have delicious varieties of fruit from the original crab apple and wild choke pear; and there exists in all cultivated fruits a tendency to variation by means of their seeds, and this variation is partly in the direction of a return to the wild type, and partly towards a more ameliorated one, so that occasionally we obtain a better fruit than the parent, and it is from these instances that we have our best varieties.

When it is desired to obtain new varieties two methods may be employed. First, by selecting and sowing the seeds from the best grown specimens of the finest sorts, to be planted out for fruiting; selecting for this purpose such as exhibit in their foliage and general appearance the greatest remove from the wild type. This appearance may not be more readily described than the countenance or handwriting of an individual, but is easily recognized by a practised eye, just as a good nurseryman or orchardist can distinguish many known varieties by their peculiarity of appearance in habit, wood or leaf, and name each of them accurately without either label or fruit upon them. Such as bear fruit unworthy of cultivation may be grafted. It is well, however, if the first fruit be only tolerably good, to allow the tree to bear several years before grafting, because the fruit of seedling trees often greatly improves as the trees approach maturity. The other method is by artificial hybridization. This is performed by fertilizing the pistil of one species or variety with pollen from the stamens of another. The seed so impregnated will produce a cross or hybrid between the two parents. This process is now well understood by horticulturists, and has been extensively practised by florists for the production of flowers;—our finest Roses, Dahlias, Camelias, Fuchsias, and many other flowers, have been originated in this way. Some fine fruits also have been produced by this method, and a great deal more undoubtedly might be done by thus combining the size, productiveness and hardihood of one variety, with the delicacy of flavor and texture of another. Hybridizing is a delicate operation, and requires care and many precautions to ensure success. Of the fruits directly obtained by cross breeding may be named Coe's Golden Drop plum, which combines in a considerable degree the flavor of the Green Gage with the size and vigor of the Magnum Bonum, its other parent. The Elton cherry was the result of a cross between the Bizarreau and the White Heart. By far the greater number of our cultivated fruits have, however, been accidentally cross bred;—that is, the product of seeds from good fruit where the pollen was conveyed to the pistil by the wind or by bees or some such mode.

It is the practice in nearly all the fruit-growing sections of this country and in other countries, to plant out seedlings one or two years old, into nursery rows, and to bud or graft them near the ground, within the next year or two;* then after one, two or three years' growth of the bud or scion, to remove them permanently to the orchard. This may be done here to advantage with such sorts as are sufficiently hardy, and vigorous growers; but there are many desirable varieties which do not generally succeed by this method; and for such it is found greatly preferable to allow the seedling stock to attain sufficient age and size to be grafted in the limbs, after being established in the orchard. This involves considerably more labor, but without it, success cannot be looked for with any good degree of confidence. The attempt will be made, when treating of varieties, to mention those, so far as our knowledge extends, which it is necessary to graft in the limbs. For this, and for many reasons I would recommend the Maine orchardist, as a general rule, to have a nursery and grow his own trees. Every orchardist ought to be acquainted with the work needful in the nursery. Scarcely any farm work is more easily learned, none is more pleasant. Sons and daughters should become familiar with it, and work in it, for, to say nothing of the gratification and profit to be derived thereby, nothing binds children to the home of their childhood more than fine fruit trees of their own care and planting. An hour or two of attention given at suitable times will keep a nursery, of sufficient size for any one family, in good order.

For this purpose, let seeds from the *hardiest* and *thriftiest* trees in the neighborhood be thinly sown in autumn, in good soil, in beds, covering the seed about one inch deep. When they grow, keep them free from weeds and see that they do not crowd each other. At the end of one or two years let them be lifted, in the spring;—select the healthiest and hardiest, and only these, be they few or many, throw the others away and plant the best in nursery rows, four feet apart. A part of the trees may be set eighteen inches apart in the rows. This is for such as are destined to be budded or grafted before removal to the orchard. The rest may be set at three feet apart, and remain until of proper size to plant out finally. The place selected for the nursery should be sheltered

*The only notable exception to this rule is in the case of apple trees propagated by *rootgrafting*, as extensively practiced in Western New York,—a method which results in trees worse than worthless for our climate—and which will be again noticed before we leave the subject.

from high winds, well fenced, and in a way not to favor the drifting of snows upon the young trees. The soil may be similar to that of the place designed for the orchard, and should be deeply worked for two years previously. If not good enough to yield fifty bushels of corn per acre with ordinary manuring, it should have a liberal dressing of compost made of leaf mould, i. e., decayed leaves from the woods, mixed with wood ashes and lime. Fruit trees, if stunted or ill fed in their earlier years, can never become what they ought to be;—on the other hand, stimulating manures are to be avoided as liable to induce a late and unripened growth of wood which cannot withstand our severe winters. If the seedlings grow well, those to be worked in the nursery may be budded in August, or grafted in the spring following; at which time the budded ones are to be headed down to within three or four inches of the bud. After the buds start, and as often as necessary during the season, rub off the robbers—that is to say, all shoots except from the inserted bud or scion; and tie the bud to the stock above in such a way as to secure it from being blown out. As it is of prime importance to secure well ripened wood, and more especially the first year, it is well to go through the trees from the 5th to 15th of August and pinch the ends of such as are still growing, so that instead of extending in height, they may devote the remainder of the season to hardening and ripening the wood already made. Clean culture and thorough loosening of the soil are to be continued as long as the trees remain in the nursery. Those which are not worked require no treatment beyond a little pruning to shape them properly. All the trees not removed to the orchard at a year from the bud should have their tops formed before removal, and if properly done, little subsequent pruning will be found necessary.

Whether grafted young or not, the evident design of nature to shield the stem from the burning rays of the sun, by means of side branches or shoots, should not be interfered with so as needlessly to expose the trunk to its scorching influence. This is a point of considerable importance, but is often thoughtlessly sacrificed to the supposed beauty of a bare, smooth stem; many young orchards have been seriously injured in this way. The lower side shoots and limbs should be *gradually* removed, and only as the tops extend sufficiently. Low branching tops are preferable to high ones, as more healthy and productive. An excuse, often given for desiring tall stems, is, to allow cattle to graze in the orchard. The excuse has no validity whatever. The place for cattle is in the pasture, and the orchard should be as much devoted to fruit as the wheat field to bread. If the grower insist upon tall stems, so that grazing or plowing be practicable, let them be formed by degrees and very gradually.

A principal reason for the recommendation that the orchardist should have a nursery of his own, is the difficulty of procuring good and reliable trees in any other way. If brought from other States they must necessarily be more or less unacclimated, besides which there is the delay, expense, and damage from exposure to various injuries attending transportation. Nurseries are neither numerous nor extensive within the State, and scarcely any apple nurseries are known to have been profitable enough to their owners to secure their long continuance, unless by the sale of trees grown elsewhere. Purchasers have been unwilling, generally, to pay a price at all corresponding to the greater cost of growing them here; including in the cost of growing, of course, the unavoidable losses from the severity of some winters, the breaking down by heavy snows, and various other contingencies; and, consequently, nearly all attempts to establish nurseries have proved failures. But to an extent sufficient to furnish one's own orchard and make gradual additions to it, the labor and expense are inconsiderable compared with the superiority of the trees thus grown, and well worth being incurred. As an acre, in rows four feet apart with half the trees at eighteen inches in the row, and the rest at three feet apart, will contain between four and five thousand trees, probably not more than an eighth to a quarter of an acre would be needed to supply any ordinary plantation; and the time required need not interfere seriously with other farm labors.

Although the matter has been already incidentally alluded to, I feel that I should be blameworthy should nothing more be said to warn the orchardists of Maine from planting Western-grown *root-grafted trees*; such as are so assiduously hawked about the State by ignorant and irresponsible tree venders. These trees are grown in the neighborhood of Rochester, N. Y., and in other places, by millions. I have myself seen hundreds and perhaps thousands of acres thickly covered with them, and they are so cheaply grown as to be sold at from four to seven dollars per hundred. Having little root, they are easily transported, and can be retailed here at from one to two hundred per cent advance, and yet at a less price than the bare cost of growing trees in a proper manner in Maine. Now a tree *can* be "rootgrafted" in such a way that it shall be as good as a tree grown by budding on a seedling stock in the nursery, but this would involve the use of an entire seedling root by grafting it at the collar, which would be nothing more or less than stock grafting at the surface of the ground, and would involve as much or more labor than the ordinary method. But these Western trees are made by working a scion on a bit of root sufficient to keep it alive until it throws out roots of its own. The work is done in winter, when there is nothing else to do, and they are dibbled out in spring, and no farther labor is given, except horse hoeing between the rows, until they are sold. When grown they are simply *rooted cuttings.** Thickly planted in rich soil, they soon run up into pretty trees to outward appearance, but when lifted are found to be furnished with only a little tuft of fibrous roots, unable to support the tree properly when transplanted, and worse still, they are destitute of the energy and *vitality* of trees grafted upon entire seedling stocks. Probably nineteen-twentieths of the apple trees brought into the State for the last ten years, are of this sort, and although in some cases they live several years, yet I have never seen an instance of what might be deemed fair success; and it is undoubtedly true that not one in a hundred has lived to come into bearing. The most successful instances are those where they die outright at once, and involve no further trouble and disappointment; but sometimes they live and linger for years, until the orchardist is fain to dig them out and be rid of the sight of them. Too often, being ignorant of the real trouble, he is discouraged, and concludes that all attempts at fruit culture are useless. Concerning the value of such trees for planting upon Illinois prairies, or in mild latitudes in other States, I have only to say that different opinions are expressed by those who have had experience with them. While many Western nurserymen claim that they are good enough, many others deny it, and point to thousands of cases of failure. At a meeting of the Western Fruit Growers' Convention,

*I have never grown the apple from cuttings, but have been informed by intelligent orchardists in the State that it has been repeatedly done, and that with care and good treatment they will attain a fair size and sometimes come into bearing; but that they are never firmly rooted, always feeble, often diseased, usually unproductive and worthless.

Mr. Williams being called upon to state his views upon the subject, said he "had paid attention to it for several years; this year had spent much time in visiting orchards and making observations. He believed that for the orchardist, trees worked standard high are better worth one dollar a tree, than to plant rootgrafted trees, receiving them and a dollar with each tree as a gratuity. Is acquainted with an orchard containing rootgrafted trees fifteen years old—have never borne well, some of them never an apple. Other trees, budded from them, in the same orchard, have borne good crops for seven years."

Mr. T. T. Lyon, in the Michigan Farmer, says: "It has long been urged by fruit growers upon prairies that rootgrafted trees are less hardy than seedlings, but never till the present season have we, in this region, witnessed occular proof to that effect. From the result of this year's experience, it is also clear that some varieties are less hardy than others, for while *rootgrafted* trees of some varieties have *suffered severely*, topgrafted trees of these varieties have *escaped entirely*."

From the Iowa Farmer we take the following: "Judge Green, of Cedar Rapids, has an extensive orchard of several thousand trees, mostly root grafts, planted five or six years since, in rows a quarter of a mile long, and extending from near the top of a ridge down a southern slope and across a gently inclined flat or bottom. * * * * The Judge, being an Eastern man, had very naturally secured a large number of Baldwins, Greenings, Spitzenbergs, Roxbury Russets, &c., perhaps most of which were planted on the low ground. Here they struggled on up to last winter, mostly living, but not doing as well as the same sorts up the slope. Thus standing, that trial winter came, and completely finished up and wiped out nearly every tree of the more tender sorts, making sad inroads upon the appearance and profitableness of the orchard. Trees of the tender kinds, up the slope were not indeed all killed outright, and should our seasons prove favorable for a term of years, they may possibly bring some fruit yet; but it would seem impossible for them to become permanently vigorous. Scarce a variety that we noticed, not even the hardiest, had done as well on the low as on the high ground. Of several tender or half-hardy sorts on the slope, *where a part were root grafted and a part budded on seedlings, in every case that we noticed, the latter were the most hardy and vigorous.*"

These statements suggest several remarks; and may also serve to throw some light on the reasons why root grafted trees have so generally failed here.

It would appear that some varieties are more likely to succeed when root grafted than others, which is also confirmed by experience everywhere else.

It seems probable, also, that some of the more popular New England varieties, such as the Baldwin, Russet, &c., are only half-hardy or tender in severe seasons, elsewhere as well as in Maine. Again, the exceptional and severe "trial winter," as it is called, was, after all, not so damaging in its effects as many which we have had; for there the Baldwin *stood well as budded trees,* while *they were killed outright when root grafted.* Now as there is no safety in planting budded trees of the Baldwin in Maine, (as a general rule,) such as there proved hardy when the same sort failed if root grafted, *the utter worthlessness of the latter for our planting* appears in a strong light.

The late William Reid of New Jersey, than whom no one was more competent to speak advisedly, in a communication to the Horticulturist writes as follows:

"I would, while speaking of the quality of trees grown in different sections of the country, call the attention of parties who are planting apple orchards to some defects not easily detected. I allude to the millions of apple trees that the country is being flooded with, and distributed in every corner of the land by persons calling themselves tree agents or pedlars, who come from Western New York. I allude to the trees known as root grafted trees. They are, to be sure, what they term them, root grafted; but the root, if root it may be called, is a very small root, or piece of a root, being only about two inches in length. A proper name to call them would be cuttings, for they are nothing more or less than apple trees grown from cuttings, the small piece of root only keeping the graft alive until the cutting begins to grow, which makes new roots of itself. The consequence will be, after a few years, or when they begin to bear, that a great proportion of them will blow down with the wind. Being only cuttings they are deficient in the strong roots which apple trees have when budded or grafted on seedling stocks above ground, and which are so necessary to make strong, healthy and permanent trees. And I would advise any person to have nothing to do with any apple tree that is not grafted above the ground. They are not only hardier but have roots to sustain them when they come into bearing and are of large size. This is one reason why so many trees now to be seen in the West that have been planted with these root cuttings are dying out in winter. Not only have they this objection, but they are nearly all more or less lurched over from the effect of the winds, and whoever plants them will be disappointed sooner or later.

It is not necessary now, if it ever was, to buy trees of travelling pedlars who have no fixed place of residence or respectability, and who are generally ignorant men, scarcely knowing the name of one tree from another, except what the circulars which they carry give them. I would again advise every person to send to a respectable nurseryman who will send them trees correct to name, who have reputation at stake, and who are generally competent to judge as to the varieties which are best adapted to the locality the purchaser lives in. I am satisfied that more loss and disappointment have been caused by pedlars selling worthless trees than would have sufficed to plant the whole Western States. In place of this they have now to begin and replant all the ground planted from 1850 to 1855." *

Grafting. The uses of grafting are many and various. The chief one is to change the head of a tree bearing inferior fruit, or of uncertain character, to another known to be desirable. We can in this way propagate choice varieties with an ease and rapidity impossible by any other method. By it we can also render dwarf certain fruit trees by working them upon different but kindred stocks which are of slower growth, and thereby attain valuable results; as with the apple upon the paradise stock, and the pear upon the quince stock. Seedling fruits, or those known to be usually tardy in bearing, can be fruited much sooner by grafting them upon the limbs of grown trees of the same species.

Not least among its uses, is its enabling us to grow successfully

---

* While revising proof, an article is observed in Hovey's Magazine of Horticulture, written by a resident of Rochester, New York, stating at some length what may be said both for and against the practice of root grafting, and I quote a sentence or two as containing the pith and point of it. "Its principal advantage is *to the nurseryman* in economizing labor," &c. * * * "The disadvantages of this mode of propagation *fall chiefly upon the orchardist*," &c. Nothing could be more frank and to the point than this.

many sorts otherwise too tender, uncertain, or of feeble growth, by grafting them upon well-grown, hardy, vigorous native trees known to be well adapted to the soil and climate.

The plant or limb upon which a graft is set is called a *stock*, (*not stalk*). The stock and the graft (be it a scion or a single leaf bud) form a partnership, the former furnishing the raw material, by the roots, and the latter, by its leaves, digesting it, and manufacturing the product. It is based on the power of union between young tissues. When similar parts are accurately fitted to each other, the sap passes from one to the other, and under favorable conditions, granulations are soon thrown out and a lasting junction effected.

Success is confined within certain limits. It is greatest between varieties of the same species, as the apple upon the apple—next between species belonging to the same genus; as the pear on the quince; and lastly between genera of the same natural order. These last are of short duration and for the most part useless. Between those less nearly allied, no union is effected. The practicable range for useful purposes, with us, extends little beyond the following: The apple upon the common apple and the crab for orchard trees, and upon the doucain and paradise for garden culture The pear upon the pear for orchards, and upon the quince for dwarf trees to receive garden culture. Some varieties of the pear have succeeded tolerably on the Mountain Ash, (*Pyrus Americana,*) the White Thorn, (*Crateagus Coccinea*) and upon the Shadbush, commonly called Sugar Pear, or Juneberry, (*Amelanchier Canadensis,*) these being all closely allied species.

Where the cherry succeeds, it may be worked either on the Mazzard for large trees, or on the Mahaleb for dwarfs. The plum has been budded on the peach, giving trees of rapid growth but short lived; and the peach upon the plum, but the trees although hardier than when on their own stock, have rarely given much satisfaction. Little success can be expected in this State with the finer cherries except in very favorable localities and soils, nor with the peach in the open air, except it be *trained very low,* so as to be covered with snow during winter.

The old adage that "the scion overruleth wholly, the stock being merely passive," needs some modifications, for to a certain extent the stock exerts an influence. A plum budded upon the peach is furnished with an unwonted supply of sap, and grows more rapidly than upon its own stock. The pear grafted upon the quince receives less than its usual supply of sap, and forms a smaller tree than if worked on the pear stock; and its growth being checked somewhat, it comes earlier into bearing. Let a row of seedling apples be grafted, a part with the Siberian Crab Apple, and a part with several free-growing kinds like the Baldwin or Greening, and it will be found upon lifting them a few years after grafting, that the former have a much greater amount of roots than either of the free-growing sorts. Let part of a row of young Canada plums (our common wild plum, sometimes wrongly called pomegranates,) be budded with the better and more free-growing sorts, like Imperial Gage, Smith's Orleans, or McLaughlin, and after two or three years, upon lifting them, it will be found that the roots of those thus grafted have not, apparently, grown at all since being budded, while those not worked have extended very much. These and similar cases I have repeatedly observed in nursery practice, and there are doubtless other influences also exerted by the stock which are not well understood—for instance, it is said that sometimes an apple, usually free from this defect, has become what is called *water-cored,* in consequence of having been grafted upon a tree, the natural fruit of which was thus affected. It is not unlikely that some other modifications of the fruit may be effected, but they are, on the whole, inconsiderable. To a very great extent it is true that the scion overruleth.

For scions we cut the twigs of the previous season's growth, selecting those well grown and thoroughly ripened. As a general rule grafting succeeds better when the scions have been cut some time previously to being set. They may be cut at any time from the fall of the leaf until the buds swell. With *perfectly hardy* sorts, March is as good a time as any, but generally my preference is for November. They may be kept in boxes with moss just damp enough to allow of no change in the moisture of the scion. Too much dampness is equally to be avoided with too little. If closely packed with plenty of moss and kept in a cool place, they come out in the finest possible condition in spring; and I have kept them thus even until another season; or they may be buried in the ground, for which purpose select a light sandy soil in a place so dry that no excess of water ever accumulates in it.

The better time for grafting plums and cherries is before the frost leaves the ground. Apples and pears a week or two before the buds of the stocks begin to swell. If need be, the latter may be grafted later, even until the buds have swollen considerably, or have leaved out; or if more convenient it may be done a month before they swell. As a matter of curiosity, grafting has been performed successfully in every month in the year.

Numerous methods of grafting have been practiced, but as a few of the simpler ones will serve all the purposes of the orchardist, these only will be described.

Cleft Grafting. This is the method most commonly in use to change the tops of grown trees. The limb is sawn off and the end smoothly pared with a knife. Then with a grafting knife and hammer it is cleft in the centre and kept open by a wedge. The scion is cut smoothly on both sides in the form of a wedge, for an inch to two inches, or as long as can be nicely fitted to the cleft. Cut so as to leave a bud just above the scarf, and the scion may be cut long enough to have two or three other buds above that one. Very large scions may be cut with shoulders, to avoid too wide a cleft. In setting the scion in the stock, be careful that *the line of union between the wood and the bark of each coincide exactly.* If the stock be wide enough for two scions, insert another on the other side, in the same way; then withdraw the wedge and cover the wound with grafting wax to exclude the air perfectly. If inserted long before growth commences, it is well, also, to wax the end of the scion. If only one scion is inserted, the stock may be cut away on the other side before applying the wax. If two are inserted and both grow, cut the weaker one away after a year or two, as otherwise there is danger that the limb eventually will split down. The most important points in all grafting are, *to have similar parts nicely adapted to each other, so that the sap may pass uninterruptedly from one to the other;* and next, that the parts be properly protected until a perfect junction is formed.

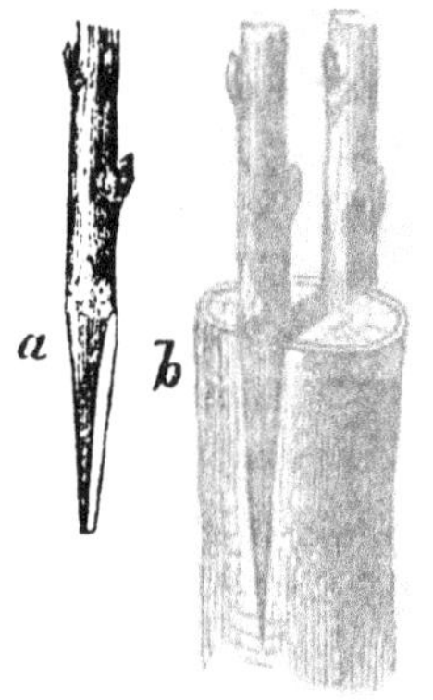

(*a*). Scion ready for insertion. (*b*). Stock with two scions inserted.

Splice Grafting. This is used chiefly in the nursery and upon small stocks. It is also employed when we desire to obtain fruit as soon as possible from a seedling variety. For the latter purpose a scion is grafted upon the end of a limb of a grown tree. In this case but little growth is attained, and little is wanted, for we cannot expect fruit buds to form on a rapidly growing shoot, because the growing and the fruiting forces are, as was remarked before, antagonistic in their character, and one or the other must give way, at least temporarily, or to a certain extent, in all cases. In splice grafting, the stock and scion are to be of the same size—each is to be cut obliquely for one or two inches, and the parts accurately fitted to each other, when a bass string is to be wound about it and covered with wax—or, better still, let it be wound about with a narrow strip of waxed cloth.

Tongue Grafting is similar to the above, except that a tongue is cut in both scion and stock, and one fitted to the other. This is one of the best methods of grafting in all cases where the stocks are not too large, say from half an inch to three fourths or even a whole inch. If the stock be larger than the scion this is decidedly preferable to the last. In this case care should be used, however, to have similar parts joined carefully *on one side*.

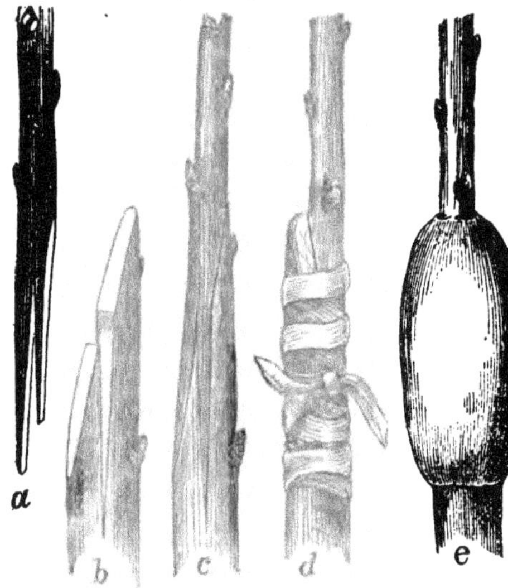

TONGUE GRAFTING IN ITS DIFFERENT STAGES.

(*a*). Scion cut for insertion. (*b*). Stock prepared to receive the scion. (*c*). Stock and scion united. (*d*). The same tied up. (*e*). Do. waxed or clayed for protection.

Saddle Grafting is more easily performed by the following method than by the one usually described in the books. Cut off the stock, which should be from half an inch to an inch in diameter, (I have seen it perfectly successful when nearly two inches in diameter,) with a sloping upward cut of an inch or two. Then, directly opposite this, cut downward perpendicularly, taking the bark and a thin slice of wood. Cut the scion upward, dividing it for the same distance into two unequal parts, leaving a bud at the top of the cut; then cut the thicker part of the scion so as to leave it wedge shaped; place this wedge shaped part into the back part of the stock and draw the thinner part over the slanting cut of the stock; fit the parts closely, tie and wax.*

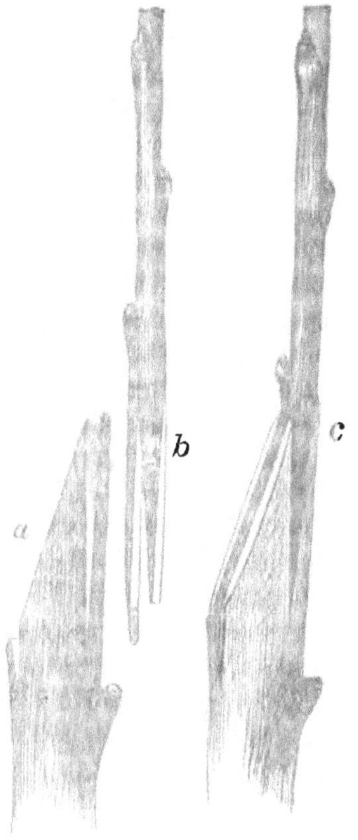

SADDLE GRAFTING.

(*a*). Stock. (*b*). Scion. (*c*). Stock and scion joined.

Bud-Grafting or *Budding*, as it is commonly called, (*inoculation* of the old authors,) is the easiest and best mode of working small stocks. It differs from ordinary grafting mainly in the use of a single bud in the place of a scion bearing several buds, and in being performed in late summer instead of spring. It may be performed in spring, as soon as the bark peels freely, using scions of the previous years' growth which have been carefully kept in good condition; but this is rarely advisable, and perhaps only when we have a very valuable scion which it is desired by subdivision to increase the chance of saving, or to work as many stocks with it as there are buds upon it.

To insure success in budding, several conditions are essential. The most important of these are, 1st, *That the bark of the stock should part freely from the wood;* for if, either by reason of the season of the year, or the feeble condition of the stock, the bark ad-

* Substantially the same method is described by Dr. Weston on page 36, as also a method of grafting under the bark.

heres to the wood, the operation will certainly fail. 2d, *That the bud to be inserted should be properly ripened;* as otherwise it will not have vital energy enough to establish itself in its new home. With ripe, plump buds and a freely flowing sap, union between the bark of the bud and the alburnum of the stock will be easily and speedily effected.

The *proper time for budding* varies with circumstances; as whether the season, be a wet or a dry one; the age and condition of the stocks, &c. In average seasons I have usually been most successful with plums and cherries from the middle to the end of July, with pears from the twentieth of July to the fifth of August, and with apples, from the fifth to the twentieth of August.

To prepare scions for budding, select well grown shoots of the present year's growth; cut off and reject all imperfectly developed buds at the lower end, and all unripe ones towards the top; then cut off the leaves from the remainder at a point about the middle of the stems, leaving part of the foot-stalk of each, by which the better to handle the bud. In this condition the scions may be kept, if need be, for a week or ten days, or be carried a considerable distance if wrapped in damp moss. Where scions are plenty, only a few of the best buds in the middle of the shoot should be used, as those below are apt to be backward about starting into growth the next spring, while those at the upper part, being easily excited, are more liable to start into growth the same season, and especially if wet, warm weather ensues; in which case the young shoots are sure to be killed or injured the following winter. When the variety used is scarce and valuable, we would take more risk and insert some which would otherwise be rejected.

The preferable size for stocks to be budded is half an inch in diameter, (from one quarter to three quarters of an inch is the usual range); though sometimes both larger and smaller stocks are worked by this mode.

There are many methods of performing this operation; but the most common and the best, is what is called shield or T budding. It is performed as follows: Select a smooth part of the stock, then with a sharp budding knife make a horizontal cut across the bark quite through to the wood; from the middle of this cut make a slit downwards an inch or more long, going also through to the wood; so that both cuts taken together shall resemble a letter T. Next cut from your scion a thin slice of bark with a little wood in the central portion of it, entering the knife about half an inch below, and bringing it out about as far above a bud. This slice of bark and wood taken together is technically called a bud—the part which grows into a shoot (i. e. the bud proper) being known as its *eye*.

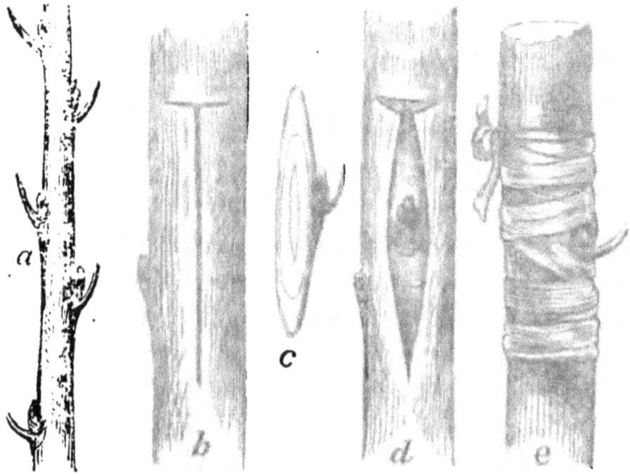

SHIELD BUDDING—DIFFERENT STAGES.

(*a*). Stick of buds. (*b*). Showing the T shaped cut in the bark of stock. (*c*). Bud ready for insertion. (*d*). Stock with bud inserted. (*e*). Same tied up.

With the ivory haft of the budding knife, or if you have not such a knife, with a wedge of wood or ivory, gently raise the bark, beginning at the corners of the slit in the stock. Be very careful that the *cambium* or sliver be not disturbed or injured in the least. Then taking hold of the bud by its foot-stalk, insert it and gently push it down to the bottom of the incision. The eye of the bud will now be about half an inch below the horizontal cut. That part of the bud, if any, projecting above this should be cut off by passing the knife through it into the transverse slit again so that a good joint be made.

A bass string, or some other which is soft and pliable, is now to be wound tightly about it, beginning at the bottom and covering every part except the eye of the bud and its foot-stalk, and tying it above the horizontal cut. The success of the operation, so far as its execution is concerned, depends mainly on smooth cuts, an exact fit of the bud to the incision made for it, and close tying. Cloudy and moist weather is more favorable than a hot sun and a dry day. In ten days or a fortnight, examine the buds and if they be found plump and full, the operation has been successful, and the string, if too tight, should be removed, and tied again more loosely, and above the bud only; in another fortnight it is well to remove the string entirely.

When the buds swell the following spring, the stock is to be cut off three or four inches above the bud. So much of the stock it is well leave in order to tie the bud to it, as it grows, to prevent the shoot from being blown out by high winds. All other shoots from the stock (the robbers as they are called) are to be rubbed off as often as they appear. The spring following the stock may be cut off smoothly close to the bud.

(*a*). Stock as left the first season. (*b*). Dotted line showing where it is to be cut off smoothly the second year.

Cuttings and Layers. Some fruits, as the quince, gooseberry, grape and currant, are propagated usually in this way. Cuttings consist of shoots of the previous year's growth, and are of any length from a single eye or bud to a foot or more long. Usually they are made from eight to ten inches in length; are cut in the fall and planted out early the next spring in well prepared soil, so that only two or three buds are above the surface. Mulching, by covering the ground with coarse manure, leaves, seaweed or litter of some sort, is useful in preserving an even moisture in the soil. The grape is sometimes propagated by cuttings of a single bud each. These should be planted in a hot-bed, nearly spent, so as to afford a gentle bottom heat.

A *Layer* is a cutting which has been prepared one or two years previously. A shoot starting from near the ground is bent down and the lower portion confined by a hooked peg and then covered with soil. Success is rendered more certain by checking the return flow of sap, which may be done by twisting the shoot at the point covered, or better still, by entering a knife on the under side and cutting upward half way through the shoot, thus forming a tongue, and fastening it open with a little soil. The sap as it returns is here stopped and forms, first granulations and then roots. When the layer is sufficiently rooted it may be removed and planted out by itself.

Trees are sometimes purposely kept headed down for raising layers, and are then called *stools.* A quince plant thus made into a stool, and its twigs layered, may be made to produce many finely rooted plants in a single season. This method is largely used for growing young plants of the quince and the Paradise apple to be used as stocks for dwarf trees.

Soil and Situation. Let us suppose the nursery work to be well advanced and a sufficient number of young trees ready for removal to the orchard; what then? Why, transplant them to be sure. But let us inquire whether we be not rather fast, for this should have been borne in mind for the past year or two, or for several years, while the young trees were coming on, and a suitable place selected and prepared to receive them. This cannot be done in a day, although some act as if they thought so, but this does not make it so, any more than because they also think that transplanting and after culture consists in crowding the roots into a small hole and covering them with the sods taken out, and thereafter letting the tree alone to struggle for existence, makes that so.

An orchard should be looked upon as *a long investment,* a crop to be harvested during half a century, and deserving of proper selection of place and preparation of it at the outset, and careful treatment all the while it is bearing; just as really as a crop of Indian corn deserves preparation of soil, manuring, hoeing and care until the harvest is finished.

The situation selected for an orchard should be good upland, with a *dry subsoil.* Side hills and elevated ridges often furnish the best, especially for apple orchards, and sometimes even where they are too rocky to admit of cultivation. These as well as other uplands are sometimes wet and springy, *in which case underdaining is indispensable.* Cold water is excellent in its place, but is not good for the roots of fruit trees, and though they may struggle along for a while, they can never thrive with wet feet the year round. As a general rule, good corn land is good orchard land, but the rule is not without exceptions, for corn sometimes does well on intervals where fruit trees would not be safe in winter.

Next in importance to dryness of subsoil, I would rank the quality and character of the soil itself. The apple will grow on a great variety of soils but it likes best a deep gravelly strong loam, alike removed from mere sand, gravel or clay, and if calcareous, all the better. It should be good enough to yield from twenty-five to thirty-five bushels of Indian corn to the acre. If not good enough to do this, make it so, or try elsewhere; unless it possesses some peculiar excellencies for orchard use, aside from what would be requisite for corn.

The ground, if not too rocky to preclude its possibility, should be well prepared and mellowed by cultivation for a year or two previous; so that the sward, if it has been in grass, be well reduced; and before planting it should be *subsoiled.* If a subsoil plow cannot be had, trench plowing, by running the plow a second time in the same furrow, will loosen the soil to a greater depth, but with the disadvantage of bringing more of the subsoil to the surface than is desirable.

Transplanting. The skill, or the lack of it, with which transplanting is performed, has so much to do with subsequent success or failure, that it is of great importance that it be done properly. Some people plant a tree as they would a post, apparently thinking that the office of the root is only or mainly to keep the stem in an upright position; but no view could be more erroneous, for the roots are the *true feeders,* as well as the mechanical supporters of a tree, and they require a pasturage ground, good enough and of sufficient extent, and also an opportunity to avail themselves of it. Transplanting, at best, is an act of violence, (unless the plant moved has been grown in a pot, so that the roots can be secured entire). It is impossible to transplant from the open ground without a greater or less mutilation of the roots, and the less the better. Very few are aware of the actual extent of this multilation in ordinary practice. The subjoined cut may help give some

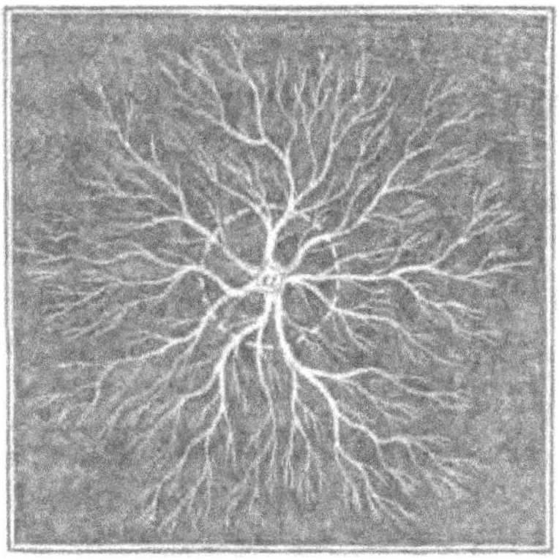

idea of it; (*a*) denoting the collar of the tree, and the dotted circle marking the extent of the roots lifted with the tree; those outside of it being left in the ground. As before remarked, the roots usually extend as far as the tops, sometimes considerably farther; and as it is only at the extremities that the spongioles or feeders are found, there is reason to believe that more than three fourths of them are usually lost in lifting. Some kinds of trees bear the loss, and recover from it, much more readily than others, as, for instance, the pear on quince root, which has the power of emitting new roots with greater facility than almost any other fruit tree; while the cherry is more uncertain because it emits new roots with greater difficulty. The following brief rules may be given as covering the principal points to be observed in transplanting:

If the trees have come from a distance, and have become dry and shrivelled, let them be buried in the earth, root and branch, until they are plump and full. Then shorten the top in some measure proportionate to the loss of roots, by cutting in last year's shoots; if the trees have a fair proportion of roots, this heading in should not be severe, and if, in addition, the planting be well done, and the trees properly mulched, it may be omitted entirely; in which case they should have a *moderate heading back the following year*, which will then result in more vigorous growth. The more top is left, if the tree does well, the more fibrous roots will be made the season following the planting. Next cut off *smoothly* the end of every root, taking away any bruised portions. A finger, amputated by a spade cut, may be expected to heal as kindly as a root so treated; both are alike portions of organized tissue, and subject to the laws of life.

The holes being large enough to allow every root its natural position, without bending or crowding, spread out the fibres in every direction as widely and evenly as possible, while fine mould is sifted among them: one person holding the tree, while another fills in. Let every root be *in close contact with the soil, and no vacancy allowed*, which would produce mould or decay. When nearly filled, pour in a few quarts of water from a watering-pot to settle the earth among the fine roots, and complete the filling with dry, mellow surface soil.

Apples and pears on their own roots, also cherries and plums (as well as trees and plants generally) are to be set *at the same depth* at which they stood in the nursery—unless the situation be a moist one,* in which case they should be set higher, and the

* If trees *must* be set where there is a liability of the ground becoming saturated with water at any season, they may be set *on the surface*, without digging any hole, raising the earth about them to the proper height.

earth about them raised in a corresponding degree. *Pears upon quince roots* should be set so that the point of junction between the pear and quince be *three inches below* the surface. *Dwarf apples* may be set so that the junction shall be *just even* with the surface.

When the tree is set, do not neglect to *mulch* it, by laying around for a distance of three or four feet, and two or three inches in depth, a covering of some kind—coarse manure and half-rotted leaves from the forest are the best materials. If these are not to be had, refuse hay, straw or seaweed answer a good purpose, and even spent tan or sawdust are better than nothing. This covering preserves a uniformity of moisture and of temperature about the roots, and is of great value throughout the whole of the first year's growth. In nearly all cases it obviates any need of subsequent watering, which as often done, is a most injurious practice; it being as easy to kill a recently transplanted tree by drowning as by drouth; and sometimes trees are killed by *drouth caused by watering*, which happens when a little is poured over the surface causing the formation of a hard crust, and thus preventing the soil from retaining moisture. If it becomes necessary to apply water, first remove the mulch and a little of the earth, and after watering replace them both.

Season. There is considerable difference of opinion whether autumn or spring is the better time for this operation. Both have their advantages and disadvantages. If set in the fall there is the danger of winter killing and crushing by the snows of one season, or, if the ground be bare, of the roots being injured by excessive freezing, or freezing and thawing alternately. On the other hand, it is a season of more leisure, and the work is likely to be more faithfully done, and if not quite so well done as it should be, the latter rains settle the earth more completely about the roots. The ground, too, is in better condition to work, and what perhaps is the chief advantage, trees set in autumn, although they do not start so early and vigorously, suffer much less from the droughts of summer. Autumn planting succeeds far better in light, dry soils than in heavy loams. In any soil it is needful to pile a little hillock of earth about the tree after planting, to be removed in spring and replaced by a mulch. If there be any doubt as to the hardiness of the tree planted, spring should be preferred. When planted in spring, *the earlier it is done, after the ground is in proper condition to work, the better.* A very common error is to defer it too long.

When trees or plants are to be procured from any distance, they should be purchased and got home in autumn, if possible, even if the intention be to plant in spring, as, by being "heeled in," they can be kept in better condition than if left in the nursery rows during winter, and the trees are at hand ready to be set on the first favorable opportunity; whereas, if left until spring, other work is apt to delay or interfere, and the order reaches the nurserymen when scores or hundreds of other orders are on hand, waiting their turn, to be executed; those sending for them all anxious to be served at once, while the period suitable for lifting and transplanting is very brief, much shorter than in districts farther south. Indeed, comparatively speaking, we have no spring here, the transition from winter to summer being so abrupt.

The "heeling in," or "laying in by the heels," alluded to, is a sort of temporary planting. Let a trench be dug in *dry soil* deep enough to cover the roots and half the tops, place them in a sloping position and cover with earth, carefully filling every interstice among the roots, and heaping the earth over them. The tops may be covered with evergreen boughs. They are thus kept in the best possible condition. When trees are received in spring, the bundles should be opened and the trees heeled in at once—at least if they are not to be planted within an hour. Never let them suffer any needless exposure in any way.

To the other advantages of procuring trees in autumn may be added that of *obtaining a better selection*, inasmuch as all nurseries, of any repute, are more or less severely thinned by a season's sale, and the stock of some desirable sorts often exhausted.

Distances between trees. It is not possible to state definitely any given distance as the best at which to plant apple trees or other fruit trees. Different sorts need different distances, some a good deal more than others; something also depends on soil, circumstances and intentions. I have seen some very good apple orchards which were planted at only a rod apart; and some others which were planted at forty feet apart. In the first, one half to three quarters of the trees had been removed by accident, disease or design. They were planted close purposely; in part to provide against losses from both unforseen and anticipated contingencies, and partly for the shelter and protection furnished by one to another.

Mature trees, of large growing sorts, like the Winthrop Greening or Yellow Bellflower, are near enough at thirty-five to forty feet asunder, for they actually need the twelve hundred to sixteen hundred square feet of surface which this distance gives. Other varieties, of smaller growth, like the Duchess of Oldenburg, Garden Royal, and the like, have as much room in proportion to their needs with a third part as much space—say at twenty feet asunder, thus giving them four hundred square feet each. For an orchard of apples of mixed sorts it may be a good plan in many cases to put the rows thirty feet or two rods apart, and the trees in the rows at twenty feet apart. This gives an average of 600 feet to each tree, and allows more room for the wagon, plow and cultivator.

Suitable comparative distances between trees of different species and on different stocks may be stated as follows:

Standard apples on free stock,	20 to 30 feet.
Dwarf apples on Doucain stock,	8 to 12 "
" " on French Paradise,	5 to 6 "
Standard pears on pear stock,	14 to 20 "
Dwarf pears on quince stock,	8 to 12 "
Cherries on Mazzard stock,	18 to 25 "
" on Mahaleb stock,	10 to 14 "
Plums,	10 to 14 "

Number of trees which may be planted on an acre at different distances:

At 4 feet apart each way, . . .	2721
" 8 " " " " . . .	680
" 10 " " " " . . .	435
" 12 " " " " . . .	302
" one rod " " " . . .	160
" 20 feet " " " . . .	109
" 25 " " " " . . .	70
" 30 " " " " . . .	48
" 35 " " " " . . .	36

Size of trees for planting. A very common error among beginners in fruit culture is to desire trees of too large size. They are very anxious to see fruit at the earliest possible moment. Such would gladly buy a ready made orchard or fruit garden for replanting, if they could. One person about to set out an orchard wrote to a nurseryman, "Send me *man* trees. I do not want any puny little children, but large, full-grown specimens." Another said, "I want the largest trees you have." "But," said the nurseryman, "smaller ones will be better in five years than these." "I don't care; I want big ones; I may not live five years, and I want fruit *now*." Three or four years later the same planter called again. Without waiting for an inquiry, the nurseryman remarked, "Well, I have some fine large trees for you now." "Don't want 'em! Don't want 'em!" was the answer; "I have had enough of large trees. They have cost me ten times as much trouble as the small ones I took from necessity, and they have not grown an inch. I have nursed them and doctored them, and they are the same size as when I got them, and they bear a little half-sized fruit. The small ones have gone by them, and are bearing fine large excellent specimens."

When the trees are on one's own land and only to be removed a short distance, they can be successfully planted of larger size than if they are to be packed and transported a considerable distance; but even then, those of six or seven feet in height are far better than larger ones, and probably others half as large would soon outstrip them. Experience is a very effectual teacher on this point, and I have never seen a cultivator, whatever his age, who had learned the lessons of ten years' experience and was still afraid of a small tree—no matter how small, almost, so it be healthy and thrifty. J. J. Thomas remarks: "When trees are to be sent some distance the increased cost of larger ones in conveyance, in risk and in packing is greater than a hasty observer has any idea of. A tree, for example, which is twice the height and diameter of another, is greater in weight in a cubic ratio. If a hundred of the smaller weigh two hundred pounds, one hundred of the larger will weigh eight hundred pounds, eight being the cube of two. A single season's growth in the nursery often makes this difference when young; but it requires many years after being checked by removal when large. There seems, indeed, to be every reason why trees should be removed small, and everything against removal when large. There is only one instance in which the larger trees can have any advantage, or can maintain it for two or three years, and this is when both large and small are treated with total neglect after setting out, so as barely to survive and not grow at all. Both remaining stationary, the larger ones will of course maintain their superiority in size. But all good cultivators discard such treatment. Sir Joshua Reynolds said if he were to paint a picture of Folly, it would be by representing a boy climbing over a high wall with an open gate by his side. Had he lived now, he might do it with equal effect by representing a purchaser selecting large trees at a nursery and rejecting young thrifty ones."

SHELTER.

Planting of Screens. The importance of shelter has already been several times alluded to, and a word may here be in place as to the better mode of securing it. It is well to have an evergreen screen or belt on all sides of the orchard; and if it be a large one, to have one or two running through it; but at least the two sides which are most exposed to injurious winds should be well protected.

Our common Spruces, Black and White, Balsam Firs and White Cedar (Arbor Vitæ) are the most available for the purpose. The Hemlock would make a more beautiful one, but it is very impatient of transplanting unless quite small, say only a few inches high. The common and almost universal error of all beginners is, to plant evergreens of too large size. Unless they have been previously grown in a nursery and several times transplanted when quite small, *none* should be set over two feet high, and one foot is much better. Let them be taken from open pastures in preference to the forests and take as much earth as will adhere to the roots. Be careful, also, that the roots do not dry in the least, and plant as soon as possible, in trenches previously prepared, and ready to receive them. A strip of land should be prepared at least one year previously, by plowing several furrows and planting it with potatoes or other hoed crop. May is the best month for moving evergreens, or until they have made an inch or two of new growth. Never prune them, and especially not by removing the lower limbs, as both their beauty and efficiency depend upon a dense pyramidal growth. Choose damp weather for transplanting. They may be set anywhere from three to six feet apart, and if you set out several rows, so as to form a dense *belt*, all the better. If the plants are small and good, and the operation well conducted, you may expect a dense screen fifteen or twenty feet high in ten or twelve years; and to be repaid, many times over, for the trouble, in the increased health, vigor and productiveness of the orchard.*

* "All who are conversant with the progress of arboricultural art in Great Britain are well aware of the necessity of protection to what we consider one of the hardiest of all trees, the oak; and that no plantation is completely successful which does not have it. For a time the opinions of planters were divided in this respect, but when Government undertook the planting of the Royal Forests of 40,000 acres, the experi-

AFTER CULTURE.

Fruit trees require attention and *cultivation*, as really as corn and potatoes; and they should have both, not merely for the first year or the first five years, but as long as they need it and pay for it.

Many a man has procured good trees, planted them skillfully and carefully, and thenceforward treated them to forgetfulness and neglect. Almost as well might he have spared the expense and trouble thus far incurred, as to leave them to struggle unaided, in competition with weeds, grass, moss, insects, and perhaps poverty also, and whatever else they may have to contend with. When good seed is put in good ground, we deem culture well begun, but not completed. Corn and carrots get attention as long as they

---

ment was fully tried, and with decided results in favor of shelter as the following report by the Government commission shows.

"'Accordingly in the most favorable soils and situations oaks only were planted at first; but in spots where it was thought doubtful whether oaks would grow, Scotch pines were planted with a small proportion of oaks intermixed; and it was soon found that in many of these spots, even under the disadvantage of inferior soil and greater exposure, such was the benefit derived from the warmth and shelter of the pines, that the oaks far outgrew their neighbors planted in more favorable soils, but without protection. After this the use of Scotch pines become more general; strong belts were planted on the most exposed outsides of the plantation, and also across, at intervals, in lines, towards the most prevailing winds, and from them great benefit was found; but in all cases where oaks were planted actually amongst the pines and surrounded by them, the oaks were found to be much the best.'

"Here we have the best of evidence of the importance of shelter even to an oak in the mild climate of England. And shall we suppose that a fruit tree needs less protection to produce its fruit aside from the mere growth of the tree? If the oak, planted with a view simply to grow timber, must be nursed while young by larches and pines, shall not a pear tree, cultivated for its delicious fruit, have equal care? The answer is plain. Every intelligent cultivator must be aware of the necessity of shelter, and he who expects to succeed without it, is wanting in that experience and knowledge which alone can insure profitable results. It is the key to the cause of many failures, of the death of trees by exposure in winter; of the loss of a crop by the dropping of their blossoms; of the spotting and cracking of the fruit in exposed situations, and in fine, the want of growth and vigor in numerous localities.

"A successful instance of overcoming obstacles of this kind and a decided evidence of the importance of shelter we have in the experiment of Mr. Tudor, at Nahant, Mass., where by means of triple palings of great height the temperature of several acres has been so changed, that while in the coldest winter the earth is frozen only a foot in depth, the soil on the outside freezes three or four feet deep; and in summer when there is scarce wind enough inside to rustle the leaves of the trees, on the outside they were moved with such violence as to dislodge them and even bruise their branches. Here, where scarcely any tree could be made to stand the blast unprotected, in the garden the finest pears are raised in the greatest perfection."—[Hovey's Magazine, Vol. XXI.

promise to pay for it. Why not fruit trees also? What matters it if no pay comes for the first year, or for the first five years, if it comes in good time, and through a long series of years, and with very large interest?

While the trees are young, the ground should be used for some crop which requires the frequent use of the plow, cultivator or hoe, so that it be kept mellow and clean; and the deeper the land is stirred, the better for the trees; but as they advance in size, *deep* stirring is less admissible, and any crop or treatment which serves to keep the land mellow and clean will answer. When too large to admit of easy cultivation, apple orchards may be laid down to grass, with a good share of clover, but *never*, on any account, *allow the sowing of oats or any other small grain.* After being laid down, unless the grass is fed off by sheep (the best way by all odds), the orchard will require manuring. Is it too much to demand double crops, and the main crop a good one, without feeding the land to meet the demand.

A common practice with some who desire to bestow good treatment is, to keep a circle of four to six feet around each tree well hoed and manured after the rest of the ground is in grass. This is good so far as it goes, and is admissible in the case of trees in grass grounds near buildings, where we cannot well dispense with the grass; but for orchard practice, and to cater for the wants of the great majority of the little rootlets, the true feeders of the tree, it would be much better to have an equal space next the tree in grass with the rest of it cultivated, (see page 141, near bottom).

By adopting the plan of planting the trees rather thickly in rows wide enough asunder to admit of easy working with the plow in one direction between them, partial cultivation of the soil may be kept up with ease for some years later than it could if the trees were at equal distances in both directions.

In the case of apple orchards on hill sides, or upon lands too rocky for cultivation, the best method undoubtedly is to occupy them for sheep ranges. Whatever the treatment adopted, let it be remembered that much profit cannot be expected unless the trees are thrifty, nor can we form a correct estimate of the real capabilities of any fruit, as to size, flavor or productiveness from the product of unthrifty trees.

Regarding the propriety of using orchards in grass for sheep ranges, I will add here the testimony of one of the best cultivators in the State, who assured me that one of his orchards now produces *ten times the value* of crop that it did ten years ago, and he attributes the improvement wholly to the fact that of late years it has been pastured with sheep, whereas formerly the grass was mown.

In the case of young apple trees (and sometimes with older ones, but less frequently), there is need of adopting some means to prevent the sheep from barking the trees. A highly esteemed correspondent and skillful cultivator writes, "My course with a young orchard is to mulch the trees well on setting, and continue it for some years. My orchards are pastured with sheep—first coating the trunks with green dung mixed with soapsuds, which is repulsive to the sheep and good for the trees; or else I take five or six laths and tack them, near together, to two strips of leather—stand the laths around the tree (having previously cut them so as to come up only to the branches) and tie them with the leather strings at top and bottom. After pasturing for five years the land becomes so rich the sheep do not like the feed. I then plow carefully and re-seed the land."

Pruning. Concerning the motion and circulation of vegetable fluids, we are very much in the dark. Although volumes have been written on the subject, no one yet knows enough to determine with certainty the best time to prune a tree. Opinions vary, and practice varies greatly. Something has been learned by experience, but what we don't know is greatly more than is known. This much is sure; any needless mutilation of a tree is injurious, and should be carefully avoided. We know, too, that severe pruning may be practised with comparative safety upon young trees; of which we have evidence in the impunity with which they are headed down in the nursery for grafting, or after being budded.

After this heading back pruning, is chiefly required, when young, to give proper form to the top, and this, if well done, obviates the need of any heavy pruning subsequently. An esteemed correspondent writes as follows: "There is one point to which I wish to call the attention of orchardists, viz., that young orchards should be early trained in the way they should grow. I speak feelingly on this point, having had to do with some trees which were sadly neglected until ready to split down, covered with diseased spots, and tops so tangled that it was difficult to get at the (often imperfect) fruit. A well balanced top is attractive to all who have an eye for beauty as well as utility. My pocket knife is an almost indispensable companion in passing among the orchard trees and take off sprouts wrongly inclined, and small branches, or to mark those to be cut off subsequently."

Pruning is an operation where more judgment is required than in almost any other operation in the nursery or orchard. Definite rules cannot be laid down to meet all cases. If the tree is naturally inclined to a close and upright head, as with the Northern Spy apple and the Buffum pear, encourage spreading shoots, and thin the top sufficiently to let in the sun and air. If, on the other hand, it incline to a spreading habit, encourage an upward growth. Aim at symmetry of development. Take away, as early as may be, all cross shoots which by and by may be chafing others.

In proportion as trees grow older, more caution is needful to effect a gradual rather than a sudden reduction of the top. When trees become stunted or unthrifty, a moderate heading back, accompanied with manuring and cultivation, will often work a surprising change for the better. If the fruit of a large tree be poor and it is desired to graft a new top upon it, let it be done gradually, beginning with the centre of the top, or if unthrifty, head in that portion, and after the emission of vigorous shoots, graft into them, and afterward into the others. Fruit, in abundance, can be thus obtained from trees not too old or too far gone, in a much shorter period than by planting young trees.

The following from Mr. Olmstead, in the Horticulturist, is an instance of success attending good management:

"These trees I commenced grafting six years ago last spring. I began on the top and grafted a third each year. I like this method better than any other for grafting large trees, as it gives the scions a good opportunity to get well started. Cutting off and grafting the top first, gives the grafts there the best possible chance, while the necessary reduction of the top throws the sap into the remaining side branches, which fits them well for grafting the following year; and the third year, the lowest branches, being made ready in the same way, may be grafted successfully. By this mode, it will be seen that when the grafts are put in the side branches they are not shaded by the heavy shoots above them and they have an unusual supply of nourishment to carry them forward. Those who have attempted to graft the whole head of a large tree at once are best aware of the great difficulty in the common mode of getting the scions to take on the side limbs.

One of these large trees so treated is probably more than seventy-five years old and has now an entirely new and vigorous head, grafted with an excellent variety. When I began with it, the fruit was fit only for cider, and it was questionable whether the tree should not be cut down. By grafting it in this manner, I have added surprisingly to its value. Two years ago (the bearing year) I obtained from it ten bushels of apples, last year eight bushels, and this year (the sixth from grafting) twenty-eight and a half bushels of excellent fruit. I consider the tree now worth a hundred dollars. The cost of grafting was about five dollars, which was repaid two years ago, the first in which the scion bore fruit."

As to the better season for pruning, may own opinion is that June is preferable for small limbs or shoots, and October when large limbs from any cause *must be removed.* Some, I am aware, differ in this, and think a tree more liable to winter kill if pruned late, but I have never seen evidence of this, while it does seem that although when pruning is done in autumn, large wounds do not heal so readily, yet they do not decay so quickly as if done in summer. Whenever any wound is made which will not readily heal over the first season, it should at once be covered with grafting wax or some other application which resists moisure. Common paint made of linseed oil and ochre answers well. The neatest application, and the one easiest made, is a solution of gum shellac in alcohol, about the thickness of paint, kept in a well corked bottle. A brush with its handle passing through the cork furnishes the best mode of applying it. It dries almost at once, and if need be, a second covering may be applied in a few minutes.

The following remarks are quoted from Downing's Fruits and Fruit Trees of America, a work, which ever since its publication, has been considered high authority:

"Pruning has the power of increasing the vigor of a tree in two ways. If we assume that a certain amount of nourishment is supplied by the roots to all the branches and buds of a tree, by cutting off a part of the branches, at the proper season, we direct the whole supply of nourishment to the remaining portion, which will, consequently, grow with greater luxuriance. Again, when a tree becomes stunted or enfeebled in its growth, the thinness of its inner bark, with its consequent small sap vessels, (which it must be remembered are the principal channels for the passage of the ascending supply of food,) renders the upward and downward circulation tardy, and the growth is small. By heading back or pruning judiciously, all the force of the nourishing fluid is thrown into a smaller number of buds, which make new and luxuriant shoots and larger sap vessels, which afford a ready passage to the fluids, and the tree with these renewed energies will continue in vigor for a long time.

This treatment is especially valuable in the case of small trees of feeble or stunted growth, which are frequently cut back to a single bud, and a new shoot or shoots, full of vigor, gives a healthy habit to the tree. In the nurseries, this practice of heading down unthrifty trees is frequently pursued, and small orchard trees which have become enfeebled may be treated in the same manner; cutting back the head as far as the place where it is wished that new shoots should spring out. *Older trees should be headed back more sparingly*, and their roots should at the same time be assisted by manure.

A judicious pruning to modify the form of our standard trees is nearly all that is required in ordinary practice. All pruning of large branches in healthy trees should be avoided by examining them every season and taking out superfluous shoots while small. Mr. Coxe, the best American author on fruit trees, remarks very truly, "When orchard trees are much pruned, they are apt to throw out numerous [superfluous] suckers from the boughs in the following summer; these should be rubbed off when they first appear, or they may be easily broken off while young and brittle—cutting is apt to increase their number.

When pruning is not required to renovate the vigor of an enfeebled tree, or to regulate its shape—in other words, in the case of a healthy tree which we wish to retain in a state of the greatest luxuriance, health, and vigor, it may be considered *worse than useless*. Bearing in mind that growth is always corresponding to the action of the leaves and branches, if these are in due proportion, and in perfect health, the knife will always be found rather detrimental to luxuriance and constitutional vigor than beneficial. The best season for pruning to promote growth, theoretically, is in autumn soon after the fall of the leaf. Next to this, winter pruning, performed in mild weather, is best, and in orchards this is the season usually most convenient. We should especially avoid pruning at that period in spring when the buds are swelling, and the sap is in full flow, as the loss of sap by bleeding is very injurious to most trees, and in some, brings on a serious and incurable canker in the limbs.

There are advantages and disadvantages attending all seasons of pruning, but our own experience has led us to believe that, practically, *a fortnight before midsummer is the best season, on the whole, for pruning in the Northern and Middle States.* Wounds made at this season heal over freely and rapidly; it is the most favorable time to judge of the shape and balance of the head, and to see at a glance which branches require removal; and all the stock of organizable matter in the tree is directed to the branches that remain."

THE APPLE.

There is little need of extended observations concerning the value and uses of this fruit. As Downing justly remarks, "The apple is the world-renowned fruit of temperate climates." No other fruit is of so universal use or so generally esteemed, and by means of the different varieties it may be enjoyed in perfection throughout the whole year.

Besides its value as a wholesome and grateful dessert fruit, it is still more so for the kitchen. This is very generally acknowledged, and yet, strange to say, and very strange it is too, that although there is quite as much preference in varieties for the latter use as for the former, many persons deem any wilding or natural fruit good enough for cooking. On no point is reform more needed than this. For pies, tarts, sauce, puddings, preserve or jelly; or for drying, or for cider, good fruit is as greatly to be prefered as for the dessert; and choice varieties are just as easily grown as worthless ones.

Another use for which sweet apples may be extensively grown is for feeding to cattle and swine. We have known whole orchards set out for this purpose. It is true the hogs get few of the apples, for none of the orchards were so extensive as to yield much more than found a still more profitable market. J. J. Thomas, author of American Fruit Culturist, remarks: "Its great value and cheapness as food for domestic animals is very imperfectly understood or appreciated. Take, for example, a brief estimate. Where land is worth fifty dollars per acre, forty good productive apple trees may be planted on an acre and brought into bearing for fifty dollars more, making a hundred in all. These will yield, as an average, four hundred bushels annually, or ten bushels per tree if the best cultivation is given. The annual interest on the orchard at six per cent. is six dollars; the annual cultivation will not exceed six more, or twelve dollars as the cost of the whole crop on the trees, or three cents per bushel. The value of sweet apples for cattle and swine has proved to be fully equal to the best root crops. No land owner need therefore fear to plant extensively with a view of being furnished with a copious supply of food for domestic animals, needing not, like other crops, the yearly attention and care of procuring seed and planting."

Obstacles. It may be well here to refer to some of the hindrances to successful culture, among which the ravages of insects hold a prominent place.

The *Apple Worm,* or codling moth—the *Carpocapsa Pomonella* of entomologists—seems on the increase, and in some sections is very troublesome. The perfect insect is a small and very pretty moth, which flies mostly by night and lays its eggs in the blossom end of the young fruit, where it hatches, and the worm burrows to the core, causing the fruit to fall prematurely. The worm then leaves the fruit and selects some crevice in the bark or other place about the tree, where it spins its cocoon, from which the moth usually emerges the next spring. Some of the earlier ones are said to come out the same season. If practicable to allow swine and poultry to run in the orchard, these worms will mostly be destroyed. Many can be caught by placing old cloths in the forks of the tree, in which the worms will collect. Open mouthed bottles filled with a mixture of molasses and water with a little vinegar, hung near the trees will attract multitudes of the moths. For this purpose June or July are the best months. Any method which will dispose of the damaged fruit as soon as it falls, will be found the most effectual means of getting rid of this pest. Removing all rough bark from the stem and limbs, and thus keeping it smooth, deprives them of their favorite lodging places, and so assists in keeping rid of them.

Bark Lice. In some situations, and some kinds much more than others, apple trees are subject to serious injury from a species of *coccus.* The limbs and twigs are sometimes so covered as to give an almost wrinkled look to them. The little oval shells, resembling half a grain of flax seed, are the deposits of eggs, usually thirty or forty in each. The insect itself is very small, and looks at first like a speck of bluish mould. They begin to hatch about the twenty-fifth of May and finish about the tenth of June. They are active only a short time, but they do a good deal of mischief in a little while, for we find the tree stunted in its growth, and its juices apparently poisoned, for the young wood beneath them, upon being cut into, is found stained. It is important to exterminate them while the tree is young, or upon their first appearance, as they multiply with great rapidity and are soon where it is difficult to reach them. If *applied in June,* I have found no difficulty in destroying them by applying whale oil soap dissolved in water, a pound to a gallon; but at any other season they resist obstinately. Dr. Fitch recommends boiling leaf tobacco in lye until reduced to a pulp, and mixing soap until of the consistency of paint. At the West, tar and linseed oil has been recommended. But the only reliable method is to attack them at the proper time, i. e., just after the eggs hatch, and then I have no doubt that even common soft soap and water would be effectual. It would appear that in other sections it is a worse evil than here. Dr. Fitch, of New York, says: "The bark louse is, on the whole, the most pernicious and destructive to the apple tree of any insect in our country. Everywhere in the Northern States it infests the orchards to a grievous extent, causing the death of many trees and impairing the health and vigor of many more. * * * Badly as this insect is infesting our orchards in the State of New York, it is scourging our Western neighbors far more severely. In those districts bordering on Lake Michigan, in particular, it is at the present time making most appalling havoc, surpassing anything hitherto recorded of this species. Scarcely a tree is free from them, and unless measures for destroying the insect are resorted to the tree is sure to perish within a few years after it is invaded."

The *tent caterpillar* has been very troublesome for a year or two past. The eggs are contained in cylindrical clusters, which encircle the smaller twigs and contain several hundred eggs. These clusters are covered with a tough leathery varnished covering which protects them from the weather. They may be easily removed by cutting off the twigs; or *as soon* as they are hatched in spring they may be brushed off, or destroyed, by soap suds or lime wash applied with a swab on a pole. If neglected they grow rapidly, and strip the leaves and thus seriously check growth.

The Borer (*Saperda bivittata*) is the most destructive insect we have to contend with and this, by a little pains-taking *at the proper time,* may be eradicated, or prevented by precautionary measures. In my last report is an article by Mr. Currier, pages 25, 26, in which this insect and the remedies are so ably treated as to leave little to say. I will add, however, that contrary to the common impression, the eggs are sometimes laid at several feet from the ground and not always near the ground. In an orchard near Bangor I saw a tree the past summer on which, in a space of a few inches, near where its largest branches started from the stem, not less than twenty of these little grubs were found from eggs laid the season previous.

Dr. Fitch says, "A person visiting me a few months since remarked that he would himself be willing to pay me a hundred dollars if, by my researches, I would discover some effectual method of protecting apple trees from the borer. Without claiming the reward offered, I informed him I had already experimented and would give him the very remedy he wished; if he would rub the bark of his trees with soap the latter part of May each year I would guarantee that not one of these borers would ever touch them."

Harris says, "The trees and shrubs principally attacked by this borer are the apple, the quince, mountain ash, hawthorn, and other thorns, and the Juneberry or shadbush. Our native thorns and Aronias are its natural food; for I have discovered the larvæ in the stems of these shrubs and have repeatedly found the beetles upon them eating the leaves in June and July. It is in these months that the eggs are deposited, being laid upon the bark, near the root, during the night."

Renovation of Injured Trees.

The winter of 1856-7 was more injurious in its effects upon trees in Maine than any other for a generation past. Not only were fruit trees damaged extensively, but I have seen in various parts of the State, beeches, maples, oaks and elms, which were killed outright. Many fruit trees which survived the first shock succumbed in the course of two or three winters following. Some yet survive, and are mere cumberers of the ground. Let such be cut down, burnt, and the ashes given to new orchards; for the ashes of the apple tree furnish *precisely the inorganic matter* which living apple trees need to appropriate to build up their own structures. Many others not only survive but seem to be gaining strength and vigor. It is an important question what shall be done to assist them?

A question of the circular before referred to was directed to this point, and the replies are in nearly all cases substantially the same, or very similar. One says, "Remove decayed wood, and suckers, *except such as are wanted to form a new top.* Shoal plowing, with moderate dressings, annually or biennially, of compost made of two parts muck and one part barn manure. Ashes, lime and superphosphate are often used to great advantage. Pasturing the orchard with sheep has been of signal benefit in my experience."

Another says, "Plow shoal, trim the dead limbs off, shorten in the live ones, scrape and wash with soap suds or some other alkaline wash, dig around the trees three or four times a year, and be sure to apply some good compost manure, and one calculated to be an amendment to the soil. Old trees bearing poor fruit, yet with sound trunks, may be grafted as soon as you get new shoots of proper size. To renovate neglected orchards requires good attention and skilful cultivation, in order to be a profitable operation. The ground ought to be cultivated and manured but not cropped with anything but apples."

A third says, "Prune, cultivate, mulch and manure."

A fourth gives judicious directions rather more in detail:

"In regard to the question of the best mode for reviving old decaying orchards, from what little experience I have had, would recommend shoal plowing, with care not to bark the roots nor bruise the bodies of the trees, and with a hoe remove the sward from the body of the tree. Then harrow and level off the furrows as well as may be, and then mulch the ground all over a few inches thick with wet strawy manure, swamp muck, or with partially rotted forest leaves. The last named is rather to be preferred as it obstructs the grass from growing more than the others and keeps the ground moister—a very important consideration—by reason of the leaves lying closer to it. Remove all the dead limbs from the tree and crop off some of the outer branches or extremities of the live limbs. Sow no grass nor any other small seeds on the ground, nor suffer any live animal to run in the orchard, and by this means, if the trees have not suffered by having their large limbs cut off at the body, thus producting decay of the tree, they will soon show a vigor of growth and yield of fruit that will richly repay the husbandman for all his labor and care.

"I find no difficulty in raising pears any more than in raising apples, but I find a pear or an apple tree will no better flourish in a state of utter neglect than a hill of corn, except that the tree is somewhat more hardy in its nature than a stalk of corn; and I would as soon plant corn in an old, worn-out mowing field, as to set it out to an orchard, and leave it without any other attention except to see it die."

The replies received which differ materially from the above are as follows:

One says, "To renovate a decayed orchard, I would cut out all decayed wood, fence it well, then turn in as many hogs as could well live in it. If kept short through the summer they will work over the surface pretty throughly. Top dress occasionally with chip manure, &c. Orchards plowed and cropped every season are likely to decay." (Is this so, unless an unripe growth of wood is caused by over manuring?)

Another says, "Scrape off moss and decayed bark. Manure as much as possible with animal manure, fish, flesh and bone dust, either put under the sod, disturbing the roots as little as possible, or covered with muck if more convenient."

Fish and flesh are doubtless good applications for old orchards, *to a moderate extent.*

A fourth writes as follows: "When I first read over your circular, I thought my experience in *fruit culture*, or rather *orcharding*, was so limited that I had nothing worthy to offer, but on a reperusal the other evening it occurred that I might give my experience as a suggestion on the *renovation* of old orchards. The method was accidental rather than theoretical, in the beginning, but it works so well that now I practice it myself and recommend it to others.

"When the limbs of a tree begin to decay seriously, I let it alone entirely, and it soon throws out shoots along the base of the limbs. These I let grow from three to five years, when I prune, selecting such as are the thriftiest and will make the best top to remain, and cut out the rest, together with the dead wood. In a few years you have a young thrifty top, bearing as well as ever, and the fruit is improved in size as compared with the old tree. I have a pear tree, a very fine seedling, that has renewed itself in this way the second time and the twigs are now bending under their load."

A fifth writes—"Where trees show strong symptoms of constitutional disease and decay, cut them down and cultivate the ground thoroughly for at least two years and transplant young trees.

There is no difficulty in raising a tree on the same spot if the ground has been carefully cultivated and well manured previously. If an orchard has been subject to the plow in previous years, plow again and cultivate with root crops of some kind. If the ground be naturally heavy, turn the furrows towards the tree so as to form a dead furrow between the rows. Clean the bark, cut out dead limbs, and wait patiently for new branches to grow. The main point is so to cultivate as to produce new wood for a series of years. Still, in a majority of cases, planting young trees between the old ones is preferable, for the young tree will be old enough to bear with profit as soon as an old tree will be renovated for the same purpose. A judicious combination of the two methods may be the best in many cases."

In connection with the opinion last quoted, I would remark that the principle upon which the practice of *rotation* is based, viz., that any crop cultivated for a succession of years upon the same spot tends to exhaust the soil of those mineral elements which that crop specially requires, is believed to hold good in regard to trees. In the operations of nature, when one growth of trees is cut down or destroyed by fire, not the same, but a different class of trees takes its place; and the policy of planting new orchards on the site of old ones is deemed to be of doubtful expediency. It is true that, with good culture of the ground, young trees will grow pretty well for a series of years. But during thirty, fifty or more years previous a severe draft was made upon the soil for those mineral ingredients which go to made up the inorganic portion of the tree and for the leaves which have been annually shed by it, to say nothing of the fruit also; and whether such an orchard can be as productive and profitable as if planted on soil previously devoted to other uses, is so far from being certain or probable that I would greatly prefer another location, if a suitable one exists on the farm.

Selection of Varieties.

No one cause has produced more disappointment in orcharding than the planting out of varieties too tender for our climate. Many persons, on beginning an orchard, have procured sorts which they know to be satisfactory elsewhere, thoughtlessly supposing that a fruit good in one place is alike good in other places. While some thus selected have succeeded well, others have not. As instances in point, we may mention the Baldwin apple and the Bartlett pear. The Baldwin is most at home in Massachusetts, where it has scarce a fault as a late keeping profitable market apple; but here it is not so hardy, and succeeds only in favorable situations, or when grown by being grafted into the limbs of hardy, well-grown trees. Out of the hundreds of thousands of young trees of this variety, budded or grafted in the nursery, which have been planted out in Maine during the past twenty years, scarcely one in ten, probably even a less proportion, is now in a sound, healthy condition, and by far the greater number have been killed outright; yet it would seem we are slow to profit by experience; for at the present time there are few persons proposing to plant trees who do not call for nursery grown Baldwins. Three winters out of four, these may escape serious injury, but this is not enough. To be satisfactory they should do this in twenty-four out of twenty-five years. So, too, with pears, we have followed too blindly in the lead of cultivators in other States, and the Bartlett has been more sought for and planted than any other. This is described in nearly all books on fruit culture as a hardy variety, and so it is where the writers had seen it; but except under very favorable circumstances, as in city gardens or other warm, well sheltered spots, with a dry subsoil too, it is quite unreliable in Maine.

If we would have fruit in abundance we must be content to learn what kinds are hardy and otherwise suited to our wants, and confine extensive culture to these. We may and ought to try on a limited scale such as give promise of excellence, as among them, doubtless, some prizes will be found, and in this way we may extend our lists until they embrace as great a variety as can be desired.

From the nature of the case, it is impossible for any one to give a list of fruits equally adapted to the different sections even of a single State. The orchardist may learn a great deal from a critical examination of the successes and failures of others in his immediate vicinity. It is not necessary that these neighbors be scientific culturists in order to give valuable testimony. What is most needed are facts, and in gathering these we should note carefully, not only what varieties succeed or fail, but also the kind of soil, the exposure, the shelter, the culture, and as far as may be, all the conditions, which, not less than the inherent qualities of any variety itself, tend to bring about the result.

Some kinds of fruits are pretty uniformly good in a variety of soils and amid other differing conditions. Other kinds depend for a profitable degree of success upon the existence of some one condition, or of several conditions, which are not essential to others.

To illustrate the influence of one of these conditions, viz., the character of the soil, let me state a fact observed in Kennebec county. Extending from the town of Monmouth, through Winthrop and Sidney to West Waterville, there is a formation of pyritiferous slate. In places, the rock is so strongly impregnated with sulphuret of iron, that copperas has been made from it. The soil, of course, partakes of the nature of the rock, which, it may be observed, decomposes more rapidly than many others. This ridge of land is remarkable for the ease and abundance with which the Roxbury Russet apple is grown upon it, and also for the size, fairness and excellence of the fruit. I was informed that although the trees were not often overloaded, they bore well and regularly, every year, so that, taking a series of years, more bushels were obtained of this Russet, than could be from the Baldwin or from any other sort. Large orchards are there to be found consisting almost entirely of this variety, which, as may well be supposed under the circumstances, is found to be the most profitable for extensive culture.

On either side, and even within a short distance of this ridge overlying the copperas rock, it is not so, and other varieties are more productive and profitable than the Russet. Cases so clearly marked, and distinctly defined, as the above, are not frequent, but something like it is by no means uncommon in many sections, and a study of the facts, in any given location, before deciding what sorts to grow most extensively, will be likely to lead to important and valuable results.

The circular before referred to, as having been sent to orchardists in various parts of the State, contained several inquiries as to the best apples for quality and for profit. In response to one as to the two best summer or early apples, Bell's Early was recommended by the largest number. This is doubtless owing in part to the fact that it has been more widely disseminated than any other as good. Next to this, and with nearly as many voices for them, are the Red Astrachan and Early Sweet Bough, each having an equal number, and Williams' Favorite had nearly as many. Next to this, Early Harvest, then High Top Sweet, and then a few for Summer

Sweet and August Sweet, intended probably either for Early Bough or High Top Sweet. Two mention Moses Wood, and one each, Barn Apple, (probably Early Harvest,) Summer Queen and River.

For autumn apples, the largest number recommend the Porter, with nearly as many for Gravenstein, about half as many for Winthrop Greening, (some calling it Lincoln Pippin, and most of them from Kennebec county). Next to this, Jewett's Red or Nodhead, then Hubbardston Nonsuch and Duchess of Oldenburg; one or two each for Fall Greening, Jersey Greening, Fall Baldwin, (meaning Kilham Hill,) Red Pearmain, Garden Royal, Aunt Hannah, Eaton's Seedling, Dean or Nine Ounce apple, Somerset, and Gloria Mundi, wrongly so called, the apple meant being a rich, sweet yellow fruit, extensively grown in Androscoggin county and popular in Lewiston market.

For the best winter, twelve named the Baldwin; eleven the Rhode Island Greening; nine, Hubbardston Nonsuch; six, Jewett's Red; five, Bellflower; four, each, Roxbury Russet and Minister; three, each, Golden Russet, Northern Spy and Ribston Pippin, with one or two each for Nonsuch, (Old Nonsuch or Canada Red,) American Golden Russet, Golden Pearmain (?), Blue Pearmain, Black Oxford, Spitzenburg.

For the best winter Sweet, Tolman's had a large majority and Danvers came next, few others being named at all.

For the three named as worthy extensive cultivation for profit, Baldwin, Greening and Hubbardston Nonsuch had the largest number; then others in the following order: Bell's Early, Gravenstein, Minister, Jewett's Red, Roxbury Russet, and Black Oxford, with one or two each for Williams', Red Astrachan, Sweet Bough, Porter, Blue Pearmain, Gloria Mundi, (the sweet apple before alluded to, true name unknown,) Porter, Nonsuch, (old,) Runnells', and Golden Russet. The recommendations of early fruits for culture with a view to profit, came chiefly from the neighborhood of good markets, and suggests the remark that they have been altogether too much neglected heretofore, thousands of barrels every year being brought from other States and sold at higher prices than winter apples bring, with all the care required before they go to market. It is true they require rather higher culture, but they pay well for it, if the market is large enough, and not too distant.

For the best single variety for profit, Baldwin had the most votes, then others in the following order: Hubbardston Nonsuch, Jewett's Red, Bell's Early, Williams', Red Astrachan, Roxbury Russet.

The replies received were not so numerous as was anticipated, and not all which came, were from persons in possession of extensive collections, which may account for the fact that so few of what may be deemed the newer varieties were even mentioned.

It is gratifying to learn that the Baldwin has so well withstood, or recovered from, the effects of the severe winters a few years ago. It is almost exclusively grown by grafting into limbs, and by this method proves hardy enough to command much confidence as a profitable variety for extensive culture.

Descriptive List of Apples.

The varieties described below are some of those which are believed to have been sufficiently tested to enable us to speak of them with comparative confidence. By far the greater number of those known to be cultivated in the State, or even of those which have fruited on our own grounds, are purposely omitted; and this for a variety of reasons. Concerning some we have contradictory testimony from cultivators in different sections, and sometimes, too, from those even on adjacent farms. Tastes differ also, as well as fruits, or opinions regarding them. We have known one cultivator to procure scions for grafting, from the limbs cut off by another as unworthy of cultivation. Concerning a portion we have too limited a knowledge, others are open to the objection of succeeding much better in some localities than in others; some are known to be uncertain bearers, or variable in quality, and of others still the omission is justified by seemingly sufficient reasons.

The variation, in most fruits, and especially in regard to quality, which is due to soil, season, culture, health and vigor of the tree, and other causes, is such that it is really no easy matter to do full justice in each case; and descriptions should be relied upon chiefly to give a general idea of size, color, form, and other characteristics, rather than minute accuracy in all respects.

Many of the illustrations, both of apples and pears, are borrowed from Hovey's Magazine of Horticulture, an excellent monthly periodical published in Boston, and largely devoted to fruit culture, and they are believed to be more than usually accurate in delineation.

American Summer Pearmain. This apple though but little disseminated in this State, has, I believe, wherever tried, proved to be of the finest quality. Medium size, rather oblong, skin smooth, yellow, mostly covered with red; flesh remarkably tender, juicy and very rich, excellent for the dessert and good for all uses. The tree is a slow grower in the nursery, but makes a very handsome and hardy tree in the orchard. Productive; begins to ripen about the middle of September and lasts a month or more.

Aunt Hannah. A golden yellow apple, sprinkled with dots, sometimes a little russeted. Of medium size, nearly globular, a little flattened. Flesh yellow, fine grained, crisp, juicy, and of a rich, peculiar flavor. It succeeds well as a nursery tree, growth moderate. Tree hardy. Season, December to February. Originated on the farm of Hannah Perkins, Topsfield, Mass.

Autumn Strawberry—*Late Strawberry.* One of the finest flavored autumn apples in cultivation; has few equals. Fruit of medium size, slightly conical and faintly ribbed, the surface mostly covered with small broken streaks of bright red. Stalk slender, nearly an inch long. Flesh yellowish, very tender, and juicy, rich, subacid, excellent. Tree very hardy, grows freely in the nursery and pretty well in the orchard, but does not attain great size. A good and regular bearer. End of September and October. It is called "late" in distinction from the Early Strawberry, which is a fine fruit, but too tender to succeed here.

Baldwin. A native of Massachusetts, too well known to need description. As an orchard tree, with the exception of hardiness, it possesses nearly all the requisites to constitute it the most profitable fruit to grow extensively for market: great productiveness, good size, color, quality, and keeping well into spring without extra care; and it is hardy enough to succeed generally in favorable situations *if grafted into the limbs of grown trees, but as a nursery tree it is not to be relied upon.* Mr. S. N. Taber, for many years a nurseryman in Kennebec county, and whose opportunities for observation in all parts of the State have since been very extensive, writes, "The Baldwin is only safe when grafted into bearing trees. Have never seen ten profitable trees of this variety in this State which were raised in the nursery." The Baldwin is more extensively grown in this State than any other variety, and it suffered more in the winter of 1856–7 than any other, and somewhat, also, during two hard winters since then. Notwithstanding this injury, however, probably a large majority of farmers in the central and southern parts of the State still rely upon it as their most profitable variety. An apple possessing all the good qualities of the Baldwin, connected with entire hardiness in the tree, in the climate of Maine, is a great desideratum. It is supposed by some that there are several varieties of the Baldwin, but there seems no doubt that the differences which exist, are due to variation in soil or seasons, or from a peculiar influence in some cases from the stock upon which it is grafted.

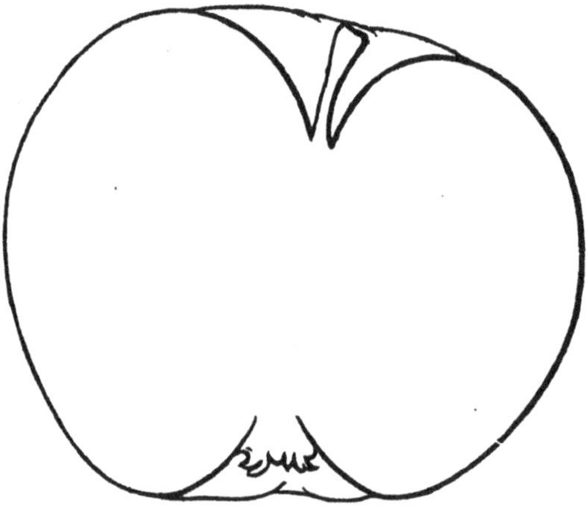

Benoni.

Benoni. One of the best early apples, ripening with the Williams' or soon after, and of decidedly better quality. Medium size, fair, smooth skin, yellow, mostly covered with deep red. Flesh yellowish, fine, crisp, tender, juicy, sprightly and rich. Tree a vigorous, upright grower and bears well, mostly in alternate years.

Ben Davis. Introduced from Kentucky and but little disseminated as yet. So far as proved, it is of vigorous growth, abundantly productive every year, keeps as late as almost any, and so hardy that scions inserted in the spring of 1856 wholly escaped injury in the following winter, a circumstance true of very few sorts. In size rather above medium, roundish, narrowing a little towards the eye. Skin splashed and striped with red, and bright red next the sun. Flavor good, rather acid. It may be doubtful whether our season be long enough to ripen it fully, but its promise is such as to warrant a fair trial.

BELL'S EARLY. A popular apple in all parts of the State, and grown to a considerable extent under several names. It may be the same as the *Sops of Wine* of Downing and the *Red Shropshire-vine* of Cole. Of medium size, roundish ovate. Skin reddish striped or splashed with dull deep red in the sun. Flesh whitish, sometimes stained with red, tender, subacid, with a very pleasant flavor. Tree very hardy, a rapid grower and good bearer, but not remarkable for longevity. August and September.

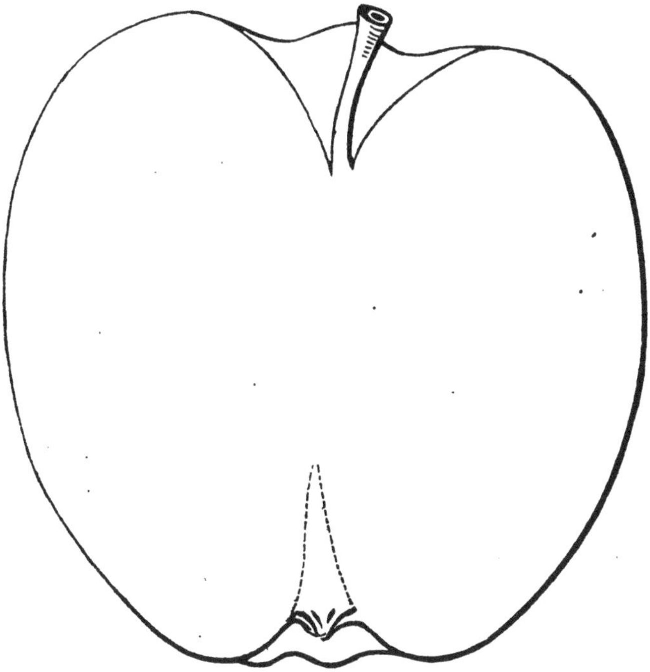

BELLFLOWER.

BELLFLOWER, YELLOW. A large, handsome, well known winter apple, of superior quality, oblong, rather irregular, yellow, with a blush cheek next the sun; the flesh tender, juicy, and crisp, with a sprightly, pleasant acid flavor. The tree is hardy, of vigorous growth, spreading habit, the limbs sometimes bending to the ground with their burden of fruit. In some localities it is very productive and in such it may be planted freely. In others it proves to be a shy bearer. Mr. F. P. Sharp, of Woodstock, N. B., near Houlton, informed me that although the wood was hardy with him, the blossom buds were either winter killed, or so badly injured that it bore nothing, while in Nova Scotia it was a favorite sort for productiveness as well as for quality. It is there known as Bishop's Pippin.

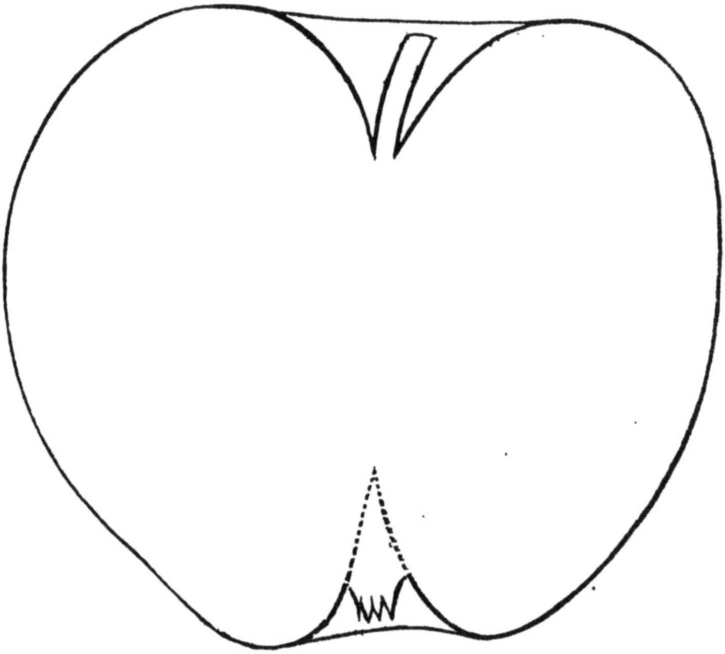

BOUGH.

BOUGH—*Early Sweet Bough—Large Yellow Bough.* A fine early apple, and one of the best of its season. Succeeds well in many parts of the State. Above medium size, sometimes quite large, oblong ovate. Skin pale yellow. Flesh white, tender, juicy, sweet and rich. Tree of moderate vigor and productive. August.

BLAKE. Originated in Westbrook, Cumberland, county. Medium to large. Roundish form, varying somewhat; greenish yellow—

yellow at maturity. Stem three fourths of an inch long, set in a deep russetted cavity, has a few russetted warts. Flesh firm, fine, crisp, juicy, subacid and well flavored; good for cooking or dessert. October to January.

BLACK OXFORD. A medium sized, roundish, deep red apple of very solid texture; mild, subacid, pleasant flavor, and keeping easily into late spring or summer. Though never rich, juicy or tender, its hardiness and productiveness are such that by many it is highly esteemed as a profitable sort to grow for market: with others it is much less valued. February to June.

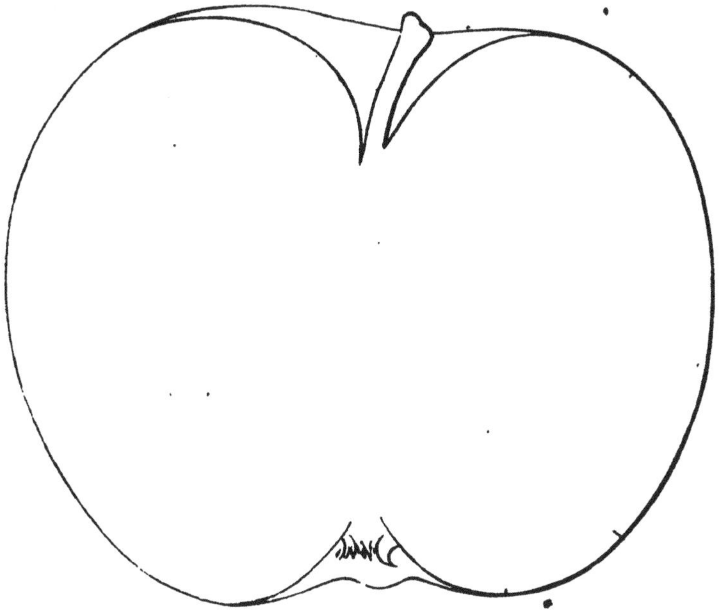

BLUE PEARMAIN.

BLUE PEARMAIN. A well known deep purplish red apple, covered with bloom, in use from December to February. The fruit is not strictly first rate, nor the tree very productive, yet from its great hardiness, its succeding in a diversity of soils and situations where others thrive less, and a frequent habit of bearing most when other apples are scarce, it is often a desirable variety to cultivate.

BRIGGS' AUBURN. Rather large and of flattened form, bright yellow skin, with a little blush. A pleasant subacid fruit which originated in Androscoggin county. The tree is very hardy and productive. September and October.

Cathead. By this name is known a popular early autumn apple in Portland market; introduced into the vicinity of North Yarmouth many years ago from New Hampshire, and quite unlike any one described in fruit books under this name. Rather large, oblong, narrowing to the eye, where it is slightly ribbed. Skin yellow, nearly covered with small dots of bright red, intermingled with a few stripes and splashes of the same. Flesh yellowish, sometimes stained with red, and of pleasant flavor. The tree is vigorous, very hardy and productive. September.

Calef's Sweet—*Magoun Apple*. Originated on the farm of Robert Calef, Kingston, N. H. Large, yellow, roundish, flattened, with some gray dots and crimson specks. Flesh white, very rich and sweet, of peculiarly fine, delicate texture. November to January.

Duchess of Oldenburg.

Duchess of Oldenburg. A Russian fruit of good size, fair quality, great beauty, extremely hardy and immensely productive. Fruit rather large, roundish. Skin pale yellow, finely streaked, and washed with bright red, with a faint bloom over it. Flesh crisp, tender, juicy, with a brisk acid flavor, of tolerable quality for the dessert and excellent for all other uses. September.

In southern Maine, the Duchess is apt to fall off before ripening, but in this, and in other respects also, it improves as we go north. It is better in Kennebec county than in York, and better in Aroostook than in Kennebec. Its value in the extreme north may be judged of by the experience of Mr. Sharp, of Woodstock, New Brunswick, twelve miles from Houlton, Maine, who informed me that out of four hundred varieties of grafted apples proved by him, rather less than a dozen succeeded, and of these the Duchess stood decidedly at the head of the list. In that vicinity it is known under the name of "The New Brunswicker." The only fault I heard ascribed to it there, was by one who objected to the necessity of building a scaffold about his trees every year—an objection not ill grounded, for unlike other apples, an excessive crop does not prevent this sort from bearing heavily the next year. Such excessive production, however, tells upon the growth of the tree. Where all the strength is given to fruit bearing, we cannot expect much growth of wood, and I do not recollect ever to have seen in Maine or New Brunswick a tree of this variety of large size, unless grafted into a tree already well grown. Had we other varieties combining choice quality and late keeping with the hardiness and half the productiveness of this, our northern counties would have little left to ask for in regard to apple culture.

Danvers Winter Sweet. A choice, late keeping, yellow, sweet apple from Massachusetts, which usually proves one of the best. It is of good size, smooth, fair, bakes well, is in condition for use all winter, and often until April. It succeeds well in the nursery. The tree is a vigorous and rapid grower, hardy and productive.

Domine. Of medium size and flattened form, the skin yellow with stripes and splashes of red in the sun, and is covered with pretty large russet colored specks. Flesh white, tender and juicy, with a sprightly agreeable flavor. February to May.

This fruit has not been much disseminated in this State, but in every instance where I have seen it, has given a high degree of satisfaction. The tree is of rapid growth and very productive, the limbs sometimes bending to the ground with the weight of fruit crowded upon them in continuous clusters. In my orchard it has also proved one of the hardiest, and is deemed worthy of more extended trial.

EARLY HARVEST. When well grown this is the very best early apple we have, so far as quality is concerned. Round, sometimes a

EARLY HARVEST.

little flattened; the skin bright yellow in the sun, pale in the shade, and smooth; flesh white, tender, juicy, and crisp, with a rich subacid flavor. The tree succeeds poorly in the nursery. Although hardy it is not a vigorous grower and requires high cultivation, as without it the fruit is inferior and often imperfect, sometimes spotted or cracked. It is a fruit of which one desires a tree or two for home use, but is not a profitable market variety. End of July and August.

ESOPUS SPITZENBURG. Above medium size, oblong, tapering to the eye, mostly a rich red, with distinct gray specks. Flesh yellow, crisp, of rich flavor and not surpassed in excellence by any other. The tree is not long lived, is rather a feeble and slow grower and less productive here than in New York, whence it was received and where it is extensively cultivated and ranks best. Succeeds best grafted into grown trees. Two or three other ap-

ples are grown to some extent under the name of Spitzenburg, **which** are much inferior in quality to the above.

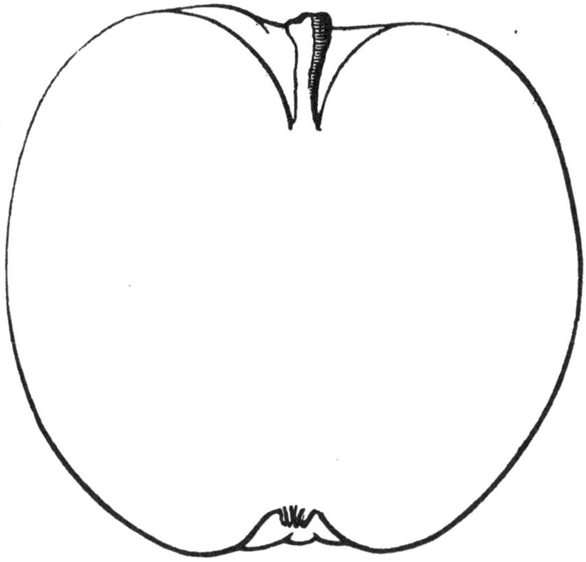

ESOPUS SPITZENBURG.

FAMEUSE.

FAMEUSE—*Snow Apple—Pomne de Niege.* This is probably of

French origin and was carried to Canada at a very early date, from whence we have received it. It occupies the first rank among Canadian apples. Fruit of medium size, or rather less, deep crimson; flesh snowy white, tender, and of delicious flavor. Tree of vigorous growth, succeeds well in the nursery and bears early and abundantly; is adapted to a variety of soils and deserves extensive cultivation in all parts of the State. Is perfectly hardy, even in Aroostook county and in New Brunswick. November to February.

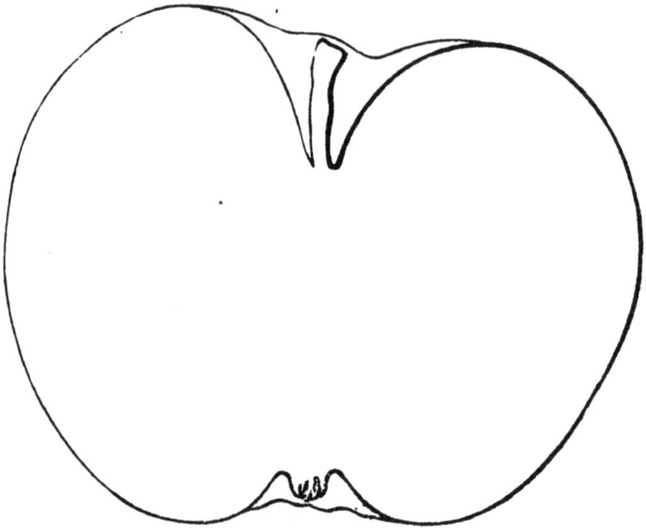

FOUNDLING.

FOUNDLING. Originated in Groton, Mass. The tree is of a spreading habit, hardy, a good grower and regular bearer. Fruit large, ribbed. Skin greenish yellow, striped and shaded with deep red. Flesh yellow, tender, and juicy, with a rich aromatic flavor. One of the best of its season, which is from the end of August to October. Has been grown in the State for twenty years or more, but is not so well known or widely cultivated as it deserves to be.

FALL ORANGE—*Holden Pippin*. Large, roundish, oblong; skin yellow, sometimes a brownish cheek next the sun and sprinkled with dark crimson dots. Stalk very short, inserted in a narrow, deep cavity. Flesh white, very tender, juicy, rather acid for some palates, but of pleasant flavor. Excellent for cooking. A very strong erect grower, hardy and productive. October and November.

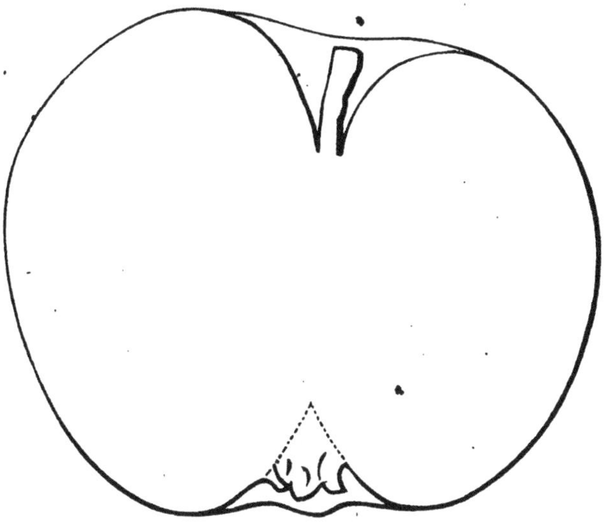

GRAVENSTEIN.

GRAVENSTEIN. This apple is more cosmopolitan than any other within my knowledge. That local character which attaches to nearly all varieties of the apple, and by which their desirableness, whether in regard to hardihood, or thrift, or quality, or production, is confined within moderate limits, sometimes to very narrow ones, seems to attach in a very slight degree, if at all, to the Gravenstein. Like the Green Gage among plums, it seems to be at home and to give general satisfaction wherever it is cultivated. It is a native of Germany, and is considered the best of northern Europe, and I know of no section of this country where it does not take a high rank, and by many is esteemed the very best autumn apple. Fruit large, rather flattened and a little angular. Skin yellow, streaked and dashed with bright red and orange. Flesh tender, crisp, very juicy and high flavored. September and October. The tree is of thrifty and vigorous growth, and productive. In regard to hardiness, Mr. A. Cushman, of Golden Ridge, Aroostook county, showed it to me in his orchard as healthy and sound as any. He esteemed this and the Duchess of Oldenburg as the two best for autumn. The only drawback to its value which I am aware of is, that in some situations (perhaps owing to stagnant moisture in the soil or subsoil) it is liable to a malignant, cankery disease which affects the wood, and soon destroys the tree.

GARDEN ROYAL.

GARDEN ROYAL. Below medium size; skin greenish russetty yellow, mostly covered with dull crimson and with large light specks upon it. Flesh yellow, very fine and tender; if fully ripened on the tree, almost melting like a peach, with a delicious aromatic flavor. With as good culture as it deserves it bears well, but is a very moderate grower, unless grafted into vigorous trees. Indispensable in a good private collection. Within a few years it has appeared in the markets of Portland in considerable quantities. September.

GARDEN SWEET. Medium size, slightly oblong; stem, short; skin greenish yellow, with blush next the sun, and dotted with light specks. Flesh yellowish white, juicy, tender, sweet and good flavored. Very hardy, thrifty and productive; succeeds admirably both in the nursery and orchard, in a variety of soils, and in many situations where few others thrive as well. The fruit, too, is uniformly fair and the tree heavily productive, chiefly in alternate years. From the middle of September, it is in use for two months or more; might be grown profitably merely for feeding swine.

GOLDEN RUSSET—*Bullock's Pippin*—*American Golden Russet.* There are several "Golden Russets" grown in the State which it is not easy to identify as distinct varieties, though probably two or three may prove to be so, and not merely differing by reason of

GOLDEN RUSSET.

soil or location. The trees are usually of fair vigor and productiveness, in favorable situations bearing well. Skin golden russet with a reddish cheek in the sun. Flesh yellowish white and tender, with a mild pleasant flavor. January to May.

GOLDEN BALL. This variety was introduced from Connecticut more than forty years ago. About twenty years ago some parties extolled it highly and it was pretty widely disseminated, but it has not given much satisfaction. It is large, handsome and good, and and the tree hardy and vigorous, but generally a shy bearer and unprofitable.

HIGH-TOP SWEET—*Summer Sweet.* An old favorite variety which originated in Plymouth, Mass. The tree is of vigorous, upright growth and productive. I found it hardy, succeeding well as far north as Patten, on the Aroostook road. The fruit is rather below medium size, bright yellow, very sweet, pleasant and rich, almost aromatic. Two or three other apples somewhat resembling it in fruit and growth of tree are grown under the same name. August.

Hubbardston Nonsuch. Origin, Hubbardston, Mass. One of the best and most popular late autumn and early winter apples, and worthy of extensive culture. Fruit of large size, roundish, a little oblong, and slightly narrowed near the eye. Skin yellowish, mostly covered with stripes and splashes of red, and often some-

Hubbardston Nonsuch.

what russetty. Flesh yellowish white, juicy and tender, with a mild agreeable flavor, mingling sweetness with acidity. The tree is hardier than the Baldwin, and generally hardy enough; a good grower and very productive. Recommended for extensive cultivation. Mr. Taber says he has sometimes seen thrifty trees killed to the scion, apparently in consequence of being grafted with this sort—an observation I have never known made by others. November to February.

Haskell's Sweet—*Sassafras Sweet.* A rather large, flattish, sweet apple of excellent quality, which originated in Ipswich, Mass. Skin yellowish, with faint blush next the sun. Flesh tender, juicy, sweet and rich. Tree hardy, vigorous and productive; bears young. October.

JEWETT'S RED—*Nodhead.* This apple originated in Hollis, N. H., in which vicinity, as well as in parts of this State, it has been long cultivated under the name of Nodhead. It is one of the best and

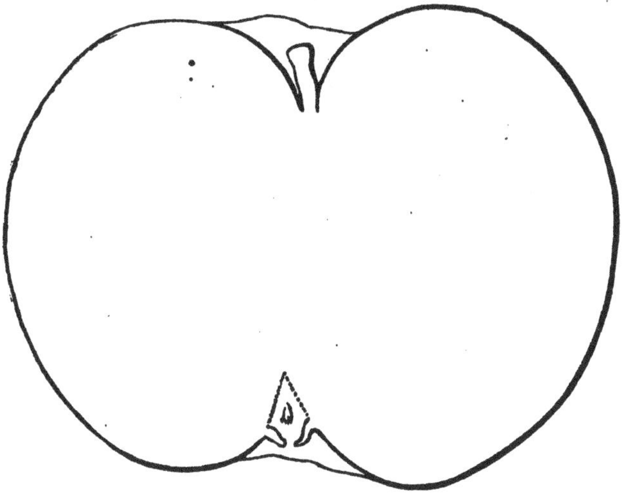

JEWETT'S RED.

most popular late autumn apples, and may be kept into winter, but with loss of its peculiarly high, rich flavor. The tree is hardy and very productive, and were it not for the extreme tenderness of the skin, rendering it very liable to injury from insects and thus causing a large proportion of the apples to be knobby and unsaleable, it would be one of the most profitable for the market. Medium size, oblate; skin greenish, striped and shaded with crimson. Stem short, set in a small, shallow cavity. Flesh yellowish, very tender, almost melting, with a peculiarly rich, mild, sprightly flavor—requires good cultivation.

JABE. Originated on the old Perley farm in Boxford, Mass. Medium size, flattened—one of the handsomest of apples. Skin smooth, light straw color, with a beautiful blush cheek, or if not well exposed to the sun, with crimson spots. Stem rather more than an inch long, set in a small, rather deep cavity. Flesh yellowish white, very fine grained, tender, juicy, melting and rich, with a rather peculiar, pleasant, subacid flavor. Thrifty, hardy and a regular and abundant bearer, giving full crops every year. End of September to early in November.

JABE.

JEFFERIS. Of medium size, flattened form. Skin yellow, splashed and striped with crimson. Flesh white, very tender,

JONATHAN.

crisp, juicy, with a rich, subacid flavor. A fair, handsome apple, ripening in September and October, which originated in Pennsylvania, and has proved of first rate excellence here. The tree is hardy, scions which were received and set in the spring of 1856, having received no injury in the severe winter which followed. Young shoots slender, growth moderate; productive—one of the best of its season.

JONATHAN. A medium sized, handsome dessert fruit, introduced to notice by the late Judge Buel. In flavor and excellence, it rivals, and much resembles, the Esopus Spitzenburg. Form, roundish ovate; skin smooth, yellow, deepening to bright red in the sun; flesh tender, juicy and very rich. The tree is hardy, growth moderate, young shoots slender, productive. January to April.

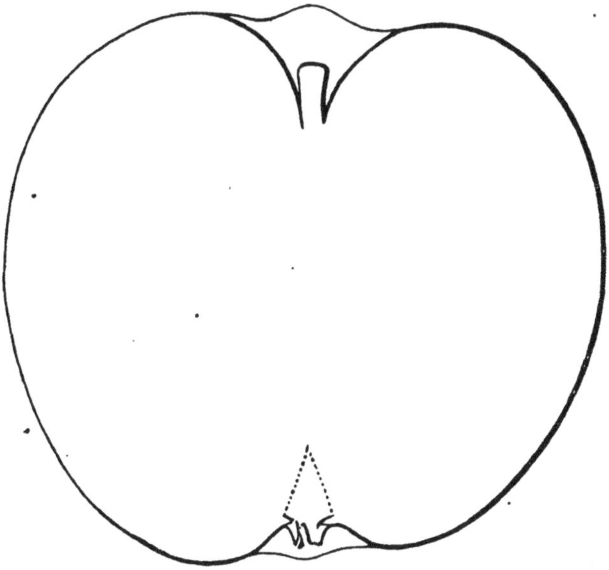

LADIES' SWEETING.

KILHAM HILL. Fruit large, ribbed; skin yellow, deepening to dark red in the sun; of good flavor when at its prime, which is about the end of November, but soon becomes dry and mealy. Tree very hardy, vigorous, of irregular, spreading growth and productive. A native of Essex County, Massachusetts. It is considerably grown in some parts of the State, under the name of Fall

Baldwin. It is *not* recommended as worthy of more extensive culture.

LADIES' SWEETING. Of large size, fine form, rich color, very sweet, and keeping late, this variety probably merits a place in every good collection. The tree is not a rapid grower or early bearer, but with age becomes very productive. In some sections, doubts are expressed of its hardiness, but it has proved hardy with me, and in a rather unfavorable situation. Fruit large, roundish, of regular form; skin fair, smooth, greenish yellow ground, mostly covered with light red and faintly striped with crimson, and dotted with numerous yellow specks; stem short. Flesh fine, crisp, tender, juicy, sweet and rich. January to April. It is quite distinct from a light colored apple sometimes grown under the same name, and also known as Vaughn's Sweet.

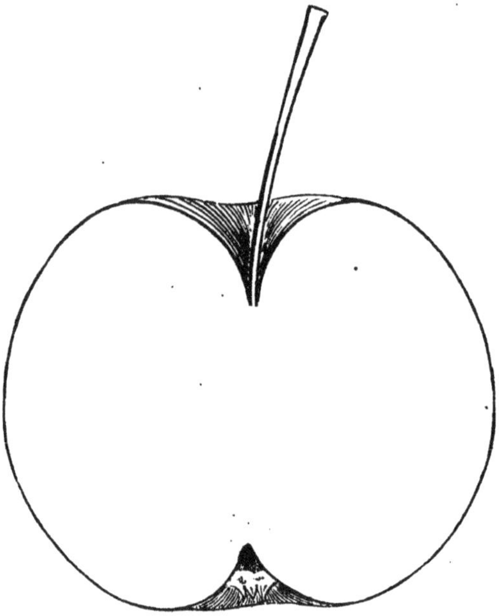

LONG STEMMED SWEET.

LONG STEMMED SWEET. Originated in Bridgton, Cumberland County. Slightly below medium size, roundish; skin yellow, covered with small stripes and dots of light red. Stem one and a half to two inches long, inserted in a rather deep and russety cavity. Flesh yellowish, very juicy, melting, rich and very sweet. A vigorous, healthy grower, of remarkably upright habit, and very productive. October.

MEXICO. Medium size, roundish; skin mostly bright crimson, sprinkled with light dots. Flesh whitish, sometimes stained with red, tender and excellent. One of the best of its season. September. Tree of moderate growth, hardy and productive. Origin, Canterbury, Conn.

MOTHER. Fruit of medium size, roundish oval; skin deep yellow, almost covered with brilliant red, interspersed with russetty dots; flesh yellow, fine, crisp, tender, juicy, with a brisk, pleasant,

MOTHER.

spicy flavor. Tree hardy, of moderate vigor, and in favorable soils productive. Originated on the farm of General Gardner, Bolton, Mass. In Worcester county it is extensively cultivated, and is esteemed among the best. It sustains its reputation here as to quality, but it may be doubted whether it can be grown profitably for market. October to January.

MARSHALL. Above medium size, roundish, a little flattened; skin deep green, mostly overlaid with a fine thick sprinkling of whitish green specks, a little blush next the sun and some crimson specks; stem short, in a narrow cavity. Little known in this State, but largely grown in some parts of New Hampshire as a profitable market apple on account of its productiveness and very late keeping. Tree very hardy, vigorous, and exceedingly productive. April to July.

MINISTER.

MINISTER. The late Robert Manning considered this "one of the very finest apples New England has produced," in which opinion we concur. It originated in Rowley, Mass., and was brought to notice by the late Rev. Dr. Spring of Newburyport, who engaged the fruit from the original tree, and his people seeing it on his table, soon gave it the name by which it has since been known. In the tenderness of its flesh and brisk vinous juice, it is not surpassed by any apple of its season. It is of good size, and though somewhat irregular in form, it has a fair yellowish skin, mostly covered with stripes of bright crimson. The tree succeeds well in the nursery and in the orchard; proves a thrifty, healthy grower and an abundant bearer. Like some other kinds, the fruit from young trees, and especially if the head be crowded, is much inferior to that from trees of mature age and open to the sun and air. Its season is about the same as the Hubbardston Nonsuch, say from November to February, or with care may be kept later. Its brisk, acid, vinous flavor forms a pleasant contrast to the mildness of the Hubbardston, and both are alike heartily commended for extensive cultivation. It often grows much larger than represented by the cut.

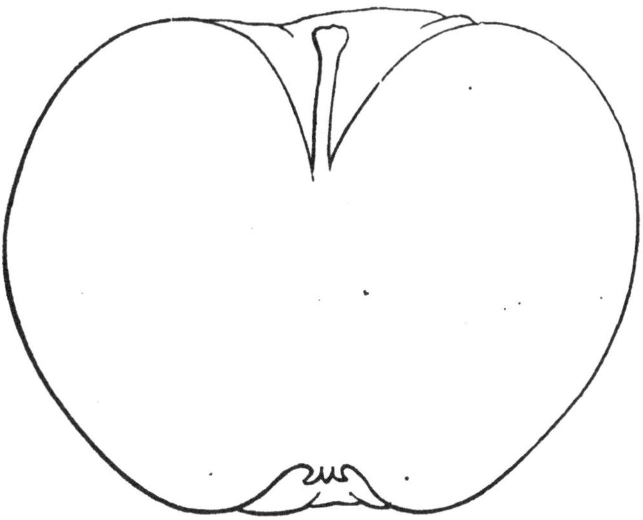

NORTHERN SPY.

MOSES WOOD. A native of Winthrop, Kennebec county, of medium size, roundish, yellow beautifully striped with bright red. Flesh white, tender, very juicy, of a pleasant, subacid flavor. Vigorous and productive. September. Were there not so many fine apples in eating at the same season, it would deserve distinguished praise.

NORTHERN SWEET. Introduced from Vermont; has succeeded well in Penobscot county and in some other sections of the State. Medium size, roundish; skin of oily smoothness, yellow, with a blush cheek. Flesh white, tender, rich and sweet; tree hardy, and an abundant bearer, mostly in alternate years; needs rich culture. October.

NONSUCH — *Old Nonsuch — Red Canada.* An old variety, formerly much cultivated, and one of the richest and highest flavored apples with which we are acquainted, but it cannot be recommended for general culture. The fruit is often spotted and small, and the tree not very healthy; yet in some sections it is still held in high esteem. A correspondent in Piscataquis county, and one in Penobscot county recommend it as one of the three best winter apples. Fruit of medium size, oblate, slightly angular; skin yellow, mostly shaded or splashed with bright red or crimson, and thickly sprinkled with greyish dots; stalk short, inserted in a broad, deep cavity. Flesh white, tender, crisp, very juicy, with a brisk, delicate flavor, which it keeps to the last. February to May.

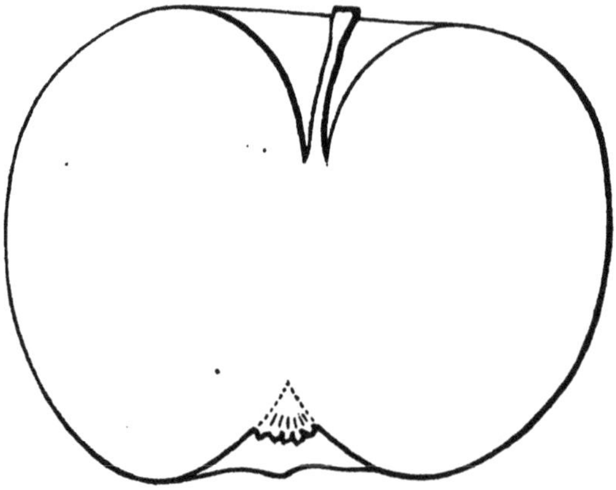

POMME GRIS.

NORTHERN SPY. When this was first introduced into Maine from New York, about fifteen years ago, it came with a loud flourish of trumpets, and was widely disseminated within a short time. Its unusual tardiness in coming into bearing disappointed many, and it came near being condemned without fair trial, but latterly it has, so far as I can learn, given satisfaction. The tree is very hardy, of thrifty, upright growth, moderately productive, and needs high culture. The fruit is of the highest excellence, fragrant, delicious, and retains a peculiar freshness, like an autumn apple, into late spring. Fruit of large size, pale yellow in the shade, with stripes of purplish red next the sun; stalk three quarters of an inch long, set in a very wide, deep cavity, marked with russet. Flesh whitish, fine grained, very tender, juicy, mild subacid, with a peculiarly fresh, delicious flavor. Origin, Bloomfield, New York. January to June.

ORANGE SWEET. The fruit known here under this name, seems to be unlike the Golden or Orange Sweet, described by Kenrick, and the Orange Sweeting of others. It is a valuable fruit, above

PORTER.

medium size, roundish ovate. Skin bright yellow, with a blush cheek in the sun, and sprinkled with small greenish dots, sometimes with larger crimson ones. Flesh yellowish, tender, sweet and rich. The tree is healthy, of thrifty growth, upright habit, and a good bearer. September and October.

POMME GRIS. The most extensively cultivated and popular

late keeping apple in Canada. It proves very hardy here, and although small, deserves a place in choice collections from its exquisite flavor. Size below medium, roundish oblate, skin rough, covered with russet, and thickly dotted with grayish russet specks. Flesh yellowish white, crisp, tender, high flavored and excellent. Usually smaller than the specimen from which the drawing was made. December to April.

PORTER. A deservedly popular autumn apple, ranking among the best. It comes in eating soon after the Williams, and is good for a month. Rather large, oblong; skin fair, smooth, bright yellow, with a little blush on the sunny side. Flesh yellowish, fine, crisp, tender, and juicy—sprightly and good flavored. Tree a moderate grower and productive. Scarcely as good here as in Massachusetts, where it originated, in the town of Sherburne, on the grounds of Rev. Samuel Porter. September and October.

PRESIDENT. A very large, handsome apple—yellow with a blush cheek. Flesh firm, juicy, subacid, and excellent for cooking. Tree thrifty, hardy and productive. September and October.

RED ASTRACHAN.

RED ASTRACHAN. A Swedish or Russian apple of extraordinary

beauty, and as hardy as it is beautiful; succeeding in the severest climates where the apple is grown at all. The tree combines thrifty, vigorous growth, productiveness and perfect hardiness. The fruit is good as well as beautiful, though not of the highest excellence, and its season is rather short; if left on the tree too long it becomes mealy; size large, roundish, a little flattened; skin fair, smooth, rich brilliant crimson on the sunny side, a little paler in the shade, and covered with a rich bloom. Flesh white, sometimes stained with pink, fine, crisp, tender, juicy, subacid. Its productiveness, beauty and good quality render it a universal favorite, and a profitable, early market fruit. August and September.

ROCK SWEET.

ROCK SWEET. Introduced from West Newbury, Mass. Rather below medium size; skin reddish yellow in the shade, but mostly covered with purplish or brownish red, and sprinkled with small light dots, except about an inch around the stem, where it is usually of a cinnamon russet color, and occasionally a small protuberance or patch of the same russet; stem slender, an inch long, inserted in a rather deep cavity. Flesh yellowish, fine grained, juicy, very sweet, with a rich aromatic flavor. No sweet apple surpasses it in quality. Tree very hardy, thrifty, and very productive—young shoots slender. November to December.

RHODE ISLAND GREENING. Too well known as one of the best

winter apples to need a detailed description. When well grown it is a choice dessert fruit, and it is also one of the best, if not the very best, of cooking apples. The tree is productive and thrifty, making a large spreading head. It is more hardy than the Baldwin, but it has sometimes suffered a little, especially nursery trees, in severe seasons. A very valuable variety, and indispensable in every collection.

Mr. C. Chamberlain of Foxcroft, one of our most skillful and experienced orchardists, writes me that in Piscataquis county they have a "variety of Greening that for cooking and eating combines more excellences than any other apple in use here. November to February. The tree large and vigorous, and is a good bearer; origin unknown—distinct from R. I. Greening."

Roxbury Russet. A well known apple, valuable for its late keeping qualities. Above medium size, flattened; yellowish russet skin, sometimes with a blush cheek. Flesh greenish white, rather dry, and of fair subacid flavor. Trees grafted in the nursery are tender, and impatient of transplanting; hence it should be cultivated only by grafting into the limbs of grown trees, and in this way it usually proves hardy. In some soils (usually deep and moist ones) it is very productive, and in others much less so. For interesting facts regarding this fruit in Kennebec county, see page 192. Spring and early summer.

Ribston Pippin. Introduced many years ago, by the late Dr. Vaughn of Hallowell, from England, where it is esteemed as the best apple. Above medium size, roundish, a little flattened; skin greenish yellow, streaked and mottled with dull saffron red in the sun, and a little russety withal. Flesh yellow, firm, crisp, juicy, with a peculiarly rich aromatic flavor. In quality it has few equals. Downing remarks that in England no higher praise can be given to an apple than to say it has a Ribston flavor. The tree is hardy, of vigorous growth and spreading habit; in some localities very productive, and in a good many others much less so, for which reason alone it is not recommended for extensive culture. December to May.

Runnells. Medium size; deep green in the shade, but mostly covered with purplish or brownish red; small protruding dots give a rough feel to the skin; stem three-quarters of an inch long, set in a deep, narrow cavity. Flesh very firm, of moderate excellence either for cooking or for dessert. Profitable as a market fruit from its hardiness, great productiveness, and late keeping; is scarcely fit to use before May or June, and will keep until autumn and later.

SOMERSET. Originated in Somerset county. One of the handsomest of apples; large, roundish, somewhat flattened. Skin bright yellow, mostly covered with splashes and stripes of bright crimson; deep red next the sun. Stem an inch long, set in a rather broad and deep cavity. Showy and saleable. Flesh yellowish, sometimes stained a little with red, tender, juicy, and of agreeable subacid flavor. Mr. Taber and others say it is a strong grower, hardy and productive. It has not fruited with me. September.

SMOKEHOUSE.

SMOKEHOUSE. Recently introduced from Pennsylvania, where it is highly esteemed, and from an experience of seven or eight years, it is recommended as promising to be a valuable variety here. Rather large, flattened form; skin yellow, shaded and splashed with red, with a few grey and brown dots. Stem rather long, and inserted in a broad cavity. Flesh yellowish, somewhat firm, crisp, juicy, with a pleasant acid flavor. Tree of spreading habit, very hardy and productive. Fruit uniformly fair and perfect. November to April.

Sweet Golden Russet. Origin unknown. Introduced many years ago from Worcester county, Mass. Medium to large, conical. Skin yellow, mostly covered with light russet; rather juicy, very rich and sweet, hardy and productive. September and October.

Tolman's Sweet.

Tolman's Sweet. Second or third rate as an eating apple, but excellent for baking, and from its productiveness would be profitable to grow largely, even for feeding swine or cattle. The tree is a moderate grower, and very hardy. Fruit of medium size, round. Skin whitish yellow, with a faint blush, often has a distinct line from the stem to the eye. Flesh white, rather firm, fine grained, not very juicy, and sweet—keeps late. November to May. Recommended for extensive cultivation.

Mr. Taber writes me of this, "I have found the tree invariably well formed, long lived, and productive; know no apple which will bear all the vicissitudes of climate better. It is the *only sort which I have even known* among the New York *root grafted* trees which lives to pay cost. In this vicinity it is a leading sort. A neighbor realizes more income from his Tolmans than from all others sent to market. They keep fresh until April. Seems to flourish best on warm soils, but thrives in as many localities as any apple."

WILLIAMS.

WILLIAMS—*Williams' Favorite.* A large, handsome, and very popular market apple, of fair quality, ripening through August and September. Always commands a high price when well grown. Oblong, smooth, red, covered mostly with darker red or deep crimson. Flesh white, sometimes a little stained with red; of mild and agreeable flavor. The tree is very hardy and productive. Needs a strong rich soil. It is a moderate and ill-shaped grower in the nursery, but forms a large tree in the orchard, with a wide spreading top.

WINTHROP GREENING—*Lincoln Pippin* (of some, *erroneously*). A native of Winthrop, and one of the most popular apples in Kennebec county. Fruit large, roundish, flattened, nearly of the form of Smokehouse. Golden yellow, partially russetted, and with a red cheek in the sun. Flesh tender, crisp, juicy, with a rich, sprightly flavor. Good from September to November, and I have seen them in perfect condition in January. In Kennebec county it is often heavily loaded with perfect fruit. In my grounds it has proved less productive, and the fruit is often blown off. Not an early bearer, but a vigorous grower, and becomes a tree of the largest size.

WOODS' SWEET. Scions of this very handsome fruit were sent me by Mr. Charles Downing, in the spring of 1856, and survived the severe winter following without injury, thus exhibiting unusual hardiness. It originated in Sudbury, Vermont, and is there considered the finest sweet apple in cultivation. Fruit medium to large, oblate. Skin waxen or oily, light yellow, shaded and striped with fine rich red. Flesh white, tender, juicy and sweet, with a delicate, rich flavor. A good grower, of upright habit and productive; succeeds well in the nursery. September to November.

CRAB APPLES, *for preserving and ornament.* Among the best of these are the Large Red Siberian, Large Yellow Siberian, the Wax Crab, and the Transcendant. The trees are objects of beauty both when in bloom and when laden with their abundant clusters of golden and crimson fruit. They are extremely hardy and very productive. The fruit of the Cherry Crab is too small for use, but it is as ornamental as any. The Chinese Double Flowering Apple has not proved hardy.

DWARF APPLES.

These have not been much cultivated in Maine. They are of two sorts. Those worked upon the Doucain stock (called Paradise by the English) and those upon the one known by the French as the Paradise stock. Upon the Doucain, which is the hardier of the two, they need from eight to ten feet room and attain a size sufficient to bear a bushel or more of fruit. Upon the Paradise stock they are of smaller growth and may be set at five or six feet apart. With a shortening in of the shoots they may be kept about the size of a stout currant bush, and bear profusely. Neither of them are suitable for ordinary orchard culture, but in the fruit garden are very desirable, being ornamental and yielding much gratification.

Their culture is easy—give a deep rich soil; plant so that the junction between the scion and the stock is *just even with the ground.* If planted deeper the scion may strike root, and the tree grow so vigorously as to lose its distinctive character as a dwarf tree. Keep the head open and thin out the fruit so it may attain its full size. To the extensive orchardist they would seem little else than horticultural toys, but to the occupants of town lots, they are both ornamental and useful, and deserve more general cultivation, especially the choice early sorts, which are rarely plenty in market. What more beautiful to the eye than the apple tree in full bloom, or loaded with its crimson or golden fruit? What more tempting to the appetite than the grateful and palatable fruit itself?

Almost all varieties are grown on these stocks, but mostly the handsome early and showy autumn sorts. Red Astrachan and Duchess of Oldenburg are special favorites.

THE PEAR.

The pear is a most delicious aud estimable fruit and its culture is worthy of more attention than it has ever received in this State. Its intrinsic importance is second only to that of the apple, and in its adaptation to various uses, and its duration, by the successive ripening of its varieties from August to midwinter and even later, it bears considerable resemblance to that fruit.

Its culture in Maine is in its infancy. Indeed the same remark might be truthfully made regarding its culture in the country at large; for although long grown, only a very few, perhaps not more than two or three, of those varieties which were highly esteemed thirty years ago, are now extensively cultivated anywhere in the United States. All those at present considered desirable are of recent introduction, and their culture in this State, for the most part, more recent still.

That the pear-tree did once thrive admirably in Maine is sufficiently proved by the existence of the large, healthy, old trees which we occasionally find at the present time in several parts of the State, * bearing, it is true, fruit of poor quality and fit only for

* In a communication from Mr. John Rogers of Kittery, he says: "Pear trees are hardy and very long lived. Many old seedling trees are standing on my farm, one in particular, which is believed to be a hundred and fifty to two hundred years old. It is a mere shell now, being decayed at the heart, but if sound would measure two

making perry and to furnish seeds for healthy, hardy stocks; but undoubtedly capable, by grafting, of being made to produce fruit as buttery, melting and delicious, as their present product is choky and austere. Have we not, in this fact, ample and conclusive proof that if we can furnish suitable location and food, and can find varieties at once hardy enough and good enough, we can compete with any portion of the world in the cultivation of pears? It would certainly seem so, and in the absence of any evidence to the contrary, we have here a sufficient warrant for strenuous exertions to attain so desirable a result. Several varieties, bearing a high character among cultivators generally, originated here, as for instance, the Fulton, which first grew from the seed in Bowdoinham, Sagadahoc county, and the McLaughlin, which cannot be traced beyond Scarboro', and is believed to have originated in Cumberland county, and more recently, a seedling shown by Mr. Nickerson, of Readfield, in Kennebec county, and named for him, gives promise of great value from its combined hardiness, productiveness, vigor, beauty, and fine flavor.

It is believed that more time, money, labor and care have been bestowed on pear culture in the vicinity of Boston during the past twenty years than upon any other spot in the world, and it might naturally be supposed that so much painstaking would afford us reliable results, definite conclusions by which to be guided implicitly; but this does not prove to be the fact. One reason for this is, because the interest there manifested has been so largely directed to the collection of numerous varieties. Every town, village, and quiet nook on the earth's surface, where the pear is grown, seems to have been searched for new sorts, and when obtained they have been put to proof of their qualities under the highest possible culture. Comparatively little attention has been given to a thorough testing of the more promising sorts under the conditions of simply good orchard treatment. The value of these immense collections is by no means to be under-estimated, for in no other possible way could the best be obtained, proved and compared one with another, and the labors of such men as Col. Wilder, Messrs.

---

feet six inches in diameter. It has always borne well, bore ten bushels the past season, and made new shoots of from one to two feet in length. An old saying is, 'He that plants pears plants for his heirs,' but it is not so on the quince root. My orchard of eighty dwarf pears, planted in 1850, has borne well for ten years, and are in good healthy condition; some of the pears weighed twelve ounces this year."

Hovey, and a host of others, some of whom possess collections perhaps never equalled elsewhere, entitle them to the gratitude of all. Still this, although a good step in the right direction, and an indispensable one, is not all which is needful. A few such collections would have answered all useful purposes for New England; and had the great majority of cultivators directed the same amount of pains and expense towards the *extensive and profitable* production of fine pears, the results would probably have been of vastly greater importance to the community, as well as more lucrative to the cultivators themselves.

Another reason is, that some kinds which have been amply proved to succeed in Massachusetts are found, upon trial, to be unreliable here. Among these we may mention the Bartlett as a notable instance. This, although not strictly a fruit of the highest quality, is the most popular in market and the most extensively grown for profit. This is due to the early and abundant bearing and vigorous growth of the tree, and the size, beauty, melting flesh and syrupy juice of the fruit; to which we may add that even the half grown fruit, windfalls or thinnings, will ripen well in the house; and there the tree is sufficiently hardy, also, in ordinary seasons, although it suffers in bad ones; but, unfortunately, it is not so hardy with us, and will succeed only in very favorable locations.

In order to be worthy of general cultivation, a pear should possess a certain combination of requisites. First of all, in this climate, it must be hardy enough to withstand severe winters; next, we desire productiveness, vigorous growth, a healthy constitution, and adaptation to a variety of soils, in the tree, and it is well also if it be not too tardy in fruiting. In the fruit we desire fine flavor, size, beauty, and good keeping qualities. Out of the thousand or more of varieties which have been introduced in the last thirty years, there are few in which all these are found in a desirable degree. One is lacking in this, another in that; a great many are wanting in a majority of these requisites. In proportion as they prevail, or are missing, is the value of any given variety for general cultivation. Practically, it is found that hardiness, vigor and productiveness in the tree, connected with tolerably good quality of fruit, are of greater value than superior flavor connected with deficiency in the other requisites. For home use, some varieties may be very desirable and almost indispensable on account of exquisite quality, while from small size or unattractive appearance in the fruit, or feeble growth or scanty bearing in the tree, they would prove unprofitable for market.

For various reasons it is more difficult to arrive at a conclusive decision regarding the value of a new pear, than with an untried apple. The pear is not so uniform in quality during a series of years in the same soil and location; one year it may give promise of high excellence, and the next prove quite poor. In one soil and location it may be all which can be asked, and in a less favorable one quite inferior. The first few years of bearing do not usually develope its full excellence,—for this we must wait until the tree has attained a good degree of maturity. In the apple the effect of an over-abundant crop is chiefly manifested in the requirement for a season of rest, while in the pear a too heavy crop is often connected with small, inferior fruit, so nearly worthless that a few dozen large perfect specimens will give greater satisfaction and will command more money than bushels of the same sort imperfectly grown; and hence the necessity and profit in many cases of severe thinning out of the fruit.

Unless the proper conditions are fulfilled, pear culture may be expected to result in failure; when they are fulfilled, a high degree of satisfaction and of profit may be confidently anticipated. Like everything else which is really desirable and valuable, pears cost something, and they readily command a price fully commensurate with the cost; usually a good deal more from their scarcity. Mr. Nickerson of Readfield, told me that the first time he offered for sale in Portland the fruit of his seedling pear a proposal was made him at once to take all he would furnish at $12.50 per barrel, and he sold his crop at that price. Mr. N. thinks they can be grown as easily as apples, and has several hundreds of trees under way.

Good pears, in our best markets, readily command from five to ten times as much as good apples, and will undoubtedly continue to do so for years to come.

The more opportunity has been enjoyed to compare the prospects of pear culture in Maine and in other sections, the more favorable do ours appear. There are obstacles in both cases, but they are very unlike. In the Middle and Western States they can grow young trees with great facility—whether they be of sorts which we call tender or hardy, and they suffer few losses from winter killing, or from crushing snows breaking them down; but when the trees come to bearing, and in fact as soon as fit to transplant, then comes the BLIGHT—fire-blight it is usually called, and sometimes "frozen sap blight"—though nobody knows either cause or remedy. Suddenly, without any premonition whatever, a limb or a whole tree blackens and withers; being a hopeless case, if it be only a limb, it is amputated, if a whole tree it is dug up and removed. This blight is an awful scourge, sometimes sweeping whole orchards, and more or less thinning almost every orchard. Here, the case is very different; our troubles are almost if not wholly past when once the trees survive the hazards of infancy and early youth and come to a bearing state.

It is not always that we are duly thankful for, or even aware of, the immunities we enjoy. This one of freedom from the blight in pears is a notable instance of such immunity. Another of considerable importance in connection with apple culture is the absence of the *canker worm*. This worm, the occasional scourge of orchards in other New England States, has never, to our knowledge, passed eastward of the Piscataqua river; yet how many of our orchardists have ever thought of it, to say nothing of being grateful for the exemption?

THE PEAR ON THE QUINCE ROOT.

A great deal has been written on the subject of dwarf pear trees, that is to say, of the pear grafted or budded on the quince root. Within the last ten years our leading horticultural and agricultural journals have teemed with animated discussions in which the most contradictory statements regarding their value have been put forth. Not a few have denounced them as worthless, while others declare that this method is attended with a degree of success unattainable in any other way. The novice, with such conflicting statements before him, both coming from those who profess to have proof from experience, is greatly puzzled, and anxiously inquires, "What is truth?" The discussion has now mainly passed by; certain conclusions have been arrived at; and I will attempt briefly to state the facts as now admitted by the great mass of intelligent horticulturists.

First—Some varieties of the pear, with proper treatment, will succeed admirably on the quince, yielding finer fruit, more of it, and at a much earlier period.

Second—Other varieties will not succeed, and such should not be worked on the quince.

Third—Between those which succeed well and those which do not succeed at all, are others, which will grow on this stock for a longer or shorter term of years, and bear more or less.*

Fourth—Some varieties of the quince, as for example, the Orange quince, which is the one most cultivated for its fruit, are unfit to be used as a stock for the pear.

Fifth—The proper treatment of pears on the quince root is something very different from what may be considered good orchard treatment of apple trees, or even from what would usually be considered extraordinarily good treatment for them. They require a more costly preparation of soil, and a higher culture.

The culture of the pear on the quince is not the novelty which many suppose. It has been practised in France for two hundred years or more, and at the present time at least four-fifths of the trees planted there for bearing (and no country in the world is so well supplied with pears as France) are on the quince root. In England it has been practised certainly for more than one hundred years. In the correspondence between Collinson and Bartram in 1763, the former, probably replying to some inquiry of the latter, says, "What I am persuaded will prevent its dropping the fruit, if some quinces were planted in the lower part of the garden, near the spring, and graft them with the pear, it meliorates the fruit. By long experience our pears are grafted on the quince stock and succeed better than on the pear stock with us." For more than a hundred years no objections were urged against the use of the quince as a stock for the pear, and its advantages were generally recognized.

Within a comparatively recent period, hundreds upon hundreds of new pears have been brought into notice. Great enthusiasm was felt regarding their excellence. Thousands were anxious to fruit these new sorts at the earliest possible period. Nurserymen, to meet the demand, worked them on the quince before it could be known whether they would succeed permanently on it or not, and the demand for stocks was so urgent that any or all sorts were used indiscriminately. Now as some varieties of the pear will grow vigorously on the quince for a year or two, but show unfitness for it plainly enough as soon as they come into bearing, and as thousands of the trees grown as above fell into the hands of

*It should be remarked that some varieties, like the Urbaniste for example, which grow slowly at first on the quince, eventually make fully as strong and permanent trees as any.

persons who knew little or nothing of the requisites to successful culture, it cannot be wondered at if disappointment and denunciation followed the results of the hasty, partial and unskillful experience of those who planted them. On the other hand, there have been those who patiently learned what sorts do succeed on this stock, and liberally bestowed high culture and good management, and the success of these, whether we regard the size, beauty, excellence or abundance of the fruit, or the prices which the product has commanded in our large markets, is very marked and scarcely credible by many who have not witnessed the results.

To the most common objection made to the quince as a stock, namely, that trees upon it are short lived, it is enough to state that many trees are known to be at the present time in active, healthy life, and promising well for years to come, which have been planted out fifteen, twenty, and some of them over thirty years, and which have borne satisfactory crops annually. The term "dwarfs," by which pears on the quince root are usually called, conveys to some minds an erroneous impression. It is true the tree is dwarfed somewhat by the influence of the stock, and thus early productiveness is induced, but the trees are not necessarily stunted, nor very small, as their trunks not unfrequently attain a circumference of fifteen or twenty inches, and sometimes more.

The principal requisites to success are:

First—A sufficiently sheltered location, either naturally so, or made so, by screens of evergreens planted for the purpose, or by some other means.

Second—A good, strong, deep, moist soil, resting upon a naturally porous subsoil, or else thoroughly drained. This should be worked twenty inches or two feet deep, and made rich.

Third—Plant trees budded either upon the Orleans or the Angers quince, and no others.

Fourth—Plant no varieties which are not known to succeed well upon the quince root.

Fifth—Plant so that the point of junction between the quince and the pear* shall be *three inches below* the surface when the planting is finished and the surface leveled. This serves several purposes.

---

*The quince *should be budded* with the pear, in the nursery, *as near the surface* of the ground as convenient—but the above rule is to be adhered to, *without regard to the height at which the operation might have been performed.*

(*a.*) The stock is thus kept soft and moist, and so swells more evenly with the pear as it grows. It also throws out roots from the stock fully up to the point of union with the pear. The quince is the only one of our fruit trees which does this freely. It should be remembered that the office of the quince in this case is simply to furnish *roots* for the tree, and if properly planted, only a few years will elapse before the *main roots* will proceed from just below the point of union. Planting dwarf pears at the same depth at which they stood in the nursery when budded, is almost sure to keep them *dwarfs*, in the objectionable sense of the word in which it is sometimes used, and to insure their being short-lived. Doing this has been a common error, and the cause of numerous failures.

(*b.*) It favors the throwing out of roots from the pear itself, thus adding to the vigor and longevity of the tree. In this case the tree loses somewhat of its distinctive character as a quince rooted tree, but by the time this takes place it has commenced bearing, and being well furnished with fruit spurs, it continues to bear as freely as if it had no roots directly from the pear.

(*c.*) The quince is as liable to the attacks of the borer as the apple tree, but as the eggs producing this worm are never deposited below, but rather at and above the surface, it is thus secured from its depredations.

Sixth—Bestow clean culture. Keep all weeds down and the ground mellow. Mulching is of great assistance. *As the roots of the quince do not extend far or wide like those of the pear or apple,* but are mostly small and fibrous, it is necessary to place a sufficiency of food within their reach. If the ground was properly prepared at the outset, this is best done by an annual top-dressing.

Seventh—Good pruning, thus giving proper form to the tree, and by an annual shortening in of the young shoots, limiting the size of the tree to the amount of its roots. The branches should be as low as consists with safety from breaking down by heavy snows.

Eighth—Never allow the trees to carry more fruit than they *can ripen to perfection, and at the same time keep up a healthy growth of both top and roots.* This involves the necessity oftentimes of a severe thinning out of the fruit in its early stages—and requires some nerve on the part of one who has not learned its necessity by experience.

If these things be attended to, the cultivator will find the pear on the quince the most delicious and bountiful of fruits, richly rewarding all his care. If they be neglected, little satisfaction may be confidently anticipated. One tree well cared for will give more satisfaction than a hundred neglected.

The principal advantages of trees on the quince over those on the pear are:

First—They can be transplanted with greater ease, and of larger size, and *with almost certainty of their living.*

Second—They come earlier into bearing, often the next year after planting, and usually within two or three years, while on the pear it often takes five, ten or fifteen years.

Third—They are more within reach and easy control; afford greater facilities for pruning, thinning out and gathering of fruit, together with less liability of its being blown off by high winds.

The facility with which the pear throws out roots of its own, when trees on the quince root are planted, varies considerably with different varieties. Some do it readily, (never, however, unless planted at the proper depth,) while others seem little inclined to do so. Generally, those which seem to be not very well suited with the quince, as a feeder, do so most easily.

Such rooting can be hastened and greatly facilitated by the following method. After the tree has had several years' growth and is well established, remove the earth from around the trunk, and with a small sharp gouge cut upward from the point of union, where the pear is usually somewhat swollen, and partially detach several strips, consisting of the bark and about a quarter of an inch in depth (in the center of each) of wood, and about two inches in length, leaving each attached at its upper part. Draw the bottom of the strips a little from the trunk, and place a little fine earth between, so as to prevent adhesion; then replace the earth about the tree. The operation should be performed a little before midsummer, and as the descending sap is thus obstructed, it soon forms granulations upon the portion thus parted, and from these roots are thrown out into the soil. It is easier done with a gouge prepared for the purpose by being bent about three inches from the cutting edge.

When rooting is thus effected, we secure the benefit of both pear and quince roots as feeders of the tree, and combine early fruiting and the other advantages of the quince with the longevity of the pear. Upon such varieties as are decidedly better upon the quince it is not advisable, but in many cases it is a great gain.

Double Working. When it is desired to cultivate a variety upon the quince which does not succeed when budded directly upon it, such sort may be grafted or budded upon some free-growing variety already well established upon the quince root;—for instance, the Seckel can thus be grafted on the Beurre d'Amalis, and so a tree be obtained which will bear much earlier than the Seckel would upon the pear root. This plan is better adapted to the wants of the amateur than for the orchardist. It can be profitably practised only to a very limited extent.

Pruning and Training of Dwarf Pears.

The pruning and training of pear trees in a way to bring them into a pyramidal form is almost universally recommended in books on fruit culture, and very minute directions are laid down for its accomplishment. As very few of our readers will be inclined to devote the time and patience requisite, it will be only briefly noticed. It is really a very pretty method, if one can afford it, though better fitted to sections where deep snows prevail less, than here, and so where less danger exists of the lower limbs being crushed.

For this purpose the trees are planted at one year old, at from eight to ten feet apart, (usually on the quince root, although those on the pear root may also be trained in the same way.) The first year's growth is headed back to within six or eight eyes. Consequently the remaining buds shoot vigorously. About the end of June the growth of all but the leading shoot is stopped by pinching the ends, and if any are not in the position desired, they are tied so as to bring them to it. The leader grows on vigorously and sometimes it is stopped the same season, and sometimes it is cut back the following year, to induce the throwing out of another tier of limbs; and so on, in successive years, until the tree has attained its full size; and all the while "stopping" (by pinching its end so as to leave an inch or two which shall then develope into a fruit spur,) every shoot which dares to start where you wish it not to grow. It involves close attention and much skill. Some sorts assume a good, regular form with much less care than others, while some are so bent on awkward ways as to defy almost any amount of skill and attention.

For our use it is well to let them grow as dwarf standards; that is, just like other standards, only with limbs as low as consists with safety from crushing snows, and the heads retained within a smaller extent. With suitable age, there is rarely lack of fruit enough without continual "stopping," and often more time is needed to thin it out properly than can well be spared for the purpose. There should be at least the annual pruning before referred to, and in doing this, if care be taken to cut *above a wood bud on the outer side* of the twig or limb, or on the side facing the direction in which it is desirable that the shoot should extend its growth, *a great deal may be easily accomplished towards improving* the form and general appearance of the tree, or towards giving it any peculiar form desired.

If any attempt is to be made at systematic training, I would suggest the adoption of the "wine-glass" style, introduced by Capt. W. R. Austin, of Dorchester, Mass., as better fitted to our needs and less trouble than the pyramidal form. It is thus described, by the editor, in Hovey's Magazine of Horticulture:

"When the young tree of two years old is planted, the centre shoot is cut out, and the side shoots are pruned in so as to obtain from the four or five laterals as many as seven or nine branches: these are preserved entire, every side shoot upon each being cut in to one or two eyes as they make their appearance; these main shoots are slightly cut in at the winter pruning, and encouraged in making a new growth each year, pinching off at all times every side shoot, by which means they are transformed into fruit spurs; as the shoots increase in length, they diverge at the top until they assume quite a wine-glass or vase shape. When of a maximum height, say ten feet, they are stopped, and are not allowed further extension. By this process, these main shoots become studded with fruit spurs from top to bottom, of which the Duchesse afforded grand examples, being covered with splendid large pears.

The advantages of this style, besides ease of management, are a more evenly balanced tree, which the wind does not affect so much as pyramids, and the sap is not directed to the top, but is distributed throughout these main branches equally; hence the trees are full of fruit from the base to the top, and at the same time it is more evenly sized. Another important thing is, that there are no lower side branches to become crowded and die off for want of a good circulation of air, as is too common with pyramidal trees. The principal advantage is in the ease with they may be managed by those who have not the skill to prune pyramids, which require a good deal of care to keep them in symmetrical shape and at the same time productive and healthy. Great judgment, also, and considerable skill are required to know when to prune, but in Capt. Austin's style, all that is important is to extend the main shoots about seven to ten in number, and no more, and cut off every side shoot (by summer pinching principally) to one or two eyes."

Trees grown in this style, seem to be, substantially, dwarf standards, skillfully and systematically trained, and the method is commended to the attention of cultivators.

Standard Pears.

The principal advantage attending the use of the pear stock is, the greater size and longevity which the trees attain. Trees on the pear stock are more suitable to be trained standard high, and planted in orchards, (rather than gardens,) than those worked on the quince root. As many sorts succeed best on their own stock, we must, with such, be content to forego early fruiting and wait patiently for them to attain a bearing age. The trees once planted, the years slip by more rapidly than we think for at the outset. Novices in fruit culture are usually in a great hurry to have their trees bear, but with ten, or twenty, or thirty years experience, they become quite willing to plant small trees, and to have them grow to a good size and attain sufficient strength and age before fruiting. Experience gives wisdom which, sometimes, is obtained in no other school.

Pears on the pear stock do not require so high culture as on the quince, but they require more care and attention than apples. They require a good exposure, with sufficient shelter, either natural or artificial, from high winds and cutting blasts. Next, a good deep strong soil and a porous or thoroughly drained subsoil, rather moist than dry, but never retaining stagnant moisture in the soil. If not so naturally, it may be amended by deepening, draining, enriching, and good cultivation. Animal manures may be given more freely than to the apple, yet *never so as to induce a late, unripened growth of wood*, which is one of the most fruitful sources of danger in our winters.

Other Stocks for the Pear. The use of the common White Thorn of our woods, (*Crataegus coccinea*, of botanists, bearing scarlet berries,) as a stock for the pear, has been attended with some success. In my own experience, the Flemish Beauty has often done well on it. Where good stocks can be readily obtained, it is worthy of a more extended trial than has been given it.

Very diverse accounts are given by cultivators regarding the results obtained by grafting the pear on the Mountain Ash; (*Pyrus Americana* of botanists, often called Round-wood.) Most fruit books, when speaking of it, direct that small stocks be grafted near the ground, and some cultivators among us have given me to understand that this practice has succeeded, but although some ten years ago, I worked several thousand in this way, and with twenty or thirty different varieties, I got no trees to succeed for any length of time, nor to come into good bearing at all; while by grafting the limbs of grown trees ten or fifteen feet high and three to six inches in diameter, I have seen them loaded with bushels of fine fruit for several years in succession; but even such trees may not be expected to succeed for any long term; a few years of bearing is all that can be expected.

As with the quince, some varieties succeed well, others but poorly, and others not at all upon the Mountain Ash. The best I have proved are, Flemish Beauty, Fulton and Belle Lucrative. The Bartlett has also done well. Even the White Doyenne, (St. Michael's), which usually cracks so badly, gave good crops on several trees.

The *Amelanchier Canadensis*, variously known as Sugar Pear, Juneberry, Shadbush, Serviceberry, &c., has also been tried to some extent as a stock for the pear. I have had no personal experience with it, and from what I had seen or heard, attached little importance to its use. But while visiting some orchards in Penobscot county, during the past summer, I found a very successful fruit grower, Mr. Jefferson Stubbs, of Hampden, had experimented considerably with it, and was highly enthusiastic in his anticipations of valuable results. He showed me some trees of great vigor and promise—one of three years growth, grafted at the ground, was fully nine feet high—another, grafted eight or ten years ago, he told me had brought him fifteen dollars for the fruit, and for premiums on it, at the time when another, of the same variety, (Flemish Beauty,) by its side, and on the pear stock, of the same age and a little larger, had yielded only eighteen pears. He had a dozen or more varieties grafted upon it and of these the

Flemish Beauty, Bartlett and Buffum promised best. In all, there might be two to three hundred trees, planted out for bearing. He transplants them from the woods, heading in the tops severely at the time, and after growing one year, grafts them, (saddle grafting as figured and described on page 166 and very skillfully done—no failures,) keeps the soil well cultivated and very rich.

A question frequently asked is, which is the best pear? Rather an absurd question it is too, for one may be best at one season and another when that is gone by; one best as regards intrinsic excellence, and another to cultivate for profit. Again, tastes differ, one favors a sweet pear, while another prefers a high vinous flavor. The question, unless qualified or limited, cannot be answered.

It is really a great desideratum to obtain a list of six, ten or twelve varieties of unimpeachable merit, which shall be really good, productive and hardy sorts, filling the seasons well, so as to furnish a supply from the earliest to the latest, and better than any other six or twelve which can be named. But unfortunately our experience is too limited to do this. As before remarked, the better sorts are all of comparatively recent introduction and they have not all been cultivated extensively enough in various parts of the State and in differing soils, to furnish the requisite evidence. It takes a good while to learn everything about any one variety which is to be learned by experience, and besides this, new sorts are all the while coming along, which as they come to proof, one after another, play havoc with lists made out a dozen years before. There is no good cultivator of pears anywhere, whose opinions have not undergone considerable change as to the relative merits of varieties within a shorter period than a dozen years.

Not less than five hundred sorts, which have come recommended as worthy of culture, have been more or less extensively proved in the State—sometimes nearly a hundred have been shown by single cultivators at our annual exhibitions. Last year Mr. Warren Sparrow exhibited eighty or more, from his grounds in Westbrook, at the fair of the Portland Horticultural society. Of these many kinds, four hundred or more have passed into oblivion or ought to; but when we come to the others it is no easy task to state accurately their relative worth.

An attempt is made below to give a brief description of such as, with the existing attainments in local pomological knowledge, are supposed to be most worthy of cultivation. The critic in such matters will notice that many sorts are omitted which are highly spoken of in almost all our works on fruit culture, as for instance, Bloodgood, Beurre Bosc, Beurre D'Aremburg, Golden Beurre of Bilboa and others, and it is believed there is sufficient reason for the omission in lack of thrift, hardiness, or other requisite for our use. Others still, as Dunmore, Dix, St. Ghislain, &c., good pears and hardy, are omitted because they have no *special* merit, and are believed to be excelled by others which are described; for it is an object not to have the list so large as to confuse and hinder, rather than help a judicious selection, and some are omitted because we do not know enough about them to say anything. A few are mentioned not to recommend them, so much as, (being popular sorts elsewhere,) to suggest caution with regard to planting these in Maine.

A word, however, may be first in place here regarding the

Gathering and Keeping of Pears.

Nearly all pears ripen with a finer flavor and texture if picked early and matured in the house. There are a few which may ripen upon the tree and be as good, like the Dearborn's Seedling for example, but the number of such is very small. Some which are nearly worthless if ripened on the tree, become rich, melting and delicious if ripened in the house. Gathering at the proper time will, in nearly all cases, prevent the *rotting at the core,* which otherwise greatly detracts from the value of many sorts, particularly early varieties. It requires some practical skill to determine the proper time to pick pears, and this must be learned by observation and experience. As a general rule early pears are best if picked about *ten days* before they would ripen on the tree; for some, a week would answer, and others are better if plucked at a fortnight before maturity. If the season is of usual and equable moisture, a good rule is to take off the fruit when the stem will part easily from the spur upon its being turned up at a right angle. If it be a dry time in August or September, be cautious about acting upon this rule, as a heavy rain at this season often causes them again to adhere firmly. They should not be picked until the full size is attained, nor on a wet day. Old Thomas Tusser in his "Five Hundred points of Good Husbandry," in treating of the labors of September, says:

> "Out, fruit go and gather, but not in the dew."

And again,

> "Fruit gathered too timelie will taste of the wood,
> Will shrink and be bitter and seldom proue good."

DESCRIPTIVE LIST OF PEARS.

Summer and Early Autumn.

Bartlett. The most popular of early pears, and where the climate suits it, perhaps deservedly so, for its combination of good qualities; but unfortunately for us, it is one of the tenderest. As in other States south and west of this, so here, it has been more extensively planted than any other variety, and its general failure

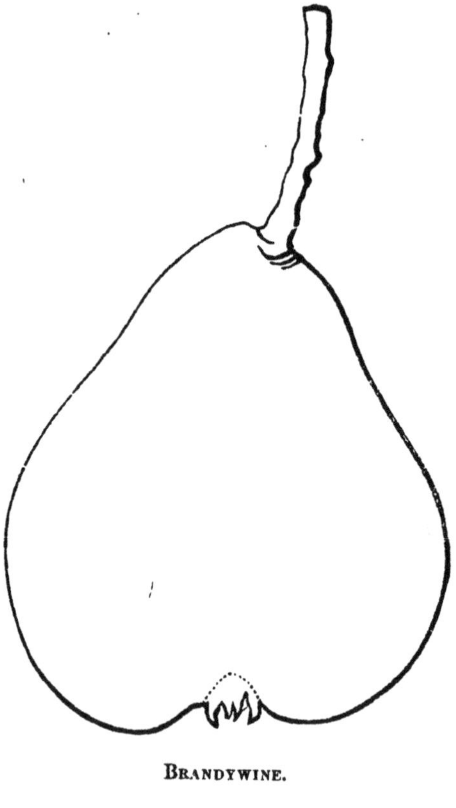

Brandywine.

has done much to discourage all efforts towards pear culture. Occasional and partial success has attended it in favorable localities and sheltered situations. We have grown some bushels of the fruit, but if our efforts—continued for twenty years, and accompanied by the loss of several thousand trees of various ages—furnish sufficient evidence, we pronounce it *unreliable*, and one which should be planted sparingly and only in city gardens or other very favorable situations.

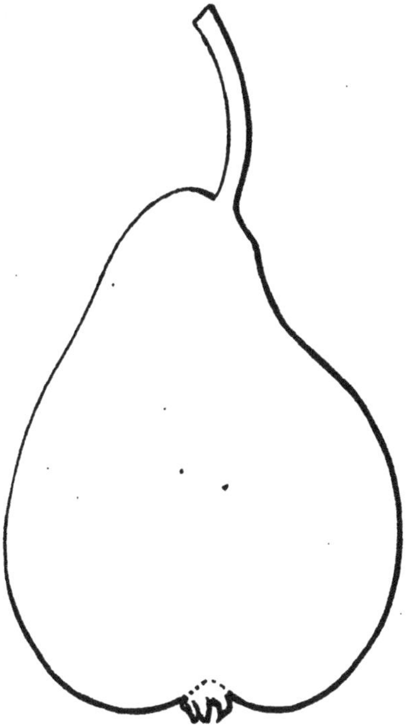

BEURRE GIFFARD.

BRANDYWINE. A native fruit of much merit, introduced to notice by Dr. Brinkle. The tree is of good form, hardy, of vigorous growth, uniformly productive and the fruit of fine quality. Rather above medium size, yellowish green sprinkled with russet and a reddish cheek in the sun. Flesh juicy, melting, sugary and vinous. Succeeds finely on the quince root. Ripens with the Bartlett. Mr. Hovey in describing it, says: "The qualities of the Brandywine are peculiarly its own, and cannot be compared with any other variety. Its flesh is slightly firm, yet perfectly melting; and its flavor, without being highly perfumed, appears to be a concentration of several sorts, being almost as sugary as

16

the Seckel, yet with the champagne smack of the d'Aremburg. It is as distinctive in its character as the Seckel."

Beurre d'Amalis. One of the hardiest and most profitable September pears. The tree is a rampant grower, irregular and straggling in its habit, and very productive. Fruit large, dusky greenish yellow and sometimes faintly russetted. Flesh rather coarse grained, melting, juicy, and in quality varying from good to very good. It ripens about the same time as the Bartlett. With some cultivators in the vicinity of Portland, it has given better satisfaction than any other, owing to its combined hardiness, productiveness and good quality. It succeeds perfectly on the quince, and is rarely grown on the pear root.

Dearborn's Seedling.

Beurre Giffard. In quality and beauty this pear is not excelled by any other early sort. Bright yellow, with a beautiful crimson cheek, melting, rich and delicious. The tree is usually a slender grower, although in some situations pretty vigorous. It can hardly be dispensed with in a choice collection, but is not recommended for extensive planting. Succeeds moderately well on the quince.

DEARBORN'S SEEDLING. A very excellent native fruit; originated by General Dearborn about forty-five years ago. In Massachusetts, and farther west and south where the Bartlett is successfully grown, its more showy qualities have greatly eclipsed the merits of this pear which ripens at about the same time. Its only fault is its size, which is below medium; while its excellences, both of tree and fruit, are such as to give it a high rank among early pears for Maine. I have seen trees of it in this State, bearing crops

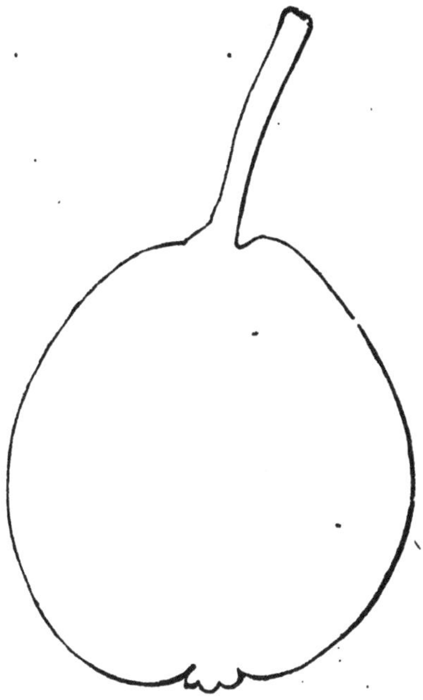

DOYENNE D'ETE.

which sold for from ten to fifteen dollars annually. The tree succeeds in a variety of soils, is very hardy and bears abundantly and regularly. The fruit has a clear, smooth, light yellow skin; flesh, white, juicy, melting, and of sprightly flavor. It deserves a place in every orchard and fruit garden. Does not succeed well on the quince.

Doyenne d'Ete, *or Summer Doyenne.* This is the earliest ripening pear worthy of cultivation. It has been considerably grown as a dwarf, but it is not well adapted to the quince, as on this stock the tree soon becomes feeble and stunted. On the pear stock it is a vigorous grower, with rather slender shoots, and an early and profuse bearer. Fruit small, yellow, with bright red on the sunny side, juicy, melting and well-flavored. It should, (like most early pears,) be picked a week, at least, before maturity, as it becomes mealy and insipid when ripened on the tree. A hardy and very desirable variety ripening early in August.

Madeleine. A very early, medium sized, pale yellow pear, juicy and good, which comes in season just after the Summer Doyenne. It has been grown in this State above fifty years and is found to succeed both on the pear and quince. The tree is hardy

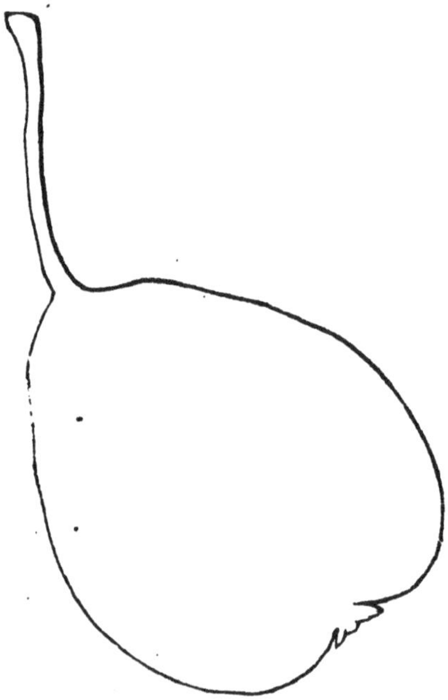

Rostiezer.

and productive, with long, erect branches. In damp, clayey soils the fruit is found to be rather astringent, and in some seasons it rots on the tree, but generally gives satisfaction.

ROSTIEZER. An early, hardy, very productive and delicious variety, of German origin. Small to medium in size, pyriform, brownish russet in the sun, and bears in clusters; stem long and slender; flesh juicy, melting, sugary, vinous and aromatic. In quality it is scarcely excelled by the Seckel or any other. Succeeds equally on the pear and quince. A vigorous grower, but of awkward and irregular habit, throwing out few and strong and often ill placed shoots; needs judicious pruning to produce tolerable symmetry.

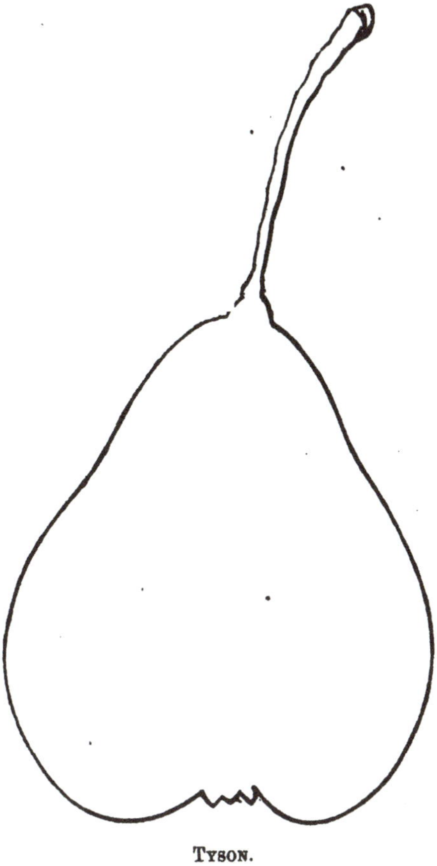

TYSON.

TYSON. A choice early pear of American origin. The original tree was found in a hedge on the farm of Jonathan Tyson, in Jenkinstown, Pa., and is said to be fully two feet in diameter. Fruit of medium size, pyriform; skin bright yellow at maturity, with a crimson cheek. Flesh fine, juicy, melting, rich, sugary and somewhat aromatic. Tree of vigorous growth, upright habit, very productive and very hardy; but is slow in coming to a bearing state on the pear stock, and, like Flemish Beauty and some others, is of uncertain propagation on the quince, as sometimes only a small proportion of the buds will grow. Trees on the quince, if once well started, however, succeed finely, so far as I can judge by ten years' experience of it. Its tardiness in fruiting is the only fault I have found, and this is fully atoned for, when old enough.

Autumn.

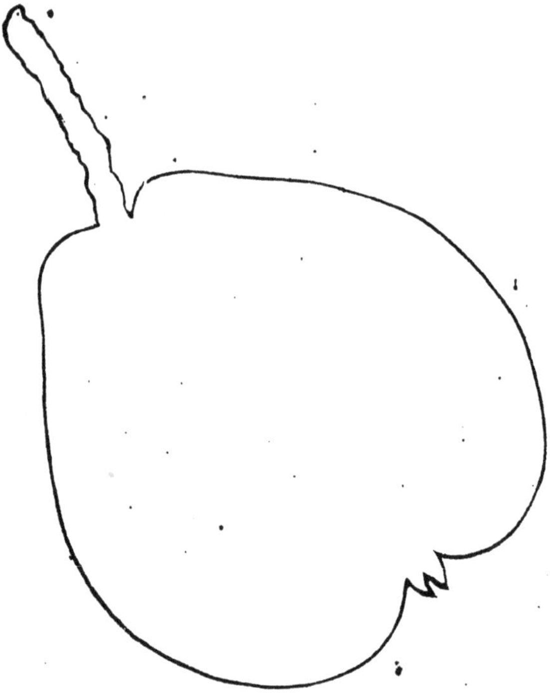

Belle Lucrative.

Belle Lucrative—*Fondante d'Automne.* Of medium size; form roundish obovate; skin greenish yellow, lightly russetted. In quality of fruit of unsurpassed excellence, being exceedingly juicy, melting, and of a rich, sugary and yet vinous flavor. Last of September and October. Tree of moderate vigor, upright habit, hardy, productive, and succeeds on both pear and quince. If the fruit was somewhat more attractive in its external aspect, and the tree a more robust grower, the Belle Lucrative would be nearly faultless.

BUFFUM.

BUFFUM. Of Rhode Island origin, from seed of St. Michael. The tree is hardy, of very vigorous growth and upright habit, bearing heavy crops of very handsome fruit, somewhat variable in quality, usually good and often very good, always salable. One of the most profitable orchard varieties, perhaps more so than any other; of medium size, oblong obovate; yellow, with a red cheek, sprinkled with brown dots; brownish green before ripe. Flesh white, melting, juicy, and of sweet and excellent flavor. Succeeds well on the quince. October.

DOYENNE BOUSSOUCK. A French pear of large size, beautiful and excellent; an early and good bearer; tolerably vigorous and usually hardy; skin rough, deep yellow, partially russetted, with a brighter cheek. Flesh buttery, melting, juicy and high flavored. Succeeds on the quince. September and October.

FLEMISH BEAUTY. Of foreign origin ; one of the hardiest of pears. The tree vigorous, healthy and an early and abundant bearer ; has

DOYENNE BOUSSOUCK.

been planted, perhaps, more extensively than any other, and is a universal favorite. Fruit of large size, obovate, somewhat variable in appearance ; in sheltered situations the skin is usually yellow with a bright brownish red cheek and very beautiful. In some seasons, and in exposed situations, it is often covered with russet, and not so handsome. Flesh yellowish white, juicy, melting, sugary and rich. Should be picked, at least, ten days before maturity, while yet green, tasteless and hard, and even before the stem parts readily from the twig, and ripened in the house ; as otherwise it becomes too soft, loses flavor and decays at the core. In my own grounds and in some others, I have noticed, for a few years past, a part of the fruit has cracked. When worked on the quince it is not sure to grow, many buds failing at times, but those which start well, make vigorous and permanent trees. It succeeds with all the different stocks upon which I have tried it, and de-

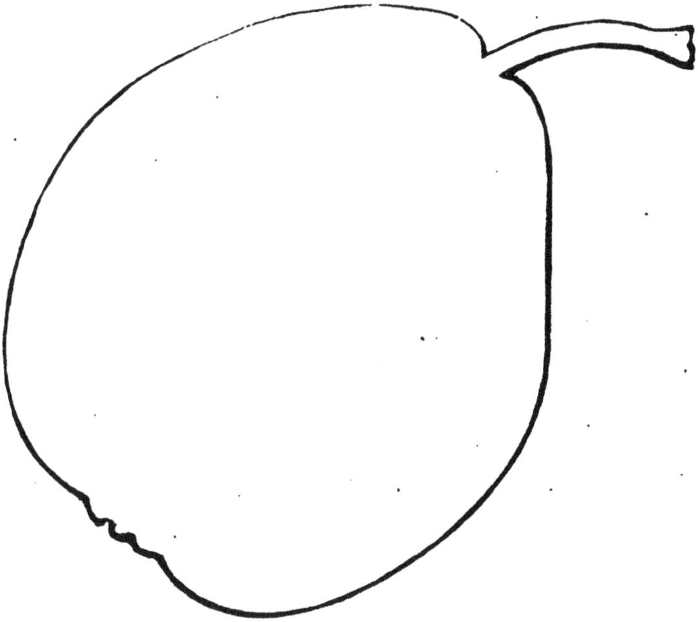

FLEMISH BEAUTY.

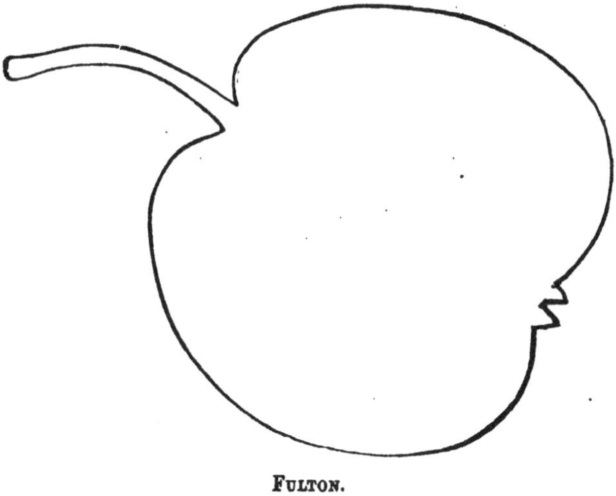

FULTON.

cidedly better upon the Mountain Ash, Thorn and Juneberry, than any other sort yet tested. Usually ripens about the end of September.

FULTON. An excellent and valuable pear, which originated from seed planted by the late Mrs. Fulton, on the farm now owned by Dan Fulton, in Bowdoinham, formerly a part of Topsham, in this State. Usually below medium size, roundish, flattened, gray russet, changing to cinnamon as it ripens. Flesh tender, rather juicy and half buttery, with a rich, sprightly, agreeable flavor; is in eating for a considerably longer time than most pears.

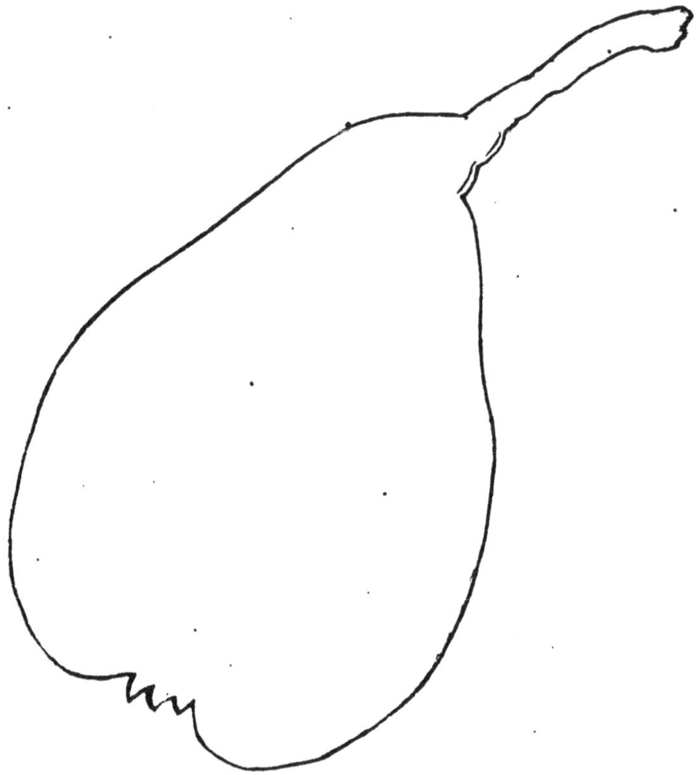

LOUISE BONNE DE JERSEY.

October, November. It should be grown on pear stock, as it succeeds but poorly on the quince. I have had fine fruit from scions set in the Mountain Ash. Rather a slow grower in the nursery, with slender shoots, but in time makes a fine tree in the orchard. It is hardy and an abundant and regular bearer.

LOUISE BONNE DE JERSEY. Few pears have given more general satisfaction than this; especially when grown in warm, dry soils, and on the quince root. In clayey soils it is often astringent. The tree is a good grower, hardy and very productive. The fruit large, pyriform, often a little one sided. Skin greenish, changing to bright yellow, with a crimson cheek in the sun, sprinkled with numerous grey dots. Flesh juicy, melting and high flavored. October.

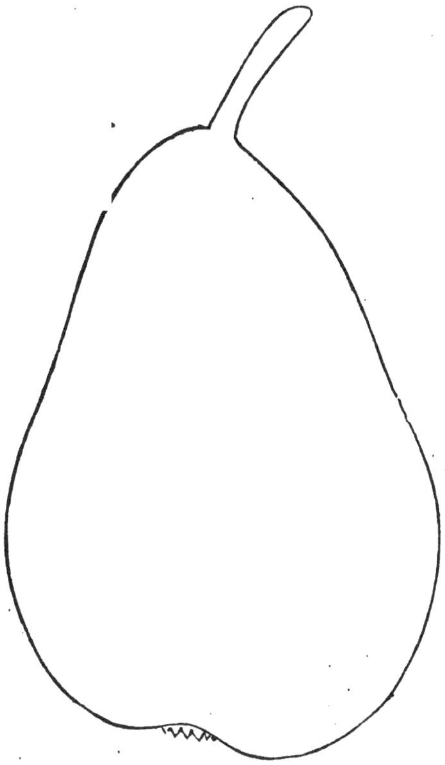

NICKERSON.

NICKERSON. A seedling which originated in Readfield in this State, on the farm of Mr. Nickerson and very little disseminated. I am not aware of its having fruited elsewhere as yet. In form and general appearance it somewhat resembles Louise Bonne de Jersey, and the specimens sent me were equal to that variety in quality. The original tree, though not old, and only about seven inches in diameter, bore three barrels in 1860, which sold at twelve and a half dollars per barrel. Young trees show vigorous growth and fine form. The evidênce of sufficient hardiness and productiveness seems conclusive. October.

SECKEL. This is introduced, not to commend its culture, but because of its great popularity elsewhere, and to caution growers from expecting too much of it here. True, the tree is hardy and the fruit *best*, the standard of excellence; but it requires a longer and warmer season, and a richer soil than ours, to bring it to

BEURRE D'ANJOU.

perfection. With the best culture we find the tree a *very* slow grower, not very healthy, and the fruit small. Some good fruit may be had by grafting it in the limbs of a vigorous, healthy grown tree, but we have never seen it here at all comparable with the fruit as often found in Philadelphia, sometimes weighing four, five or six ounces, and report says sometimes larger still.

LATE AUTUMN AND EARLY WINTER.

BUERRE D'ANJOU. This noble pear, introduced from Europe by Col. Wilder, possesses qualities which place it in the front rank. The tree hardy, vigorous and productive, the fruit large, fair, rich and keeping well, it deserves extensive culture. Succeeds equally well on the pear or quince root. Fruit large to very large,

BUERRE DIEL.

roundish obovate, often larger on one side than the other. Stem short and thick. Skin greenish yellow, sprinkled with russet and brown dots. Flesh melting, very juicy, with a rich, brisk, vinous flavor. It is usually in eating through the whole of November, and some years I have kept them in perfect order till the twentieth of December.

Buerre Diel. A magnificent Belgian fruit raised by Dr. Van Mons. It is a pretty general favorite, being rarely absent from autumnal exhibitions where pears are shown. The tree is very vigorous and usually proves hardy, bears just about enough not to require much thinning. Succeeds best on the quince root. Large, obtuse pyriform, at maturity yellow, with large brown dots and markings of russet. Flesh rather coarsegrained towards the core, but juicy, rich, sugary, and half melting. I would not advise planting it extensively, as it sometimes cracks or otherwise does not succeed well. October and November.

Beurre Hardy.

Beurre Hardy. A vigorous growing tree on both pear and quince. Seems particularly adapted to culture on the last named stock. Fruit rather large, often a little one-sided, like Beurre d'Anjou. Skin greenish yellow, russetted and shaded with brownish red, and sprinkled with brown dots. Flesh buttery, melting, very juicy; vinous flavor, and perfumed. Of comparatively recent introduction, but has, wherever proved, gained a position among the best. October—November.

DUCHESSE D'ANGOULEME.

DUCHESSE D'ANGOULEME. The largest good pear we have—sometimes weighing a pound or more. Skin greenish yellow, often with a red cheek, sometimes partially russetted; surface uneven and knobby. Flesh melting, very juicy and rather coarse towards the core; of rich aromatic flavor, and is in eating condition a good while. It is so much better on the quince, that it should be grown only on this stock. The tree is a vigorous grower but not perfectly hardy, neither can it be considered a very tender sort, as it succeeds generally, but suffers in very severe winters. It is irregular as to production, sometimes bearing very heavily, and again bearing little or nothing. In my own experience, barrenness has often followed a very abundant bloom. The trees appear to be exhausted by excessive flowering, and a severe thinning out of the bloom buds as they begin to swell, remedies the evil, and a large crop sets. It needs severe thinning out to attain full size. October, November. Succeeds best in warm, dry soils.

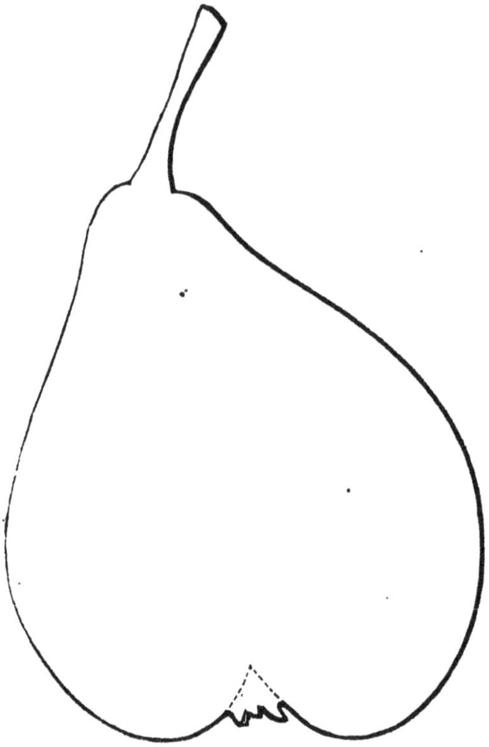

NOUVEAU POITEAU.

NOUVEAU POITEAU. Of foreign origin, being a seedling raised by Dr. Van Mons; one of the most vigorous of growers, and proved hardy enough to withstand the winter of 1856–7, with scarce any injury. It forms a fine shaped top and is very productive; promises to be a valuable orchard variety; succeeds perfectly on the quince. Fruit large—sometimes twice as large as the figure here given of it; skin green, covered mostly with russet. Flesh white, buttery, melting, with a vinous, refreshing flavor, usually rich, but in some seasons rather less so, and the texture of the flesh has occasionally proved soft. November.

OSWEGO BEURRE.

OSWEGO BEURRE. A Bergamot shaped pear, which from its great hardiness and productiveness may prove a valuable orchard fruit; medium size, roundish, cinnamon russet. Is in eating condition a long time. Has proved variable in quality, some seasons being very fine indeed, and in others decidedly inferior. November, December.

SWAN'S ORANGE—*Onondaga.* A seedling of Connecticut, whence it was carried to New York, and thence brought to notice. It is said to vary in quality in different situations, but here it has uniformly proved one of the best of its size and season. Extremely hardy, vigorous, and very productive. Large, melting, buttery and rich; deep yellow, sprinkled with russet dots, and from its shape and

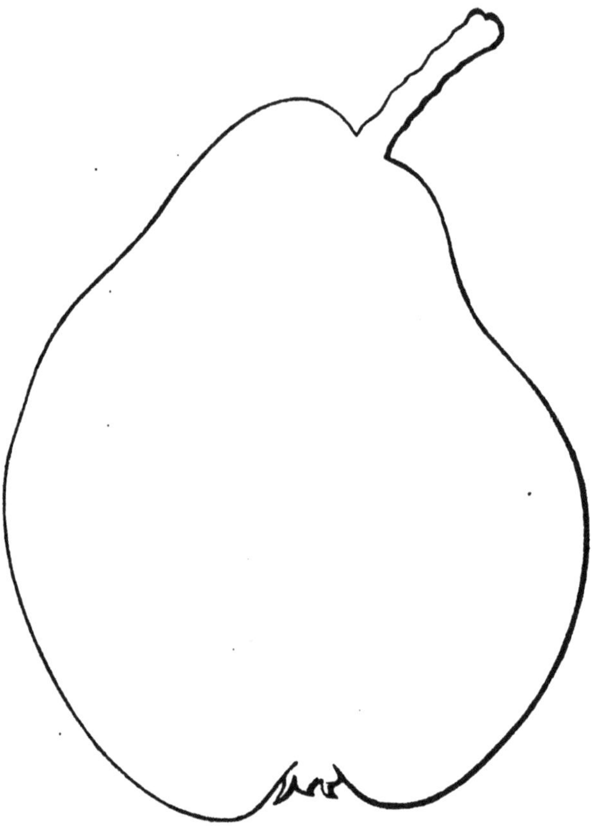

SWAN'S ORANGE.

color was called Orange. Said to do best in a strong loamy or clayey soil. Succeeds on the quince. A very valuable orchard pear. October and November.

URBANISTE. Upon the pear root, this has proved unproductive. I have a tree more than twenty years old which has never borne half a peck in a year; but upon the quince root it is one of the most desirable; and this, too, notwithstanding in its earlier years it is of slow growth and refuses to bear until it has grown to good size and has laid by capital enough to do a good business.

It then begins at once to bear full crops of most estimable fruit which remains a longer time in eating condition than most others. The tree, when once well under way, is a vigorous grower and

URBANISTE.

forms a symmetrical top; while in healthiness and hardihood, it is unequalled by any other, and it promises the same in regard to longevity. Fruit medium to large; fair, smooth, pale yellow, spotted with grey dots: melting, juicy and of rich flavor. October, November.

WINTER.

The quality of late pears depends very greatly on the perfection in which they are grown, and the way in which they are ripened off. Inferior specimens are not often worth the trouble of harvesting, no matter what care is given subsequently. Hence, one reason for good culture and thinning out of the fruit early in the season, to secure size and quality. They must not remain too long on the tree. Most kinds lose, rather than gain, if left on after the first week in October, and none should be left after the middle. Handle with care; gather on a dry day and put in a cool cellar, not damp and not too dry; if wet, they rot; if too dry, they shrivel. Where there are but few, the better mode is to put them in barrels or boxes, between layers of apples. When within a fortnight of maturity, bring them into a warm room, and keep in close drawers. In this way they will soon develop the richest hues, the most perfect texture and the highest flavor of which they are capable.

The number of winter pears which has given satisfaction in this State is very limited, and there is greater need of acquisitions to it, than to the number of those ripening at any other season.

EASTER BEURRE. This is mentioned here because it has often been extolled too highly. When perfectly well grown and ripened, it deserves all the praise given to it, but this cannot be done in Maine. Although hardy, it requires a longer and warmer season than ours, to arrive any where near perfection. In a very few instances it has ripened tolerably well in warm gardens.

GLOUT MORCEAU. Few pears, really so good as this is when in perfection, have given so little satisfaction in Maine. If planted, it should be only on the quince root, for which it is peculiarly adapted, and then as much patience must be exercised as for almost any pear (except the Dix) on pear root. After a lapse of ten or twelve years or more, I have heard cultivators here pronounce it the most valuable of any. The tree is vigorous and very hardy. The fruit, in perfection, is large, of excellent quality, and keeps late into winter, but until the trees are near maturity, the fruit is usually worthless.

PASSE COLMAR. Very hardy, a good grower; fruit of very good quality and keeps late. Succeeds on both pear and quince. Its fault is excessive productiveness, requiring altogether too much thinning out to secure specimens of good size; and small ones are not worth growing. January, February.

LAWRENCE. One of our best late keeping pears; of American origin. Tree of moderately vigorous growth, regular shape, exceedingly hardy, very healthy, bears early and produces well. When well grown the fruit combines beauty, rich flavor and gen-

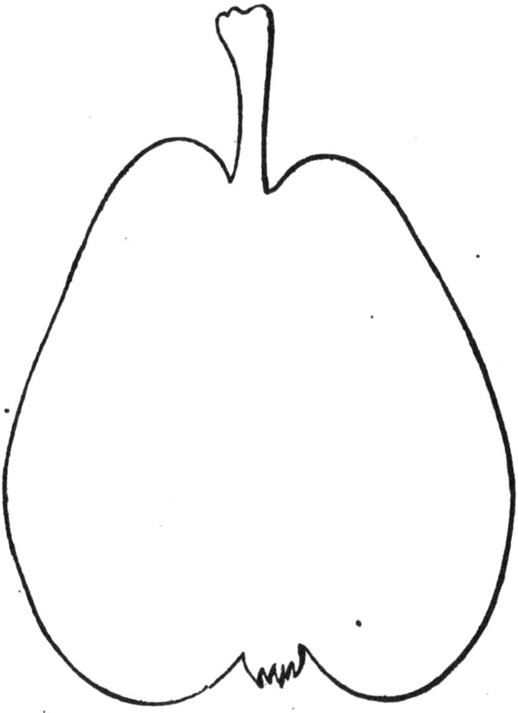

LAWRENCE.

eral excellence, with the keeping qualities of the Vicar of Winkfield, and often keeps later. Unlike many winter varieties, there is no difficulty in ripening the fruit with ordinary keeping in a cellar. Fruit of medium size, obtuse pyriform; skin lemon yellow, covered with small brown dots. Flesh white, a little granular, and melting, with a rich aromatic flavor. Succeeds tolerably well on the quince. Needs high culture on either pear or quince. December, January.

McLAUGHLIN. There seems to be little doubt that this is a Maine seedling. It cannot be traced beyond the old trees on the Mc-

Laughlin farm at Beech-Ridge in Scarboro', Cumberland county, although the oldest trees now standing there are grafted ones. It was shown to the Massachusetts Horticultural Society many years ago, and was at first supposed to be the Brown Beurre.

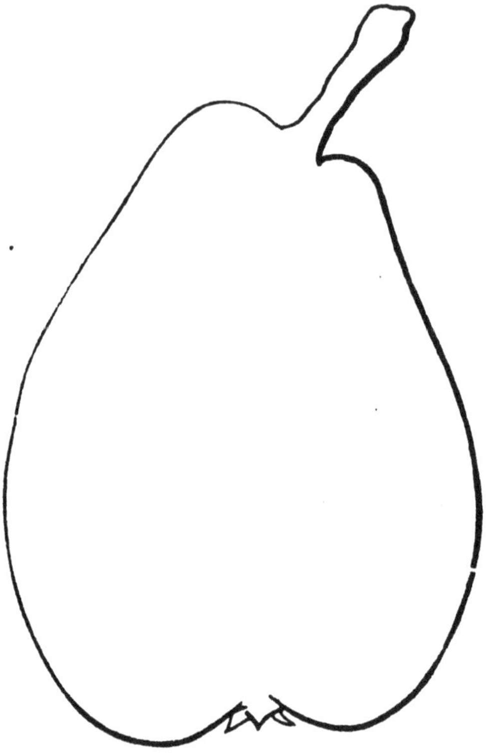

McLaughlin.

Subsequently, (about 1842,) I exhibited specimens, in December, which attracted admiration, and scions were also furnished the next spring. It has, I believe, given general satisfaction. At the last meeting of the American Pomological Society, Mr. Carpenter of New York said he was much pleased with it as a thrifty tree and good fruit, keeping into winter. The President assented fully, and said it had been too much overlooked. Messrs. Downing and Barry expressed the same opinion. The trees in Scarboro', standing in a low, undrained situation, pretty moist, if not absolutely wet, suffered severely in the winter of 1856–7 ; but the fact that they lived and bore well for scores of years previously, is evidence of a good degree of hardiness and general adaptation to our climate; while the price which the fruit always bore in Portland market shows the estimation in which it was there held. The fruit is a little variable, but in good seasons is unsurpassed by any other of its season, which is usually November to December.

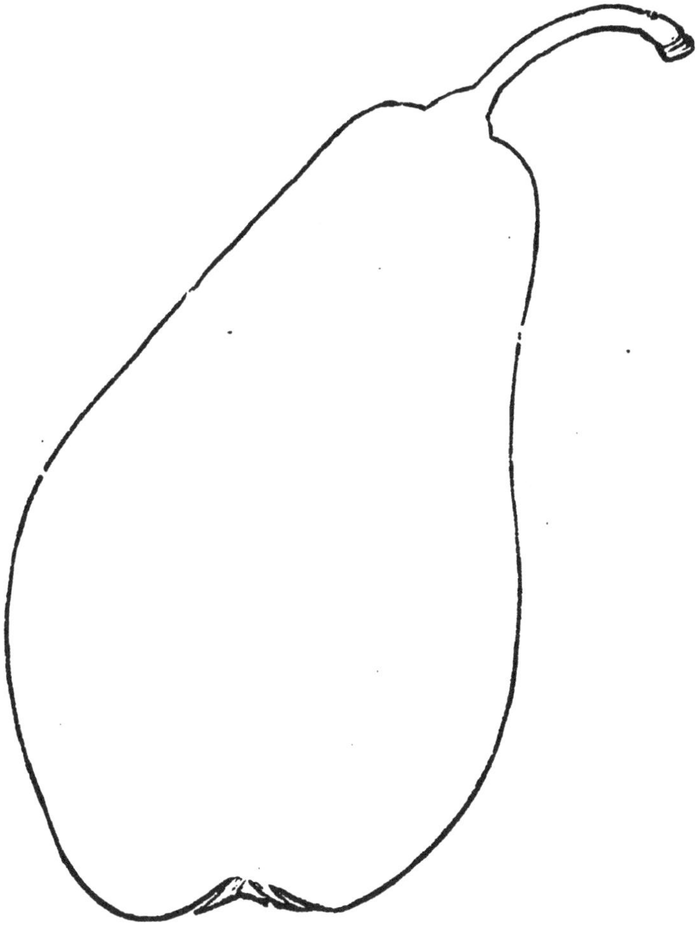

VICAR OF WINKFIELD.

VICAR OF WINKFIELD. Worthy of extensive culture as the best cooking pear we have. When negligently grown it is nothing more than this, but with suitable treatment it can be, and sometimes is, made a very good dessert fruit. For the latter purpose, the largest possible size must be attained by severe thinning out, (connected with good culture,) and the fruit should remain on the tree as late as the middle of October; then pick carefully and put in a cool dry cellar until near the time it is wanted to be eaten; then bring them, a few at a time, into a *warm room* and keep for a week or fortnight in a closed box or drawer. By this method, although never melting nor high flavored, it is crisp and tender, perfumed, abundantly juicy, and of pleasant flavor; while its

WINTER NELIS.

coming after the autumn pears are gone gives it peculiar value. They should be eaten before becoming soft enough to be easily indented by the thumb.

It possesses qualities specially fitting it for a market fruit for cooking purposes, the tree being hardy, a great grower, an early and profuse bearer, and will bear more than almost any other without severely checking its growth or lessening materially its ability to bear the year following. It succeeds best grown on the quince. Fruit long pyriform; pale yellow at maturity. Like the

Minister apple, this fruit seems to have been named for the clergy. It was first discovered in the woods of Clion, a natural seedling, by a French curate, and is universally known in France at the present time as "Le Cure." Soon after its discovery it was carried to England, cultivated and disseminated by a clergyman of Winkfield in Berkshire county, and received his title, by which it is now most commonly known both in England and America.

WINTER NELIS. When well grown this pear, of Flemish origin, is the most delicious of all our late varieties; it needs good culture and severe thinning to get them of good size. The tree is hardy, healthy and productive, but as it is a feeble and straggling grower when grafted in the nursery, it should be grown by grafting into the limbs of grown trees, and then, with care in pruning, we may have good shaped and vigorous trees, which will bear regularly and well. Fruit of medium size, roundish obovate; skin greenish yellow, covered with dots and patches of gray russet. Flesh fine grained, very melting, juicy, and of honied richness. Middle of December to end of January.

NEW VARIETIES OF HIGH PROMISE.

The foregoing are not supposed to comprise all the desirable sorts. There is a large and constantly increasing number of new varieties which promise well, but which have not been sufficiently proved here to enable us to speak with certainty of their adaptation to the soil and climate of Maine; and yet mention of some of them should by no means be omitted. As better sorts make their appearance, the standard, by which we judge whether one be worthy of cultivation or not, rises. A sort which would have been thought very good twenty years ago, may not now be admitted as worth growing. We do not want more kinds unless they are better in some important respect. A few of the more promising of the new ones are:

BEURRE SIX. Of foreign origin. Tree vigorous and productive. Pyriform, with angular sides. Flesh greenish white, exceedingly fine grained, melting and juicy, with a peculiar and very pleasant flavor. It has fruited in at least two collections here, and may be considered hardy enough, as in both cases the trees withstood the winter of '56-7 without injury. Succeeds on the quince. November—December.

Beurre Clairgeau. Large, rather one-sided; yellowish fawn color, partially russetted. Flesh somewhat granular—juicy, sugary and vinous. Seems to be rather averse to the quince, but succeeds if double worked. Is an early and productive bearer on the pear stock. November.

Church. Originated in New Rochelle, N. Y. Rather below medium size, roundish; yellow, juicy, melting and of very rich flavor. September. Another, named the Parsonage, which originated near it, (both on land belonging to Trinity Church,) is said to be a fine pear.

Clapp's Favorite—(*See frontispiece.*) This fruit has been disseminated the present autumn for the first time, and a large number of young trees have been sold at five dollars each. Of course, it promises well; and the prospect is good that the promise will be fulfilled. It is believed to be a cross between the Bartlett and Flemish Beauty, and to possess the hardiness of the latter. The tree resembles the latter and the fruit resembles the former, but as grown in Dorchester, where it originated, is both handsomer and better. For several years past, its fruit has been shown at the exhibitions of the Massachusetts Horticultural Society, and there is every probability that it will prove a decided acquisition.

De Tongres, *or Durandeau.* A foreign fruit, raised by M. Durandeau; of peculiar appearance and excellent. Bronze colored, with a russetty, uneven surface, and striped with red next the sun. Flesh melting, vinous, subacid and rich. Growth moderate. Said to be difficult to transplant successfully. A pear imported under the name of Colmar d'Artoisenet, fruited here this year for the first time, and more nearly resembles the above than any other, yet it appeared to be distinct.

Doyenne d'Alencon. A very late keeping pear, which has elicited high praise; medium size; russetty green.

Dana's Seedlings. Mr. Francis Dana, of Roxbury, has originated a number of very promising seedling pears, several of which have been named and lately disseminated. *America* is about as large as Beurre Diel, and is said to be preferable to it in some

DANA'S HOVEY.

respects. December. *Hovey* is of medium size; yellow, russetted, melting, juicy and very rich. November and December. Others are known as *Excelsior*, *Admirable*, *Shawmut*, and *Augustus Dana*.

HOWELL. From New Haven, Conn. Large, handsome, melting, juicy and good. October.

KIRTLAND, *or Kirtland's Seckel.* Supposed to be grown from seed of Seckel, which, in some respects it resembles. Yellowish, russetty, melting, juicy, and of aromatic flavor. Must be picked early. September.

SHELDON. Medium to large, roundish; smooth, yellowish brown, with a deeper cheek; juicy, melting, rich and high flavored.

THE PROPOSED AGRICULTURAL COLLEGE.

At the last session of the Legislature, the subject of Agricultural Education came up in connection with the question of accepting the grant made by act of Congress to endow an Agricultural College in each State. The grant was accepted; but nothing farther was decided upon; doubtless some action will be taken during the coming session.

The subject was fully discussed before the Board of Agriculture, and the result of the deliberation may be found in the resolutions unanimously adopted, as given on page 57. The report accompanying these resolves treats of the subject more in detail, and shadows forth many of the essential features of the proposed institution in so able and thorough a manner, that it seems unnecessary here to dwell farther upon it, or to recapitulate the views and arguments there presented.

The deliberations of the Legislature, aside from the question of acceptance, took little farther range than whether or not to accept a proposal made by Waterville College to the State; which was, substantially, that the donation of lands be made over to that institution, and in consideration therefor, a specified number of pupils were to be instructed at this institution, in applied chemistry, civil engineering and other branches of learning more or less intimately connected with agriculture, without any charge for tuition; and for this purpose to establish two professorships additional to those at present existing in the College. This proposal was not accepted; and, chiefly, if the reasons are correctly apprehended, because, first, the grant by Congress, *was not made to increase, or to extend the facilities for instruction in any existing literary institution*, but, in the language of the act itself, for "the endowment, support and maintenance of at least one college where *the leading object shall be*, (without excluding other scientific and classical studies, and including military tactics,) *to teach such branches of learning as are related to agriculture and the mechanic arts*, in such manner as the Legislatures of the States may respectively prescribe, in order to promote the liberal and practical education of the industrial classes, in the several pursuits and professions of life." The proposal made by Waterville College, being simply *to embrace in its course of study* the branches of learning related to agriculture and the mechanic arts, and not to make these the "leading aim" of the institution, it seemed to fall short of the evident design of Congress in bestowing the grant. The second reason was, an apprehension that the agricultural features thus blended with or engrafted upon a literary and classical institution might, in time, lose their distinctness and prominence: and thus the intention of the grant be defeated through absorption into the former and prevaling aims of the college.

It is not proposed here to enter at length upon the arguments, pro or con, regarding the advantages attending an independent and wholly separate existence, or of connection with some existing institution; but only, and very briefly to offer a few suggestions.

A cursory glance at, and a thorough examination of the act of Congress, alike show, that a separate existence best corresponds to the intentions of the grant; nor can any doubt exist that the Agricultural College might be best conducted in this manner. Standing by itself, it will excite greater interest in the classes for which it is intended; will draw pupils more numerously from them, and will more readily and to greater extent raise up for itself friends and benefactors. As a separate institution it will appear more conspicuously both as the educator and the organ and representative of the industrial classes; nor will there be any peril of its being overshadowed or absorbed by any other.

The interests of such an institution would in no wise clash with those of the existing literary colleges; there would be no competition between them, save a generous rivalry to accomplish the greatest possible good; and that such a separate and independent existence would be the unanimous preference of the agriculturists of Maine there can be no doubt. But doubts do exist in the minds of some, whether it is practicable for an independent Agricultural College to be suitably maintained upon the income of the fund to be derived from the sale of the land scrip which falls to our share as a State;—and an unwillingness also exists with some, either to rely upon the voluntary benefactions of the friends of agricultural education, or to ask aid from the State. The amount which may be realized for an endowment, from the proceeds of sale, is very uncertain. Possibly, any fears of its sufficiency may prove groundless, or suitable effort may elicit private donations hereafter, to an extent sufficient to make good any possible deficiency; in either of which cases, an independent existence is practicable without State aid.

But if it must, from economical considerations, be connected with another, cannot some way be devised by which many of the advantages of a separate and independent existence may be secured? This seems possible, for although it may, in order to save expense, be put under the supervision and management of the *Trustees* of some existing institution, it may still have,

1*st*. Its own course of study and recitations, entirely separate from the institution with which it is connected, and adapted solely and exclusively to its own wants, precisely as if the connection in question did not exist.

2*d*. Although there may be some lectures in common, yet even here the wants of the pupils may be supplied by such extension of the lectures and such practical applications of the truths taught, as their peculiar circumstances demand.

3*d*. Its *Faculty* may also be distinct from the college Faculty, being composed of its own professors and teachers alone.

4*th*. It may be known distinctively, as THE AGRICULTURAL COLLEGE OF MAINE; as the Maine Medical College is known as such, though connected with Bowdoin College.

The Medical School, just named, affords a good illustration of the sort of connection which may exist with another institution, and yet retain many of the advantages of separate and independent existence, viz.: that of mere government and direction by the same board of trustees; with opportunity to avail itself of the benefit of books, apparatus, and to a limited extent, also, of the instructors of the institution with which it is connected, while *for all other purposes*, it is conducted separately.

As the act of Congress allows five years in which to "provide" the college, (reckoning, probably, from the date of approval by the President,) there remains yet three years in which to decide what shall be done and to do it. While, therefore, there is no occasion for unseemly haste, or inconsiderate action, the time is short enough for due reflection, thorough maturation of plans, and for giving efficacy to them.

It is rare that any subject of greater magnitude calls for legislative deliberation. Upon the action which this receives, depends, in large measure, not only the extent and degree to which agricultural knowledge shall be disseminated among the farmers of the State, but also the degree of progress which shall be made in all the arts of life; the future development of our untold natural resources; in a word, the productiveness of our whole domain, and its position and power as a State.

Questions pertaining to the existence, integrity and honor of our common country, and to moral health and prosperity alone take higher rank. May Infinite wisdom guide the deliberations to the best possible results.

S. L. GOODALE,
Secretary of the Board of Agriculture.

JANUARY, 1864.

INDEX.

INDEX.

CPSIA information can be obtained
at www.ICGtesting.com
Printed in the USA
LVHW100444110522
718424LV00003B/218

9 783375 006532